Flanders sat up and saw that Lachlan was already awake, watching her intently. She couldn't read the look in his eyes, but she felt suddenly shy and turned away from him to dress.

"You have to kill me, don't you?" she asked with her back still to him.

Without answering, he stood up and walked to the mouth of the cave. Slowly, Flanders followed him. Streaks of color pierced the night sky until, with a blaze of light, the orange fireball of the sun climbed over the edge of the plains.

"If I let you live, can I trust you not to betray me?"

His eyes never left the sky. At first, in fact, Flanders couldn't believe that he was addressing her. She'd already given up the hope of living.

Finally, she managed to say, "I'll never betray you." Her voice trembled. She felt as though she were taking a solemn oath—an oath that involved more than her word.

It was an oath that would bind her heart.

New South Wales

RUM COLONY
FIRST FAMILIES
FREE WOMAN
THE PIONEERS
THE WILDINGS
THE DIGGERS
THE SEEKERS

THE DEFIANT

by

Terry Nelsen Bonner

Dell Publishing, Inc. * * * * New York

Published by
Dell Publishing Co., Inc.
1 Dag Hammarskjold Plaza
New York, New York 10017

Dell ® TM 681510, Dell Publishing Co., Inc.

ISBN: 0-440-01863-3

Printed in the United States of America

First printing—September 1983

1

ON the afternoon of July 10, 1862, the lumbering Cobb & Co. coach was traveling south through Queensland, Australia. It drove across the plain known as Darling Downs, a sun-baked plateau that stretched toward a horizon so distant it could well mark, as the aborigines believed, the edge of the world.

The coach followed Claxton Crossing Road, really no more than a dirt track that cut through the bush. The road wound around giant slabs of purple and gray rocks and the more formidable clumps of gray-green bushes. It seemed always in danger of disappearing altogether under new growths of scraggly brush or outcroppings of stone that drivers swore appeared overnight specifically to overturn their coaches.

The driver on this afternoon was a creature as rough and burly as the four stocky dray horses he urged on with shouts and curses. He added the encouragement of frequent lashes from his six-foot long stock whip.

He wore a cabbage-tree hat made of plaited palm leaves with a broad brim to protect him from the blaze of the sun. His shirt sleeves were rolled above his elbows because, although it was July, the middle of the Australian winter, the temperature in this tropical area was already over 70° Fahrenheit.

The Cobb & Co. coach normally carried only mail and cargo as it traveled down the western side of the Great

Dividing Range, crossed the mountains through Cunningham's Gap, and drove east to the coastal city of Brisbane.
Today, though, the coach carried a passenger. The company permitted this because the lady in question had insisted
that her cargo required her supervision. Also, she was
willing to pay the company double its usual rate.

The driver had picked her up in the morning at her
Toowoomba home. He'd admired her pretty face and form.
At first. That was before she began ordering him around
and insisting he wasn't being careful enough with her
things. She strode around the coach checking and recheck-
ing everything he did. By then he'd decided any man who
tangled with her would be sorry. She must be one of those
women who came to Australia with family money, for
God knew what reasons. More money than sense, he
figured.

Flanders Wilde bounced from side to side as the coach
bumped along the rocky track which substituted for a
decent road out in the bush. How long would it take, she
wondered, before she accepted the fact that in Australia it
was impossible to do anything while traveling except to
stare at the passing terrain? Forgetting this fact, she had
planned to use this two-day coach ride from her home in
Toowoomba to the port at Brisbane to write the long
overdue reply to her old professor's letter.

She really should have known it would be impossible to
write a civilized letter while sitting on a hard wooden
bench in a stagecoach that threatened to fall apart at every
jolt. The letter would have to wait. Not only because the
jolting of the coach would make her writing illegible, but
also because the clouds of dust which billowed in through
the uncovered windows made her eyes burn and tear until
she could hardly see. If she pulled down the shades, the
heat and lack of air would probably make her faint. Instead
of covering the windows, she held a lace-edged hankie
over her nose and mouth to keep her coughing to a

minimum. She would write the letter, she decided, as soon as they stopped for the night. She must not put it off then, though, no matter how tired she felt, because the following day she would be shipping her first report along with a collection of her samples off to London. A letter to Professor Thorenson, who had been so kind to her, who had taught her everything, must accompany them or his feelings would be hurt.

She rummaged about in the petit-point travel satchel that lay on the seat beside her until she found his letter to her. She unfolded it. The date at the top read June 25, 1861. Today's date was July 10, 1862! More than a year ago! Flanders felt pierced by guilt at not having answered sooner. But the mails were so slow that it had taken months to get to her, and since its arrival she had been totally preoccupied by her scientific work. Her reasoning didn't completely ease her conscience.

She began to read the letter in her hands. She had read it so often she almost had it memorized.

> My Dear Flanders,
>
> Surely you can satisfy your desire for adventure nearer to home! I appreciate the fact that you want to do original scientific work, but, my dear child, there is no need to live the life of a barbarian. You have been in that wilderness nearly a year . . .

Flanders paused in her reading. The letter was a year old, so she had already been in Australia two years. When she'd undertaken the long journey from England, it had been the rash and rebellious gesture of a young woman who refused to be considered just another maiden on the marriage market. She wanted to be taken seriously. None of her friends had as much education as she, and none of them would have dreamed of putting the education they did have to any practical use! Well, she was different. She

wanted to be accepted by the scientific community, but the
men insisted on treating her like an adorable decoration.
That was when she'd made up her mind to come to
Australia.

Reports—almost rumors, really—had drifted back to
England from Baron Sir Ferdinand von Mueller, the botanist,
who was supposed to be doing fabulous work in Australia.
Flanders figured she would follow his example; she told
herself she had always wanted to make momentous
discoveries. When she announced her plans, she'd met
with opposition and disapproval on all sides, but it was
Professor Thorenson's demurrals that had actually unnerved
her. Still, she didn't dare back down then, and run the risk
of being dismissed as yet another of the scatterbrains so
typical of her sex. So, with her heart in her mouth, but
filled with fierce pride and determination, she'd embarked
for Australia.

Of course, she had planned to make those momentous
discoveries in short order, then to hurry home to praise and
rewards. She would be able to take her place as a famous
naturalist. The equal of any man! Well, she had made
momentous discoveries all right—the London scientific
world would soon discover just how momentous. But her
calculation of just how much time she would need had
been way off. Besides, the longer she lived in Australia,
the less desire she felt to return to England anyway.

She gazed out the window. Through the dust kicked up
by the horses, she viewed the parched earth with its scrubby
clinging plants, plants that refused to give up and die
despite the absence of water. Their pastel tones dotted the
pale gold ground. She spotted a clump of eucalyptus trees
in the distance—she had already catalogued thirty different
varieties of these gum trees, she thought proudly. She
could close her eyes and the names would fill her mind
like a litany or like favorite lines of poetry: Blakelyi,
Bridgesiana, Camphora, Cinerea, Fastigata, Pauciflora.

The coach gave an enormous bounce, and Flanders'

head slammed against the roof. Her eyes flew open. She rubbed her head. Soon they would be at the gap—God willing—and once through it they would stop at an inn set up just for the coach run. She would be glad to stop for the night. She could certainly use the rest after this ride.

Flanders swept the dust from her salmon velvet skirt with a gloved hand. Her coral silk shirtwaist was now the same color as the seat beside her and the world outside the carriage window—dust beige. These clothes, so pretty in London, were nothing but a nuisance in the Australian bush. How she wished she could dress in the free and easy manner that men did.

With an impatient sigh, she forced herself to return to the letter she still clutched in her hand.

> I confess your descriptions of what you are finding intrigue me greatly, but surely you have already collected enough material. Write up your findings here in England. Do come back at once. Wild Australia is no land for a woman alone.
>
> I dread that something will happen to you there, and for that I could never forgive myself. After all, I am the one responsible for your training—training that, I fear, turned you into a naturalist first and a woman second.

There was more, but Flanders refolded the letter along its original creases and stuck it back in her bag. His accusations hurt. He was unfair, she told herself. She had a woman's heart. It trembled for all the living creatures of the earth!

What did it matter that it had never been touched by love of a man? She'd never been able to understand all the swooning and giggling that her girl friends had done over boys back in England. And as for the men of Australia—in two years she'd hardly met a one who came close to being her equal. To be sure, men like this rough and ready driver abounded—the country fairly crawled with similar coarse creatures eager to lay claim to the women they so greatly outnumbered. But what was that to her? Far far better to be alone! That was what she really intended to do anyway. She paused in her thinking. Maybe the professor had been right, after all, in calling her more of a scientist than a woman.

The coach had entered Cunningham's Gap. Magnificent mounds of rock rose on both sides of the coach. These rocky mountains, striped in unnumbered shades of brown, stood in bold relief against the brilliant blue sky. Flanders smiled. She was learning to love this land in all its forbidding aspects. The last thing she wanted was an easy life, an ordinary life, and by coming here she had put that danger far behind her.

The gap path was narrow and boulder-strewn, and the horses had to slow their pace to pick their way across the difficult rocky path. The coachman cursed them in his guttural voice. Then he cracked his whip on their backs. Flanders winced. Without a doubt, this driver was the coarsest man she had yet come across in Australia. Even the look of him had repelled her. His rolled-up shirtsleeves revealed thick hairy arms that were none too clean. In fact, none of him looked any too clean. His grizzly beard made his head appear unnaturally—and to her, unattractively—large, although it was his manner rather than his looks that had really offended her. He'd looked at her as though he were taking off her clothes with his eyes, but worse than his treatment of her was the way he handled the horses who pulled the coach. Every minute he seemed to be whipping them or cursing them or sawing at their mouths. It had made her sick to watch him with the horses when he was loading the coach, and even though she couldn't see him now, she knew he must be brutalizing the poor creatures in the same way as they drove along.

Suddenly she heard his voice burst out in a new blast of

curses, ending with, "What the bloody hell! If this don't beat all. Son of a bitch."

The horses whinnied nervously, and the carriage shuddered to a stop. Flanders' body imitated the shudder. She wondered what was going on and hoped that nothing was wrong with the carriage. She didn't relish the idea of spending the night in the outback with this brutish man.

The driver's curses had continued, but now they were interrupted by another man's voice.

"Never mind your curses or my parentage, mate."

The voice had a hint of Scottish brogue to it.

"Throw down your guns," it went on. "Throw down your bloody guns before I blow your bloody head off! Is that bloody clear enough for you, mate?"

Despite the heat of the day, Flanders found that her arms were covered with goosebumps, but she cautiously stuck her head out the window anyway. The first thing she saw was a gorgeous roan stallion. Then she noticed the man sitting astride it—a wild-looking creature who seemed to be another kind of animal, and equally magnificent. He wore a black, body-hugging shirt and a pair of tight leather trousers that emphasized the leanness of his long, slim body. In his hand he held a long, slim black pistol, which was aimed steadily at the driver's head and which looked like an extension of his body. Flanders had no time to examine him further, because at that moment he spotted her and shouted, "Get your bloody head back inside that coach where it belongs or I'll blow it off!"

Startled, Flanders jumped, then cast him a disapproving look that she hoped showed withering disdain rather than the terror she actually felt. She retreated within the relative safety of the coach's interior.

"You're only supposed to be carrying cargo," she heard the bushranger berate the driver. "Why the hell do you have passengers? And how many of 'em are there?"

"Just that one. Just her," the driver grumbled. He'd

dropped his guns to the ground. "She got some kind of special permission to ride along with her stuff."

"Damn it all to bloody hell, I heard about a special shipment, but there wasn't a word about any female. Climb down off that box," he demanded of the driver. "Nice and slow, mate, with your hands where I can watch 'em."

Flanders slid back over near the window so she could see out without being seen.

The bushranger was on the ground now, and so was the driver. He'd picked up the driver's guns and stuffed them into his belt. Across his chest he wore a crossed band with a garish display of bullets. Without looking away from the driver, he slipped a coiled rope off his saddle horn.

"Go give that tree a nice hug." His gun never shifted position. If it went off, the driver would have a neat hole between his eyebrows. He lashed the driver's hands together. "How long you been a driver? I haven't run into you before."

"No surprise, this being only my third run. I just come over from America. But I know you, I think. Unless I miss my guess, you're the terror of the territory, 'Bad' Lachlan."

"Right you are, bucko, but with you all trussed up like a wild boar on a spit, I think you better mind your manners and call me Mister McKenzie."

The driver struggled against the knots, which only grew tigher on his wrists. "Damn you. I've never heard tell of any Mister McKenzie. Only a bushranger called 'Bad' Lachlan."

Lachlan threw back his head and laughed. It was a laugh both melodious and inhuman, Flanders thought. He could probably kill them both without a single stirring of conscience. The hair at the back of her neck stood at attention. She hoped he'd just forget about her.

"Watch your tongue, man," he said, growing serious, "and you might live to make a fourth coach trip."

He turned from the bound man and ambled toward the

carriage. In a single movement, he opened the coach door and leaped inside to sit beside Flanders.

In fact, although Flanders jumped back when she saw him heading for the coach door, he ended up sitting half on top of her. She pulled away from his touch as fast as she could, but he only gave her a slow smile.

"Well, well, well," he said. "A fiery lass, eh? I like that in a woman—a little fight! I guess my booty is going to be a little more fun than I'd figured on. A little extra treasure."

He reached over and pulled her to him, but before he could give her the kiss he intended, she pulled free of his grasp.

"There's no treasure for you here," she asserted, surprising herself with the steadiness in her voice, despite the pounding in her heart. "These boxes and bags contain material I'm shipping off to the British Scientific Society." She ignored the implication that she herself was part of his loot.

His voice turned to steel. "You may be telling the truth." His eyes seemed to pierce her. "I hope for your sake that you're not! I wouldn't like to be disappointed in today's take. In any case, you and your things are coming with me. I'm one of that peculiar breed of men who check things out for themselves. If you know what I mean." He leered at her, his eyes resting first on her face, then on her breasts which rose and fell with her frightened breathing, and finally on her hips. She was afraid that she knew exactly what he meant!

She also knew he could just as easily shoot her as reason with her. She'd heard tales of the bushrangers. There'd been quite a scandal about the murder of a newspaper editor who had been writing editorials urging citizens into organized resistance the bushrangers who were making the roads such a hazard.

She'd also heard specifically about Lachlan McKenzie. He was something of a folk-hero in the saloons. Many a drink was drunk to his continued health. Rumor had it he only robbed the very rich, and the common folk seemed to think that helped even things out a bit.

She hadn't heard anything about his raping women, but in this male-dominated land maybe that wouldn't be the sort of thing anyone would bother to comment on. Maybe that was understood as a part of the bushrangers' way of life. Her heart was beating so hard it actually hurt.

Lachlan jumped back down to the ground, swung the coach door shut behind him, then leaned back toward her to warn, "Don't do anything foolish. I've never shot a lady, but I have no objection to starting now!"

What a loathsome creature, Flanders thought. How could she have found him so handsome when she'd first seen him through the window? She had to escape. But there wasn't really anything she could think to do. There was no one to hear her if she screamed for help. If she jumped from the carriage and made a run for it, there wasn't any place to go—even if he didn't shoot her in the back. Her only recourse was to bide her time and try to get away later on.

"Hey you ! Driver," Lachlan called as he tied his horse to the back of the coach. "Someone should be by here in the next day or two." He gave another of his blood-chilling laughs as he climbed up into the driver's seat. He snapped the reins, and the team of horses began to move.

"My name is John Parker," the tied-up driver screamed after him as they began to pull away. "You better remember it, because it's going to be on your tombstone as the man who brought you down."

"Don't take it so hard," Lachlan called back. "Everybody has bad days." His laughger rang out and echoed and bounced against the rocky canyon walls until it seemed there were a dozen men laughing.

Flanders covered her face with her hands, as though that would make everything disappear. But when she took her hands back down, there she was in a runaway coach, bounding across the Australian outback at the mercy of a madman. Well, Flanders my girl, she told herself, you wanted adventure in your life. Now adventure is what you've got. I hope you're satisfied. I also hope you live through it, she added, and tears were beginning to sting her eyes.

2

ALTHOUGH it was only the middle of the afternoon, the flickering gaslights gave the Red Raven Saloon the soft look of evening. Calculated to keep the drinker drinking and the gambler gambling, Rosie Sullivan thought as she smoothed the bodice of her form-fitting satin gown. And to keep the men coming back for more.

"How do I look, Bart?"

She leaned toward the barman. He had a full view of the expanse of creamy bosom above her gown. Rosie knew the royal blue color brought out the blue of her eyes and constrasted strikingly with her black hair, but she wanted to hear him say so. As she was pinning up her hair just a few minutes earlier, she had discovered a gray strand, the first, and it had depressed her.

"Ah, Rosie, you're an awful flirt, and you know it. You're always beautiful to me."

"It's been a long time since you last asked me to give up my wild ways and marry you."

Bart cupped the back of her neck in one hand, took the cheroot from his mouth with the other, and gave her a wet kiss on the forehead. "It does me no good," he said. "Ain't you drinking today, sweetheart?"

"When I'm not, you'll know I'm either sick or dead. Give me a spider."

"I don't know how you can ruin good brandy by adding lemonade to it." He blew smoke into a cloud which hung between them, then drifted lazily up toward the ceiling. "But if that's what you want, that's what you'll get." He clamped his teeth around the cheroot, and squinting one eye against the irritation of smoke, he mixed her drink.

Rosie strained to see herself in the gold-flecked mirror behind the bar. Giving up on that, she took a small mirror from the black silk bag that hung from her wrist. After a few moments of careful scrutiny, she decided she looked all right. Her skin was clear. She was lucky about that. Some of the girls were always fighting off blotches. Just a fluff of cornsilk powder and some rouge, that was all the makeup she needed. Rosie caught up a few loose strands of hair and pinned them in place. Then she put the mirror away.

"Drink up, my darling," Bart said, "and I'll give you a toast. To Rosie—young, beautiful and rich!" He pounded his fist on the mahogany bar, making the glasses jump.

Rosie's laugh was more like a snort.

"Can you believe it! When I came over, that's just what I intended to be? Young, beautiful and rich, within the year. Married to some digger who'd struck gold. With a passle of kids around my skirts soon after." She paused and took a swig of her drink. "Here I am, five years later, nothing but a. . . ."

"Don't say that!" Bart gripped her wrist, making her wince. His voice had become tight and serious. "Don't ever let me hear you say anything bad about who or what you are. There's plenty others always willing to do that."

"You're right about that." She finished off her drink in a swift gulp.

Bart, his striped shirt sleeves rolled above his wrists so that the curly red hairs on his forearms showed, poured her another and poured himself a shot of rum. Rosie watched her friend. "Tomorrow's my birthday," she said. "I'll be twenty-eight, but if you dare repeat that, I'll swear you're a liar. I tell the customers I'm twenty-four and hope that they have weak eyes!" She shook her head. "This is gloomy talk. Why don't you take me out to lunch tomorrow to celebrate?''

''Good! We'll go someplace fine and play the proper lady and her gent, what do you say to that?''

Rosie didn't get to answer, because just then a young boy came crashing into the saloon on the run, shouting, ''Hey, come on down to the dock. You're missing all the excitement. A ship come into port with plague or something. There's a mob down there already.''

The only customers in the place were two diggers comparing tall tales over in the corner. They stood up, clamped their dusty hats on their heads, and hurried out the door.

The boy tugged on Rosie's fingers. ''Come on,'' he urged. He was slim and olive-skinned with scraggly hair that stuck out from under his hat. Rosie knew him because he came into the saloon almost every night to try to earn money by shining shoes or running errands. He was only ten, but he was already a little man. Old before his time, Rosie thought, like so many of the Sydney kids. She knew his parents lived in a shack a few blocks away and had eight kids to feed. They needed the money he earned.

''All right, Sam,'' she said, disengaging her hand from his. ''I'll be there in a minute. You go on.''

He was out the door almost before she finished speaking.

''I don't suppose you can come along,'' she said to Bart. ''The other girls aren't down yet.''

''There ain't one of them worth anything. I wouldn't leave the bar in their care. They're just kids, really. My luck, Mr. Smythe would come in and I'd be out of a job.''

''Well, I'll play the reporter and bring you back the news. The plague indeed! Probably seasickness. Have you ever seen the likes of these Sydney siders for being proper fools?''

She slid down from the red velvet bar stool, Mr. Smythe's latest attempt to give the place some class. Rosie smoothed her tight skirt along her hips and made sure the flounce of ruffles at the bottom could swing free around her ankles.

She figured you never knew where your next customer would come from. She waggled her fingers at Bart in farewell and headed for the swinging wooden doors.

The day had a glassy calm to it. The sun shone down on the variety of buildings along the Sydney streets. Most of the houses were single-story wooden constructions. The two-story brick saloon hinted at the solid comfort to be found inside. Rosie took a deep breath and began cheerfully down toward the Circular Quay. She picked her way along, taking care that her high heels didn't get caught in any of the ruts along the unpaved street. At each corner she could see the blue waters of the harbor.

The ominous noises of the crowd reached her before she turned the last corner, and when she did, she saw that the dock was crowded with people. Still, with the water slapping gently at the sides of the little boats and making a foamy nest around the larger ships anchored there, it was hard to feel that any real trouble was in the making.

The center of attention was the *H.M.S. Three Winds*, a large windjammer that looked to be a ship of a thousand tons or more. Its masts were furled; its heavy timbers creaked as it rolled on the small swells.

Rosie spotted the frowning captain up on the deck.

"Listen to me, I say," he shouted, but his words were barely audible above the angry mutterings of the crowd.

"What's going on?" Rosie asked the woman beside her, a hefty creature in her thirties with two small tots tugging at her full skirts.

"There was sickness aboard. Most of the passengers is dead. The men won't unload. Nobody wants to let the folks still alive onto the land."

Next to the captain, clutching his hand and crying piteously, Rosie saw a young girl who looked not much older than Sam, the shoe-shine boy. Her terror probably made her look younger than she was, but she couldn't be more than twelve or thirteen.

"Go back!" one man shouted.

Others agreed, hollering up at the captain about how they didn't need more problems, and how he shouldn't have come into Sydney Harbor.

The captain, dropping the girl's hand, held both his own out in a calming gesture to signal that he wanted to speak.

"Plenty of you folks know me. I've been making this voyage from England to Sydney a long time. Do you really believe I would bring you disaster? I swear I wouldn't!"

"Yah," a young boy scoffed, "you brung us a death ship. Death Ship! Death Ship!" he began to shout in a rhythmic way.

The chant was picked up by others. "Death Ship!" "Death Ship!" The words rang out across the calm waters of the bay.

"I have people on board who need a doctor," the captain shouted. "Others need to be buried. But it's no death ship. Just people who got sick and died. It happens that way sometimes during the months at sea."

He wanted them to understand that there was no plague on board, but he didn't dare utter the word for fear of adding to their hostility. He dreaded mob hysteria. He had heard stories of what it could do. He knew of ships that mobs had burned. He knew of captains, good men, who had been lynched.

The symptoms indicated the disease was some sort of dysentery. That was no surprise, considering the length of the journey and the poor provision for sanitation and the difficulty of keeping a safe water supply. He'd seen it plenty of times before, though this was by far the most disastrous outbreak in his experience. He himself had just been lucky, he figured. Or maybe his repeated exposure had somehow made him immune.

He struggled to make himself heard over the shouts of the crowd, but only the few men standing closest to the edge of the dock heard his words. The girl beside him buried her head in his side. Poor lass, he thought, both her parents dead and now faced with this dreadful scene.

Rosie looked at the faces around her contorted with rage and fear. Many of the men were just out for trouble. They had no jobs, and the afternoon seemed dull, so why not mash a few heads? She saw a hefty man a few feet to her side pick up a sturdy plank and hold on to it like a club. His face turned into a snarling mask as she watched. He was the kind of man she avoided whenever possible. The kind who liked to smash things up. Things or people.

Other men began looking around for objects to use as weapons, and there was plenty of debris lying around the streets to provide them with a complete arsenal. The glint of light playing off a knife's blade caught her eye.

Rosie knew she had to act and act fast or there was going to be a blood bath—as likely to destroy the tenuous peace of Sydney as any possible disease. She'd have to speak out. She pushed through to the front of the mob where a group of barrels formed a kind of platform she could get up on. She turned to one of the men nearby who was sucking on his pipe and not really involved in the jeering. "Give me a hand up, won't you, mate?" she asked.

He looked her over appreciatively, taking in her form-fitting clothing and the look she had of being available.

"Both hands, luv," he answered, "and any other parts you want." He put his hands on both sides of her waist and swung her up onto the barrel top. She leaned a hand on his shoulder to steady herself as she straightened.

"Hey," she shouted, "hey!" But her voice got lost in the general hubbub. The man who had hoisted her raised two fingers to his lips and gave an ear-splitting whistle. Then a second. Then a third. The noise died down enough so that Rosie could make herself heard.

"What kind of fools are we?" she asked. "We're acting like lunatics. How did any of us come to be in Sydney? Most of us because we weren't wanted elsewhere, if you know what I mean!"

"Get the whore down," the man with the snarling face cried out. "We don't need no woman to call us names!"

A knot of men moved toward her, and Rosie's heart began to hammer inside her. Someone threw a rock, and although she ducked, it grazed her cheek and slashed it open.

"Wait!" she shouted as the warm trickle of blood made its way down her face.

The man who'd whistled the crowd to silence shouted, "Let her talk! Are you such cowards that you think beating up a woman will make you men?"

His words were met with muttering, but no one edged toward Rosie.

"It wasn't many years ago that everybody in Sydney was a criminal," Rosie started again. "Many of our mums and dads, for that matter."

"So what?" a woman screeched. "We don't want more trouble."

The noise of the crowd again surged at Rosie, and she considered getting down and letting the mob do their dirty work. But she felt she had to try at least one more time—if for no other reason than the girl who stood on the deck beside the captain. Somehow that child's pure face, a face that would become beautiful in the woman she'd be a few years from now, touched Rosie's heart. She couldn't let any harm come to her if she could help it.

"You're right," she shouted. "You're right that we don't need any more disease. Because we have plenty of our own!"

A few men chuckled at that. There was a lot of head-shaking that gave Rosie a feeling maybe the worst was over.

"But a few more sick people won't make no difference either, will it? And what are we being so uppity about anyway? Look at the streets around you, friends. When we don't have mud, we have dust! And don't forget our beautiful open sewers."

By now the men who had armed themselves were dropping the planks and stones back to the ground. The few women in the group were nodding toward Rosie in encouragement. A few people on the fringe of the crowd even began to walk away, as though whatever happened here no longer interested them.

One man in the plaid shirt and brown work-pants of a digger called out as he turned away, "Aw, what the hell, bring the baggages ashore and the folks along with 'em. Some of us will earn some money from that anyway. That still leaves me with a powerful thirst!"

Amid hoots of laughter, he trudged up the street toward the saloons.

"I'll join you, mate," called another digger from the middle of the crowd, "if you'll shout me to a brew."

"Go to the Red Raven," Rosie called after them. "Tell Bart, the bartender, I said to give you drinks on me! That goes for the rest of you, too. The first round of drinks on me!"

She knew that offer would win a lot of the hard-drinking Aussies. It would cost her. She'd have to spend a hell of a lot of time on her back to pay the bill. But it was worth it.

The mob started to break apart with people moving off in all different directions. She'd won! She leaned over and gestured to the man who'd hoisted her up, indicating she wanted to get back down. As he lifted her down, his hand slid part way up her leg under her petticoat. Well, Rosie figured, everything has its price. He gave her a sly wink.

"I'm comin' to see you at the Red Raven," he said. "Get that free drink." He laughed, and she knew it wasn't a drink he was after.

Rosie pushed her way through the remaining people to reach the gangplank.

"Captain Thornburg," she called. Already he was busily shouting orders to his men in preparation for disembarkation. "Captain Thornburg," she called again to catch his attention. She knew the man from other trips to Sydney. He often came and shared a drink with her, though they'd never shared anything more than that. "May I come aboard?"

"Indeed you may," he called back to her, "and mighty welcome too."

He watched admiringly as she strode boldly along the rough wooden planks toward the deck.

"You're a brave woman," he said when she drew close enough to hear him without his having to shout. "You saved the day. I wasn't having any luck at all before you came along. But your face is cut! Come along and let me tend to that."

"Oh, it's nothing, I'm sure," she said, nonetheless allowing him to draw her by the hand toward his cabin.

"Come along, child," he called to the girl, who still stood, pale and shaken, by the railing.

"I did my best, Captain," Rosie said as he settled her in his chair and got out his medicine kit. "I hate to see people making fools of themselves."

"You went far beyond that," he answered, dabbing her face with ointment. "And please don't call me Captain anymore. My name is Daniel, but I'd be honored if you'd call me Dan."

Rosie smiled at him and he smiled back, and a strange warm feeling came over Rosie that made her blush, a thing she'd thought she'd forgotten how to do.

"What's your name, young lady?" she asked turning the conversation to a safer arena. She reached out and stroked the blond tresses of the girl who stood close by the captain. The girl had yet to utter a sound. The tracks of her earlier tears still showed on her cheeks, but now her face was calm.

"Anne Finch," the girl answered in a clear voice.

"You wouldn't happen to know a good woman who might like to raise this dear child," Dan Thornburg asked. "She's a real darling, she is. I'd keep her myself if the life of a sea captain didn't prevent such a thing." Then he whispered in Rosie's ear, "Both her parents died during the trip over."

"I think I know just the woman," she cried impulsively.

"Me! I was thinking a while ago that tomorrow would be my birthday and I had neither husband nor child. And to tell you the truth," she leaned conspiratorially toward the Captain, "of the two, it's not having the child that makes me saddest. Anne, you could be my birthday present to myself. The best present I could ever get. Would you like to come and be my girl?"

The two grownups could see that the child had to struggle to swallow a new round of tears. No doubt her thoughts were with her parents, lying dead in a cabin beneath their feet. But she tried to smile bravely, and she answered, "You're very pretty, ma'am." Anne stretched out her delicate hand and softly patted Rosie's skirt.

"She certainly knows the right things to say," Rosie joked. She hated to admit that her own voice was half-choked for the poor child arriving alone in this strange new land. "Come along then," she said, taking Anne by the hand. "Captain, I mean Daniel, why don't you join us for a late supper when you've completed your work here."

"Count on it. I'll be along as soon as I can."

He watched the woman as she walked away, round and ripe as a luscious fruit in her tight gown that seemed ill-suited to the bright afternoon sun. The girl walked carefully step by step behind her. They made a strange, but handsome pair, he thought, the one so fair and the other so dark. He had certainly not intended to turn Anne Finch over to a woman who sold herself to men, but he didn't know how to find anyone else. Besides, at least this woman really wanted a daughter. That must surely count for a lot. He sighed. Anne Finch would have to be responsible for her own growing up to a great extent here in Australia. It was a rough land for anyone, but especially rough for the young and vulnerable.

He had come to know Anne Finch during the long journey. Before the sickness began to strike people down, she had been a bright and lively imp, skipping everywhere, always asking him questions about the way the sails worked and needing to know the name for everything on the ship. She would be a handful to raise. She was entering that particularly difficult period between childhood and woman-hood already. Twelve years old, she had told him. In this pioneer land that would be almost a woman.

It hurt him to have to hand her over to someone else, but he knew she needed a mother. Besides, a sea captain could never hope to raise a child. He thought about her sweet face with the rosebud lips, her sparkling eyes full of tears these last days. She would be breaking hearts before too long. He hoped Rosie Sullivan would be able to help her. Rosie seemed to be a good-natured sort. Her speech today showed she had spunk and brains as well. It was a lucky stroke, he thought, that she'd come down to the dock when she had.

Well, he couldn't spend any more time lost in thought. He was already half a day behind schedule. The faster he worked, the faster he would get to relax with Anne and her new momma, Rosie. Maybe they would be his adopted family. He had none of his own, having never been on shore long enough to arrange it. An adopted family in Sydney, Australia, the thought cheered him.

As he turned from the deck to shout orders to his crew who had been hiding out of sight when it looked like trouble was brewing, there was a faint smile on his face.

3

IF Flanders found the coach ride rough with the company's driver, she found it terrifying with Lachlan holding the reins. Once through the gap, he turned sharply off the road and drove directly over the rugged land. He headed north along the eastern side of the Blue Mountain chain that made up part of the Great Divide. The horses seemed willing to stretch out for him in a way they wouldn't for John Parker. They galloped along; the landscape whizzed past, and Flanders squeezed her eyes shut. The carriage, though solidly designed with four widely spaced wooden wheels, now careened across the countryside mostly on two. The dazzling series of twists and turns Lachlan maneuvered had never been envisioned by either the carriage maker or the coach company.

Flanders' earlier sense of adventure shifted to a dull realization that she would very likely not survive the night. In some ways that reduced her terror. Once she accepted her inevitable death, she could stop worrying about the coach tipping over and crushing her. It seemed no worse than a bullet in the back—or whatever other death lay in wait.

She could even stop worrying about whether her specimens were being hurt by the wild ride or how the British scientists would react to them. No doubt, the scientists would never see them. She knew science could go on perfectly well without her work. Her feelings of self-

importance seemed foolish now. She had actually believed the work she was doing was so important she
couldn't leave Australia.

The carriage made a sudden lurch to the west. Flanders
could tell the direction by the shift in the sun's position.
They seemed headed straight at the rocky base of the
mountains. Well, she thought, the damn fool was going to
destroy them both by crashing into rocks so old that scientists had not yet established their age. If the rocks had
spirits, as the aborigines believed, they would surely laugh
at the recklessness of these two white creatures casting
themselves up like some ritual sacrifice.

Then, as though the mountain had parted like the Red
Sea did for Moses, they were past the rocks, and the
carriage stopped. Flanders could only dimly see where she
was in the murky gloom. She waited for her eyes to adjust
to the change of light after the bright sunshine out on the
plains.

They seemed to be in an enormous cavern, but she knew
of no caverns on this side of the mountain. The sense of
new knowledge dispelled for a moment her awareness of
how she had gotten there. Then the door was thrown open,
and she remembered everything.

"Get down if you like, or stay in there," Lachlan said.

He stomped away before she could think of an answer.
No use being indignant, she decided. Her curiosity made
her climb down from the carriage. She saw that Lachlan
had turned his attention first to the animals. The four coach
horses were in a lather from their uncommon exertion. He
had unhitched them and was rubbing the sweat from their
flanks with soft cloths. His own horse, a beautiful creature
obviously more used to Lachlan's speed of travel, remained temporarily tethered at the back of the coach as if
patiently waiting his turn.

This was an interesting aspect of the bandit that Flanders
had not heard about in the stories. He preferred animals to
women or even to loot. If she got back to civilization

alive, she must be sure to spread the word. That would ruin his reputation! Still, Flanders couldn't help admiring the very characteristic she was making fun of. Hadn't she been thinking earlier that she herself preferred the creatures of this earth to the human beings who walked upon it?

Ignoring her, Lachlan had led the horses from the cave, no doubt to let them graze. Flanders untied the bow of her bonnet and threw it in on the coach seat. She took off her gloves and tossed them in on top. Then she walked over to Lachlan's horse, talking to him soothingly as she approached.

"There, boy, good boy," she said. He took a single nervous sidestep, jerking his head up and away from her. "Easy now." She ran her hand down his gleaming side. He was hardly sweating at all. His owner certainly kept him in peak condition. He lowered his head, and she patted his nose. He pressed against her hand for more. "You know you're a handsome devil, don't you?" She had just untied the reins when Lachlan's sharp voice called, "Bandit!" The horse wheeled away from Flanders and trotted to where his master stood framed in the mouth of the cave.

"I hope you weren't planning to try to escape on Bandit," he said. "He won't let anyone on his back but me."

To Flanders amazement, she realized that escape hadn't even entered her mind! She felt disappointed in herself. She had always thought of herself as heroic. If this kidnapping was a test, she thought glumly, she was certainly failing it. At least, though, she wouldn't show him that she was afraid. And she positively would not cry. Flanders had a romantic nature which had brought her a lot of teasing as she was growing up. She would burst into tears in the middle of her classes if they were reading a sad story. She had finally learned to control that excess. At least she hoped she had.

"I wouldn't steal your horse, Mr. McKenzie," she said

in what she meant to be an insulting manner. ''I simply
untied him to be helpful.''

''Good,'' he answered, unimpressed. ''If you want to
be so dang helpful, how about taking a look at the food
supply over in them bags by the rocks and see what you can
fix us for supper. I'll start us a fire. It'll be plenty cold in
these caves by nightfall. Meantime, you can use it to cook
on.'' He paused and gave her a slow, scrutinizing look
from the top of her russet hair to the tip of her high-button
boots. It made her feel like a piece of dress goods on sale,
but she stood perfectly still. She would not allow him to
see her discomfort. ''God knows, I hope you can cook.
You sure ain't much of a looker.'' Despite the crudity of
his words, Flanders was taken by the curve of his lips as
he uttered them. She felt sure he was just teasing her and
wasn't really passing judgment. Anyway, she reminded
herself as she turned away in a huff, what did she care if
this highwayman liked her looks or not. She certainly
didn't care.

She went over to the food supply. He obviously spent a
fair amount of time in this cave—there were enough provisions to last a month or so. There was even some dry forage
for his horse. This must be his hideout, she realized with a
sinking feeling. If he took her to his hideout, he surely
couldn't let her live. Until she felt a drop of water fall on
her hand, she didn't realize she was crying. The very thing
she had just vowed she wouldn't do. At least Lachlan
McKenzie hadn't seen her, she thought, as she brushed the
tears from her cheeks with the backs of her hands and
gathered up the ingredients to make some sort of boiled
dinner.

Outside, Lachlan made sure the animals were all safely
out of sight of anyone passing on the road. Since no one
ventured off the road in these parts, he knew that was all
the precaution he needed to take.

He plucked a wild oat and stuck it in the corner of his

mouth. No need to rush back inside. His prisoner sure
wasn't going anywhere. As he leaned back against a rock,
he tried to think how he was going to get himself out of
this predicament and began to rue the impulsive decision
to bring the girl along. He certainly hadn't planned on ever
bringing anyone back with him to his hideout. Kidnapping
wasn't his specialty, that was for sure. That mail coach
wasn't supposed to take passengers. Why did they have to
go and make an exception this time?

Not that he wasn't used to his plans turning into a mess.
The fact that he was one of the most famous criminals in
Australia was the end-result of one mess after another.
Half the people in Australia were criminals or criminals'
kids, but not him. His folks had been good, respectable
people. The picture of his family back in Edinburgh,
Scotland came to his mind. He could see them all gathered
around the table and sharing the blessings before eating
their Sunday supper.

His father was a minister, and his mother a proper
minister's wife. Lachlan was the first-born of six kids. He
had always had to toe the mark, always had to set the
standards for the younger ones. He could still hear his
mother scolding him, "You have to do better, son. We've
raised you to be a gentleman and a Christian."

But he'd wanted to be a sailor, so at sixteen he ran away
to sea. Could it really be that long ago? He'd turned thirty
on his last birthday, and it depressed him.

Everything that had happened to him since that decision
to leave seemed mostly happenstance. And he didn't have
much to show for it. His ship had eventually put in at
Sydney Harbor. He'd heard wondrous stories of fortunes
in gold and had had enough of sailoring, so he'd decided
to try his hand at prospecting.

Of course, it didn't take him long to learn that, although
diggers were many, finders were few. He'd had no more
luck than most others, but he'd at least been smart enough

to give it up. He'd seen too many diggers growing old dreaming of the big one. Not him. That's when he took to the highway. Figuring that if he couldn't find gold of his own, he'd just help himself to a portion of everybody else's. Not the behavior of a gentleman and a Christian.

He knew his folks must still worry about him and remember him in their prayers. He had always planned to go back home a success, but when he turned thirty, he'd faced the fact that that dream was over. He doubted he'd ever make it back. He didn't even know if they were still alive, but he figured they'd probably outlive him. Bushrangers died young.

He hoped his folks' prayers would help him. He could use some help now, with this lady on his hands. He didn't know what he should do about her and cursed himself for a fool for saddling himself with her in the first place. He should have tied her up with that brute of a driver and to hell with it.

Then a tantalizing smell reached him, the smell of a sturdy stew simmering away. Lord, it had been a long time since he'd had a good hot meal! Most of the time he just cut up some vegetables and swallowed them down raw with chunks of black bread and a bottle or two of lager. Tonight, though, smelled like it was going to be a treat. She might mean trouble in the long run, but tonight he was going to enjoy sharing a good meal with a woman.

She would mean trouble. He might as well recognize that. He'd have to kill her for sure. And the murder of a woman . . . well, even the barbarous Aussies might find that hard to swallow.

What the hell! No matter what, he was going to have himself a night with a woman! In the morning he'd take care of disposing of her.

Not that he had any trouble getting women—he always had enough pretty trinkets to buy himself one for a night. But this woman was different. She was clearly a lady and, if what she had said in the coach was anywhere close to the truth, an educated one at that. It could be an amusing dinner. He headed back to the cave's almost-hidden entrance. He would worry about what to do with her once he'd gotten some use out of her.

He stopped to let his eyes adjust to the cave's dim light. When they did, he saw the woman bent over the cookpot. She was more capable than her fancy outfit indicated. She'd managed to start the fire on her own and had even made a clearing to cook in. She had rolled up the sleeves of her blouse and opened the collar. By the fire's light he could see the damp tendrils of her hair, almost the color of Bandit's coat, stuck against her forehead. She was a damn fine looking creature, never mind the remarks he'd made to goad her. Her nose was long and straight, her skin fair, her lips full. But her most outstanding feature was her eyes which, as she raised them to him now, were large and luminous.

"Well, don't just stand there," she said, "come in and make yourself useful."

"You sound like my mother when you say that," he laughed. "Though I can't picture my mother down on her hands and knees in front of a campfire."

"She probably would be if you had your way!"

"While we're on the subject of mothers," he retorted, "what do you suppose yours would think of your life here in the wilds of Aussieland?"

Flanders stood up and put her hands on her hips, leaving smudges of soot on the velvet of her skirt. She answered, "Indeed I often wonder about that myself. You see, my mother died shortly after I was born." She immediately regretted her words. She had wanted to make him feel bad, but instead it was she who felt bad. Was she trying for his sympathy, she wondered.

Lachlan stood looking at her in silence.

"I've set plates inside the coach," she said. "It seemed

the only semi-civilized setting for our meal. Is there something to drink? I think the food's about done. I cut everything small for speed.'' She smiled at him.

''I have some Australian beer in the back of the cave. There's a stream there that's always cool. By the way, miss, where's the knife you used on that food? I'd rather not be cut up in small pieces!''

''Back in the bag. I'm not as devious as you. I never thought about sticking a knife into your ribs. But maybe I'll learn from you!'' She heaped her words with as much scorn as she could muster.

''If you live long enough.''

Her confidence wilted at his ominous words. In the firelight, Flanders thought, his face looked quite evil enough for those words to be a serious threat.

''My name is Flanders Wilde,'' she said more sedately. ''Please don't call me 'miss.' It makes me feel old.''

''Your food smells good, Flanders. I confess I'm starved! Could we call a truce long enough to share a meal? We can get back to being enemies after we've eaten.''

''Good,'' she said. She held out her hand to shake on the deal.

That surprised him, but he shook her hand solemnly. She was certainly different from any woman he'd known. She had a wild, free spirit, which he admired, and the manners of a man. He wondered, too, how much woman was buried under that brusqueness. Slowly, he raised her fingers to his lips.

At the soft, moist touch of Lachlan's lips on the back of her hand, Flanders shivered. Her free hand flew to her mouth, where her fingertips rested lightly on her lips. She closed her eyes, told herself not to be foolish. But when she opened them and gazed into the dark coals of Lachlan's eyes, she felt a tightness close around her chest that she'd never experienced before.

''You can serve now,'' he whispered. Her parted lips

gave him the answer to his question. There was plenty of woman to Flanders Wilde. "I'll be right back with the beers. You do drink beer, don't you?"

Unable to utter a sound, Flanders nodded. Lachlan smiled and turned away.

4

THEY ate in silence, sitting opposite each other in the coach. When either of them moved, their knees touched. They seemed to share the comfortable silence of old friends. An outsider would never have dreamed they were kidnapper and victim.

The glow on Flanders' cheeks came only in part from the flicker of the fire. With each passing moment, her attraction to this dark outlaw grew stronger. She told herself that she was being a silly fool—falling for someone who would as soon kill her as look at her. But no matter—even though she was completely at his mercy, she found him utterly mesmerizing.

His curly dark hair hid most of his face as he bent over his plate. She remembered the depth of his eyes. Surely he couldn't be a murderer, couldn't simply murder her.

"Are you going to kill me?" She hadn't planned to ask. The words just came from her.

Her bluntness caught him off-guard. He stared at her. He knew he was going to *have* to kill her, but he couldn't see any point in sharing that piece of information with her. It was really a shame. She was the kind of woman there should be more of. But a bushranger's life didn't allow for sentimentality.

"You weren't in my original plans," he answered. "I don't know what to do with you."

She lowered her fork to her plate.

"You came as quite a surprise to me, too," she said.

"Were you telling the truth about what's in the boxes?"

"Yes."

"Rocks?"

"Scientific specimens. Some of them are rocks. Some are dried plants."

"All those boxes?"

"Yes."

"Damn! What kind of a lady are you anyway?"

Flanders recalled the words in her professor's letter: more of a naturalist than a woman. Here was this outlaw saying pretty much the same thing.

Lachlan pushed his plate aside and climbed out of the coach. Flanders tried to go on eating, but she couldn't swallow. She put her plate down and followed him. Flanders watched him dragging down the boxes and bags from the top of the coach. He must still be hoping she was secretly shipping gold.

"Please be careful with my things," she said quietly, not wishing to arouse his anger. "It was to safeguard them to the dock that I made this journey in the first place."

He turned from his precarious perch on the side of the coach and glared at her.

"I'm sorry." She felt chilled suddenly. She wasn't sure whether it was because of the sight of her two years' work being chucked about or because night had fallen. "It's just that I've spent two years gathering that material." She lapsed into silence. Lachlan turned back to his work.

She moved closer to the low fire and added some branches. It blazed up. In the brief bright light, she thought she spotted a drawing on the cave wall, but by the time she got to it, the fire had died down just enough so that she couldn't see it clearly. Flanders pulled one of the partly lit branches from the fire. She held it over her head to examine the painting. It was the authentic work of an aborigine tribe. She could make out the figure of the sacred snake and of the yam, the staple aborigine food.

"What are you doing over there?" Lachlan asked, coming up to her.

"Did you know there were drawings in your cave?"

"Sure. I'm not blind. I've wondered about them, but if the aborigines that made 'em are still around these parts, they don't seem to mind sharing this space. I've always had more reason to fear the white man than the natives."

"But this is a real find!" Flanders' voice trembled with excitement. "This should be studied. Someone should copy it. . . ."

Lachlan had grown ominously silent. Here she was babbling on about bringing people to his hideout. Her every word guaranteed her death sentence, she realized.

"I didn't mean . . ." she began, then stopped. "If you let me go, I promise I'll never reveal your hiding place to anyone." She held her hand up like a little girl promising to tell the truth. The man looked at her in silence.

"We'll see," he said finally.

The stick in Flanders' hand had just about flickered out. Lachlan took it, walked back to the fire and threw it in. She turned her head to follow his movements and gasped in dismay when she saw the contents of her bags and boxes in heaps on the cave floor. The things she had so carefully sorted and labeled.

"Junk," he snarled when he saw the look on her face. "The whole lot's not worth a single shilling."

"Fool!" She bit the word out with contempt.

He strode up to her and slapped her so hard that his fingers left red stripes along her cheeks, but she was so furious that even that didn't stop her.

"Those packages contain something rarer than gold. There's more value there than in half the goldfields in Australia. But only for those who have eyes to see it. Now that you've made it all a mess, I hope you're finally convinced that I told you the truth."

"Yes, the truth. Not much comfort for having risked my neck. And ending up with nothing but trouble—a coach

and horses, and a loud-mouthed crazy woman who collects
rocks that *don't* have gold in them!''

They glared at each other. Then the humor of Lachlan's
description of her welled up inside Flanders, and she
couldn't resist the laugh that bubbled up and burst from
her. Lachlan joined in.

''Come on,'' he said, ''let's take a walk. You've never
seen anything so beautiful as the sky out in the bush.''

''I live in the bush,'' she protested. ''Outside of
Toowoomba in Darling Downs. I've walked out under the
stars plenty.''

It offended her that he thought her some delicate city-
bred lady, although her sojourn in Australia not withstanding,
that was exactly what she was. She wanted to make him
admire her. On her own terms. As his equal.

''You live on the Downs, eh?'' he asked as they strolled
along the footpath beside the mountains. As if by agreement,
they both stopped and stood staring up at the enormous
inverted bowl of blackness agleam with uncountable glitter-
ing stars. The moon, a perfect silver ball, seemed tangled
in the arms of a distant tree.

''It's hard to think of this as winter, isn't it?'' Flanders
asked.

''Right, there's not much resemblance to the bitter chill
of home. You're from England, aren't you? I'm Scottish.
Still, you're shivering. I've got a blanket you can use as a
shawl. Back in the cave.''

''Don't go!'' She touched his arm. ''I'm all right, really.
It's so magnificent, this land.'' She left her hand where it
was. It felt good to touch another person. She wondered
why she'd never noticed that before.

They began to walk again, setting a slow dreamy pace.
Then Flanders caught her foot in a mole burrow. She
started to fall. Lachlan grabbed for her, pulling her to him.
She was against his chest, feeling the hard muscles of his
body. Then he bent down his head, and his lips found
hers. She told herself she ought to resist, but instead she

threw her arms around his neck in a passionate response. When at last they pulled apart, she was shaken with confusion and embarrassment, and half turned away.

"You certainly are full of surprises," he said, turning her back toward him. "Let's try that one more time."

He placed his hands on both sides of her narrow waist and gently kissed her lips, then her eyes, then the soft skin of her cheek. Finally he held her to him and rested his chin against the top of her head.

"Let's forget about that walk," he said.

A terrible war raged inside of Flanders. All the precepts and standards of her upbringing—modesty, purity, chastity—locked in combat with the waves of desire that rushed through her body. She had been taught that she must fight to retain her honor above all things. But this was a word learned in another country in what seemed tonight to have been another lifetime. Honor. What did that have to do with the pounding she felt in her throat, the tightness in her stomach, the sweet ache in her breasts?

"I've never. . . ." she began, but his fingers on her lips hushed her.

"I know," he said.

Lachlan put his arm around Flanders' waist, and she leaned her head against his shoulder, as they made their way back to the cave.

Once inside, Lachlan led her past the coach which almost blocked the entrance, past the dying fire, toward the back of the enormous cavern where his bedroll lay spread out beside the wall.

"Wait here," he said. "I'll stir up the fire to keep us warm. Although I'm sure we can provide each other with heat enough."

The pressure of his fingers on her arm reassured her, and the darkness of the cave hid the blush that rose to color her cheeks. She sat primly, her hands folded in her lap. In a moment, it seemed, he was beside her, pressing her down onto the blanketed floor.

"Wait," she said, "wait."

Her voice was breathless and scared.

"What is it?" he asked, then realized she was just afraid. "Give me a kiss, girl, why don't you? Relax."

Lying under the weight of this stranger's body, Flanders thought again that he still might kill her. At least, though, she'd die knowing what it felt like to be a woman.

To her surprise, he didn't tear her clothes from her. Instead, he went on kissing her—gently at first, then more deeply. His touches and kisses began to work their magic. She forgot about being new and nervous, and just surrendered herself to the moment and to the man. She heard the trickle of the stream, the crackle of twigs in the fire, and then she heard nothing, saw nothing, became part of a wild surge, like stallions galloping across the plains.

Slowly and with infinite tenderness, he undressed her. Each article of clothing, as it was removed, earned a kiss, a touch, a gentle caress, until her body was on fire.

She felt no shyness, and she could see admiration in Lachlan's eyes. She leaned over, lightly kissed his lips, and began to unbutton his shirt. He smiled and began to help. When they were completely undressed, they stretched out on the blanket. The firelight created beautiful sunset tones across their bodies.

Lachlan drew Flanders on top of him. They were soon joined again in the double shape of love. Then, cradled in each other's arms, they fell into a sleep that lasted until the whinny of the horses announced the dawn.

Flanders sat up and saw that Lachlan was already awake watching her. She couldn't read the look in his eyes, but she felt suddenly shy and turned away from him to dress.

"You have to kill me, don't you?" she asked with her back still to him.

Without answering, he stood up and walked to the mouth of the cave. Slowly, Flanders followed him. Streaks of color split open the night sky, until, with a blaze of light, the orange fireball of the sun climbed over the edge of the plains.

"If I let you live, can I trust you not to betray me?" His eyes never left the sky. At first, in fact, Flanders couldn't believe that he was addressing her. She'd already given up the hope of living. At this hint of release, her breath became painful in her chest. She could hardly speak.

Finally, though, she managed to say, "I'll never betray you." Her voice trembled. She felt as though she were taking a solemn oath.

"Make coffee," Lachlan ordered.

As she turned away, he added, "I'll get you as far as the main road. Just leave the horses on a loose rein and they'll carry you straight to town. They know the way."

Flanders didn't dare raise the question, now uppermost in her mind, as to when, or if, she would see him again. No matter what, she wouldn't play the frail female. But it was with a heavy heart that she began somewhat haphazardly to repack her boxes. By the time the coffee was ready, her boxes were tied, her bags refastened, and her emotions closed away where she knew they would have to stay. At least she was alive.

They drank their coffee in silence. When Flanders was only half-finished, Lachlan said, "Time to go. If I wait much longer, there's likely to be a scouting party on the road."

"I'll have a long ride before Brisbane, I imagine."

"Most of the day. Tonight, though, you'll be able to sleep in a real bed. Not on the floor of a cave."

"I have no complaints about my last night's sleep," Flanders said softly, but Lachlan had already walked away from her and was busy hitching up the horses to the coach. He spent the next few minutes getting her things in place, then he called to her that he was ready to head out. He helped her up to the driver's seat.

"Don't be afraid," he said as he led the horses out.

"They'll behave. They'll be glad to have your light touch, I'm sure, instead of that brute of a driver's."

He handed her up the reins and whistled for Bandit, who was already saddled and came galloping up at his signal. Lachlan hoisted himself onto Bandit's back and called to Flanders, "Follow me. When I point ahead, you'll know you're almost at the road. Then I'll turn around. At the road, you head east and just keep on going. Eventually you'll get to Brisbane and the sea."

He rode ahead of her coach, gracefully seated on the loping horse as though he were a natural extension of the animal. Flanders felt she could ride on this way forever. When he pointed ahead, though, she saluted and kept on without a backward glance. No use, she told herself. Thank goodness she had work to do and couldn't give herself over to tearful brooding. The horses, glad to be back on the familiar road, moved along at a good clip, and Flanders found herself daydreaming about the last twenty-four hours. By the time she reached the outskirts of Brisbane, she was shocked to realize it was already late afternoon.

Her arrival prompted a flurry of activity as the coach company representatives came out to question her about her adventure and tried to assure her that the company would do everything in its power to capture and punish the bushranger. They only hoped she had not been harmed. She assured them she had not been. Could she provide them with information as to the whereabouts of the bushranger, they asked. She assured them that she had been blindfolded the entire time and hadn't the vaguest idea where she had spent the night. When the excitement finally died down, she settled herself into a room at the Olde Cove Inn. With a sigh of relief, she closed the door on the bustle of the port town and threw herself across the bed, overcome with memories and longing.

5

ROSIE Sullivan put the girl, who had hardly spoken through-out the day, to bed as soon as it grew dark. The strain of the difficult journey showed clearly on Anne's tense young face. Even dining with her friend, the captain, hadn't been enough to raise more than a fleeting smile. Anne wore one of Rosie's old slips as a nightgown. She was already beginning to fill it out.

"Sleep well, Anne Finch," Rosie said as she tucked her in, leaned over, and gave her cheek a tender kiss. "I'll be right in the next room during the night in case you get scared or need anything. Don't you worry now. In the morning we'll get your trunks unpacked, and you'll have your own clothes to wear."

Rosie looked at the young woman who lay on the oversized four-poster bed. She remembered the years when she herself was caught between wanting to grow up and wanting to remain a child. But time has its way with us, she thought, no matter what it is that we want. Anne Finch would soon be a woman. How Rosie hoped she could help her become a strong person. She prayed the memory of these past terrible days on board ship would fade from her.

"Good night," she whispered, and tiptoed from the room. She left the door open a crack so that the light from her own bedside kerosene lamp would seep into Anne's room and shield her from any nighttime terrors.

A short time later, Anne began to toss and turn in her sleep.

"No," she moaned, "no."

Rosie, though, was down at the bar by then. She joked with the men who came to the saloon for a laugh or two along with their liquor. It was her job. She didn't hear that the child's dreams had turned to nightmares.

In her dream, Anne was back aboard the *H.M.S. Three Winds*. She lay in bed beside her mother. Outside, a storm raged. The black sky rumbled, and then a terrible crash echoed in her ears. She sat up and stared out the porthole, but she could see nothing. Suddenly, a jagged white line ripped open the darkness and filled her eyes with a vision of waves as big as snow-covered mountains.

"Momma," she screamed, but the woman in the bed beside her didn't move. Anne scrambled over to her. "Momma," she sobbed again and shook her. The blanket fell away from the woman's shoulders, but it wasn't her mother. It was a skeleton. The skull grinned up at her. Anne tried to scream, but no sound came from her lips. Frantically she fled from the cabin out into the fierce storm.

She staggered along, clinging to the rail so that the wild wind wouldn't catch her and fling her overboard.

The rain soaked her. The deck beneath her feet was slick with rain and the wash of waves. She had to reach the captain. He would save her. She pulled herself hand-over-hand along the railing toward the front of the ship.

She saw him ahead of her. The captain. Only he was lashed to the huge main mast. Then she realized it wasn't the captain. It was her father. He stretched his arms out towards her, calling to her. But his words were blown away on the wind.

Then there was a crack so loud it sounded as though the ship had split in half. The mast, with her father bound to it, had been torn from the deck. Anne watched in horror as a monstrous wave lifted it and hurled it into the sea. She raised her hands to her face to hide from the hideous sight, and at that instant a wave swept her from the deck. It raised her up in its powerful grasp. Up and up and up. She struggled to keep her head above water. The wave crested. Anne tumbled down in its foam, sank deeper and deeper, and the black coldness of water closed over her.

She woke up with her heart pounding. She lay in a dry bed. She tried to think where she was, and it came to her that she had landed safely in Australia.

Then she remembered what she didn't want to remember and what she would never be able to forget: her mother and father were dead. She was alone in the world.

A face appeared at the door. It was the woman who had been so brave down at the dock. It was Rosie Sullivan, the woman who was now going to take the place of her mother. But she never really would. No one would ever take the place of her real mother, Anne silently vowed. Still she was relieved to see the concern on Rosie's face. Someone in the world still cared about her. Anne began to weep.

Rosie hurried over to her. She hadn't heard Anne call out in her sleep; the barroom sounds had made that impossible. She had simply come upstairs to check on her new daughter.

"Oh, poor Annie," she murmured. "I know you've had terrible sorrow for your young years. But I'm going to do by best to make things right for you. Just you wait. Everything's going to be all right."

Anne tried to smile at her. She wiped the tears from her face and lay back down in the bed.

"Thank you, Rosie," she said. "I'm all right now."

Rosie sat with her another few minutes, until the girl drifted back off to sleep. She was already beginning to realize how many changes having this girl would bring to her life—the bad as well as the good. But at the moment, seeing the twelve-year-old's innocent face, the good seemed to far outweigh any bad that might come.

"Anne Finch, my daughter," she whispered.

* * *

Anne awoke to a day full of sunlight shining through her window. She remembered that she was in Sydney, Australia, her new homeland. And for whatever reason—the fine day, a good night's rest, the natural resilience of youth— her heart felt lighter than it had in days. She got out of bed and went into the next room where she saw Rosie Sullivan still asleep. Rosie had one arm thrown up over her forehead, as though to fend off the invasion of the light. She had taken her long black hair down, and it lay like a fan around her pale face. Anne went over and sat down on the bed beside her and patted the woman's cheeks. Rosie's eyes flew open and for a moment stared blankly at the child. Then she broke into a lovely large grin and reached over to draw the girl to her. Anne smiled back and then began to giggle. It was the first time Rosie had heard her sound like a child.

"Happy birthday, Miss Sullivan."

"Why, bless your heart, you remembered it was my birthday! But please call me Rosie, at least, if not mum. I know I can never take the place of your real mother, but I want to be as good to you as she would have been."

The child seemed playful as she bent over, kissed Rosie's cheek, and said, "All right, mum, but it's time to get up now so we can celebrate your birthday."

"You rascal. All right. I'll get up, but it'll be hours yet before we can go on the picnic that Bart . . . uh, Mr. Nettleton, promised us."

She threw the coverlet off the bed and stuck her feet over the side. The girl slid to the floor and matched up her little bare feet to the woman's larger ones.

"When I grow up, will my feet be as big as yours?" she asked.

Rosie laughed out loud. "You do make me laugh, child. What a question! I suppose your feet might be as big as mine when you grow up, although I always fancied that I had rather small feet, until this moment when you compared them to yours."

"Oh, I didn't mean to hurt your feelings. I want to grow up and be just like you."

Rosie kissed the child's head, then took her hand.

"You'll be a hundred times better than me in every way, I'm sure. But thank you for the compliment. Now let's go get some breakfast." She wrapped a kimono around her nightdress and led the way down to the communal kitchen.

The morning disappeared in a flurry of activity involving the unpacking and organizing of Anne's possessions. Rosie had set up the picnic time with Bart, and he had assured her he would take charge of everything, even the preparation of the food.

So in the early afternoon, Rosie and the young girl who had just become her daughter stood hand in hand before the Red Raven and waited for Bart to come collect them in the carriage he had hired for the occasion. Rosie, looking like a proper lady, wore a white muslin gown decorated with small embroidered pink rosebuds. The dress fitted her well and emphasized her firm bosom and small waist before falling away in a full swirl of skirt. The child wore a long white dress, too, but one with ribbons that hung like banners down along the skirt. Both of them wore sunbonnets, and Rosie carried a pair of sweaters in case the day turned chilly.

"Here he comes," she said excitedly to the child when she saw Bart pull into view around the corner.

Soon the three of them were comfortably seated in the small phaeton and the horses were cantering out of town.

"Where shall we go?" Rosie asked.

"I thought we'd go to the far side of the Botanical Gardens, eh? The plants are so lush and really beautiful there that they're bound to please out little visitor."

"You're a good fellow, Bart." Rosie smiled up at the man beside her. He gave an extra flick to the reins, flushed with pleasure by her warm approval.

It wasn't long before they had reached the gardens. Bart pulled the buggy to a halt and tied it up under the shade of some trees. Then he handed the ladies down and retrieved the picnic hamper from its hiding place beneath the seat.

"Are you hungry yet, or would you prefer some time to wander around?" As he asked the question, Bart saw that Anne had already run off to investigate a cluster of exotic flowers, leaving Rosie and him behind. "Well, I guess she'd rather play a while," he smiled, confirming the obvious. "That will give the two of us a chance to talk some." He lay the hamper on the ground, withdrew a ground blanket from the buggy and spread it out. "Come sit with me."

Rosie arranged her skirts prettily around her as she lowered herself to the ground. Bart lounged beside her, stretching out his full length along the blanket and propping himself up on one elbow.

"Now, Rosie, since you are to be a momma, have you given any new thought to my offer to join you in your endeavor? You know I love you. Marry me, and we'll make a proper family for Anne Finch."

Rosie Sullivan looked away. A slow flush began to creep up her neck and into her cheeks, but she remained silent.

"I can't marry you, Bart," she finally said. "It wouldn't be fair to either of us."

"Don't go giving me that blather about the kind of life you've led, woman," Bart interrupted. "I know you. No matter what, you're as good and pure as any virgin back in Ireland.

"No, it's not just that. Although that is a big part of it, I admit. But there's more. I'm fond of you, Bart. You know I am. But I don't love you. I'm sorry that I don't, because I know you'd make me a good husband and Anne a good father, but there's no help for it. I hope you'll forgive me and we will be able to go on as we have . . . the very best of friends."

"Oh, Rosie, I could marry you on those terms. Maybe you'd even come to love me in time. Besides, even if you didn't, your affection would be enough for me. I have enough love to make up for your share."

For reply, Rosie gave a brief, negative shake of her head. Bart began to say something else, but just then Anne came running up to them with a bouquet of wildflowers in her hands.

"Happy birthday, mum," she said, thrusting the flowers into Rosie's hands. "I picked 'em just for you." The child stood before them smiling proudly, and the grownups dropped their conversation and turned their attention to her.

"You're a love, Anne," Rosie said. "I couldn't have a better present."

After that they ate their roasted chicken with its accompaniment of rolls and salads, and then the three of them wandered through the park-like gardens enjoying the perfume of the orange-flowers and the colorful array of plants. As they stood at the top of the hill and gazed down on a lovely peaceful bay, the darkhaired man and woman, both young and handsome, and the fair child seemed to represent the hope of the Australia-to-be, strong and capable and optimistic about the future.

By the time they were on their way back into Sydney, Bart and Rosie were back on easy terms, any bad feeling inspired by their cross-purposes about marriage plans having lifted. The child prattled on about the flowers and the waters of the bay. Rosie only half—listened, being totally preoccupied with thoughts about her new role as Anne's "Mother." She must find out about schools. This child was too bright not to be taught. She must rearrange the rooms she took customers to, also. She couldn't bear to think of Anne walking in and finding her in bed with some stranger. It amazed her how quickly she had come to think of herself as Anne's mother. Something deep inside her must have been yearning urgently for a little girl of her own. Twenty-eight years old, she thought, but somehow, with Anne beside her, the number didn't seem so terrible any longer.

6

DESPITE her good spirits at the picnic, Anne awoke from sleep with bad dreams the next night and the next. She began to dread falling asleep. Rosie would tuck her in, and then she would lie there willing herself not to fall asleep. She dreaded having to relive the voyage in the darkness of dreams. Even as she lay in bed awake, though, she could see her mother's face as it grew paler and paler, until finally it turned grey. She saw over and over the way her mother's laugh became only a ghostly smile, then finally disappeared into a grimace of pain.

Anne tried to remember the last time she had spoken with her mother. It was the night before the big storm, and more than a week before they arrived at Sydney Harbor.

Her father, who had refused to leave his wife's side, called her to come over to the bed.

"Your mother wants to talk with you alone, Anne dear. I'll be right outside." As he stood up, Anne saw him stagger and catch himself against the wall of the cabin. He hadn't appeared to be sick during the weeks that her mother had lain restless and fevered in her bed, but now Anne saw how pale his face was.

"Daddy," she said, "are you sick the same as momma?"

He smiled at her gently and placed his hand on her shoulder. "I think I'm sick at heart is all."

She hadn't known what he meant, though his tone of voice made her tremble in fear.

"Momma," she said softly, standing beside the woman who appeared to be sleeping. At the sound of Anne's voice, the woman's eyes flickered briefly, then opened and focused with difficulty on her daughter.

"Come closer, daughter," she managed to say, licking her dry lips. "Sit by me on the bed so I can talk to you without raising my voice."

The child obeyed at once.

"If I don't get better . . ."

"No, momma, don't even say that," the child said and fell weeping on her mother's neck.

"Anne, you must be brave. I know you are only twelve years old, but you've always been very mature. Now listen to me, I don't know how much longer I'll be able to talk to you this way."

The child sat back up. She rested her hand on her mother's arm and could feel how hot her mother's skin was.

"You must take care of your father for me. Do you understand?"

Anne nodded numbly.

"You must grow up to be a lovely lady, pure and good. I want you to study hard so you will be smart as well. Australia is a new land and you are a new life for it. I want you to grow up in such a way that you represent the very best product of this new world." She could speak no more; her words were broken by a fit of coughing, and when it passed, she felt too weak to continue. "Oh, I wish you were old enough to really understand . . ." was all she managed. Then her eyes closed, and she turned her face away from where the child sat with tears streaming down her face.

"Daddy," she called, "Daddy," and her father was soon beside her. Silently, they stood together looking down on the form of the woman so much loved by them both.

Now, as Anne thought back to that night, tears welled in her eyes. Her mother had died the next day, falling into a

peaceful sleep from which she never awakened. Then her
father took her mother's place. He seemed not to care
whether he was sick or well, alive or dead. She didn't
know if he had died of disease of heartbreak. All she knew
was that, within another day or two, her father was dead
and she was an orphan.

Rosie, peeking in to see if Anne was all right, saw the
child's tears. She came and sat beside her.

"Anne," she said. "It's all right to cry when you have
such terrible sorrows. Cry now, dear, then try to put your
tears aside for a little while and go to sleep."

The child, swallowing the last of her tears, nodded
miserably.

"Shall I tell you a story?" Rosie asked.

Again the child nodded. She would be glad not to think
about herself for a while. Maybe Rosie would tell her a
story about some other little girl, some happier little girl.

Rosie tried to think what story she should tell to cheer up
Anne. Then it came to her! Cinderella. That was a story
about a girl who was all alone in the world, but who,
because she was good, had wonderful things happen to
her. Rosie would play down the wicked stepmother. Instead,
she would make the stepmother into the fairy godmother.
She would be able to leave out the wicked stepmother all
together. So she began the story of the poor girl without a
mother or a father, and before she came to the place at the
end of the ball where Cinderella meets the prince, Anne
was sound asleep.

Please let her sleep without any bad dreams, Lord,
Rosie prayed. If she were just kind and patient enough,
surely the girl would be able to overcome this tragedy. As
quietly as possible, she left the room.

An hour or two later, Anne awoke from a pleasant
dream in which she had been at a fancy dance. She turned
on her side, not wanting to fall right back asleep. She
enjoyed the feeling of the bed under her and the warm
gleam of the soft yellow light from the doorway, the light

from Rosie's room left on so Anne wouldn't awaken in the dark and be afraid.

Anne lay in bed and thought about that first night in Sydney. She had eaten dinner with the captain from the *Three Winds* and the pretty lady from the dock, the one who had taken her home, Rosie Sullivan. As he was leaving after dinner, the captain had whispered to her, "You must be a good girl, Anne. Promise me that you will be. In return, I'll make you a promise. I promise I'll come back and visit with you on my next trip to Sydney, and I'll bring a wonderful present with me."

Of course, she had promised him that she would be a good girl. She knew he would keep his promise, too, and visit her. She wondered what the present would be. Well, it would be a long time before he came back. She remembered how very long a time she had spent on the ship coming over. He had to go back to England and then return.

Anne slipped from the big bed and headed toward the light in the next room. It was Rosie's room, but Rosie wasn't in it. The bed, still unmade with its crumpled sheets and piles of pillows, tempted Anne, but she was suddenly curious about the room downstairs where Mr. Bart worked. Uncertain as to what she would discover, she opened the door slowly and quietly. A man's hearty laughter rolled up to her on a blast of music. She walked out on the landing and leaned over the shiny bannister to look down into the crowded bar.

She had already noticed in her walks around town how many hotels and saloons there were in this city. Rosie had answered her questions by saying that drinking was the basic pleasure for the men who came into Sydney from the gold-fields or from their great land holdings and for the Sydneyites themselves.

"Child," she had said, "there must be a hundred licensed houses of one kind or another in Sydney. That's a lot of drinking!"

"Why, mum? Does it taste so good?"

"I suppose different folks would give different answers to that. Some drinks are mighty tasty. Remember the first night when I gave you that glass of sherry? That tasted good, eh? But more than that is the fact that it makes people feel jolly. If a man has had bad luck at the diggings and feels he's never going to get anywhere . . . you know what I mean? If he feels he's given up England or America, wherever his home is, to come way out here and make his fortune, and now he begins to think there is no fortune . . . Well, that man will come to town to drink and forget his troubles."

"It's like medicine then," Anne answered, and Rosie had laughed out loud.

Now Anne looked at the room full of noisy men and women from her vantage point on the second-floor landing. Everyone seemed to be laughing and talking at the same time. There were little clusters of men, usually around one woman. Anne noticed the player-piano in the corner. It always attracted her when she passed it. It had a tinny sound that somehow matched the flocked red-velvet wallpaper and the glitter of the huge gaslight chandelier hanging in the center of the saloon. The bar itself was a lovely length of gleaming mahogany. She saw the glasses hanging upside down from their perches above the bar where Bart reached for them whenever a customer placed an order. She liked Bart with his droopy mustache that made his face look so sad and old. She liked this whole place. It was really quite a happy place, full of music and laughter and people.

She thought the whole saloon scene was a great deal more appealing than the dull parties her parents had given back in England. Then, too, she would creep out to the top of the stairs, but the grownups back there were ever so much quieter. There was no music and no loud talk and nowhere near as much laughter.

She began to think she was going to like it here in her

new Australian home with this cheerful lady who had taken her in.

Anne yawned so wide that her jaw ached. She leaned her head against the rails and closed her eyes. She felt herself falling asleep. Oh dear, she thought, I mustn't fall asleep here. Rosie might get mad at me. She forced herself to stand up and go back to the bedrooms. In Rosie's room, the bed tempted her again with its cozy look and the piled up quilt. She climbed into it and breathed in the fragrance of Rosie's lavender sachet. Within moments she had fallen blissfully asleep.

7

"CHARLIE Burrows," Rosie said, leaning toward the man beside her at a corner table ,"you're not only one of the richest squatters around here—you're also the naughtiest. That's no kind of a joke to be telling a lady!"

"That's right," he roared. "That's why I didn't tell it to one." He playfully slapped her rump. "You're a fine piece of meat, though, girl. How about a little fun?"

"You want some fun, eh?" Rosie knew better than to take offense at his words. She'd known Charlle a long time, or anyway a long time by Sydney standards, where friendships came and went with the seasons, as people were always heading out to find a place of their own inland, while new settlers kept pouring in on the ships.

She noticed the fine lines that crisscrossed the back of Charlie's neck. Funny, she hadn't noticed them before. He must be pushing forty, she realized. She remembered when he was just a big bluffer talking about the strike he was going to make like a million others who passed through the Red Raven's swinging doors. They'd shared a lot of nights, including the big one after he'd struck gold just like he swore he would. It had been drinks for everyone then, until everyone was drunk and Charlie the drunkest of them all. Crazy drunk. Sick drunk.

That was the one and only time he ever told her he loved her. Of course, that was only the booze talking, she

58

knew that. The next day he couldn't even remember how he'd spent his money.

She looked at him more carefully now. He was a short, stocky man, no more than five-feet eight-inches tall. Even with his beer belly, though, anyone could see his bulk was mostly muscle.

He had a half dozen convicts assigned to him as servants by the government. They worked in exchange for room and board, and they considered themselves damn lucky not to be in the prison house. One of their regular duties was to wrestle with Charlie in the evenings. He despised men who let themselves get soft after coming to Australia.

"If we don't stay in fighting shape," he told anyone who would listen, "the damn felons will take charge. They'll take over this whole place, and it will be our own fault."

Charlie Burrows was a man who wanted to be in charge. He left Surrey, England for Australia as soon as he heard they'd found gold in the fields. He always knew he'd succeed no matter how many others failed. When he'd found gold, he enjoyed being an instant celebrity, a rich man overnight.

His only regret involved the wife he'd left behind in England to care for their two sons. She was already carrying a third child when he boarded the ship for Australia.

"I'll send for you as soon as I'm settled," he'd promised. "By then, you can come to our new home with our family of three fine children! We'll be regular pioneers." He'd kissed her fondly and brushed away her tears. "We'll be together again before you know it," he'd said.

But he'd been wrong. By the time he got settled, his wife had died in childbirth. The new baby, who would have been his only daughter, died the same night. He'd brought over his two boys, Hugh and Edmund, but even his wealth couldn't make up to them for not having a mother. It didn't make up to Charlie either, for not having a wife. But he'd made do. So far. Soon all that would change. He could hardly wait to tell Rosie the news.

"Come on, girl," he said, holding out his arm to her.

He stood up with a gesture that screeched the chair back along the tiled floor and made two or three men at the next table turn his way. Charlie Burrows's movements were all big movements.

At the top of the stairs, he pushed open the door to Rosie's room, saying, "I look forward to your taking these boots off my feet. I feel like a man who walked across the desert today." He plunked himself down on the side of her bed and felt something squirm under his hand.

"Why, what the devil?" He jumped back up and had his gun drawn before Rosie could manage to say, "Shush, Charlie, don't be a fool." She pushed him aside, peeled back the covers partway, and revealed the form of a child. "Come with me," she said, "we can't stay here."

Rosie beckoned to Charlie to follow her. She turned off the kerosene lamp beside the bed and left the room.

"What the hell's going on?" Charlie spluttered.

"I'll explain," she whispered.

They went to a plainer room at the end of the hall, usually kept available for the others. Those girls didn't have a special suite like Rosie did. Smythe set it up that way because they didn't bring in as much money as Rosie. Sort of an incentive, was how he put it.

"What's that kid doing in your bed?" Charlie blustered.

"She's the surprise I wanted to tell you about. She's mine."

"Yours? You never told me you had a kid."

"Well, I didn't until a week or so ago. She came in on Thornburg's windjammer, alone. Her folks died during the voyage. So I took her in. She's my own little girl now."

"You can't raise a kid here!"

The tone of his voice cut her. He didn't think she was good enough to be a mother. Maybe he had already forgotten what a scrambler he was until he made his strike not so long ago.

"Haven't you seen what blood parents have been doing to their own kids here in Sydney? Why two of our new girls here at the saloon—the real young ones that sat together over by the bar tonight, giggling to each other—Ed Smythe took them from their folks as payment for debts they owed him!"

"You're crazy, lady. Smythe wouldn't do that. Why, he's the stuffiest man in town. Our banker!"

"Charlie, our banker owns this place, doesn't he? Ed Smythe owns the Red Raven Saloon, although he shows up less and less often, I admit, and seems to be trying to keep it quiet."

"But sell your own kid?"

"Not only sell them, but sell them into this life. Sell them into drinking and whoring. It's true. But nobody better ever touch my little Anne—that's her name, Anne. I'll kill the man who does!"

"But how are you going to take care of her?"

"I'll send her to school. She's a real smart little thing. Not as young as she looks. Wait till we get some smiles on her lips, then you'll see what a lady she's going to be one day. I thought maybe you could help me figure out about school and so on, since you've been raising two boys alone."

"How old is she?"

"She'll be thirteen in December. I thought she was only about ten when I first got her from the boat, but that was probably because she was crying and had on some old too-big dress. I noticed when she was having a bath this morning that her form is starting to fill out, if you know what I mean. She's getting round all around." Rosie felt embarrassed to be talking about her daughter's body with Charlie, especially because of the kind of relationship she had with him. She had been thinking about Charlie a lot lately, and about the fact that he had two boys and now she had a little girl. If they threw in their lot together, wouldn't it be best for everyone? She wasn't sure how to raise the subject. Then Charlie started to talk. He had something else on his mind.

"I have some big news for you, too, Rosie. I've got me a new wife coming in on the ship that's due the next day or two! How's *that* for a surprise?" He slapped her on the shoulder and guffawed. She tried to cover her distress with a question.

"What are you talking about, a wife?" she asked.

"Yup. That's right. A real lady, too. Bring a little breeding to my homestead. I worked it out through the newspapers. Her family's got an old name, but no cash. I sure got no name, but I dare any man to snicker at my gold, eh?"

"You mean you bought her!" Rosie's outrage was in good part just disappointment and envy. She saw her own plans falling apart. "Sight unseen, at that," she added.

"Hell, she's too young to be too ugly. Why she's younger than Hugh, my oldest. She's sixteen!"

"So you'll be married again soon."

"As soon as the ship docks. I'm bringing the preacher along with me to meet her. We'll tie the knot on the spot." Delighted with himself, Charlie rocked back and forth on his haunches. "Why are you looking so down, Rosie girl? I'll be married to a proper lady. Can't you give your old friend Charlie a smile?" Rosie smiled at him, but her heart wasn't in it. "That's better," he said. "Now how about a little kiss? Or something a little more than a kiss . . ."

He reached over and pulled Rosie to him. At first, his kisses made it hard for her to breathe. She felt like her chest was about to burst. So, she never would be Mrs. Charlie Burrows. That had been her dream. Now it was over. Charlie's hand circled her breast. Usually his touch aroused her, but tonight she had to force herself to respond. Tonight he would be just another customer—tonight and from this night on. She closed her eyes and kissed him back. "Oh, Charlie," she whispered, "why?"

If he heard her, he ignored her. He pushed her down onto the bed.

She knew they could have been happy together. They were both from the same backgrounds, both trying for a better life than their folks had had. Part of Charlie's effort, she saw now, was to be accepted as part of the upper class. But he wasn't married yet, she realized with excitement. Maybe she could change his mind tonight. She had this one last chance.

"Charlie, let's play married tonight," she said, sitting up so abruptly that he was forced to sit up too.

"What foolishness is this?" he asked.

"Come on. It'll be fun. We'll play like we used to as kids, only this time knowing the real part of the playing-house game." She stood up, pushed at him until he stood beside her, shook the coverlet from the bed, folded it neatly, and then began to unlace her bodice. "Get undressed," she urged. "All of your clothes. I will too. Then we'll crawl between the sheets like proper lovers. Okay? Let's give it a try. You know you've always had a special place in my heart, Charlie. You're not like the others to me. I really care about you." As she spoke, she slid her top from her shoulders. "Untie my cinch," she said, and Charlie obeyed. He watched as she slipped her dress down over her full hips. It fell with a sensuous rustle to the floor. She stood before him now with her lovely bare breasts, and only the white display of her petticoats barred his view of her other treasures.

"Why, Rosie, you're a real looker. Whatever this new game is you're playing, I like it." Charlie hurried to undress while Rosie slid between the sheets, took off her petticoat and tossed it out of the bed. Charlie climbed in beside her. This time when he reached for her, she gave herself to him completely.

Late in the night, he sat up and began to dress in the dark.

"Charlie," she said sleepily, "why don't you stay the night?"

"I got to get back. It wouldn't be good for the master of the estate to be staying away overnight, sweetheart. But we'll have plenty of other times."

"Charlie," she began again, "why don't you take me for your wife, instead of that foolish child you're bringing over?" She held her breath waiting for his answer. Only the darkness allowed her to speak so boldly.

"Ah, that would never work," he said. He patted her hip under the sheet. "Besides, it's all arranged. They have the gold and the girl's on her way. It won't ruin our romance, Rosie. She'll just be my wife."

Some romance, Rosie thought. Cash left on the bureau; him creeping away in the middle of the night. She had a bitter taste in her mouth, as though she had been sucking on a coin. Charlie bent over, kissed the top of her head, and said, "Wish me luck." She couldn't answer, but he didn't seem to require it. She heard him open and shut the door. He was gone.

8

FLANDERS Wilde paced the length of her room at the Olde Cove Inn. She stopped to look out the window at the clear waters of the bay. Then she started up again. She was fuming over the delay in getting her material off to London.

She had arrived in Brisbane weeks ago, the day after her night in Lachlan's cave. At that point, everything was in too much disorder to be sent off as scheduled. She'd spent days redoing the work she'd already done once, almost weeping with frustration over the waste of precious time. Then she had to wait for the arrival of another ship. Fortunately, the *H.M.S. Three Winds* had been in dry dock in Sydney for repairs. It was about to return to England, and the shipping clerk had promised her he would notify the captain to stop in Brisbane on its northward passage. It was due this very afternoon. Her boxes were already at the dock.

Oh no, how could I have forgotten, Flanders groaned, as she realized she hadn't yet written her answer to Professor Thorenson's letter. She had been so distracted, and the days so busy, that it had slipped completely from her mind. There was still time, though. If she wrote a letter at once and hand-delivered it to the captain personally, surely he would make certain it arrived safely.

She put the date at the top of the page with a flourish: August 1, 1862.

Dear Professor,

Please forgive me for not having written much, much sooner than this. I shall not bore you with my excuses. No matter how valid, other people's excuses always sound like lies, while our own sound like the essence of truth. I believe you taught me that lesson when, early on in my studies, I failed to prepare adequately for one of your examinations. I suppose I frequently disappointed you during my student days. That is in the past. All disappointments will end when you reap the harvest of my work in Australia.

This entire continent is one huge laboratory. It is impossible not to make discoveries if one has open eyes and the training really to see. You have never been fully appreciated for your own work, but I am confident that my work here will bring us both a deserved reputation for important discoveries. Truly, it will be yours as much as mine, for what am I, after all, but the end-product of your amazing mind?

The same windjammer that brings this missive to you carries my preliminary report, boxes and boxes of plant and rock samples, and a portfolio full of my drawings of the Australian animals—all addressed to the British Society.

The assortment of marsupials here is beyond belief. Surely nowhere else on the earth can one find such a range of creatures who carry their young about in pouches. They range from tiny rats to kangaroos that tower over me. What conditions made the mammal population so overwhelmingly marsupial in Australia? That is a question which requires a serious theoretical response. Please give this matter your best attention and write me your thoughts. Perhaps we can publish jointly a scientific monograph on the subject.

That indigenous creature, the kangaroo, is worthy of a paper alone. Local people describe it as the animal that ''jumps when it walks, sits down when it stands up, and carries its young in its pocket!'' The infant kangaroo is born in the common mammal manner, but then must make an arduous journey up the momma's belly to her pouch. The climb can take as long as an hour. Once safely inside, the baby finds the nipple to suckle.

There is an even weirder category of creature here than the marsupials—a ''living fossil,'' the platypus. It has a duck-bill, lives along the banks of streams, and is amphibious. It has webbed feet, but the toes have claws on them. Its fur is brown on top and silvery underneath. Most surprising is the fact that, although it lays eggs, the creature nurses its babies. The mammary system is so rudimentary that the milk comes not from a nipple but oozes from its pores!

How I would love to show you all these wonders at first hand.

Flanders raised the pen from the paper. She realized there were few people with whom she could speak as frankly as she could to her old professor. Having been raised by her father alone after her mother's death and later tutored privately by Professor Thorenson, she knew she lacked the delicate refinements English society demanded of its girls. Neither her words nor her manners were ladylike enough. She had raised eyebrows, even when she was younger, on any occasion that her father took her into polite society.

''Imagine that,'' she had overheard a matron whisper once, ''he has reared that daughter as though she were a son! What a shame he never married so she could have a mother.''

''It's a good thing he has money,'' came the answer, ''or she would never make any sort of match.''

Flanders knew they would shake their heads in self-righteous disdain if they learned she was spending her inheritance on a life alone in the Australian bush.

The evening she had overheard that conversation was the first time Flanders had given any thought to the fact that her father had money, and a good deal of money at that. When he died, she greeted the news that she was an "heiress" with astonishment and little satisfaction. The price was too high! She had just turned twenty and had nursed her desperately ill father in his final illness for more than a year. His death released him from suffering and she thanked God his ordeal was over at last, but how terribly she missed him!

After his death, she found herself with a great deal of money and her whole life stretching emptily before her. She didn't want a ladylike life. She wanted adventure!

Other women her age were marrying as though life offered no other alternative. But she couldn't imagine taking such a step. Devote herself to some man who was probably not interested in seeing her use her mind? Never. But what then *could* she do?

She had heard rumors about Australia, that wild land that had been established as a penal colony. Some members of the scientific society had said that flora and fauna abounded there and was of such an exotic nature that it had no equal anywhere else on the earth. She might be able to make a name for herself in a place like that. It wasn't a ladylike idea—ladies didn't go off to explore wildernesses alone. But that was all the more reason for her to go.

Surely, being ladylike wouldn't be very important in a primitive place like Australia. So her lack of domestic skills and womanly graces would go unnoticed. Besides, what an amazing opportunity Australia afforded her to be recognized as the equal of any man in both brains and courage! With that thought in mind, she decided to make the journey. How she had flourished since she landed in Australia! She was really putting her scientific training to the test, and she believed in herself as a naturalist now.

With that thought came an almost tactile memory of Lachlan's hand cupped over her breast. She leaned back in the chair, closed her eyes, and allowed herself to relive those precious moments in his arms. "You're lovely," he had whispered, and for the very first time in her life, she felt lovely. His fingers traced the curve of her eyebrows. Then he stroked the length of her straight nose, the bow shape of her full lips, the small cleft in her chin. It was as though his touch taught her what she looked like more truly than any mirror had ever done. He had said nothing about seeing her again, except for the bit of a poem he had quoted early in the morning. How did it go? Flanders struggled to remember. When he had said it, she vowed never to forget. Oh yes, "If I should meet thee, after long years, how should I greet thee? With silence and tears."

Tears glistened in Flanders' eyes now, as she straightened in her chair and turned her attention back to the letter she was writing. She forced herself to continue.

Won't you please reconsider and come to visit me in this "barbarous isle," as you call it? I have a lovely homestead with a goodly amount of acreage, which I acquired at practically no cost—so eager is the colonial government for settlers. A man and his wife live on the grounds as servants. You would be quite comfortable, I assure you.

Locally I am known as a squatter, a term with none of the negative connotations it might have in England. As a squatter, you see, I am a member of the group of wealthy landowners in Australia. I think it is a good way to spend my inheritance, at least a portion of it. I believe there is a great future in store for this Australian land, and it thrills me to be part of it.

Although you request that I hurry home, I do not find myself ready yet to return to England. The fact is, Professor, I am beginning to think of my homestead in Toowoomba, Queensland, Australia as my

true home. As to your fears for me, they seem quite
unfounded. I might be in greater danger in the streets
of London than I am here amongst the aborigine
natives.

I did have a misadventure with a highwayman who
held up my coach, but it was far less terrifying than
those words indicate. At least in retrospect. I must
hurry to get this letter down to the dock so it will sail
with my goods, or else I would tell you more about it.
Perhaps in my next letter, which means you must quickly
write me again. Please do not be the shamefully
delinquent correspondent that I have been.

My warmest regards, your student, Flanders Wilde
P.S. Let me know the reaction of the British Society at once, won't you?

She sealed the letter with a blot of saffron wax and
pressed her initialed stamp into it, FW. She rose from the
desk, wrapped a mauve cashmere shawl around her
shoulders, and hurried from the room. At the front desk,
she made arrangements for a buggy to drive her down to
the bay. She knew the ship would not be setting sail until
the winds picked up. They had gone dead calm during the
night, so she was in no danger of missing the departure.

She settled back in the buggy and enjoyed the luxuri-
ance of the flowering trees. A coastal area, Brisbane had
adequate rainfall to produce flowering trees of all sorts—
jacaranda, bouganvillea, hibiscus. The buggy passed a
sugar cane plantation and Flanders felt anew the wonder of
Australia's enormous variety. The sensuousness of the
tropical vegetation was almost too much, she thought,
preferring in some peculiar way the sparser region she had
chosen for her home. Here there was too much of everything.
She found it a distraction.

They were approaching the bay now, and she craned her
neck to see which ship bore the name *H.M.S. Three
Winds*. The shipping company had informed her the captain's

name was Daniel Thornburg and that he was one of the best. At dinner one night, though, she had overheard two men at the next table talking about how, on its voyage into Sydney, his ship had lost almost half its passengers to some virulent disease. Well, that was surely not the captain's fault, Flanders reasoned. Moreover, disease would be no problem for her cargo. The thought of sick rocks made her smile.

The buggy drew to a halt.

"There it is, miss," the driver said, pointing with his whip. "You want me to wait for you?"

"Yes, if you don't mind. I want to check on my parcels and then speak with the captain, but I shouldn't be longer than an hour or so."

"You'll find me in the saloon over yonder." He pointed with his whip again, only this time back along the street that fronted the wharf.

"Fine. I'll collect you when I'm ready."

She climbed out of the buggy and shaded her eyes against the sun as she scanned the waterfront. The wharf was bustling with activity. Some men and boys lounged about on piles of goods, and an aborigine family squatted in the dirt, while dock-workers lugged carts full of crates to and from the ships. She spotted a rugged man standing near the prow of the *Three Winds* and she hoped he was the captain. Stepping as close to the edge of the dock as she dared, she called up to him, "Hallooo, are you Captain Thornburg?"

The man stopped in the middle of shouting orders to someone behind him and regarded the slim woman on the land.

"Captain Thornburg, at your service," he replied.

"I'd like to speak with you, if you have a moment. Shall I come up or can you come ashore?"

"You wait right there," he said, then disappeared from sight into the interior of the ship. She could hear his voice giving orders about the securing of cargo. That reassured her. He was a captain who took pride in his ship. He strode down the gangplank with a jauntiness that belied his fifty-some years.

"I have the impression that you must be the Miss Flanders Wilde whose boxes and cartons were delivered to me with the direst warnings of consequences should they be mishandled. Am I correct?"

Flanders smiled. "I am Flanders Wilde," she admitted, "the same. I suppose I overdid it a bit with my lectures to the drovers at the inn. But, you see, the material you are carrying to England for me represents so much work." She ducked her head as she realized how foolish her words must sound to this man who made his living carrying cargo back and forth to England. "It is two years' work," she added, hoping that would mitigate her obsession over her specimens' safekeeping.

"Very good, ma'am," he said. "I intend to give it my best effort. Is that what you wanted to hear?"

"No, as a matter of fact, it isn't. She had almost forgotten the letter again! "The shipping clerk already reassured me that you were the best captain afloat. I wasn't going to come here about my cargo at all," she lied. "I came because I realized there was a letter I must send at the same time. I've brought it with me in the hopes that you would carry it personally."

She held out the letter. The captain took it from her and tucked it inside his jacket pocket.

"I'll carry it with me with pleasure. Also, I received the special carton that you wanted placed in a cabin so it would remain dry. You see, all your orders have been conveyed to me."

"Oh, Captain, you make me ashamed," she finally cried. "But that material is an important report of the animals and plants I've been studying here, along with some drawings I've made. If it got wet, it would be ruined. I can see I've made a perfect nuisance of myself."

"Not at all. I'll do my best to deserve your faith. I

know how hard it can be to hand over something that is special to you. I had that experience myself in Sydney, with an orphan girl who was my passenger. It hurt to say good-bye.''

The captain straightened his jacket and added, ''Is there anything else, Miss Wilde?'' He was back to being the brisk man of the sea, perhaps embarrassed to have said something so personal.

''No,'' she said. ''Thank you for being so understanding.''

He touched his brow in a sort of salute and turned away, saying, ''Good-bye for now, then.''

''Safe journey,'' Flanders replied as she watched him make his way up to the deck of his ship. ''Safe, swift journey,'' she whispered. Then she went in search of the buggy driver. Tomorrow she would start out for Toowoomba, anxious now to get back home and to get back to work.

9

JUST as in Britain, Australia's social center was the saloon. When Flanders swung open the doors of the one where she expected to find her driver, she confronted a microcosm of Brisbane society, if not of all Queensland. Three or four groups of men were trying to outtalk each other on the concerns of the day. A solitary drinker would have been an oddity, and today there was none. The bartender was kept busy refilling glasses, since fast talk and flamboyant gestures raised powerful thirsts.

Flanders stood in the shadows to survey the scene. To her right, four or five diggers boasted about the hardships they'd endured, the area they were going to work next in their search, and the latest story of someone finding a nugget as big as a fist. Someone else, though, not them—someone they'd heard about, but hadn't actually talked to themselves.

Directly ahead, a larger group clustered around a seated man who bent over a paper straining to read it aloud in the dim light.

"The land selected will have to be lived on and improved. Small holdings of 40 to 320 acres are to be sold for a pound an acre."

"Whoa, Gil, what does that mean?"

"It means," the reader answered, looking up, "that we have a chance to break into the squatters' land holdings. It means maybe we can have a piece of land of our own."

The man speaking was probably under thirty, Flanders thought, but he had a worn, lined face that gave him the look of someone older. From his yellow leather vest, he drew a pipe and lit it in a leisurely way.

"But you say they passed that law in New South Wales. How does that effect us up here in Queensland?"

"How are we supposed to be able to pay a pound an acre if we have to buy at least forty and then spend a lot more on improving them?"

Both men addressed their questions to the reader, who seemed to be the leader of the group.

"By planning," Gil Tyler answered, leaning back in his chair and letting the paper fall to the table. "What's good for New South Wales is good for Queensland. It'll be coming. We're lucky enough to get this advance notice so we can do some planning. Save money. Get together with others to combine forces."

"Wait a minute, you mean like to live together?"

"I mean plan ways to maximize our economic strength. The squatters aren't going to say 'Here you are, fellows, we've been hoping you'd come and take over some of our land, as we have too much anyway.' "

The men around him laughed.

"You're right about that! We'll only get some of that land if we're more clever than them. Otherwise, the squatters will end up with it all—fair or foul, law or no law!"

Flanders, listening from a few feet away and out of sight of the men, realized she herself was one of the wealthy squatters they hated and feared. If the land went up for sale, as Gil Tyler suggested it soon would, she would have to insure her continued holdings somehow. There must be ways. She was already there on the land; they couldn't just walk in with their grubby goods and take over. With a shock she realized that she had already begun to think of them as the enemy.

She heard the Tyler man trying to explain the complex-

ity of borrowing money to buy land by giving title to the
land in surety against a default on the loan.

"Then, in a way," one of the men said, "the bank
would be better off if we can't pay. That way they'd get
cheap land for theirselves."

"Right," another answered. "Soon the squatters would
have new neighbors all right, but it won't be us as selected
the land. No, it won't be selectors. It'll be bankers!"

"I'm glad to hear you've started thinking, Rooney,"
Gil said. "It'll take a lot of ideas to make this thing work
for us. If we don't start saving and planning now, you
could be one-hundred-percent right."

"I been trying to save since I was freed," another man,
silent up to now, said. "During my prison days—first in
London, then here—I vowed I'd get out and make so
much money the judge who sentenced me would tremble
in his boots. I still don't have a pound to hide in my shoe
or my sugar bowl."

"I know it's hard, but if we want our own land, Ned—
and who here doesn't —we have to find a way."

For the millionth time in her life, Flanders wished that
she were a man. If she were a man, she could slip into this
group and join their discussion. The whole issue of land
rights was crucially important—to her, to these men, to the
growth of Australia. But women weren't supposed to join
the men in serious discussions. In fact, as she looked
around, Flanders realized she was the only woman in the
saloon. There wouldn't be any way she could remain a
simple anonymous member of any group. As soon as the
men noticed a woman was present, everything would
change—what they said, and the ways they said it, too.
She raged against the unfairness of it inwardly, but what
was there to do about it? By living alone in the wilderness
and carrying on with her work, she had made the best
accommodation she could imagine. Maybe someday it
would be different, she thought, but she doubted it.

Then she remembered it was her driver she had come to

find. She spotted him in the far corner drinking with another man. As she walked toward him, she entered the better lit portion of the saloon. Her driver's companion caught sight of her and pointed at her excitedly.

"That's her!"

Flanders stopped in her tracks, recognizing the coachman who had been so unceremoniously tied to a tree the last time she'd seen him.

"She'll tell you how Bad Lachlan got us. She was my passenger!"

Suddenly, Flanders was the focus of every eye in the saloon. The promise of a new tale of the bushrangers excited everyone's fancy.

Oh no, she thought, just what I didn't want—to draw attention to myself.

John Parker and her driver came toward her, their drinks in their hands. Other men from the far side of the bar came closer as well. The diggers edged in. Only Gil Tyler's group went on with their talk of land laws after a short pause to see what all the excitement was about.

"Come here, miss," Parker said, leading her up to the bar and urging her to take a seat on one of the bar stools. "Now you tell these folks how it was. I was fired, you know, because of that scoundrel. John Parker was fired for not protecting the company property well enough." His injured pride showed clearly through his words. There was a fierce gleam in his eyes that Flanders didn't like.

"Mister Parker," she said, choosing her words with care. "there was certainly nothing you could have done about the holdup. I am sincerely sorry to hear that you lost your post because to it. If there is anything I can do in the way of talking to the company officers, I will gladly do it."

"No, thank you anyway. I have my own plans for setting matters straight! I'm going to get Lachlan McKenzie."

"Don't be a fool," Flanders' driver interrupted. "He's

outwitted the best shots in the territory. How can you hope to shoot him down?''

"I ain't going to shoot him," Parker snarled. "See this?" He whipped out a Green River knife from a hidden sheath behind his neck. "I been practicing with it in my spare hours and I'm going to keep it with me every moment. Watch this." At that, he jerked his arm back behind his head, and holding the knife by the tip of its blade, with a snap of his wrist he released it toward a knot-hole on the far wall. The knife whizzed through the air, entering the exact center of the target.

Flanders felt the hair rise on her arms. Lachlan was going to be killed by this repulsive ruffian, she just felt it. This man who sat before her wearing a smelly leather jacket over his none-too-clean shirt. This man whose grizzled face looked like he enjoyed nastiness, like he was a boy who tore wings off butterflies and laughed. She realized he wasn't much more than a boy now, but he had an ageless look that reflected all the barbarism of which human beings were capable.

As he went to retrieve his knife, Parker was stopped by a burly man who had been sitting at a far table.

"You sound like a man I could use," he said. "Are you interested in a new job?"

Flanders, watching from her bar stool, saw that the man who spoke was well known to just about everyone in Queensland. It was Harris Wakefield, probably the richest of the squatters and the one with the largest holdings of land. She hadn't noticed him when she first came in, or else he had entered during the knife-throwing exhibition. He was as close to Parker's opposite as a man could be—older, smoother, with a kindly face that belied his ruthless nature, if rumors were to be believed. He sat waiting for Parker's answer with his right hand hitched into his belt and his left hand holding a fine cigar. In front of him on the table was a bottle of rum. He wore a fine linen shirt in a soft beige and over it a suede vest.

"What kind of work?" Parker asked, his voice suspicious and hard.

"I have lots of land and lots of work. Drover, in part. But mainly," he leaned forward to add emphasis to his words, "I want you to keep on practicing with that knife—and with a pistol, too. Be a kind of bodyguard. Things are changing around here and a man can't be too careful. I don't plan to give away anything that's mine. Not to a bushranger. Nor to anyone else." He shot a pointed glance at the group of men who had been listening to Gil Tyler, then glared at Gil Tyler himself. Then, as though he'd just noticed him, Wakefield raised his hand in a half-salute. The handsome Tyler nodded in return.

"What kind of pay'll you give me?" Parker asked, drawing the man's attention back to himself.

"We shouldn't discuss that here, but I can assure you that no one who works for me has any regrets. I take care of my own. But I expect absolute loyalty in return. Well, Mr. Parker," said Wakefield as he stood up and held out his hand, "is it a deal?"

"Hell, yes," Parker said enthusiastically and grabbed hold of the older man's hand to give it a vigorous shake.

"Hey, Blade," Flanders' driver called out, "you didn't stay out of work long, eh? Not in Australia. That's what I was telling you. A man can always work in Australia."

Parker turned back toward him. "Blade you called me," he said. "I kinda like that. I think I'll hang onto that moniker. Blade Parker. In the employ of . . ." He turned to Wakefield again. "I don't know your name, boss."

"Harris Wakefield."

"You lucked out," the driver said, coming up to them. He slapped Blade Parker on the back. "You just hooked up to the biggest man in the territory. I've got to get going now, but I'll see you around. Don't forget your old friends, now that you've made it big."

Parker grinned at his drinking buddy and ducked his head.

"You've stood me to a few drinks. I won't forget," he said. "I won't forget about Bad Lachlan either. His name is on my knife."

"Shall we go now?" Flanders called from across the room. Her driver waved and held his hand out so she would walk in front of him to the door and the street beyond.

She was conscious of the men's eyes upon her, evaluating her. She straightened her shoulders and, remembering her training, moved slowly across the rough wood floor toward the door. As she passed Gil Tyler's table she heard him say, "Big Harris Wakefield is the kind of squatter we'll be up against. He's already making preparations to resist, did you hear? He's the biggest, but there's many another squatter around just as determined that no poor men will take away what they view as their own."

Flanders winced to think that she was one of those squatters. And that he was right. She had no desire to give away her land. Then she was out the door and back in the day's light where she could hear no more of the issue, but her time in the saloon had given her much to ponder on her ride back to Olde Cove Inn.

No sooner was the buggy rolling smoothly along than the driver turned toward her, and said, "Kidnapped by that bushranger, that must have been terrible for you."

He was fishing for a story, she knew. Her escapade with Lachlan had given her a kind of instant notoriety. Everyone who came in contact with her in Brisbane had more or less asked her the same questions. What they all really came down to was: what is Lachlan McKenzie like?

"It's already forgotten," she lied. "No harm was done. Although that Mr. Parker wouldn't agree, I suppose."

Her driver seemed glad for a chance to talk, and she hoped she might get some idea from him as to just how dangerous this "Blade" Parker would be to Lachlan.

"He's a bad one, that Parker. A deserter. He told me he was a soldier in that war going on in America with the

North against the South. When his commander gave him an order he didn't like, he strangled him. Killed him and took off. That's how he made it to Australia. Figured they'd never find him here."

"Do you think he's telling the truth?" Flanders asked, horrified. "He seems like a proper braggart to me."

"Maybe. But I wouldn't want to make him angry, not me."

"Well then, it doesn't sound as though Mr. Wakefield has gotten himself a very reliable bodyguard."

"That depends. If Wakefield can get him in line, he's got a killer on his side. And I've heard that Mr. Wakefield is a generous boss—his men stand by him."

They both fell silent then, lost in private thoughts. Flanders sent her thoughts out to Lachlan, wishing him well. She asked herself if she was thinking about him so constantly simply because Brisbane found him such an interesting topic of conversation. Or was it something more? No, she would not allow herself to be foolish. She probably wouldn't ever see him again. Probably. Once she was back in Toowoomba and back at work again, thoughts of him would no doubt fade from her mind. She hoped so. Because living the way she was now was painful. The moment she closed her eyes, she would see his face. As she drifted off to sleep, she would feel his body against hers, his breath stirring the tendrils of hair along her cheek. Longing for him, she would wake from dreams of their passionate lovemaking.

But what was she to him, she wondered. Did he find himself thinking of her? Or was she just one of the many women he had taken somewhere along the road? She hoped at least that wasn't true, hoped she was somehow special to him, even if she were never to see him again.

Never see him again. The thought made her heart feel like a lump of stone. Then the carriage stopped, and she was back at the inn. Tomorrow she would start for home.

10

WINTER gave way to spring, and it was November, 1862. Flanders counted off the time as she walked across her land and enjoyed the seasonal changes of nature all around her.

It seemed that all she did these days was wait. She was awaiting news from London regarding the safe arrival of her report, but she knew it was too early even to hope for that. She was awaiting news of Lachlan McKenzie, but she knew that would require a trip into town where the latest stories always circulated.

Most of all, she had spent these months since her abduction counting days, and each day confirmed more her suspicion that she must be pregnant. At first, the idea seemed so horrifying that she refused to think about it. Then, even before the changes in her body forced the thought upon her, she began to think that having a child might not be all that bad. By the time she realized that her breasts, more tender than usual, were growing larger, she had begun to anticipate the birth of Lachlan's baby. Lachlan's baby, that was how she thought of it.

She had toyed with the notion of returning to his cave in order to tell him the news, but the prospect of *that* was too degrading to contemplate. What would it be to a man like him that she carried his child? No doubt the countryside was littered with his bastards. She winced at the word, but did not try to kid herself about its aptness.

All things considered, She could hardly demand that he behave honorably toward her and marry her. Anyway, she didn't want to be married any more than he did.

So, instead, she went on with her work. As best she could calculate, the baby wouldn't be born until April. No sense in wasting these months, she thought. She could still wear her regular clothes, although soon she would have to talk to Elizabeth, her servant, about making some alterations. Such thoughts filled her mind as she meandered across the scrubby earth around her house and headed for the porch.

As she approached the porch, Flanders saw that someone was waiting there. It had to be Elizabeth's husband, she decided, because nobody ever came to visit—she lived too far from any neighbors and also very much valued her privacy. She'd have to have a talk with him. There was too much work to be done for anyone to spend time lounging on the porch in the middle of the day.

Yes, there was definitely a man sprawled in her porch chair with his feet lazily up on the railing. Flanders decided her eyes must be deceiving her, but it certainly looked at this distance like Lachlan! She knew it couldn't be. Just wishful thinking. After all, she hadn't heard a word from him since that July night. Still, she hurried along toward the house at a faster pace—almost breaking into a run.

The man took his feet from the rail and stood. The graceful elegance of that simple movement told Flanders all she needed to know. She could no longer doubt. It was Lachlan. For a moment she stopped dead in her tracks. My God, she thought, it really is him. Then, with her heart pounding, she started running toward the house.

She held her skirt gathered in one hand so it wouldn't trip her, and she raised her other hand high over her head and waved and waved. The man gave no indication that he saw her, although she could tell from his stance that his eyes were on her.

"Lachlan McKenzie!" she exclaimed, as she climbed the three steps up to where he stood.

"None other. At your service, Miss Wilde." He made a mock bow, then in a single swift move swept her into his arms and held her pressed to him. "Kiss me, lady," he ordered, and she was glad to obey.

The pressure of his lips carried Flanders back to their moments together that night. She wrapped her arms around his rangy back, feeling the bones through his shirt. She wanted the kiss never to end. When they pulled apart, she laughed with happiness.

"You're too thin, man," she said, adopting a casual tone that was new to her. "Why don't you come inside and let me make you some food." She had planned and planned for this moment in her mind, and in her plans she was always cool and indifferent, always the lady. Now that he was really here, it seemed a foolish game. She didn't care why he had come to her, only that he had come.

"That's what drew me back to you—the promise of a good meal." He smiled at her, and his words were like a caress, his smile another kiss. Flanders turned from him to hide her confusion. She led the way into the house. Lachlan paused just inside the door to admire the sturdy and simple construction. The hardwood floors were bare and shone from polishing. The walls were whitewashed without the normal touches of affectation that most squatters enjoyed— flocked wallpapers imported from England and paintings of family groups adorning every bare space.

In the parlor the chairs were comfortably padded, but obviously bought for utility, not style. They had heavy wood arms and were obviously locally crafted. The single painting on the wall was of some kind of iris magnified until the single bloom filled the canvas, which was at least four feet square.

"I've never seen anything like that," Lachlan said.

"Do you like it?"

"I must say, I think I could grow to like it. It's a whole new way to look at a flower, that's for sure. I'm used to those pictures of ornamental bouquets where you never look at the flowers themselves, if you know what I mean."

"I painted it. I wanted to show the true beauty of a single bloom. You're right, we seldom look. That's one of the things I'd like to do—train people to see what's right before their eyes."

"One of the things? I suppose you came to Australia with a list of improvements you planned to make!"

"That must have sounded foolish. I do have a list of improvements in mind, but mostly they're improvements on myself. I'm quick to get carried away with my enthusiasms. If you get to know me better, you'll see that." She paused, wondering if she were being too forward, hoping that he would say something about planning to get to know her better. But he wasn't about to be led into any traps. That's how he survived on the range and that's how he planned to survive in her house. He'd make any statements in his own good time.

"How about that food," he said.

They went together into the kitchen at the back of the house, which like the rest of the place had a solid practical look to it.

"Who else is here with you?" Lachlan asked.

"Only my two servants, Elizabeth and her husband Allen. They are loyal, I'm sure. If I tell them not to see you, they will pretend that they don't. Besides, around here who is there to tell?"

Lachlan only nodded. He had grown to distrust "loyalty." But there was no way to live without taking some things on trust. This woman, Flanders Wilde, seemed as trustworthy as anyone he had met. She hadn't betrayed him or his hiding place when she had the chance in Brisbane. There seemed no reason to suspect her of treachery now.

"Elizabeth's a good cook. Do you want me to call her to make you something?"

"No. You're a good enough cook for me. I want you to make me something." There was a light in his eyes that made Flanders blush. It seemed like he wasn't talking about food at all. She wondered why it was that, when she was with him, she couldn't keep herself from wishing he would kiss her, couldn't keep herself from thinking about his lips, his touch, his body.

"I can make you a cheese omelet and some biscuits, if that will do."

"Sounds mighty tempting," he answered, that strange smile still playing on his lips. "Mighty tempting."

She moved around the kitcen with a starling awareness of her body. Every gesture became a part of some elaborate dance with Lachlan's eyes upon her. She was also acutely aware of the changes in her body since the last time he saw her. She felt the fullness of her breasts strain against the broadcloth of her bodice. She knew there was a new roundness to all of her.

Would he notice, she wondered. If he didn't, shouldn't she tell him? She practiced ways to tell him in her mind as she prepared the meal under his watchful eyes.

"I'm having your child," she might say.

Or, "We've created a new life together."

"Soon there will be a true Australian brought into being because of us."

No, that all sounded awful. She'd wait a while and see if the right words would come to her.

"I met that coach driver again," she said instead.

"Still driving?"

"No, the company fired him." She swirled the eggs around in the bottom of the skillet. Her back was to Lachlan.

"Good for them. He was a rotter. You could tell by the way he treated the horses. Always judge a man by that."

Flanders slipped the eggs from the pan onto a bright blue plate. She peeked into the oven. Naturally, the biscuits were not nearly done. She never had been any good at making things come out at the same time. Too impatient, Elizabeth told her.

"Well, you can start with eggs and coffee," Flanders said, placing the plate before Lachlan. "The biscuits will take another few minutes."

"Another thing," Lachlan added, stuffing the fluffy yellow eggs in his mouth, "he swore too much. After all, there was a lady present." He smiled up at Flanders who had remained standing beside him.

"He's nothing to joke about," she said, waving the spatula in her hand at him. "I heard him threaten to kill you in a saloon full of men. He's got to at least make the effort in order to save face."

"He's an American, I hear. Probably can't shoot the side of a barn."

"He's not planning to shoot you." Flanders sat down across from him, poured herself a mug of coffee from the pot in the middle of the round table, and took a sip before going on. "He's been training with a knife. An ugly, long thing that he stores behind his back."

"A knife, eh? Probably a Green River. Many a man has been sent down that river!" He finished the last mouthful of his eggs and pushed the plate from him. That reminded Flanders of the biscuits. She would soon have been reminded without that cue by the thin trail of smoke that was just starting to rise from the ridge of the oven door.

"Oh no," she wailed. "I've burned the biscuits. Again." She rushed to the oven, barely taking time to grab a potholder to prevent her usual burned hand. She flung the door open and curlicues of smoke happily escaped toward the high ceiling. Flanders pulled out the baking tin and dropped it on top of the stove. The biscuits looked salvageable. She picked them up one by one and scraped the bottoms where they had turned black. Lachlan had come over to stand beside her and chuckled.

"That's quite a sight," he said. "You've got enough

little black crumbs on your hands and your clothes and your face to be a chimney sweep!''

She turned to face him angrily, but when she saw his soft eyes, she could only return his smile.

''They'll taste pretty good, if you don't mind much about the looks.''

''Good, bring 'em over and share a few with me. We'll have another cup of coffee and biscuits and talk some more, but not about that driver. I've even forgotten his name.''

''They're calling him Blade now, because of the business with the knife.''

''Well good for him. But don't worry your little head about me. He'll not bring me down. Especially now that you've warned me about the knife and its location. I'll watch out.''

''Please do, Lachlan,'' she said, the pleading look in her eyes adding urgency to her words.

''Do you care so much?'' he teased.

Her eyes met his and held.

''Yes,'' she answered.

It would have been hard to say who moved toward whom. They simply melted together. Then they were kissing, and Flanders felt the wonderful comfort of having Lachlan's arms around her. How often she had dreamed this scene, but never had she dared hope it would come true.

''Would you like to see the rest of the house?'' she asked when she could catch her breath.

''You mean like the bedroom?'' he whispered.

She nodded. She told herself that afterwards she would tell him, no matter what. But she didn't know then that, afterwards, he would be running for his life and she would be telling lies to men with guns in the hope of saving him. No, all she knew then was that her heart seemed to throb with each step they took toward the upstairs, which held her bedroom and her study and the extra room she had already labeled the nursery.

He looked around the large square room she led him into. It was so simple that it was elegant. The large double bed had four posts that were hand carved and shone as though they received loving care. The bed was covered by a spotless white quilt. Other than the bed, the only two pieces of furniture in the room were a six-foot tall armoire and a rocking chair. There wasn't even a mirror on the wall. He liked it. It made him feel more comfortable than all the overstuffed chairs and gaudy crucifixes in all the bedrooms he'd ever been in could ever make him feel.

"The room's a beauty," he said admiringly. "I wondered how you might live."

"I've found myself wondering now and again whether you were still alive!"

He placed his hands firmly on her waist and said, "I'm immortal."

She wondered if he could feel the new thickness in her body. No, she figured, he didn't know her well enough. Surely his hands couldn't remember. Then he pulled her to him and kissed her cheek and her neck and her ear, and she herself almost forgot. Flanders almost let herself forget the reality that had dominated her every waking moment over the last several months: that she was going to have Lachlan McKenzie's baby. She let herself be led to a bed she had slept in alone for the past two years. At last she would be able to share its spaciousness. No matter what else happened, she would have that memory to keep with her—that of Lachlan, here in her house, sharing her bed.

"Lachlan," she spoke through lips already parted in passion, "how long I have dreamed that you would arrive here like this."

As she spoke, he was undoing her linen shirt, loosening the belt of her full black skirt. Her blouse was a bright crimson which slid to the floor like a flame in a campfire.

Everything seemed to replay their night in the cave in
Flanders' mind.

He fondled her breasts as he whispered, "I've had that
dream a few times myself." Then he pressed her down
onto the bed and stretched himself out beside her.

"Then why," she cried, unable to restrain herself, "why
didn't you come to me sooner?"

He looked at her in silence for a moment, propping his
head on one hand.

"Perhaps," he said softly at last, "I was afraid to
discover that our night in the cave was the dream. It
occurred to me that I mightn't be welcome into your real
world."

"You fool," she sighed happily as she wrapped her
arms around his neck. "You perfect fool."

Flanders nuzzled his neck. She surprised herself with
the ease with which she accepted him back into her life.
How easily she found herself aroused and longing for his
touches. Only a sense of shyness kept her from pulling his
body on top of her. Fortunately, he had none of that same
shyness.

He rolled from his side onto her willing body. His long
legs enclosed her legs as though he were astride a mare;
then, with a smoothness that made each movement appear
as natural and inevitable as the sun rising in the morning,
he placed his legs between hers. Another moment, and he
was inside her. The suddenness made Flanders cry out. He
held her tight against him and didn't move.

"Hush, darling," he whispered. "Wait a bit now. Let's
just lie like this."

"Oh, Lachlan," Flanders sighed. "I can hardly believe
this dream is real. To have you here. To be with you once
more."

Then Lachlan began to move within her, and the mount-
ing excitement of their lovemaking silenced any further
comments.

Afterwards, Lachlan lay so still beside her with his eyes closed that Flanders began to imagine he'd fallen asleep. She thought that a peaceful sleep was probably a rare treat for a man on the run. Just as well, too, because she had to decide whether to tell him about the baby or not. This was her chance. They'd never be any closer than they were right now. And she'd promised herself that she would tell him.

"Lachlan," she said. He opened his eyes and smiled at her. Flanders leaned over and began to kiss his cheek softly, when the sound of feet pounding up the stairs made them both jump.

Lachlan was off the bed and into his pants before the knock on the door came. He reached for the pistol he had placed under the pillow.

"Miz Wilde, Hurry!"

Flanders recognized the voice of her servant, Allen, although she had never heard it sound so breathless or frightened before.

She signaled to Lachlan with a finger to her lips.

"A moment, Allen," she called, hurrying back into her clothes.

Lachlan speedily completed his dressing at the same time.

"What is it?" Flanders asked, opening the door a crack, shielding Lachlan with her body. "What is it?"

"Men coming this way. Galloping. I saw your gentleman friend stable his horse and I figured that's who they might be after."

Lachlan moved to Flanders' side, in plain view of the man at the door.

"Where did you see them?" he asked, his voice tense.

"Out on the Three Notch Road. I was with the sheep. I took the shortcut back here to warn you. I've got your horse ready out back. If you hurry, you might have a five-minute lead. No more than that, I'm sure."

Lachlan was already racing down the stairs, taking them two at a time.

"You're a good man," he called up over his shoulder. "Thanks."

Not a final word to Flanders. Not a word. She stood biting her lip. Then she took a deep breath, told John to get to work around the house, but to stay nearby. She hardly needed to caution him to remain silent about her visitor.

"I'll go blur the tracks," he said. "I'll be nearby if you need me."

She made an effort to smile at him. He was a good and trustworthy man, no matter that he and his wife had been shipped over as convicts. They had paid their debt to society, and had proven their loyalty to her in a hundred different ways. They were as much friends to her as servants.

Damn! she cursed to herself in silent frustration. Lachlan was gone, and she hadn't yet told him that he was about to become a father in a matter of months. She sighed. No time to think about that now. She stepped off the bottom stair just as the men Allen had spotted were hammering their way up the porch stairs. They pounded on the door making a fearful row, and in their excitement pawed the porch almost like a nervous group of horses. Flanders looked at them in an amazement that was only half-feigned. No such hostile party had come to visit her in her two years in Toowoomba.

"Gentlemen," she said, "have you come to announce the start of war, that you are so agitated?" Her voice shook as she spoke, but she hoped the men would put it down to the frailty of woman.

The largest man, who seemed to be acting as the leader, took off his hat and punched the man beside him so that soon, like the motion of birds taking flight as a group, every hat was off its owner's head.

"Ma'am, we been on the trail of a bushranger spotted coming this way."

THE DEFIANT

"Well, I assure you that no stranger has been here today!" She gave herself credit for managing to speak truthfully, although she knew she would gladly lie for Lachlan without a moment's hesitation.

"We'd kind of like to have a look around, if we can," he replied, ducking his head like an embarrassed schoolboy.

"Are you doubting my word?" Flanders asked haughtily.

"We're coming in—with or without your leave," a man standing near the back of the pack called out stridently.

Flanders saw a pistol waving around, aiming nowhere in particular. God, she thought, they might shoot me. Shoot me just for fun and claim it was an accident. Lots of such things must happen, she figured. She knew that a lot of men were just no-goods looking for a little action. They hated the squatters. But they feared them, too—feared the power the squatters' money represented. That's what she had to remember and wield against them. Also, she had to buy time for Lachlan. After all, if the men went away now, they'd probably pick up his trail in no time.

Taking a deep breath to calm the terror that made her body shake, she said, "Remember your manners, gentlemen. You are addressing a lady. Although it is absurd to think that a criminal would be hiding in my house, I will allow you to come in and check that out for yourselves. But do try not to break anything!"

Her confident words, like whistles in a graveyard, calmed her miraculously. The men, affected by her calmness, became a little less restless themselves.

"What made you think this bushranger might be here?"

"We've been following his path of victims," the leader said. "He seemed to be moving toward Toowoomba, a new area for him. So we're searching all the main homesteads. Yours was just first in our path."

What luck, Flanders thought. What rotten luck!

"Come right in, then," she said, opening the screen

door, which had been between them during this conversation, so that they could enter. While two of the men strode off to talk to Allen, who was busily repairing a fence post, the other four tramped past her into the house. The leader told two of them to take the first floor while he and his partner went upstairs. Flanders wondered frantically for a moment whether Lachlan could have left anything behind, anything that would give him away.

"Just a moment," she said, "I'll lead the way." She brushed past the two men on the stairs. "I'm not sure my bed has been made yet, you know how lazy servants can be," she said, silently begging Elizabeth to forgive her for this lie that maligned her good character. It's in a good cause, she told herself.

She opened the door with the sinking feeling that Lachlan had left his hat on the rocking chair. She was almost positive. And the way the men were crushing after her, there would be no way to hide it before they barged into the room. Her eyes fastened on the chair. She drew a deep breath in relief. There was no hat there. Quickly she scanned the room. Empty. The men were past her now and roaming around, handling her things. The closet door was open.

"Out of there, fast," one of the men said to the shape inside.

"Don't shoot, mister!"

It was Elizabeth!

"I was only straightening out Miss Wilde's clothing. Is there some law against that?" Still grumbling, she pushed her way through the men and left the room. Satisfied that no one was lurking in the closet, the hunters left soon afterward. Flanders followed them down the stairs and out onto the porch.

"Come on, boys, before his trail gets too cold," the leader said.

"Can't see a sign of any tracks," one of his boys answered.

"Damn. We've lost him again," another added. "Might as well give it up and head back to town."

"Don't be a quitter, Jake," the leader berated his comrade. "We'll stick to our original plan and go from homestead to homestead. I'm going to get that bastard!"

His voice had a menacing tone to it that made Flanders shiver. "Sorry to disturb you, ma'am," he said to her. "But we hope you'll rest easier knowing that we ain't gonna let no bushrangers terrorize our women!"

She nodded, unable to risk an answer that might betray her nervousness. She watched them ride away. She doubted their visit would in any way improve the quality of her sleep. She dreaded the thought that they were after her Lachlan. Then she turned toward the kitchen to find out what Elizabeth had really been doing in that closet. The room had been cleaned up hours earlier, and it wasn't like the woman to decide midday to do such organizing.

When she found her, Flanders learned that she was right. Number one, Lachlan *had* left his hat on the rocker. Number two, Elizabeth hadn't just decided to reorganize the closets but had scurried up the stairs before the men in order to make sure there would be no such evidence in sight.

"Thank you, Elizabeth," Flanders said with heart-felt gratitude. Then, because she had to tell someone, and because Elizabeth was the only woman she knew in Australia, and because soon she would need help in planning, Flanders told Elizabeth that she was carrying the child of the great outlaw who had just barely escaped with his life.

To her surprise, Elizabeth acted as though she already knew that her mistress was with child. Claimed she'd guessed as much for weeks. Her response, so warm and ready to help in any way she could, touched Flanders deeply and brought her close to tears. She found herself on the verge of weeping frequently these days. It must be a part of the pregnancy, she decided, and wouldn't let herself feel how deeply hurt she was by Lachlan's departure.

Elizabeth, sensing her mistress's unhappiness and guessing at its cause, said, "I'll stand by you."

Flanders blindly stretched out her hand, and Elizabeth grasped it in her own good sturdy one.

11

THE months that followed had a dream like quality for Flanders. She tried to rouse herself and focus on her work, but mostly she felt as though she were just waiting. Waiting for the moment when she would give birth to her child—to their child, hers and Lachlan's.

She also kept waiting for Lachlan to reappear. Then there would be no need for words. He could take one look at her and know everything. But he didn't return. At times she worried vaguely that he had been caught and that their child would be born a dead man's child. But the torpor that had descended on her as her pregnancy advanced had robbed even such speculations of their sting. She spent her days in an idle reverie, imagining how things might be . . . someday, someday when she and Lachlan were together with their child.

Then she awoke one night in the grip of a contraction so powerful that it practically lifted her off the bed. She tried to relax and fall back to sleep, figuring that she would need her strength, but she was too excited to sleep. This was it! She was about to have her baby.

She got up in the dark and groped for her bathrobe. She would make herself some tea. No need to awaken Elizabeth yet. Soon enough she would need her help.

''Help me! Help,'' Flanders moaned ten hours later, as she lay tossing and turning in her big bed. Elizabeth stood beside the bed and spoke in soothing tones. "Just try to relax, love. It won't be much longer now."

Flanders buried her head in her pillow. Her mountainous body restricted her movements. She'd be glad to be rid of this burden. No, she mustn't say that, she thought. Mustn't even feel that. It was unwomanly, monstrous. Then the pain hit again, wave after wave of it, like a gathering storm, until there was nothing left in her universe but pain. There was no Flanders, no baby-to-be, no Lachlan. There was no room, no homestead in Toowoomba, no scientific work. There was nothing but pain, a round howl of pain.

When she'd first felt the tightness that came and went and told her time must be near, she'd felt ecstatic. No one, she'd thought, in the whole world is more pregnant than I am. Soon I'll be a mother. For a while, she'd gone about her morning chores with renewed energy. But eventually she had been taken over completely by the increasingly intense and urgent contractions. Could that only have been this morning, she wondered. It seemed an eternity ago, an eternity of increasing tightness until, overcome, she'd climbed laboriously, with Elizabeth's arm to support her, into her bed. Since then, there had only been pain.

"I can see the baby," Elizabeth cried, "it can't be much longer now, girl. Just a few good pushes."

And Flanders pushed and pushed, and the contractions went on and on, and the baby seemed no nearer to being born. Flanders had never known such exhaustion as she now felt.

"Something's wrong, Elizabeth. I just know it must be."

Elizabeth mopped the beads of sweat from Flanders' worried face.

"It seems to want to come into the world backwards," she answered. "Typical enough for a true Australian, I guess." Her effort at a joke was weak. She felt worried, more worried than she dared to show. She had assisted at dozens of births over the years, but she'd only once seen a breech birth. And that baby hadn't lived. She wished now she'd insisted that Flanders go over to Sydney and find a doctor when she came near her time. But it was too late for those thoughts now. There wasn't a doctor within a day's ride of them.

She held a hurried conference with Allen in which they agreed that there was no possibility of getting any outside help. They would just have to do their best and leave the rest in God's hands. Then Flanders screamed, and Elizabeth hurried back over to her. What she saw horrified her. The baby's buttocks and one little leg dangled from Flanders' body.

"Help me, Elizabeth! Help me, God!" she cried.

Elizabeth said a silent prayer to God to guide her hands as she grasped the baby's ankle and then tried to find a way to keep the little body aligned as she eased it out of its mother's body. She breathed a sigh of relief when she saw the other leg appear. Now the baby's lower body lay half outside of Flanders, and Elizabeth tugged gently on it to locate the arms. If she could just get the arms safely delivered, she felt sure she could manage the shoulders and head. But the arms seemed so firmly wedged that at first she despaired.

"The baby is almost born," she said reassuringly, with a confidence she surely didn't feel. "Just pant. Pant now. Don't push!"

Elizabeth reached up inside of Flanders to feel for the little arms. She maneuvered them into position against the little chest and, holding the arms pressed together, eased the body from its imprisoned position. Though she worked at fever pitch, it felt as though she were working at some unreal, double-slow time. Finally, after what seemed like a lifetime, the baby was completely free except for its head. It was a boy, but Elizabeth hardly took notice of that as she struggled to bring the baby to a live birth.

"Just one more push, love," Elizabeth said to the exhausted Flanders. "Just one mòre push and your little son will be born!"

With that encouragement, Flanders made an enormous effort and the baby was thrust into Elizabeth's waiting arms. Elizabeth held her breath, as she saw the blue color of the baby's face. Would it be born whole only to be pronounced dead? But she gave him a business-like slap on his little rump, and then the sweetest sound in the world filled the room—the wail of the newborn baby. It was alive and well and they could all give thanks for that miracle.

Elizabeth then shifted her attention to Flanders herself. The woman who had always been so vital and full of spirit lay like a pale ghost against the plumped-up pillow with her russet hair strewn around her face like a sunset. The moment she heard the baby's cry, which assured her of its health, she closed her eyes with a sigh that seemed like a precursor to death. Elizabeth was near panic. More frightening than her exhaustion was the fact that Flanders was bleeding heavily, and the older woman knew that she must somehow stop the flow of blood or her mistress would surely bleed to death.

"Allen," she said in an urgent voice to the man who stood not more than a foot from her. "Quick, bring some brew for the missus. And some of those nice linen towels I have hanging in the kitchen. Quick, I say."

The man, aware of the dangers of the situation, needed no urging and hurried off to fulfill his wife's requests.

While he was gone, Elizabeth cleaned the baby a little and wrapped it in a blanket. Then she held him close to his mother's cheeks and whispered, "Try to nurse him. It would be good for both of you." But Flanders seemed not to hear. "Flanders!" the woman said sharply now, "your baby needs you and you need him. You must struggle to help me finish this birthing!"

At first she thought the woman had not heard or would

not respond, but then she heard a whisper as soft as the sigh of rain outside the house.

"Surely it's finished," the voice said.

"No, it isn't, not quite. You must nourish the child. He needs to suck. That will help you to stop bleeding as well." Elizabeth placed the baby on the bed beside his mother's head. She loosened the gown Flanders still wore loosely over her shoulders. Now the baby could reach its mother's breast and Automatically started to nuzzle her. The sweet, soft feel of his little form made Flanders struggle to open her eyes and assist his efforts. By then Allen had returned, and Flanders eagerly drank the beer that he offered her. Elizabeth, meanwhile, had delivered the after-birth and packed Flanders with clean cloths. She hoped the nursing that the baby was doing would make the difference. There was nothing more to be done now but wait and see.

"What will you name him?" she asked as she straight-ened the room a bit. Soon, she thought, they would all be able to sleep. She hadn't realized during these long hours how tired she herself had grown.

"For a while he must simply be 'baby,' I suppose, until I get some sense of who he is. I want a name that shows him to be different from us, you know what I mean?"

"I'm not sure I do."

"Well, he's Australian-born. A true Australian! So I think he needs a special name." Then she fell silent, utterly drained by her ordeal. Allen left the women alone then, and Elizabeth once she'd finished up, lowered the lamp and settled into the chair beside the bed. Her mistress was already asleep by the time she moved the baby to the cradle that they'd had waiting for more than a month now. Silence settled on the household, and as Elizabeth drifted toward a well-earned sleep, she thought she heard Flanders' soft voice say, "Thank you, Lachlan, for our son."

She knew that the father of this baby didn't even know he had a son. He would certainly have a surprise waiting for him the next time he returned to Toowoomba.

12

FLANDERS named her baby Tarleton Wilde because she hoped that he would represent the best of the new breed of Australians. He was born on April 10, 1863, at the beginning of Australia's fall season. During the remainder of the year, his care absorbed the attention of the doting household so completely that they remained oblivious, for the most part, to the raging controversy that was taking place between the squatters and the men who wanted a piece of land for themselves, the men who owned nothing and felt that they deserved better. New laws, known as Land Selection Acts, had a noble democratic goal: that every man had the right to own a piece of land.

There were a lot of unemployed diggers around now that gold rush fever had abated, and the powers-that-be felt that, for the time being, it was more important to get them settled on the land than to appease the squatters. The hope was that, with these men on their own land, they would become an asset to Australia rather than a liability.

Many of the huge tracts controlled by the squatters went essentially unused. Worse yet, a great deal of land was being abused either by planting the same forage crop over and over on the soil until it was completely depleted or by allowing sheep to graze so long in one spot that the plant life there was totally destroyed for years to come.

Discussion of the new laws filled the mouths of people of every level—from the rich in their private clubs and swanky homes to the poor in taverns, public houses, hotels and hovels. As so often happens, though, the spirit and the letter of the laws were far apart. It was the selectors' goal to gain land from the squatter, and the squatters' goal to hold on to that land by hook or by crook. And the hooks and crooks were many.

Gil Tyler, the man Flanders had heard explaining the principle of land selection to his cronies in the bar in Brisbane almost a year ago, was one of the first to try to make his pitch for land ownership, and one of the first to encounter head-on the formidable strength and power of the wealthy. In particular, Gil Tyler came up against Big Harris Wakefield, and they both lived to regret it.

When the Land Selection Acts first passed, the squatters worked out a number of ways to get around the law. Their favorite ploy, perhaps, involved the use of "dummies," or people who would pretend to select the land for themselves but who were really acting for the squatter and would immediately turn around and transfer the land back to him. In one area alone, out of one hundred twenty lots, all but ten were selected by dummies. The next most popular method to defeat the purpose of the laws was the technique known as "peacocking." In peacocking, the squatter would pick the choice "eyes" out of the tract of land—the best land, the water holes, the water frontage—and buy them up. In effect, this would make the rest of the land virtually useless so that the squatter would have no competition for it. There were other strategies, too, all with the same goal, to keep the selectors to a minimum and retain the power of land-ownership in the hands of a wealthy elite.

As for Big Harris Wakefield, he made such extensive use of dummies that he began to be referred to jokingly as the ventriloquist. He owned land that stretched from the edge of Brisbane proper to deep inside Darling Downs. When Gil Tyler registered for his piece of land, he violated Harris' territory. It would be nice to be able to say that Gil Tyler was just picking a choice piece of land and it had nothing to do with Harris from the very start, but that would be a lie. He knew perfectly well that the land he had chosen was a part of the land that Harris viewed as his own. He didn't exactly want trouble, but he wanted to make a point of his own about the rights of the little fellow in Australia.

Gil Tyler had always been a fighter. Born the youngest of fifteen kids in a poor family, he had learned early on that the best way to defend himself from attack was to attack first. Somehow he couldn't give up that old pattern, even now when at twenty-four it was no longer appropriate. As he was a charismatic fellow, people tended to back down when they encountered opposition from him. But that wasn't Wakefield's way—to back down.

Big Harris Wakefield had also been raised rough and tough. He'd been the only son in a well-to-do family, but his father believed that a boy should know how to defend himself in every way. Wakefield knew his way around both boxing rings and banks. He behaved with equal ease in either situation. Although his personality was not so appealing as Tyler's, he had the force of his wealth to counter any lack in personal charm.

Where Tyler had drifted from one occupation to another, Wakefield had continued steadily to strengthen the power base which his father had established for him. He was close to forty, almost sixteen years older than Tyler, and Wakefield knew that he could probably buy and sell a dozen Tylers. Besides, was there really any question as to who was more valuable to the struggling young colony? Not in Wakefield's mind, there wasn't.

When Wakefield received the news that the upstart Tyler had selected a piece of his land and resisted efforts by Wakefield's persuaders to sell it, he smiled to himself. He was ready for a good fight. He had no doubt who would be the victor, but he was going to enjoy hell out of getting there. God and Mammon were both on his side. He knew he'd win!

Over breakfast, his daughter Louisa, a romantic fifteen-year-old, listened with eagerness to every detail of the story of Gil Tyler as her father reported to her mother the tale of Tyler's treachery.''

"I'll get his ass!" Wakefield chortled ignoring his wife Bertha's remonstrances about speaking so coarsely in front of his children.

"Never mind," he insisted. "They might as well learn the facts of life now as later. I'm going to talk with that fancy banker from Sydney, Ed Smythe. He's opened up a branch in Brisbane. He seems to be a man who knows his way around a dollar. I'll see what we can dream up together to get that land away from Mr. Tyler." He spoke the name with a sneer. He looked over at Louisa who sat ignoring her breakfast and staring at him. "Don't you worry, punkin," he said. "Your daddy's going to protect every acre of land for you and yours."

Never did he imagine as he spoke that Louisa cared nothing at all for the wealth he was safeguarding for her, and that her eyes burned so brightly because she was caught up in the romance of the renegade he spoke of with such loathing as "that no-good Tyler." Instead, Harris beamed at the assembled group—his oldest daughter Virginia, Louisa, his only son, the delight of his heart, Stephen Gray, and his wife Bertha—confident that here in the bosom of his family he had nothing but true-blue supporters. How differently he would have felt had he known his vendetta against Tyler would embroil his family in the only genuine calamity they had ever experienced.

"Well," he said, picking up his hat and starting for the door, "I can't sit here all day gossping like a lazy woman." He leaned over and bussed his wife on the cheek to show her he was only fooling. "I've got to ride over and talk with Smythe and settle some other matters in town. Then I'll make a check here and there to make sure all is well on our water-edge land out by the gap."

"Be careful, love," his wife warned. "I worry about

the rumors I hear about murderous bushrangers. Why not take someone with you?''

He laughed at his wife's concern, but was secretly pleased to have her fussing over him.

"All right," he conceded in the age-old manner of men placating their womenfolk, "I'll take that Parker fellow along with me. He's just yearning for a chance to put a hole through one of those road bandits. Maybe I could have him put a hole through Tyler while I'm at it, and that would be an end to that issue."

"Oh Father, don't even say such a thing," Louisa remonstrated in a horrified voice. "That would be murder!"

He patted his daughter's braided hair.

"It was just my little joke," he assured her, taking no notice of her intense concern. Then he was off.

"Finish your food, children," their mother scolded, "then get on about your lessons. And don't forget your chores. You know your father wants you all to be smart as well as beautiful!"

The mood at the table was cheerful as the children finished eating, lovingly kissed their mother, then set off for their daily activities. Throughout the day, though, Louisa found herself dreaming of the man her father had described with such distaste. In her imagination he became Robin Hood and Romeo rolled into one, and she determined to meet this man as soon as possible.

Meanwhile, Gil Tyler was discovering that having saved enough money to put down the required twenty-five percent of the purchase price of a pound per acre was only the barest beginning of his expenses as a landowner. He was busily making arrangements with storekeepers to extend him credit for the purchase of seeds and supplies. It was a time of excitement for him because at last he was on the verge of fulfilling his lifetime desire to be an honest-to-goodness man of property. He whistled "Waltzing Matilda" as he made his way along the streets of Brisbane from merchant to merchant gathering up the goods he had decided he would need to settle in for the coming winter. He'd have to work like hell to build himself a shelter for the coming winter and to prepare the land for next spring's planting. It all seemed like an exciting challenge to him, and there was a special lilt to his walk as he realized he was really going to do it! He was really a landowner! He smiled at everyone he passed, and most of the folks he passed smiled back.

Later in the day, though, as he headed toward his favorite saloon for a drink to soothe his parched throat, he passed by a group of men who had no smiles to spare. He reckoned they were all squatters, especially when he saw them disappear into an exclusive club patronized by the town's so-called elite.

He didn't really give their goings-on much thought as he entered the cool sanctuary of the pub, but if he'd known what they were up to he would have felt greater alarm. Wakefield had gathered the group together and suggested the meeting. Now, in the comfort of the Brisbane Club, he told them his plans regarding the Mister Gilbert Tyler who was such a source of consternation to him.

"These damn selectors have to be put in their places," he said to his listeners. "I think if I make a good example of this Tyler fellow and you do the same with any particularly troublesone folks who've selected land that belongs to you, we'll soon be able to rest easy again."

"But once they've got the acreage fair and square, what's there to do?" a short fellow with a pencil line mustache asked. He was known for his pious sentiments, acting as a part-time preacher out in the bush upon occasion, and Wakefield had hesitated to have him join the group. There was no room for faint hearts at a time like this.

"Don't be a fool, Bertie," he roared. "These men don't know anything about land ownership. They're just no-goods who want to get in our hair—drifters who hope they can make a quick buck and force us to buy them out. Why, without any action on our part at all, they'd be handing the land back over—and at a discount, too—within the next few years. We'll just help them hurry the process along.''

"Well, what's your idea, Harris," one of his friends and neighbors asked. "You tell us what you have in mind and we can have something concrete to consider. Australia's not the place to talk theories. Give us some specifics. I'm right on the border between New South Wales and Queensland and these laws are a pain in the butt to me for sure, I can tell you. There are some selectors I could as easily shoot as give the time of day to. In some of the remote land spots, they'd best watch out, too, or that's exactly what's gonna happen to them!''

There were some murmurs at his comment, some of the half-dozen men agreeing, others feeling that that was going too far.

"Well, the remotest sections shouldn't worry us too much," Harris answered. "Before we have a chance to notice them, I'll wager just about any thing they'll be off chasing rainbows somewhere else—maybe further inland. It's plain to see most of these rag-tags have no staying power." He harumphed sententiously.

"But the ones that somehow get good land, that's another story," he continued. "This thorn in my side, Tyler, for instance. I was just talking to Smythe, the banker from Sydney. He told me how they've been handling the upstarts in the capitol. I think we have a lot to learn from them."

"Come to the point, man," another man said. Harris was known as a good man to drink with, because he always had a story to tell, but that same trait became a nuisance in the middle of a busy day.

"Tyler has already been to see him about a loan on his land. The papers haven't been drawn up yet, though. When Smythe draws up the papers, he's going to bury a clause in it that gives him the right to demand full payment in three months. That'll be before he's even got his first crops fully in the ground. No way he'll be able to, pay."

"So the bankers will soon own all the selectors' lands, if that idea spreads," Bertie said. "What's the good of that? We'll be in a worse fix than we are already."

"You're right that's a danger," Harris said. "He told me the banks are doing just fine in the land business these days in New South Wales. But as I say, we should benefit from their experiences—and that means not make the same mistakes, too. I made him a little deal under the table. The bank itself will never have that land. The deal will be a straight cash-benefit program between me and Smythe. Only bank paper will make it all look official. Then I'll have my land back again. Maybe in better shape, if the Tyler man gives it some good attention getting it ready to farm before he loses it."

Wakefield beamed at his compatriots. He had decided to share his big news with the other squatters nearby because he like being considered the man with vision and foresight. Now, as he saw some of them looking dubious, he questioned the wisdom of his candor. His main concern, after all, was to get his own land back again. Helping the rest of them was just icing on the cake.

His friend Henry, who had holdings to the south of Wakefield's, chimed in now. "We could make similar arrangements with the storekeepers. Pay them a profit for charging men a higher rate. Or promise to buy any of the land they get their hands on in exchange for supplies. At a good rate. If we don't, we'll soon find the selectors gone but all the selectors'land owned by bankers and shopkeepers. That might be worse. After all, there has to be some advantage to having come here first. We made this land ours. Sure, lots of folks would be glad to take it over now, but we're the ones with the money and the land. That gives us the power and let's not forget it."

"Right," Harris Wakefield said. "We better not forget it, and we better use it to good advantage or we'll find we've lost it. Every damn freed criminal will soon be in politics and what kind of rules do you think they'll be making?''

The talk continued along these lines as the men ordered another round of drinks. Big Harris Wakefield let his mind drift back to the very satisfactory conversation he had had that morning with Smythe. They were going to get along just fine. He could tell that. And Tyler's days as a land-owner were numbered.

Tyler, meanwhile, had gathered a few folks of his own together as he sat drinking in the saloon not more than a hundred feet down the street from the Brisbane Club.

He was feeling concerned that he was getting himself so deeply into debt he'd never see his way out again. He hoped some of the others who had talked about getting land might have some ideas he hadn't thought of. But instead he found the few who had actually gotten hold of some land turning to him. The others, most of the folks, hadn't been able to get any land yet and were still trying to save up for another round of selections. They counted on the laws helping them. Gil had the feeling they'd better all help themselves.

He fell silent and let the others go on with their stories. Perhaps, he thought, he'd bitten off more than he could chew by taking on Big Harris Wakefield. The elation he'd felt only a short time before had all but evaporated. But wasn't that always the way, he reasoned. Reality just never could live up to dreams. He was still a young man, only twenty four. Why then, he wondered, did he feel so terribly, terribly old?

13

LOUISA Wakefield, Harris's youngest daughter, sat many miles away feeling terribly, terribly young. When will I ever grow up, she wondered. She sat daydreaming about the concerns of the real world, the world she imagined she would enter when she found true love.

That was the most important thing in life—more important than the sums she was supposed to be doing now, more important than the chores she was supposed to do as soon as she finished her sums. More important than anything.

Louisa had grown up on romances. Despite the rugged and exacting land in which she'd grown up, which seemed to urge toughness and practicality on one and all, Louisa treasured a different vision of herself. She saw herself as the heroine of every penny romance she could get her hands on. As her mother said, she always had her nose stuck in a book. More than once, Louisa had been punished for neglecting her work in favor of finishing just one more chapter in whatever novel she happened to be devouring at the time.

She went over to the mirror and gazed at herself. She wasn't a child anymore, no matter what her parents said. Her breasts were full and round and her hips curved provocatively. That was the way her favorite novelist, Harriet Arnold, would have described it. She thought about her face. Was it the face of a heroine? She had asked herself that same question a thousand times before. She didn't have rosebud lips, whatever they were. But her lips were full and pink. Her eyes were grey. She would have preferred blue, but at least they were in the same family. Her worst trait, she decided, was her hair. But the fact that she had ignored it, because it wasn't a "fiery mass of ringlets," was probably making things worse. She took down the braids that she usually wore wound around her head and brushed and brushed. After maybe five minutes of solid endeavor, she was pleased to see that her hair flew around her head like a swirling cloud. A soft brown cloud. She looked like the woman in one of the paintings her mother had hung in the parlor. Yes, this would do nicely. She would wear her hair loose and full like this from now on.

She thought once more about Gil Tyler. She didn't really understand why her father hated him so, but it excited her. She also felt afraid for him. Her father was a tough man—not mean exactly, but certainly tough. She hoped that Gil Tyler could defend himself. In her mind she began to imagine a story where she would save him. She would protect him from her father. She would risk her life for him, and, in gratitude, he would marry her. She smiled.

Except for her notions about romance, Louisa was a serious girl. She had a thoughtful nature, essentially gentle and sensitive. Both her sister Virginia and her brother Stephen Gray turned to her to lead them. She was adept at finding compromises for their youthful imbroglios and dilemmas. That trait alone, the ability to conciliate, was so atypical of the Wakefield manner that her parents always wondered how she'd ever come by it.

"Lou, you playing 'mirror, mirror on the wall?' "

She whirled around and faced her little brother, just eleven years old.

"Come here, brat," she said.

Stephen Gray walked over to her and buried his head on her lap. He wrapped his thin arms around her waist. Then he began to tickle her until, gasping for breath, she pushed him away from her.

"Silly!" she said. "What are you doing? Want me to read you a story?"

He looked up at his sister and his eyes grew larger for a moment. She knew he loved it when she read to him. Louisa's heart melted when she looked at his darling face. He seemed almost like an angel to her. It scared her sometimes, as though he were too good to be a part of this world. And she knew that she wasn't the only one who felt that way. Everyone loved Stephen Gray Wakefield. Even their father, for all his teasing and roughness, virtually melted at the sight of Stephen.

"Daddy, I'm so glad you're home," he'd say when Wakefield returned, tired and disgruntled, at the end of a typically taxing day. The gruff patriarch couldn't help but let the child know how much he adored him.

The girls loved their father, too, but their love was always tempered with the respect bordering on fear that he had instilled in them. Not so with Stephen Gray. His love for all the members of his family was joyfully pure. And, of course, they loved him in kind.

Louisa tousled his sandy hair.

"C'mon, then," she said. "I'll read you a chapter of *Pilgrim's Progress* before we go on with our chores. Okay?"

The boy grinned and nodded. She took his hand and they headed toward their favorite reading place, a bay window that had been fitted up as a cushioned seat, where they could cuddle together and he could follow along with her or watch the pictures as she read the words.

Far away in the Red Raven Saloon in Sydney, another young woman was hidden away in a secret nook reading, too. The girl was Annie Finch, who had become quite the young lady during the year since she'd arrived in Australia a homeless orphan. She was reading a letter that had just arrived in a package sent to her by Captain Dan.

The package contained a number of drawing tablets of different sizes and a collection of colored chalks. Anne was delighted. She had always fancied herself an artist back in England. But she'd only been a child then, she thought now, with just a few watercolors to her name.

Dear little Ann, she read, as she turned once again to the letter.

The moment I landed back in England, I hurried to an artist's shop to buy you these supplies. I decided that it would be too long for you to have to wait for a present—if I waited until my return. The reason I chose this particular present is that I was struck with the lively way you looked at the world around you when we were on board ship together. With such a fine eye, you should either be a sea captain—and a good one, you would be, I am sure—or an artist. Since the life of a sea captain is a wearisome one—even for a man, let alone for a lively young woman—I decided you might prefer to try your hand at art!

I must admit this gift was also inspired by a young woman I met in Brisbane shortly before the ship sailed. She was a scientist of some sort, but her work involves a great deal of drawing. I saw some of her renderings, and though I'm no judge, her talent struck me as prodigious. I'll try to arrange a meeting between the two of you upon my return to Australia—I think you'd like each other. Her name is Miss Flanders Wilde, and I will write to her as soon as I post this letter so she will know of you. I must write her some bad news in regard to her shipment of goods anyway. Your name will brighten the pages. I can

hardly wait for the time when I can greet you
again in person. But, until then, my friend, I
remain

> Yours most sincerely,
> Captain Dan

There were tears in Anne's eyes as she finished the
letter. Hearing from the man after so long a time brought
back unsettling memories of her parents, and the grim and
untimely manner of their deaths. But, in truth, these brooding recollections weren't with her very often anymore.
Mostly, she now went on with her life as though it had
begun the day she stepped onto Australian soil. She remembered the first sight she had of Sydney Harbor. What a
vision! It was like a heaven on earth, particularly after the
fearful hell of that journey. When they'd finally entered
the glistening and peaceful cove, it was as they had left all
dangers behind them. Sydney Harbor—that would be the
subject of her first drawing. She'd start on it first thing in
the morning.

While Annie sat lost in the currents of memory and
feeling that Captain Dan's letter had evoked in her, her
adopted mother was sharing a far more down-to-earth
scene with a discouraged Charlie Burrows.

"They say a good wife is like precious rubies," he
muttered. "Well, I'd hate to tell you what I compare a bad
wife to!" He was half-drunk, although it was only the
middle of the afternoon. It was an effort to lift his head up
and meet Rosie's eyes. "Get me another drink, love," he
said, as the walls of the room seemed to close in and reel
around him.

"Charlie, I don't like to see you like this," Rosie said
solicitously. "You'll not solve anything by drinking yourself blind, you know. Besides, you've weathered far worse
storms than this one. Don't tell me you can't control your
own wife, for heaven's sake."

He shook his head with a vigor he instantly regretted.

Pressing his hands to his throbbing temples, he practically moaned, "Oh Rosie, she's beyond everything. I should have married you when I had the chance. But I was caught up in respectability then."

Rosie blushed, remembering the night she'd tried every trick she knew to lure him into marrying her, all to no avail. It just wasn't meant to be. She had long ago accepted that, and had resigned herself to their being "the best of friends."

She had heard rumors about Charlie's new wife. Men joked that she was too much of a lady to be a woman. Then they'd nudge each other and wink knowingly. Charlie himself had dropped hints that he wasn't happy in the way he'd expected to be with his new young wife. Until today, though, he had never spelled out his misery. Now, as he drank down the fresh drink Rosie had gotten for him, he told her a detailed story of the sorrow his first year of marriage had brought him.

"She's got the longest face in the known world," he moaned. "A day doesn't go by that she doesn't curse her new land and yearn for England. She's no good in the homemaking department, and as for her wifely duties—I think she'd rather be burned alive than give me my due."

"Maybe she just needs a little more time," Rosie suggested. Now that Charlie had confessed how unhappy he was with his new bride, she could afford to be a bit charitable toward the little twit. She'd only met her once, when Charlie had brought her around to meet the gang at the Red Raven. His little Clara. Well, his little Clara had turned up her little nose at everything in sight. Rosie could have scratched her eyes out for treating Charlie so shabbily.

"More time!" he roared. "She took to her bed a month ago and refuses to do anything. She rings a bell when she wants something, and the servants are supposed to drop everything and run to her side. No, it'll never be any good. If I don't murder her, she'll be damned lucky. But she probably thinks I'm such an old man that she'll just wait around for me to die and then have all my money and run back to England." He dropped his head down on his arms. Rosie wasn't sure whether he was crying or whether he had fallen asleep. She was almost afraid to touch him. She racked her brain to think of the right thing to say or do. After all, she reminded herself, this was good old Charlie Burrows. They'd been friends a long time. But no brilliant ideas came to her.

"Charlie," she whispered finally. "You don't have to put up with it, you know. You've already paid your dues. You can ship her home. From what you say, that won't break her heart, although it might upset her greedy little plans. You don't have to stay married or wait around for one of you to die. There is such a thing as divorce."

"Don't talk that way, girlie," he said gruffly, raising his head to regard her with bloodshot eyes. "How would it look if I divorced the child I'd sent all the way to England for? People would think me a proper fool, no doubt about it."

"Oh, Charlie, you're being a *real* fool to tolerate such misery! Who cares what people think or what they say? You're rich enough to thumb your nose at all of them. Most of them would just be jealous in the first place. Just please yourself. I hate to see you this way."

Charlie staggered to his feet.

"Sit back down," Rosie insisted. "You're in no condition to get on a horse. Let me make you some coffee and we'll talk about happier things. You haven't told me a word about your boys."

Charlie sat back down heavily and a smile crossed his face. Rosie knew she'd finally found a way to lead him out of his unhappiness, if only temporarily. Charlie's boys were the soft spot in his heart.

"Wait just a minute," she said, "I'll get the coffee and be right back." She rested her arm on her friend's shoulder. She wanted to show him somehow that he was dear to her, that she wished him the best, whether she was part of his life or not.

Soon they were drinking coffee and he was telling her about Hugh and Edmund. Rosie thought Edmund was a wonderful name, but his father always called him Eddie. Now he said, "Eddie has a real fondness for the sheep. I can't decide if he's a natural born sheepman or if he's just lazy." Then he threw back his head and laughed, and Rosie knew that the crisis about his wife was over for the moment.

"How old is the boy now?"

For a moment Charlie looked startled, as though he couldn't remember. Then he answered, "Why, he's sixteen now, I think. I don't pay much attention to birthdays. Dammit, if I had a real wife, that's what she would be doing!"

Rosie stopped this train of thought at once and steered the conversation back in the direction of the children.

"My Anne is thirteen, you know. Maybe we should introduce them. I've tried to have her meet a variety of children, but I have to confess she doesn't seem to care much for people her own age. She much prefers the conversation of adults."

"Why, then they're alike as two peas in a pod, except Eddie doesn't even care much for adults! What's the matter with these kids anyway?"

Just as he finished uttering those words, Charlie turned at the sound of clattering feet approaching.

"Momma," the young lady hurrying toward their table cried. "Momma, look what was in the package that Captain Dan sent me." She held the offering out in her arms and insisted that her mother and Charlie gaze at the pads of paper and the art materials she had been given.

"Anne," her mother reproached her. "Don't you see that I'm entertaining a guest? Remember your manners, please." Though she tried, Rosie couldn't make her voice very harsh. Just to look at the girl's sweet face brought a smile to Rosie's lips. She stood up and wrapped her arms around Anne.

"Anne, you remember Charlie Burrows, don't you?"

"Oh, of course, I do," the girl said making an artful curtsy. "I'm so pleased to see you again Mr. Burrows. You're one of mother's favorite friends."

Both adults found her artless ways quite charming. Anne told her mother about her plans to spend the next day practicing her drawing.

"But Anne," her mother said, "what of your lessons?"

"They're so boring, Mother. Please let me take the afternoon off to do some sketches. I promise I'll make up the assigned work over the weekend."

Rosie sighed. She never could hold out against Anne's wishes. She was lucky the girl was such a good child. Otherwise, there would be bedlam, she was sure. "Very well," she said. Anne hurried off to put away her things, and Rosie sat back down next to Charlie. "Well, what's to be done?" she asked. "Youth will be served."

Charlie grabbed her and gave her an enormous kiss. He was feeling a bit more sober by now and far less maudlin than when they had begun their conversation.

"You make me laugh," he said, "talking as though you're a hundred years old!"

"Sometimes I feel it," she retorted with a grin. "I am getting pretty old never to have been married. Imagine that, Charlie, a charmer like me! Never married," she teased.

"Thank your lucky stars for that," he said darkly. "Well, you've been a friend indeed today, but now I have to head back home. I'll remember you for this one, Rosie. Love you, sweetheart." He kissed her again before leaving. When he had gone and Rosie was carrying their coffee cups back into the kitchen, she found a big bill folded under the saucer. Charlie had wanted to thank her with more than words, but was afraid to offer her money for fear of hurting her feelings. She tucked the money into the bosom of her dress. Once she had wanted his name and his love. Now she had a daughter to raise, after all, and she couldn't afford any false pride. The money would come in useful.

14

THAT gift from Daniel Thornburg marked the real beginning of Anne Finch's life in Australia, the true beginning of her passionate life as a woman. And it led to the deepest love she was ever to know, her love for a young man she met one day near the beginning of 1864, in the heat of summer.

She had taken to the art work with total absorption, and Rosie quickly realized that the child had a genuine gift. Anne took to drawing naturally, joyfully, and only the sternest demands could force her to attend to her other studies. Her art came before everything. No sooner would she awaken than she would be begging her mother for permission to go here or there in order to do some sketching. After a while, Rosie realized there was no point in fighting such a serious devotion and allowed Anne to make her own schedule and to ignore any other schooling.

"It's a gift from God," she said to Bart, the barman, as they sat together. "She was meant to be an artist, I suppose. But it's a damn good thing she's a woman and won't really have to earn her keep at it, I can tell you!"

"Why do you say that, Rosie?" he asked, drying his hands on his apron and coming around the bar to sit down beside her. "She's good enough, I think, to be very successful."

"Good enough! Hah! Since when does ability have anything to do with success?"

"Oh, I see what you're driving at. There's no money in it, right?"

"Exactly! As a hobby for a lady it ain't bad, though, I suppose." She drank down her beer and stood up. "I guess it's time to get dressed for the afternoon crowd. You know, Bart, I'm getting tired of this life. I've been thinking of talking to Mr. Smythe about putting me in charge of the girls and letting me stay out of the beds. I run this place anyway—he might as well make it official. The pleasure's most definitely worn off. Soon the customers will be sure to notice, and then there will be complaints. What do you think? Will he buy it?"

"Why not? The men come more for the pleasure of your company and your lively talk than for anything else. They might not care whether it's you or one of them childish chippies Smythe's been bringing in between the sheets, but they know the difference when it comes to sharing time outside the bedroom! Smythe's no fool. Talk to him."

"I will. I've been thinking about it for a while now. Maybe as long as since I first brought Annie home with me. I'd rather die than live to see the day she'd be ashamed of me."

Bart nodded his head and shifted the cigarette he was always smoking from one side of his mouth to the other.

Rosie went slowly toward the stairs that led up to her room. At that same moment, off in the hills on the outskirts of town, her daughter climbed slowly and laboriously up a steep incline to reach a particularly beautiful rock formation. When she reached it, she paused to take in the view on the other side of the hill. There, gathered in a picturesque arrangement, she spotted a cluster of pure white sheep. Anne settled herself on a boulder and began to draw, only to be startled by the sudden appearance of a man approaching the sheep from the far side. She wished she could be invisible so that she could add him to her sketch without self-consciousness. He looked so much like the perfect shepherd it almost seemed as if the scene had been prearranged by an invisible hand for her personal satisfaction.

As he neared the sheep, the man stopped, but he seemed to be lost in thought and remained totally unaware of Anne sitting not more than a hundred feet away further up the hill. She was delighted by this obliviousness on his part and good fortune on hers, and began busily making sketches of him. He was a good six-feet tall and so lean it looked like even more. He had blonde hair and a slight mustache, which she felt sure he affected because he believed it made him look older. She couldn't see the color of his eyes, but she imagined them a deep brown, and that was the way she drew them. He wore a white cotton shirt that laced up the front, but which—no doubt due to the heat, she reasoned—he left open, so his manly bare chest was exposed to her view. His breeches were a rough-textured brown cloth and fit snugly, outlining strong, muscular thighs.

"Holla!" he exclaimed, suddenly spying her at her work, and by then she had grown so involved with her sketching that he startled her over again. She tried to cover her embarrassment by hurriedly putting her pad aside, and gathering her skirts together, she stood and made him a pleasant curtsy.

"Holla back to you, sir," she said primly.

"Sir, is it, lass? Well, you do be the first lady to give me that lovely title."

"I believe an honest workman is as good as any gentleman," she replied, borrowing a line she had lately read in one of her mother's story magazines.

Then, as though they both shared some wonderful joke, or perhaps simply from the joy of being young in the summer season, they both broke into laughter. The young man quickly covered the ground between them and stood at her side.

"I'd like to introduce myself," he said, "if I may."

"Oh, please don't," she said. "Let's enjoy this mysterious meeting for just a little while before we bring it down to earth with all that tedious business of names and so on. Wouldn't you like that? A bit of pretend? You shall be my loyal shepherd, and I'll be your artist!''

What an odd girl, Edmund Burrows thought. But entrancing, too. He had to admit to himself that it was refreshing to be mistaken for a shepherd. More often than not, he found his father's wealth and position as much a burden as anything else. He'd play along with her for a while and see where it led.

"So you're to be my artist, are you? I thought you would have said, 'my lady fair.' Isn't that more in the manner of things?''

"Oh, dear, I see you must have been reading too many stories. You see, I am a perfectly modern woman! I must be an artist first, and only then a lady fair.''

Edmund sensed that under the playfulness of her manner this young woman was probably quite serious.

"Well,'' he said, throwing himself down on the grass and indicating that she should seat herself once more on her rocky perch, "I don't know that a shepherd has much use for an artist. Nor for a perfectly modern woman either, for that matter. Can you cook?''

"Why . . . I can . . . Why you . . .'' she spluttered.

He held up his hands in mock distress to stop her from going further. "I wasn't serious,'' he said. "Really!'' He saw that two red circles had appeared on her cheeks. They added to her appeal, he thought, but still regretted that he had so obviously distressed her.

"Let's begin again,'' Anne said, struggling to regain her composure.

"Excellent,'' he agreed. "Why don't you show me your pictures and explain about them? I know practically nothing about art. You can be my teacher. Do you fancy that?''

"Oh yes,'' she said. "But you must be my teacher as well.''

"But what can I teach you?"

"Oh, about the world of the countryside. I've spent my entire life in cities. You can help me see. That will help my art work as well." She paused and glanced up at him with sparkling eyes, "I shall be ever so grateful."

They spent the afternoon lost in happy chatter, but though they managed to reveal a great deal about themselves, as young people will when they first discover each other, they never once mentioned their parents or very much about their home lives. The omissions were calculated on both sides. Edmund and Annie both being glad to keep their backgrounds for the moment in the shadows. Encroaching darkness forced them to part, but before they did so they made definite plans to meet again. In the very same spot. Their hill, they already called it.

That evening Anne went about her chores whistling with such a distracted air that Rosie wondered if she'd taken leave of her senses. She could hardly wait for bedtime so she could be completely alone in the dark to try and relive every moment they had had together. She saw him walking up the hill toward her over and over. Her fancy was that he had been drawn toward her the way ships are drawn toward safe harbor. That idea made her smile, and she turned over in bed until her small nose was positively buried in the down pillow. Then she fell into a deep, peaceful, dreamless sleep.

Edmund, on the other hand, couldn't seem to fall asleep no matter what position he took. He tossed and turned until his older brother Hugh screamed that he'd kill him if he didn't stop "moaning and messing about." Then Edmund lay still, rigidly staring up at the ceiling over his head. He had never in his life given a girl more than a passing thought. Oh, he was popular enough, and, with his father's urging, he had taken various girls to the dances his father's club sometimes organized. But they were all "nice, proper" girls—that's how his father described them—and

Edmund had soon realized that those words were nothing but synonyms for boring.

This girl, though, was different. Not that she didn't seem nice, and proper, too. But she seemed so much more than that. She seemed—Edmund hunted for the right word to express what he was feeling—she seemed odd, he decided. Odd and interesting. He had the notion, although he had no basis for it, he assured himself, that his father wouldn't approve of her. Maybe he was just looking for trouble. No sense in that, he told himself. And finally, with the coming of the first light, Edmund fell into a heavy sleep.

That was the first night. It set a pattern as truly as a dressmaker marks her ideas on tissue and then follows the lines she has drawn with the sharp blade of her shears. Anne and Edmund became a part of each other's lives as simply and naturally as sunshine nourishes the growth of plants or one season flows into the next. They met almost daily and became best friends. There was no talk or thought of romance when they were together—and almost nothing but romantic notions in their fevered time apart. It was the strangest feeling that either of them had ever known. They began to talk about a future together as though they would go on meeting like this forever. They knew each other's names now—Edmund and Anne—but not the significance behind those names. Not the fact that he was Charlie Burrows's son. Not the fact that she was an orphan and her adopted parent was a less-than-respectable woman. No, they knew the essentials only. They knew only who they were inside.

15

CAPTAIN Thornburg stood near the prow of his ship, the *H.M.S. Three Winds*, as it neared the Brisbane coast. He scanned the dock to see if he could pick out the fair shape of Flanders Wilde. He had written her months before to ask her to meet him upon his arrival. He had decided that news of her shipment's misadventures would be better delivered in person than by post. Besides, he had a letter to deliver to her from Professor Thorenson. Most important of all, he hoped to convince her to come with him to Sydney to meet Anne Finch and become her special teacher. He thought for a moment that he saw her, but then he noticed that the woman he thought was Miss Wilde had a child in her arms. No, it must be someone else.

Then he had to turn all his attention to docking the ship. It was almost an hour later when he strode down the gangway to the shore and again sought out the face he could only vaguely remember from the single meeting he had with Flanders almost two years earlier.

"Oh, Captain," a sweet voice hailed him.

He spun around to see the young woman he had noted from shipboard advancing on him—the woman with the child in her arms. The smile that radiated from her face was mirrored on the face of the small boy she held.

"It's me, Captain Thornburg. Flanders Wilde. Has it been so long that age has transformed me beyond recognition?" Flanders' smile never wavered. Actually, since the birth of her son Tarleton, she found life so pleasant that she almost always had a smile on her face.

"It has been a long time," he said. "But the transformation I see on your face has nothing to do with age. It seems to have something to do with happiness, though. Maybe something to do with this little fellow, eh?" He reached over and patted the little boy's rosy cheek. The boy reached up and grabbed the man's fingers.

"Yes," Flanders admitted, extricating the man's hand from Tarleton's tight grasp, "he's certainly responsible for a lot of changes in my life! But let's not tarry here in the street, sir. Shall we go to the inn across the way and share an afternoon tea?"

"Yes, that would be splendid. It's grand to have solid land under my feet again. We'll have our talk, and then I'll finish up my work aboard ship."

As they walked, the little boy babbled his own private secrets to the air. The jolly sound cheered both adults and charmed many a person they passed as well. In the inn, Flanders turned his care over to Elizabeth, who had come along for just this purpose. Then Flanders and Dan Thornburg sat at a small table over a pot of Earl Grey tea and talked of the things that were really on their minds.

"Your shipment seemed to have a strange destiny. A unique destiny, I might say," the captain began apologetically. "It arrived safely enough onto British soil, that I can vouch for. I turned it over to the longshoremen myself. Your drawings and the letter you gave me, though, I took it upon myself to deliver by hand. Well, it turns out that I made a wise decision in that regard. Quite by accident," he added modestly. "You see . . ." Here he paused, took a long drink of tea, and seemed embarrassed to continue.

"Yes, yes?" Flanders' eager voice urged him on.

"Miss Wilde, those items were the only ones to reach their destination, I'm afraid. No one seems to know what happened to the boxes, but they never arrived at the Society! Nor back at the ship either." He fell silent a moment, and

Flanders sat before him gaping. Impossible, she thought. My work never arrived. I've waited all this time. She was momentarily shocked beyond feeling.

"I'm so sorry," he said helplessly.

Flanders pulled herself together. This man was surely in no way responsible. She mustn't make him feel any worse than he obviously did already.

"No," she said. "You have nothing to apologize for. But wait, you say you delivered the letter and my drawings, is that right?"

He nodded.

"Well, then there's no real harm done. The specimens were only additional evidence. You wrote me that my professor was preparing a letter for you to bring to me. He'll surely tell me the reaction my work received. Quick, man, where is the letter?"

The captain reached inside his jacket pocket and drew out a thickly stuffed envelope. Flanders reached for it with such speed that she spilled her tea onto the linen tablecloth, and there was quite a to-do before everything got straightened out so that she and the captain could settle down again to their meeting. Then Flanders turned imploring eyes on Captain Dan.

"I really can't wait. Would it be too terribly rude if I excused myself now in order to read my letter? I know you have work to do. I have decided that, if my son can come along, I will accompany you to Sydney when you sail tomorrow to meet your Anne Finch. I have work to do in Sydney anyway. The ride with you will be a delight. I had only thought of the overland route. But for now, I'll bid you adieu."

The captain stood at once and assisted Flanders to her feet. She felt at ease with him. He had a kindly face, she thought. She would like to know more about his life. Did he have a love tucked away somewhere in his background as she did? Well, he was kind enough not to inquire about Tarleton's father, about why she was still unmarried, so she would respect his privacy also. But she looked forward to getting to know him better. Meanwhile, though, she hurried to her room to see what her professor had written.

As she read the words, a short time later, her hands began to tremble. The color faded from her face. Elizabeth, who was sitting nearby playing with Tarleton, noticed the change in her mistress and put the child on the floor with some little soldier toys. She came over to Flanders and stood above her silently.

Flanders crumpled the letter and sat rigidly in her chair. Elizabeth grew alarmed.

"Can I help?" she asked. "What is it? Has someone died? Flanders, you look so pale. Please, speak to me."

"I can't talk about it just now," Flanders said through clenched teeth. "Please take care of Tar. I'm going for a walk. I must have a breath of air."

"Of course."

"Momma, look, momma," the boy said with delight, having made two soldiers stand at attention.

"Not now, Tar," Flanders said. "Momma loves you. She'll be back in a few minutes. You be a good boy for Elizabeth. Tomorrow you and Momma are going on a great big ship together."

"Ship," the boy said in imitation. "Ship."

Flanders, with tears blinding her eyes, walked past him and out the door. She still held the letter crumpled in her hand. She held herself stiffly erect. Breathe deeply, she commanded herself. Breathe deeply, walk firmly, don't think about it. Those were the rules she gave herself as she made her way out into the busy Brisbane street.

It wasn't until after dark when everyone else had gone to sleep that Flanders allowed herself to smooth the letter out and look at it again. She leaned close to the kerosene lamp which she had kept low in order not to disturb her boy who slept on a little cot beside her bed. The noises of the inn were distant, but heightened her already keen sense of being away from home.

Dear Flanders, dear child, she read. Just those few
words and already she felt the tears rising to her eyes. She
drew a hankie from her pocket. (She insisted that Elizabeth
sew pockets into every item of clothing she owned—even
her nightgowns. She couldn't understand how other women
made do without them.) She blew her nose noisily and
dabbed at her eyes. Then she went on with the letter:

> By the time you read this, news of my death will
> already be in the papers if any of the papers care
> to make note of it. They certainly cared little
> enough to make note of my life. No, that's the
> self-pity of an old man talking, Flanders. For-
> give it. I write to give you news of your recep-
> tion here, and tell you that I am not long for this
> world. You, my friend, must understand. As for
> the rest of the world, they never will nor ever
> can. Understanding is beyond them.
> Your material arrived, and I at once shepherded
> it through the entry procedures at the Scientific
> Society. Then I awaited a call for me to come
> and explain its significance to the committee.
> Instead, I received a call to come and pick it up.
> The voice on the line sounded angry, so I in-
> quired what might be the trouble. The committee's
> report would tell me all, I was informed.
> Naturally, I went at once. The report denounced
> the fraud perpetrated between us—you and me—in
> the rudest terms. No such creatures existed as
> you described, it said.
> Fools!
> You must not take it too much to heart, Flanders.
> Just do your work and do not concern yourself
> with the regard of the fickle world.
> As for me, my life is done. I have no more
> useful work to do. Besides, my doctor informs
> me that I am seriously ill. I do not favor a

lengthy period of decline accompanied by who knows how much pain. No, I'd rather choose my own time and manner of exit. In fact, I sent my own epitaph to the London papers. They may print it if they wish. To you, I wanted to say more. I told them: "To Science he gave the best efforts of his mind, and to the world a few good students to follow after. Hail and farewell!"
Flanders, a final thought. Don't return to England just now. There is much vicious talk about "the scandalous lady in the provinces" who sent the Society a pack of lies. It will all die down, of course. Someday your work will receive the recognition it deserves. My love is always with you to sustain you. We shall not meet again on this earth, but I believe we shall greet each other again in heaven.

It was signed in his most formal manner with a great flourish. Dead! Flanders couldn't believe it. Dead. And all her work mocked and disregarded!

Well, he need not warn her against returning to England. Her decision was irrevocable—she would be an Australian and Britain be damned! Besides, with the professor dead, there was no reason to return.

Toowoomba was her new home now. She had only been away for a couple of days and already she missed it. But at least she had Tarleton with her. Her darling son. She could hardly believe that he was over a year old and Lachlan still didn't know of his existence. She worried at times that Lachlan was dead. Must she lose all the men in her life? Or perhaps he just didn't care. She had even planned to return to his cave, but then the letter from the sea captain arrived, so she put it off until after her Sydney trip. She badly needed more art supplies, and they could all use a little sojourn in the big cosmopolitan center. Moreover, she was intrigued by the story of Captain Dan's talented young lady. Perhaps it was her turn to take a student. Perhaps that would be her way of making it all up to Professor Thorenson. She remembered the words he had left as his epitaph: "To Science he gave the best efforts of his mind, and to the world a few good students to follow after. Hail and farewell!"

Flanders turned down the light until it flickered and went out. She felt her way to the bed and crawled beneath the covers. Even if I can't sleep, she thought, I'll lie here and rest. Almost as soon as she had thought that, though, she fell into a deep sleep that lasted until morning. Then she had to rush about and make all the last-minute preparations for her journey that she'd meant to take care of the night before.

She spent most of that journey chasing after her son, who seemed to have no trouble toddling about on the shifting decks of the ship.

"He's meant to be a sailor," Captain Dan cried, scooping the little boy into his arms. Tarleton threw back his head and chortled as the captain's beard tickled his cheek.

Flanders, who had spent some time brooding over whether she would end up the way her professor had—disillusioned and suicidal—realized, as she looked at them, that she would never be so saddened by the world as long as her son was in it. He connected her to life in a way that felt much more profound than even her work, which had been for so long the very bedrock of her existence.

The captain came over to her and she took the boy from his arms.

"We're almost there," he said, pointing ahead to where the two rocky outcroppings marked the entrance to Sydney Harbour.

The dancing sunlight on the blue waters delighted the eyes of both mother and child. They laughed aloud at the sight of the little skiffs and sailboats bobbing about. As they drew closer, Flanders became aware that the sky over the city was holding a cloud of grey that seemed to be the result of plumes of smoke rising from a number of manufacturing concerns. These were signs of new industrialization she had been hearing about, no doubt. More to argue over. Was it good for Australia to turn its back on its own natural resources and rely on imports—except for sheep and wool—or should it develop a national group of industries with the possibility of true independence? Well, she hated to see the dirty air, which already reminded her of London, despoil her beautiful adopted land. But everyone spoke of Progress as though it were a God, and there was no way to fight the popular idea whose time had come.

A short time later, Dan and Flanders were entering the restaurant whose picture windows overlooked the glorious waters of the bay.

"There she is," Dan cried. "My God, she's a young woman!"

With Flanders rushing along behind him, he hurried across the floor toward a table in the corner. She was both amused and touched by the man's concern for the child he had brought to Australia almost two years earlier. Then she was being introduced to a young woman—was she fourteen, maybe fifteen?—Flanders wondered. Surely no more than that. A young woman with clear and direct eyes and an honest, open face. They nodded to each other in response to the introduction and exchanged smiles. Flanders found herself quite taken with this Anne Finch.

"I hear that you have an interest in art. And in the art all around us in this beautiful homeland of ours," Flanders said, as they all sat down and prepared to share a lunch.

"Oh, nothing quite so grand as that, I'm afraid," Anne stammered, blushing. "I'm afraid my dear friend Captain Dan brags about me." She smiled over at him and reached across in the most natural of gestures to take his hand. He beamed back at her in response. "But," Anne went on, "I am eager to learn, and I understand that you have both training and talent. Perhaps you would not take it amiss if I asked to see some of your work."

"Not at all. I'd be flattered. I have brought a small sketchbook along with me . . . I never can bear to travel without one, it seems. For fear of missing the perfect picture, I suppose." Flanders made a wry grimace. "I'll be glad to exchange viewings with you," she added. "The captain tells me you have been drawing for quite a while now."

"Oh yes, daily, since his wonderful present arrived more than six months ago. You know, Captain Dan, I'm fourteen now!" she bragged.

Then the talk turned to the commonplaces of the day, including the transocean crossing that Dan had just completed. Flanders chose these moments to scrutinize the girls manner, which seemed totally natural and refined. She had a lively wit as well, and they were soon all laughing and chatting like old friends. Yes, Flanders decided, she would make an excellent pupil.

A marvelous idea suddenly occurred to her. Perhaps she could start a training institute. Perhaps this girl would only be the first student among many. Well, that would be a life's calling. She'd have to think it through more fully. But it added a high color to her cheeks as she went busily to work on the lovely poached salmon that was set before her.

She would have to plan her time well if she was to spend time with this girl, order her supplies, and be ready to board the ship that the captain had assured her would be leaving the following day or the day after. Not his ship, though, for he intended to rest up for a week or so and visit with Anne and the woman who had adopted her.

After Dan had called in on Rosie, Anne spent the remainder of the day tagging along with Flanders. She learned a great deal about supplies just from listening to her talk. She also enjoyed comparing views on the way forms should best be represented by the artist's hand. For the first time she began to think she might really be able to make something of the talent to draw pictures—with this woman's help.

On her part, Flanders enjoyed having someone to talk to who felt these concerns—concerns with shape and hue and composition—were important. That had been the single element missing from her life in Australia. When she looked over Anne's sketches, she was struck by the unusual sensitivity to natural design she saw there. Yes, this woman would make an excellent student. She had a keen eye. Now Flanders' mind raced, trying to think up ways to make their association workable. After all, the distances between them would make frequent contact impossible. From what Dan had told her, Anne's adopted mother would probably not be willing to part with her darling either. Well, there would be ways, she'd just have to think them up.

Meanwhile, Dan and Rosie were having a cozy reunion. She had been afraid that, when she saw the actual man in the flesh, her fantasies—fed by distance and time—would be painfully far from reality. Instead, she found him more handsome than she remembered and every bit as nice. He wasn't really the old man she had once thought him.

On his part, he was struck by how warm and real Rosie was, compared to the more proper women he had as friends in England. Warm and real and pretty. But, more than that, he was impressed with the fact that she hadn't let her hard life get her down. No, indeed. This lady had real spunk!

They began to talk about the way they imagined the next decades would change Australia. Oh, they had some high-flying ideas on that. They didn't talk much about their personal plans, although, by the end of the afternoon, some ideas had started to form in each of their minds. The only hint either of them gave to these more secret thoughts came in Dan's parting comment.

"May I take you to supper tomorrow night?" he had asked, and after she'd agreed and was walking him to the door, he added, ''Another few years—well, less than ten anyhow—and I'll be retiring, you know. I'm beginning to think that Sydney might be the place I'd like to come settle down in. What do you think?''

He could almost swear he held his breath as he waited for her answer. Now, doggone it, he told himself, don't go making a fool of yourself.

''Why, Dan, that way we can look forward to a real friendship,'' she said. ''Not like now, with months and years between visits, but something we can rely on day-to-day. That sounds downright splendid to me!'' She laughed and patted his shoulder. He joined her laugh and kissed her cheek before he left. Out on the street, he thought he had never seen so fair a day.

By the time Flanders left Sydney, she had given Anne a group of assignments she was to execute and then post to her at Toowoomba. Flanders would make comments, then return them with new assignments. They would get together for some live instruction as soon as Flanders could figure out a feasible way for them to do so.

Both Anne and Flanders felt their meeting had been a major event, one that would significantly influence both of them. As impressed with each other as they each were, however, neither of them realized just how fully their lives were to be intertwined in the years ahead. For now, it was enough simply to have met and talked, to have found another person with whom to share one's dreams of beauty.

After Anne had seen Flanders off, she hurried to change her clothes and made her way to the secret meeting place where she promised Edmund she would arrive the very moment she was free. The day was crisp, and she covered her shirtwaist with a sweater knit from native flocks and a heavy shawl. The wind whipped at her hair as she rushed up the hillside where she knew Edmund would be waiting. Whenever she was away from him for very long, she got an eerie feeling that something was wrong. It always came as a great reassurance to her to see him standing or lounging near their meeting place. Today, though, her anxiety increased when she arrived and found that he was not there. During their last visit, they had openly declared their love for the first time, had shared their first kisses. Perhaps that had scared him away!

"Edmund," she called, "Edmund."

There was a rustling in the bushess off to her side and she started. Turning, though, she saw that Edmund was there, standing before her. How beautiful he looked, she thought. She rushed to him, and he opened his arms to welcome her. They came together in a tender kiss.

"My love," she whispered, "my love."

Had Flanders who was at that moment standing at the ship's rail bound for home been privy to the happiness of her new protegee, she would have found much in it to envy. Her thoughts were filled with her own lost love, and they were anguished and depressing. Oh Lachlan, she cried silently, why haven't you come back to me? She had fought off the feeling that he might be dead a number of times before, but today it seemed oppressively strong. Maybe the sound of the slapping waves that fought against the ship's progress brought the doleful note to her mind.

In any case, she decided quite definitely that she would not wait any longer. If there was no news from Lachlan when she returned to Toowoomba, she would go out in search of his cave. Even if he had no interest in her—or in his son, for that matter—she must tell him about the birth. And she must know for sure whether he was alive or dead. Yes, she told herself, she would set out as soon as she settled the baby back at home.

16

GIL Tyler stood overlooking his freshly planted land and told himself he was going to make it. It was the start of 1865, Australian summer again, and he had his crops in the ground, had planted his own land for the first time in his life. He'd made it!

Harris Wakefield had promised him trouble if he didn't agree to get off "his" land, but so far he hadn't seen any. Unfortunately, other selectors among his friends hadn't fared so well. One man had been shot right on his own property. No one made too much effort to find the killer either. Another family had gone into so much debt for supplies that the shopkeeper had taken over their land. Tyler grimaced. This was his first crop that he'd put in. He had to have time to reap it if he was to have any hope of profit. Not profit to keep either, but just enough money to keep his creditors at bay. The last time he'd been to town, the banker had sent for him and begun making threatening noises. Gil thought that he'd made it clear that he couldn't pay anything until his first crop came up, but the banker wasn't so easily pacified. If he demanded money, Gil was in trouble.

Wakefield was behind it. He had no doubt about that. Wakefield and the new so-called association of squatters that had sprung up. Wasn't that typical, Gil told himself resting his hands on the sides of his waist, the rich banding together to aggrandize themselves still further, and be damned to whoever got in their way.

As for the poor . . . Gil shook his head. He couldn't understand the fear of group action that he ran into every time he tried to get the selectors to work together.

He walked slowly across his fields toward his shack. Next year, maybe, he'd have time and resources to build a real house. For now, though, this filled all his needs. He had a bed, a cookstove, a table. But he had no woman, he admitted, as he felt a pang of loneliness well up in him at the sight of the empty hut. Well, all in good time, he supposed. First, of course, was the joy of the land, owning his own land, working his own land.

He stomped the mud from his boots before he went in the house. Time to make himself some grub. Then back to work. He put up a kettle of water. A cup of tea always made him feel better, made him almost forget the troubles he had, not the least of which was a meager supply of food. He had almost gotten used to listening to the growling of his stomach; he was getting used to going to sleep hungry.

While the water was heating, Gil sat down at his table and picked up the pamphlet he had been reading last night before bed. It was written by an American named Thomas Paine. It made damn good sense too. He went back to the passage he had underlined.

> Tyranny, like Hell, is not easily conquered; yet
> we have this consolation with us, that the harder
> the conflict, the more glorious the triumph.

Suddenly there was a ruckus outside, and Gil heard a woman's voice calling out for help.

"What the . . . ?" He rose hastily, the heady words forgotten, and rushed out the door.

A huddled shape lay on the ground near the boundary of his tilled fields. At first, Gil had no idea how she—it was undoubtedly a she—had arrived. A gift from the heavens, he thought sardonically. Then he saw a puff of dust in the distance that revealed the escape route her horse was taking in its flight. It must have thrown its rider and run. That's gratitude for you, Gil thought as he rushed over to the woman who raised her head and looked at him imploringly.

"Are you hurt?" he asked.

"Help me up and we'll see," said Louisa Wakefield, who had contrived this meeting after absolutely ages of plotting and planning. He's as handsome as I imagined, Louisa thought, and her heart pounded as she felt his arm around her waist. He lifted her to her feet; she leaned heavily on his arm.

"It's my knee," she said.

"Lean on me, and we'll get into the house where I can take a look at it."

Louisa limped along beside Gil toward his cabin. She already loved him. She'd loved him ever since the day her father first cursed him at the breakfast table. He was all the underdogs who never got a chance, all the misunderstood men of the world. Despite her father's best efforts, Louisa had grown up with a strong social conscience, larded with heavy doses of romanticism. When he grew aware of her leanings her father blamed them on the fact that she always had her nose stuck in a book, and he might have been right. Certainly, she had never gotten her ideas from her parents. Now, as she limped along leaning on the arm of the handsome Gil Tyler, Louisa felt that her own true romance was coming to life.

Inside the house, Gil sat her down on the chair where he had been reading. His tea kettle, neglected while he rushed to the damsel's rescue, was shrieking. He went over to the stove and turned it off.

"I was about to make some tea," he explained, feeling quite foolish. "Would you like to join me in a cup? It's soothing."

"I'd like that very much." She smiled.

As he brewed the tea, Gil covertly examined the woman who had landed in his field so unexpectedly.

Her pale face appeared delicate within the cloud of hair that surrounded it almost like a soft halo. Her accident certainly didn't seem to have done her much harm. She didn't look the least bit ruffled, and her slightly rapid breathing made her chest heave in a way that called attention to her lovely bosom. She was young, he noted, but she was not a girl. No, indeed, she was all woman. He felt a coil tighten in his stomach somewhere in the neighborhood of his belt buckle, and he knew it wasn't from hunger. At least not from any hunger for food.

He came toward her with the pot of tea. Then he got his mug and the single other cup he owned, and set them on the table in front of her.

"I have honey, if you'd like, but no biscuits, I'm afraid."

She smiled, revealing a row of even white teeth that spoke of good health and good eating.

"A cup of tea with my savior would be a sweet enough treat," she murmured.

Gil had never heard such talk in his life. What a charmer this young woman was.

"I'll check your knee after we've had our tea," he murmured, sitting down opposite her.

"I suppose I should introduce myself. I'm Gilbert Tyler. My friends call me Gil—and some of my enemies too, I suppose. In any case, you can call me Gil."

"I'll call you Gil gladly, but only if you include me in the camp of the friends who do so . . . Not the enemies."

Their eyes met. Louisa tried to send him the message she felt in her heart. He had dark brown eyes that looked pained and vulnerable to her. How she yeared to take care of him, to erase the pain.

"My name is Louisa," she said. "My family calls me Lou, but I'd rather you call me Louisa."

"It does suit you better," he agreed. "Lou seems somehow too real, whereas you seem a creature of the air. I almost believe I must be dreaming, that you're here at all.''

Louisa closed her eyes a second to keep herself calm. She knew from his words that he would come to love her. It was going to happen. She had found her prince.

''I'd better check your injured leg,'' Gil said to hide his own confusion. He hadn't had much time for women in his life, and it was easy to see that he felt ill at ease. He knelt in front of Louisa, who raised her skirt up slowly along her slim ankle and calf until finally she revealed her knee, which was, in truth, a bit swollen. The fall from her horse had been real enough, even if she had engineered it. At the touch of Gil's cool hands on her leg, Louisa quivered.

''Oh,'' she sighed.

''Have I hurt you,'' he asked, alarmed.

''No, not at all.'' she insisted, reaching for his hand. Now his heart was beating as fast as hers.

Still on his knees, which brought his head in a line with Louisa's, Gil leaned toward her. She stretched forward to meet him. They came together in a tender, tentative kiss. He pulled back almost at once and stood back up.

''Forgive me,'' he muttered. His hair fell in dark strands across his brow, half-shading his eyes. He reached up and pushed it away from his face. Louisa, steadying herself on the table, stood too. She reached out her hand and, more gently than Gil had done, brushed the few remaining strands of hair from his forehead.

''Gil—you said I might call you Gil—please don't ask me to forgive the first kiss I have ever received from a man. To forgive I would have to forget, would I not? And I would never promise that.''

Gil had never experienced such a rush of emotion as he now felt. This woman seemed so gentle and yet so—well, he had to say it—so available. What should he do? She was surely a lady and must be treated with courtesy. Yet he wanted to grab her and crush her against him. How he wanted that!

"Tyler! Tyler!" The voice shouting his name seemed vaguely familiar, but Gil found it hard to shift his attention from the woman beside him. But the voice was coming closer. "Tyler, damn you!"

Louisa blanched.

"It's my father," she said.

"Your father? Who's your father?"

Before she could answer, the horseman reined in his mount outside. Gil and Louisa turned toward the door just as Harris Wakefield burst through it.

"I knew you weren't any damn good, Tyler. Get your hands off my daughter or I'll blow you to kingdom come."

In fact, Tyler didn't have his hands on Louisa as her father spoke, but Louisa had her hands on him! She'd reached for his arm as soon as she'd recognized her father's voice.

"Daddy," she said, "Mr. Tyler has saved me. Don't yell at him like that."

"Your horse came back without you, Lou. We knew you were in trouble, so I came out looking for you. Your pony led me here. Then I knew you were in worse trouble than I'd even feared. This man is nothing but trouble. But I'm not going to stand for it, Tyler. Get out of here, Lou. Your horse is outside. Go get on it."

"Mr. Wakefield," Gil began, "your daughter . . ."

But he didn't get to speak further, because with a bold few strides Harris advanced on him, struck him to the floor with a single blow, and wrenched his daughter from Tyler's side. Tyler, half-unconscious, watched the man drag the sobbing young woman after him out the door. He heard the horses' hooves as the two of them rode away. He continued to lie where he was, trying to clear his head and make sense out of what had just happened.

He could hardly credit the fact that it had been less than an hour ago when he had heard the piteous voice of the young woman calling for help. Louisa Wakefield, of all people! And what was worse, he couldn't help but remember the sweet words with which she addressed him, the sweet touch of her hand, her lips. Oh God, he groaned, Wakefield's daughter!

He climbed to his feet. The blow Harris Wakefield had delivered had hurt nothing but Gil Tyler's pride. The worst pain he felt had nothing to do with fists, however. He feared that the daughter had struck a greater blow than the father. Already he missed her. He hardly knew her, yet he felt that he must see her again. He knew it was foolhardy even to think that way, but there was no help for it.

Gil Tyler had always been a loner. He'd never given much thought to women. He'd always believed that he was too plain and too poor to interest them. Now, suddenly, this young woman had forced him to consider her. As innocent as she was, Gil was her equal. Her love was formed by her romance books, his by his dreams. They were right for each other as two characters in a fairy tale.

17

FLANDERS had spent days searching for the right cave among the rock walls in the area she remembered. How foolish she had been to imagine that there would only be one cave in the vicinity. When would she learn? Still blundering your way through life, Flanders old girl, she scolded herself.

She was almost ready to give up and return home when she decided to try one more rock formation a bit further south. Something about their reddish cast in the late-day sun chilled her spine like a cool wind across a sweaty neck. She had to trust that feeling. It just might lead her back to the place where she had spent the most glorious night of her life.

Then she saw the cave. She was certain it was the right one at last. She hesitated in the entrance; this just had to be it. Her eyes searched the walls. If she could find the aborigine cave painting, that would confirm it beyond a doubt.

Yes, there it was. She could make out the snake figure and the magic circle. A tightness that had been crushing her chest like a metal band finally let go its hold. She could breathe again. She'd found her Lachlan's hideout. She shivered in the cold air. It was May and getting on toward winter. May, 1865 . . . three years since her night with Lachlan! Where had the time gone? She must be getting old, she thought, to feel that time was racing by her too fast, much too fast—Season after season, year after year. And she was growing older. She was twenty-seven already, twenty-seven and alone. She shivered again.

She forced her thoughts back to the immediate matters at hand. Where was Lachlan? He was clearly not inside the cave. Where were his provisions? She hadn't brought much with her, riding sidesaddle on a lone horse, expecting to help herself from his storehouse whether he was around or not.

Toward the back of the cave, she came across the stream that had provided musical accompaniment to their night of lovemaking. His food had been to the right of it, she remembered, over by the wall. Yes, there were still some goods here, though not much. She saw branches, too, to make a fire with. That would be her first goal. She would obviously have to spend the night here. At least one night. First of all, it was already turning dark. But most of all, now that she had found Lachlan's place, she didn't intend to return to her homestead without learning something of his whereabouts. Maybe he'd show up during the night. Or in the morning. If not, maybe she could figure out when he'd last been in the cave by some process of detection. But she couldn't do that tonight, not in this dim light. No, now she'd just make herself as comfortable as possible for the night. In the morning she'd make a fresh start.

Within a short time Flanders had a fire roaring. The wood had obviously been there for a long, long time drying out. She chopped some of the dried foods up and put them on to boil. It reminded her in an eerie way of the last time she was here doing these very same things.

That night, the night Lachlan kidnapped her, she wasn't sure she would live through the night. Well, at least she had no doubt about that this time.

While the food cooked, she took care of her horse. After her meager supper, she prepared for the night. She had remembered to bring a bedroll so that she would be warm and cushioned from the cave floor. Flanders wasn't tempted to go back out in the night alone, so, when she had finished with her chores, she prepared for sleep. Please, she prayed silently, please, Lachlan, come back to the cave tonight. A feeling of calmness came over her, as though her prayer had been heard, as though Lachlan were somehow watching over her. Then, within minutes, she fell asleep, exhausted by the days of wandering in search of this spot where now she lay.

Hours passed. The night grew colder and blacker, and the fire dwindled down to embers. Sometime after midnight, at the blackest and bleakest time of the entire twenty-four hours, Flanders was suddenly awakened by the frantic whinny of her horse tethered outside the cave. She opened her eyes but saw nothing. She crawled from the sleeping bag and over to the fire. She blew on the embers until they flew up into flames again. Then she saw a sight that drained the air and also the hope from her.

At first, it was only a strange wild smell that snapped her head up from where she was bent over the fire. Then she caught the red gleam from their eyes, like miniature fires. Light glittered on their fangs, which shone like brandished knives. Flanders was inside a circle of creatures that looked like monsters from the mouth of Hell. One of them raised his snout and began to howl. The others joined him.

Their circle enclosed her in a radius of maybe ten feet. She couldn't make a run for it, she knew. They'd tear her to bits before she ever got near the cave mouth. Then the boldest one, the leader, began to edge in toward her.

There was a whirring in the air, a brief hysterical shriek from the creature, and then he fell dead not three feet away from her.

Now the animals, their leader vanquished, were just as confused and terrified as Flanders. They snapped at each other or bayed at the roof of the cave. A few just turned in helpless circles chasing their tails. Before the momentary panic passed, a human shriek, at least as high-pitched as that of the animal who now lay dead on the ground, split the air. Then a shape hurtled through the air, landing beside Flanders in a crouched position and hissing at the animals.

Flanders recognized the shape as human, though unfamiliar. The small brown man, an aborigine she now saw, stretched out his hand and grabbed for a firebrand. His other hand held a dagger. He waved the burning stick in a slow and graceful circle over his head.

He half-chanted, half-sang words in a language Flanders had never heard before. But the animals were obviously affected by it and began to back off, still snarling and drooling as they did so. The aborigine, still crouched low so that his head was on the level of the wild creatures', followed them toward the cave mouth and made sure they turned and were on the run before he returned to the amazed Flanders' side.

He threw the stick back in the fire, returned his dagger to its sheath, and raised both hands in a gesture of peace as he said, "No fear. No fear me."

"Thank you," Flanders whispered hoarsely. The adventure seemed to have left her almost speechless. "What were they?" she asked.

The aborigine shook his head to show that he hadn't understood. Flanders pointed to the dead animal at her feet.

"Him. What name?"

The aborigine bent over the dead animal in order to retrieve his boomerang, the curved wooden weapon he'd used to kill the beast.

"Him dingo," he said as he dragged the body over to the side of the cave out of the light. "Dingo wild like crazy man when hungry. Pack would eat you."

Dingoes. Yes, Flanders had heard tell of the wild dogs called dingoes. She'd never seen one, though.

"Flanders Wilde," she said, pointing to herself.

The aborigine, to her great surprise, extended his hand in the European manner.

"Doogalook," he said, pointing at his chest with his free hand. They shook hands solemnly.

For the first time, Flanders noticed that it was already growing light. The animals must have awakened her shortly before dawn. How lucky she was that this man had come to her rescue. How hideous it would have been if this cave, the scene of her greatest happiness, had also become her tomb!

"Doogalook," she said, "come here." She led him over to the cave painting that had so fascinated her the first night she'd seen it. "Do you know this?"

"Yes, my tribe paint. I don't stay by tribe more. Now I work for digger mens. But I run away from them for they beat me. Now I come home to tribe."

So, Flanders thought, that explains why this man has some English. Her own knowledge of the aborigine languages was next to nil. She had tried to learn, but the tribal dialects were so disparate she scarcely knew where to start.

"Beautiful," she said now, pointing to the painting again.

Doogalook smiled at her praise.

"Yes," he agreed, "it's good. Painting good."

Flanders had an idea. Perhaps Doogalook would be interested in coming back to Toowoomba with her. He could work on the land, lend a hand to Allen and Elizabeth. But most importantly, she might be able to train him to work in the aborigine art forms. This fortuitous meeting might prove to be a blessing in more ways than one. He had saved her life, and might now become her second student!

But first she must convince him that he should come back with her to Toowoomba. She knew enough about the tribes in this area to realize that she must not seem to be offering charity. His pride would never allow him to accept that.

"You saved me. Thank you, Doogalook. Will you come with me and protect me where I live?" she asked.

"Work for you?" He seemed to be considering the idea. "Work for woman," he said thoughtfully.

"Protect me," Flanders hurried to add. "Keep me safe."

"Yes. I come with you," he said finally with a firm voice. "Keep you safe from bad mens like them who came to cave."

"Men came here? To this cave? Bad men?" Flanders' mind turned in a flash to her fears for Lachlan's safety. "Who? What did they do?"

Doogalook seemed unable to comprehend Flanders' questions. Her agitation made him back away. She realized she was scaring him. She forced herself to act calm.

"Tell me," she said.

He raised his eyes to the ceiling roof. "Bad men," he repeated. "Blood. I hide."

No matter how much she urged him to say more, he refused to elaborate. Bad men, Flanders thought. Blood. Oh no! Her heart became a lead ball that crashed heavily to earth and carried all her hopes with it. Her worst fears were true then. Lachlan McKenzie was dead. They had somehow found him in his cave and murdered him. That would suit the pioneer sense of justice. No need to waste time or money on a trial when they already knew he was guilty. Well, she couldn't break down, not now, in front of this stranger. She must make plans to return home. She'd found out what she wanted to know. It was time to head home.

"Doogalook, can you leave at once? Do you need anything?" Even as she spoke, the words seemed foolish to her. Here she was asking this aborigine, who had lived his life almost totally naked, with nothing but his weapons and a bowl as property, whether he had to pack.

"We go now," he replied with dignity. "Doogalook come with wild woman."

Flanders smiled at his misunderstanding of her name. "No," she started to explain, but then realized it would make no sense to him. Well, he had agreed to work for a wild woman. That was probably more accurate than he knew.

She was anxious to get back to Tarleton, especially now that he was all she had in the world.

18

DURING the remaining months of 1865, Flanders redoubled her efforts at cataloguing the plants and animals of eastern Australia. She made no further attempt to have her work sent back to England, however. No, now she thought of herself as one-hundred-percent Australian. She would develop a nautral science of Australia for Australians themselves! No need, she thought, for us to be constantly turning back to England for legitimation and approval.

Now that she had given up hope of ever seeing Lachlan again, she found it easier to put her energy back into her scientific projects. She divided her days among a number of activities. First came the care of Tarleton. He was two-and-a-half now and bright as a shiny coin. She loved to nuzzle the soft skin at the back of his neck, but she knew she must not neglect his training either. Just cuddling wasn't enough. So it was that she allotted a time period each day to give him lessons. He could recognize his letters and could read a few words as well. Also, she encouraged him to notice the creatures around him and to try to draw them the way his mommy did. They made it a game. They would often spend an afternoon together drawing pictures.

Flanders also spent as much time as she could spare with Doogalook. Although he was short and slight, a build typical of his tribe, he was no boy. Flanders estimated from comments he made that he was about thirty years

old. He agreed that she was right in wishing to preserve the
native art forms before they disappeared forever. She was
helping him improve his English, and he was teaching her
his tribal language. She also showed him ways to make
tracings of cave art in order to duplicate it. They were
enjoying their time together. They were becoming friends.

The last of the extra duties for which Flanders tried to
find time in her day was her long-distance training of Anne
Finch. The girl completed the assignments Flanders gave
her in record time, and she was always eager for more—
more knowledge, more work. In her last letter to Anne,
Flanders had broached the idea that Anne might come to
Toowoomba for a visit. Then they could work together
intensively; Flanders was waiting for Anne's reply.

While she was thinking of Anne, Flanders hit on an idea
that struck her as an ideal solution. A railway line had
recently opened between Sydney and Brisbane. Maybe
Anne would enjoy the adventure of a train ride north along
the southeastern coast of Australia. They could meet in
Brisbane. Flanders herself welcomed the prospect of spending some time in a city. She would lease a suite of rooms
at a good inn and the two of them could spend a few days
together. It would be a holiday for both of them. It would
also allow her to talk to Anne about establishing an Australian Art Institute. This idea had been developing in Flanders'
mind for some time now. If she could convince Anne to
join her at some point, train Doogalook to handle the aborigine arts, and really invest her own energies in the
project as well, they might really start something that
would become a national treasure, once people had the
leisure to look around them and appreciate the country
they were living in. She decided she would contact Anne
at once. They would meet in Brisbane.

With that plan in mind, Flanders went about her days'
routines with a lighter heart. It gave her something concrete to look forward to. That had been what was missing,
she told herself sternly—plans for the future. In truth, she

knew she was putting it too simply. It wasn't an absence of plans for the future *per se* that was making her life feel empty. In fact, she actually had plenty of those. It was the absence of Lachlan. She had grown used to having him as the cornerstone of all her dreams for the future, and however unrealistic this may have been, she was finding it damnably difficult to readjust her deepest hopes and longings. Well, she'd just have to see her way clear to doing just that, wouldn't she? On to Brisbane, she told herself firmly.

And, in truth, the days until she was to meet Anne did seem to fly with an unfamiliar and welcome lightness. In seemingly no time, she was on her way. She'd even left Tar behind so that this time with Anne could be devoted competely to art and science and planning.

Flanders arrived a day early to make sure everything was in readiness. Then, once she'd settled in her rooms, she turned to her journal, which she had been neglecting, and wrote:

> The original treeless plains are being disrupted by the pastoral nature of the land usage by squatters with large herds of sheep. The new land use by selectors who wish to pursue agriculture will also affect the natural grasses of the plains. None of the communities of grasses in which Spear Grass and Wallaby Grass co-existed with Kangaroo Grass is now in existence as it was just a few brief years ago.

Her concentration was interrupted by a great blast of noise outside her windows. She placed the book down on the table, open so that the ink wouldn't blur, and went to see what was going on.

In the street below, a group of men circled a wild horse at a safe distance from his flying hooves. They shouted orders to one another about how to get close enough to hold him. He had a number of ropes around his neck, but their ends were loose and went bounding about with each leap or buck the horse made.

The horse was a beautiful creature. His roan coat shone in the sun like a glorious sunset. Suddenly stunned, Flanders realized that she recognized the animal—it was Lachlan's Bandit! One of the men lifted a whip high over his head, getting ready to beat the horse into submission.

"Wait!" Flanders shouted out the window. "Don't touch that horse. I'll be right down."

Astounded, the men turned toward the window, but she was already hurrying down to join them. She rushed out to the assembled men, almost as furious as Bandit.

"Who owns that horse?" she demanded. "Who brought him here?"

An enormously fat man with a leather bushranger's hat pulled down halfway over his face strode forward to demand what the hell business it was of hers.

"Do you own that horse?" Flanders asked him, not the least intimidated by his overbearing attitude.

"Yeah, it's mine. I brought him here to sell. You want to buy the damn creature, lady? He's more trouble than he's worth, I can tell you that."

'Where did you get him?" she pressed, then softly said, "Easy, Bandit." Though still nervously pawing the ground, the horse had stopped rearing up when Flanders appeared. She approached him slowly. The men, sure the horse was about to trample her to death, backed away.

"Easy, boy. You remember me, don't you?" She held her hand out toward the stallion's quivering nose. He snorted and bucked, reared high in the air. Then he landed stiffly on all four feet and stood trembling. Flanders advanced on him, still murmuring comforting words. She grabbed hold of one of the dangling ropes that held tight against the pull which she knew would inevitably come when the horse felt himself constrained.

"Well," she demanded then, turning back to the fat

man who stood with his mouth agape, "where did you get him? I know you didn't buy this horse from his owner. He'd rather have died than part with this beauty."

"Beauty, eh? There's not a rider in Australia who could get in that brute's saddle, I warrant. Some beauty!"

The crowd began to break up, leaving Flanders, the fat man and the roan stallion alone in the street.

"But you still haven't told me how you got him!"

"Some wrangler sold him to me in with half a dozen others. There warn't nothing special about buying this one. I thought they were all half-wild horses. No one cares too much about papers on these critters, you know."

"Well, I want to buy him from you," Flanders said. "He can't be too expensive since you can't even find a rider for him. You have to admit he's pretty useless to most anyone else."

"He seems to be pretty important to you, though, lady," the fat man said, spittle glistening on his thick lips. "You seem to want this horse pretty bad, I'd say."

Flanders could almost smell his greed. This was the worst of Australia, she thought—the attitude that whatever way you could make a profit was an acceptable way, the attitude that said it was every man for himself in this world. But she had no time for moralizing. She had to have Bandit. She didn't know the whys and wherefores of his being here in the first place, but it didn't matter. She had to save him from the brutality that would surely await him under anyone's hands but Lachlan's.

Lachlan. He would never have parted with Bandit, not if he were still alive. She knew that finding Bandit like this was the final proof that Lachlan was dead. But she would save his horse. That would at least be something.

Although it was true that Lachlan would never part with Bandit voluntarily, Flanders' conclusion that he must be dead was false. In fact, at the very minute that Flanders was negotiating a price for the wild stallion, Lachlan was trying to figure a way out of his latest mess—a ten-year sentence in Darlington Jail. Darlington Jail, not more than a mile from where Flanders stood on the main street of Brisbane, was the most dreaded spot in Australia. The solid stone structure bore mute testimony to the suffering of numberless villains as well as innocent folk misused by the law as well. It was dark and dank, and it promised to be there long after the fellows incarcerated inside were buried in their graves. At the northern end of the building was an attachment that became, on special days, the entertainment for the community, men and women alike. The only person not amused by the structure was the criminal who was bound to be the center of attention, the man doomed to hang on the gallows—for it was a gallows that was the attachment to the jail proper. This same gallows was the only thing that Lachlan could see from the small barred window in his cell.

For most men, this would have been a powerful deterrent to any thoughts of escape, for to attempt this and fail meant certain death. But Lachlan put the thought of recapture resolutely from his mind. He must escape for the simple reason that he could not live behind bars. That was all there was to it. The only question was the manner of his escape. And that topic obsessed him.

At least most of the time. There were moments, though, when he found himself unable to sleep and thoughts of the lady naturalist came floating into his mind unbidden. He tried to keep them away. Especially the thoughts of how her breasts gleamed in the fireglow, or how ardently she had given herself to him that second time in Toowoomba. Thoughts like that were deadly to a man in prison. He could almost feel himself inside her sometimes, and often he awoke from a dream sure that he was holding her soft body. Those times were the worst, when he would come gradually up out of sleep hardly remembering where he was and reach over for his woman, only to discover that she was nowhere near. The reality of prison would come to him then in a way almost too bitter and painful to bear.

His woman. It was funny, in a way, that he should think of her like that. Not only because they had had so little time together, but also because he had had so many other women in so many ways and in so many places. Yet this woman had touched him in a special way. Whenever he *did* think about her, he thought of her as "his woman." He wondered if he would ever see her again. It had occurred to him to write her a letter explaining where he was, but when he'd asked the jailer for pen and paper, the man had guffawed.

Lachlan pushed that memory away and turned his mind once again to thoughts of escape. If he pretended to get sick, he figured, maybe they'd transfer him to a hospital somewhere. The key to all his various schemes was to find a way to make them move him outside the jail walls. Once outside, he'd manage to get away, he had no doubt of that. He considered the possibility of convincing his fellow convicts to rise up against their jailers. But that would take too long. No one was a fiercer individual—resisting collective action—than a petty crook. Also, people more readily withstood evil situations than risked their lives to succeed or fail on a grand scale. He'd better do this thing by himself.

The stronger prisoners, he knew, were used to build the squatters' roads. Perhaps he could become one of that number. He'd have to curb his surliness to the guards, of course, and make up to them when possible, so that they would be on his side. Also, he should probably do some body building and show off his muscular development at every possible chance.

With this thought in mind, Lachlan began a rigorous campaign of friendliness to the guards. He knew he could charm them if he really tried. His reputation as a blackguard would make it more difficult, but he could do it.

In addition, he began to do push-ups, sit-ups and a variety of other strenuous exercises that would serve the double purpose of improving his body and calling its strength to the attention of the guards every time they passed his cell.

He thought about what things he missed most in jail. The broad open sky above his head was probably the most important one. Then others: Bandit, his stallion; Flanders, his woman. And books. Imagine that, you old rogue, he told himself, you're barmy over books! When he'd been dragged from his cave by the posse, he'd managed to secrete a volume of verse in his shirt. After they'd stuck him away in this cell, an old guy had given it back to him.

"No harm in this, I suppose," he'd said.

Well, there might be no harm in it, but there was the greatest joy. Lachlan read and re-read passages from the Romantic poets, Byron and Shelley and Keats. He'd have the whole book memorized, if he didn't get out soon. He opened the book to his favorite, Byron, and read: "If I should meet thee, after long years, how should I greet thee? With silence and tears." He'd spoken those words to Flanders. "After long years." God, the words seemed prophetic as he thought about them now. He let the book fall shut on his lap. Flanders, he thought, I must find you and take you in my arms once again! I must get out of here, and I must return to you.

19

FLANDERS purchased Bandit, and took him to the shed behind the inn where travelers' horses were sheltered.

"I'll need a private stall for him," she explained to the stocky man who greeted her there. "He's been badly treated, and I'm afraid he's terribly on edge." She'd managed to calm the animal somewhat, but he was still visibly skittish. Nonetheless, the man who took the reins from Flanders' hands was unperturbed.

"Easy, boy," he said in a voice both soothing and authoritative. "A bit high-strung, but a beauty."

His voice and manner further soothed not only Bandit, but Flanders as well. Thank God, she thought, a man with a love for horses. Bandit will be all right until I can make arrangements to take him back to Toowoomba with me.

Anne was due in shortly. Despite all the commotion the horse had caused, Flanders was determined that they would use their time wisely and well. Who knew when they would be able to meet again?

As for all the feelings about Lachlan that this chance encounter with Bandit had churned up, she strove resolutely, to put them aside.

Anne Finch noticed that they were getting close to Brisbane and tried to pull her thoughts away from her last meeting with Edmund. It had been disturbing, and it was one of the main reasons that she was so glad to have this chance to get away. Flanders' request couldn't have come at a better time as far as she was concerned.

She and Edmund had met as they always did, and she had no hint that the meeting would be in any way different from any of their others. How wrong she had been!

Edmund and she had begun to talk about their parents. It had all started when Anne began to reminisce about her life before she came to Australia. She had tried to describe her mother and father and, in the process, had discovered that the memory of her actual life with her real parents was fading from her. It horrified her to realize that she wasn't actually certain whether what she was saying was true or only a fairy tale she had invented to console herself.

"I understand that," Edmund had said. "I used to pretend that my dad was a poor but honest man, instead of the powerful squatter he is."

At his words Anne had felt a chill. They'd never before discussed Edmund's parents, she realized. Why was that, she wondered now. She had spoken of her British parents so often, and she'd also expressed the love and gratitude she felt for Rosie Sullivan.

At first, that had worried her, the fact that her mother was the kind of woman she was, but Edmund had accepted her statement that Rosie was a good, kind woman without seeming the least perturbed by the way she earned her money.

"Edmund," she said, "I don't think we've ever talked about your father. I know your mother died long ago, and somehow I always assumed that your father was just a worker on this land. You're not telling me that he owns it, are you?"

"I'm afraid I am. My father is Charlie Burrows. Somehow, I thought you knew." He paused and looked down at a clump of brownish grass at his feet before continuing. "That's not true, Anne. I knew you had no idea. I admit I enjoyed playing the role of the poor shepherd boy a bit. But now I need you to know the truth, because something has come up." Again he paused. "Oh, Anne. . . ."

He began to kiss her neck. Just remembering the passion of those kisses made her blush, reliving the way he moved up her neck and kissed her cheek, then turned her face toward his and at last pressed his lips against hers. The intensity of that kiss was like no other they had yet shared. It had made her tremble. Something must have happened to put him in such a strange and powerful mood. It was almost as though he were saying good-bye.

"What is it, darling?" she had asked. "What's the matter?"

"My father wants to send me away."

She felt faint. "Away!" she gasped. "Where? Why?"

"He says I have to look to the future, that it's time to start making something of myself. He insists I go back to England for a while. He wants me to become a gentleman, something I guess he always wished he was, even though he's more remarkable than any proper gentleman could be. He also wants me to find a 'lady' to take for my wife! We had quite a row."

"And?" Anne urged, as Edmund sank into silence again.

"I never mentioned you. Cowardice, I suppose, but our love seems so special . . . so private . . . I was afraid he'd ruin it somehow." He took her hands in his and gazed into her eyes as he said, "The end-result was that I am to leave for England within the month!"

"Oh Edmund, no," she cried. "I can't live without you." Then she stopped, abashed at her own boldness. She had never spoken directly of her strong feelings for him.

"I don't know what to do," Edmund admitted. "I've been crazed all day, trying to think the situation through. The idea of parting from you . . . Well, that's the very worst aspect of the entire situation. If you were with me . . ." He began to pace. His mood was agitated and tense, in striking contrast to his usual calmness. He strode across the grassy hill, circled around the single eucalyptus tree that marked its crest, and turned back toward where Anne sat. He bore down upon her with such energy she cried out, ''Stop!'', fearing that he might trample her in his progress. He stopped abruptly, threw himself down on the knoll beside her, and announced, ''That's it! That's my decision.''

''What? What's your decision? Edmund, you're not making any sense.''

''I'm making perfect sense,'' he insisted. ''The best sense I've ever made, in fact. I'm asking you to marry me, Anne.''

At that moment, the whole world seemed to stand still. The two young Australians made a lovely picture of youth and vigor as they sat close together on the hillside. The young woman's ruffled white shirt covered with tiny pink flowers emphasized her innocence, but it couldn't disguise the womanliness of her full breasts rising and falling with each breath. Her young face was open to experience, eager for life to happen to her. Two red circles appeared on her cheeks.

The man, not much older than she, nonetheless drew her toward him with the strength of his desire. He wore a black suede vest over his loose shirt. It combined with his dark hair and the dark look on his face to give him the semblance of a handsome desperado.

Anne, who had just gotten the letter from Flanders inviting her to Brisbane, turned away from Edmund's question.

''My tutor from Darling Downs wrote me,'' she said, drawing the letter out of her skirt pocket. Her strained voice held only a hint of the nervousness she felt. ''She asks me to come to Brisbane by train and spend a holiday with her doing art work. I think I should go.''

Her words came out in a rush. She'd already gone through the process once—with Rosie. Her mother had finally, but reluctantly, agreed to the trip. Anne couldn't help but realize Rosie felt jealous of Flanders. Anne dreaded a repeat of that scene now with Edmund.

To her surprise, though, he agreed at once to her plans.

"Good!" he said. "You can use the time to think over my offer. My father has set up a round of chores for me for the next few weeks that would make our meetings difficult, if not impossible anyway. We'll both attend to other duties for a while. But promise me that you'll keep my proposal uppermost in your mind." He squeezed Anne's arm affectionately, but she winced from the pressure.

"I wish," she answered in a voice just a shade above a whisper, "that I could put it aside for a bit. But I'm sure I won't be able to. Your sweet words will be my companions every moment that we're apart. I promise."

They hadn't seen each other again before Anne left. The train's jolt, when it pulled into the station, brought her back to the present. She could see Flanders waiting for her. The woman's warm smile made Anne smile back, and she hurried to meet her hostess on the train platform.

Within the hour the two women had placed the concerns that troubled their solitary hours aside, and they were busily comparing notes on their work.

Anne had been devoting her efforts to harbor scenes in the fashionable manner of the plentiful, but uninspired draftsmen of Sydney. Flanders pointed out to her that there was never any use in doing what had already been done, and that, moreover, the natural beauties of Australia's hinterlands far exceeded all of the man-made attractions of city life. She was preparing the way to invite Anne to join her in Toowoomba. Anne, quite taken with Flanders' animation, thought that before she left for home, she must really do a portrait of her friend. In addition, she spoke to Flanders about the new art of photography that was attracting some attention.

"Perhaps," she offered, "if I can learn something of it in Sydney, I could be of help to you with your tasks of cataloguing the plants of the region in which you live. A photograph, after all, is even more accurate—though perhaps less soulful—than a painting. And faster, too, I believe.''

Flanders was delighted with Anne's enthusiasm. It helped to renew her own. Also, the topic of photography, thus introduced by Anne, provided a natural bridge for Flanders to make her suggestion regarding Anne coming to Toowoomba.

At that suggestion, however, Anne burst into tears, leaving Flanders quite at a loss as to what to do or say. Rather than rush in without any understanding, she sat quietly by until the storm of emotion had passed. She patted Anne's hand, and then she offered her a lace hankie.

"If you care to explain, I'd be glad to listen," she said, "but don't feel you have to tell me anything."

"Oh, but I must tell someone," Anne replied. "You may be the perfect person to tell." Then she proceeded to tell Flanders about her love affair with Edmund, including all the complications of their respective backgrounds.

"If you love him, then you better find a way to stay together," Flanders said, giving advice that, up until the time she met Lachlan McKenzie, she would have never imagined herself giving to a young woman. "But I have a plan that—if you have any interest in it at all—might resolve a portion of your dilemma. You say that you two would have to escape from his father's dominating influence . . ."

"His father will never allow him to marry me! He doesn't even know that we know each other. If he did, he would already have forbade Edmund to have anything to do with me, I'm sure. Even though the man spends wanton nights with my mother, he's set his sights far higher for his son. Oh dear, that doesn't sound very nice of me, does it? Flanders, you must understand that I love my adopted mother with all my heart. She has given me everything.

She's a good warm person, but there's no denying that she'd not be welcome in polite society. Especially by the very people who slink around at night in order to be with her!''

Flanders was surprised to hear this innocent-looking person speak out in such a worldly-wise way. No doubt, she thought, Anne's saloon upbringing has been unusually broadening. To Flanders' surprise, she realized it had not had a negative effect. Anne Finch was a delightful creature who was both spontaneous and intelligent. Maybe other parents should take a lesson from the direct, realistic methods of Rosie Sullivan.

Flanders had decided that she would suggest to Anne the possibility that, if she married Edmund, they might make their home with her and work with her on establishing a native artifacts museum and a museum of natural history. It was a grand scheme she envisioned. With the help of Anne and Doogalook and Anne's young man—if he proved to be as worthy a person as Anne described—it just might become a reality. She'd spend her last cent on it if she had to. She believed completely in her dream.

This new machinery that Anne had mentioned—the camera—excited her tremendously. Perhaps she could master it; in fact, it might be the answer to restoring her shattered reputation in England. She had put that out of her mind for a long while now, but it still hurt. How could they deny the evidence of photographs? It would be like denying their own eyesight. Flanders felt a growing excitement over the way things were taking shape. Only when she thought of her newest acquisition, Bandit, in the hostelry down the road, and her concomitant realization of Lachlan's loss did she feel glumness steal back upon her. She wouldn't let gloom take hold, she told herself. She had lost too many of the important men in her life, it was true—her father, her professor, and now her lover—but she still had her own life. She still had her son Tarleton.

She still had her dreams of an Australian cultural center. No, she would not despair. Life was for living.

Nor would she let Anne despair, Anne whose love was alive and ready to claim her for his own. Flanders wanted so much to help these two whose fresh, youthful love, she knew, would warm her own life.

20

GILBERT Tyler learned, as had so many other farmers before him, that the earth can be cruel as well as kind. No matter how hard he worked his land, he was plagued by bad weather—if the earth wasn't parched with drought, it was flooded.

Equally vexing was his frustration over Louisa Wakefield. He was desperate to see her again, but had no way of getting in touch. He sent her letters under various guises, but her father had so well warned the household to be on the lookout for anything having to do with him that no word ever reached her. Worst of all, he had just been given final notice that he must come up with the cash to pay off his mortgage at the bank or face eviction. He knew it was the same old drama that he'd watched happen to selector after selector who had been unable to keep the land they'd acquired. Now it was his turn to lose unless he could find a last-minute escape.

Gil decided to go into town and see if he could round up some of his old cronies. There was an idea beginning to form in the back of his brain. He'd have plenty of time to formulate it as he rode into town. He knew the resistance he'd have to overcome; it wasn't easy for independent Aussies to join forces. But he also knew that he could find the right words if he tried. People had listened to him before—why wouldn't they listen to him now? God knew he wasn't the only one in trouble. If his plan didn't work, he'd lose his land. But, by God, he'd go down fighting.

Once in town, he made his way from saloon to saloon in search of the fellow selectors he knew had either already been driven off their land or hadn't yet gotten hold of any. He set up a meeting time. Then he went around the town from merchant to banker to tradesman. He gathered every piece of paper he could that would show how much he had been forced to borrow and how much he was being charged for it, the totals and the terms. Folks were always impressed by the look of things on paper.

Then it was time. It was the moment when his words must not fail him. He started out by greeting his old friends. Now that he'd become a land owner, he seldom had the time to sit around as he'd used to do. He missed that. A farmer's life, especially for a single man in the prime of his life, was damn gruelling and lonely. But he couldn't waste any time worrying about that just now. If his plan didn't work, he'd have nothing *but* time!

He began to recount to the gathered group the usury that had been driving him deeper and deeper into hopeless debt. There was a murmur of general agreement. Others in the group knew from experience the punishing string of high interest rates.

"Some of you who have yet to get some land probably think you'll find a way to avoid this trap. Well, we all thought that once, and we were just kidding ourselves. The only way we'll beat this thing is if we join forces and work together!"

"You mean a union?" someone asked scoffingly.

"Or a club like them swells has got? That would do us a lot of good. Give us a place to drown our sorrows together is all," said another.

"No, I don't mean either of those. I mean pool our resources so we have enough to beat them at their own game. Together, we could maybe put together enough money to match a squatter—or anyway at least enough to save some of the land for the purpose it was intended: a home and a small farm for the poor working stiff.''

"That sounds fine enough, but get down to some specifics."

"All right. I'll speak to you plain. From my heart, I assure you. My land is going in the well if I can't raise a powerful amount of cash, more money than I've ever seen in my life. I know I've been put in this position by Wakefield, because he's determined to drive me off what he thinks of as his private property.''

"He thinks of all Australia that way," someone interrupted. There were some smiles at that comment.

"Well, if some of you will put in with me, we can pay off these debts and I'll make you part-owners in the land. There's room enough for us all to have a share."

"You mean band together like gypsies? You mean all live together?"

"Don't say it like that," Gil insisted. "Band together like free men who intend to show their strength as free men! That's what I mean. You'll have part of something, rather than all of us ending up with a bunch of nothing for our effort, the way it looks now."

"I'm with you, Gil. I have to get out of my place within the week anyway. What little I've got left you can have gladly. And I'm a good worker."

"Me, too. I'll buy in. I was just ready to put down my money on an acreage, but I'll give it to you instead and maybe buy myself a chance to make it."

Others chimed in with their agreement. Some few, however, went away disgruntled, mumbling that it was all cockeyed and futile. But when Gil made a list of the available monies, he found that his idea was going to work! They would have enough to pay off the most pressing debts, particularly the one at the bank. "We'll make ourselves into a fine community," he announced. It will even make life less lonely—a side benefit, he thought.

After the meeting broke up, a chaos of thoughts filled

Gilbert Tyler's mind as he wandered down the street. He was so preoccupied that he took no notice of the woman coming toward him until she was directly in his path and he was forced to stop stock-still in order to avoid a collision. Only then did he raise his eyes from the ground to see who was blocking his path. And his heart stopped. It was her—Louisa Wakefield! Just as though he had summoned her from his dreams into reality.

"Louisa! Is it really you? I've tried a dozen times to reach you since that night at my place. Did you know that?"

Mutely she shook her head no; tears sparkled in her clear eyes. Tears of happiness, that was clear from the radiant smile that played on her lips.

"I've wanted to see you again as well," she said, "but I'm watched constantly. I'm virtually a prisoner in my own home. Only the necessity of having someone do the town chores has made this day-trip possible. And to think we should simply meet like this! It's a miracle."

Whenever Louisa became flustered, as she was now, she talked in the strangely stilted manner that she had learned from her romance novels. It gave her the confidence that she would otherwise have lacked in tense situations. Gil, somehow sensing that this unnaturalness would soon ease if he could get her off alone somewhere, only smiled.

"Can you spare me the time for a shared cup of tea? Our last one was so rudely interrupted." Without waiting for an answer, he took her elbow and began to lead her toward the coffeehouse across the road. They both looked about nervously as they moved, certain that if they were spotted there would be a rip-roaring scene to match the last one. Fortunately, though, no one noticed them, and within moments they found themselves cozily seated in the bay window table of the shop over cups of steaming coffee.

"God, that smells divine," Louisa said in a manner

quite unlike that of one of her heroines. "Do you think I could have a plum tart too?"

Good, he thought to himself. She's beginning to relax. He purchased the desired pastry, and they were soon chatting away as if they'd known each other all their lives and had been apart only a matter of days. Gil told her of his troubles with the farm, but Louisa already knew, having been aware of her father's machinations during the past months. What she didn't know, until now, was the course of action that Gil intended to pursue. She took it as a tribute to his faith in her that he would share such a secret with the daughter of his worst enemy.

Finally, but too soon, Louisa felt the need to mention the lateness of the hour. The afternoon had raced past. She had to leave for home, or they would be out searching for her. Couldn't they somehow meet again, she asked.

Gil wanted that more than almost anything, but he couldn't think of any way for that meeting to take place.

"There's no future in it for you, I'm afraid," he added. "Your father hates me, first of all. But second of all, I'm a poor man and probably always will be. You're used to better."

"There's nothing better than the feeling I have when we're together," Louisa whispered shyly.

Gil lifted her fingers to his lips and kissed them reverently. What good luck had brought this jewel of a girl to him, he asked himself. When they parted, they agreed to do everything in their power to meet in two weeks at the same time and place.

"Perhaps you could write me occasionally," Louisa suggested. "I know you can't deliver the letters, but when we see each other next we could exchange them and then read them over when we're apart."

Gil agreed instantly, and on that note they parted.

His happiness at the reunion with this charming girl stayed with Gil most of the way home. Then the problems of establishing an entire new living arrangement began to press in upon him. If only he could think of a way to make Louisa part of that life, his happiness would be complete. But no, he forced such thoughts from his mind. She was too young, and his life was too full of troubles. Maybe some day . . . But it was foolish to allow imagination to play games that way. He wasn't normally a dreamer. He was a practical fellow. At least he'd always thought so. He began to think in terms of dividing up the land among the half-dozen or so families who would be joining him. There would be time enough for thoughts of love in the future.

21

WHEN Anne Finch boarded the train to return to Sydney, she had even more on her mind than she'd had when she arrived. During their days together she had grown to understand Flanders' vision of an Australian Culture Center. She had also grown to love the intensity Flanders brought to every project.

Anne let herself imagine what life in Toowoomba as Edmund's wife would be like. Edmund's wife! Flanders had said she would help them build a house of their own near the main house. It wouldn't matter that they had no money, she'd said, because she had enough for them all to be able to live comfortably. The money issue was important because Anne had the definite feeling that Edmund's father was not about to give his blessings to their marriage. Or any of his money either. And she had no money of her own. Edmund had told her not to worry about that. He felt sure his father would love and accept her without money. Anne hadn't been able to bring herself to tell him that she'd already met his father at the Red Raven, and it was unlikely that he would want her to become his son's wife.

By the time the train arrived in Sydney, Anne had decided that she would accept Edmund's offer. And Flanders' offer, too, if Edmund agreed to it. She hardly took time to change her clothes and kiss her mother hello before she rushed off to their pre-arranged meeting.

"Edmund," she called as soon as she came in sight of him. "Edmund, here I am. Home to you, darling."

And then she was in his arms. Their embrace went on and on until she felt she was a part of him and couldn't tell where Anne ended and Edmund began. Truly they would be one body, one soul—soon.

Feeling suddenly shy about telling him she wanted to marry him, she asked instead about how he had spent his time while they were apart. Following her lead, he asked her about her time with Flanders.

"Oh Edmund," she cried, her natural avidity overcoming all efforts at restraint. "It was wonderful! And the most wonderful opportunity has grown out of it—an opportunity for us. Oh Edmund, what would you say to a life in the Downs? A life devoted to the development of an Australian cultural center?"

"Wait a minute. Slow down. You say a life for us, eh? Does that mean what I hope and pray it means? Have you decided to become my wife, Anne?"

She looked down at her folded hands, enjoying the moment's drama. Then, overflowing with laughter, she raised her face to his and answered his question with a simple nod.

The moments that followed are the moments that live on in lovers' memories for a lifetime. The tender sighs they exchanged mingled with the delightfully cool breeze that floated through the day. The words might someday be forgotten, foolish phrases of adoration, but the feeling behind those words, the feeling of being more alive than any other people in the entire world, that feeling would remain forever.

"I'll talk to my father at once," Edmund said. "I know this will alter his feeling about my having to be exiled to England. Are you going to talk to your mother? Or have you done so already?"

"No, I haven't yet, but I shall. But Edmund, my mother is not the real problem. I must warn you again not to expect a happy reaction on the part of your family. And then what?''

''It will make no difference, darling. Of that I can assure you. We are going to be together, no matter what.''

With those words, they fell into each other's arms, and all thoughts of Edmund's father were temporarily forgotten. When they parted, though, they agreed to talk to their respective parents at once. Edmund was to bring his father to the Red Raven that night, so that they could sit down and make plans together.

Anne rushed home resolved to talk to her mother first thing. As she pushed open the swinging doors to the Red Raven, though, her courage faltered. Her mother would recognize only too clearly the problems ahead; she knew Charlie Burrows' dreams for his sons better than anyone. So, instead of saying, ''I have to talk to you about something important. Right away,'' as she had planned, she waited for her mother to speak first. When Rosie said, ''Anne, come tell me about your Brisbane adventure,'' Anne was only too happy to do just that, omitting, of course, any mention of moving to Toowoomba or of her plans to marry Edmund Burrows. Even as she spoke, she cursed herself for being so faint-hearted.

She looked closely at her mother and felt a rush of such pure love for her that she felt quite overwhelmed. The tiny wrinkles at the corners of Rosie's eyes when she smiled only made her more beautiful to her daughter. Nonetheless, she couldn't help but notice that her mother was getting older, that she had changed a great deal in the four years since Anne's arrival in Australia. Often her mother looked tired, and sometimes close to weary. Could she really go off and leave her? Should she?

With a sense of alarm, Anne asked, ''Are you ill, Mother? Is there something you're not telling me?''

''Not at all,'' Rosie answered. ''I'm just tired of this life is all, I guess. Don't you worry your pretty head about it. Just having you back makes me feel better already.''

The sharp afternoon light had softened into the foggy mauve of early evening as they'd sat talking. Suddenly Anne realized that it was she who was doing what she accused her mother of—holding important things back. Also, she realized that if she didn't speak soon, it would be too late to speak with Rosie alone at all.

"Mother," she began, forcing herself to speak. "Mother, I have something terribly important to talk over with you."

Rosie's face paled at these words. Alarm flared up in her eyes, but she said nothing, only waited for her daughter to continue.

"There's a man—a young man—I met him one day while I was out making sketches. . . ." Every word was an effort for Anne to speak and for Rosie to listen to as well. Rosie could sense well enough what was coming. She had always known she would lose her daughter to a man; that was the natural order of things. But not this soon. She wanted more time. She'd had so few years. Where was the fairness in it, she wondered.

Anne, on her part, told herself she was saying it all wrong. Only the knowledge that Edmund and his father were due soon forced her to continue. "He wants to marry me," she said abruptly, unnerved by her own audacity. She bit her lip as she waited for her mother's response.

Rosie clapped her hands together and laughed. The sound was a bit forced.

"Thank God, that's all it is," she said. "I was afraid it was something really serious. Love! Love is great! Puppy love. But marriage—no. You're too young to talk about marriage. Don't even think it."

"Mother, stop!" Now is was Anne's turn to pale. "I've already given my answer to Edmund. I told him I would marry him."

"Edmund? Edmund who? Who is this young man?"

"Edmund Burrows," Anne admitted and lowered her head.

The sound that came from Rosie's throat was like a roar.

"Never!" she cried. "Charlie Burrows will never let his son have anything to do with a child of mine! You know that!"

Even though she'd expected a strong reaction, Anne was stunned by her mother's ferocity. She wanted to find out what was behind it, but before she could begin to question her, the door burst open and in charged Charlie Burrows himself. If anything, he was even more enraged than Rosie. They faced each other like two prize fighters in the ring circling for the advantage.

"Did you send your tramp daughter out to grab my son when you saw you couldn't grab me, Rosie? Did you think I'd fall for that, huh?" he shouted.

The two of them were oblivious to everyone and everything but each other. It was as though they were the sole inhabitants of a private universe. The passion that at times had bonded them now separated them. They spoke not for themselves, but for those extensions of themselves—their children. Rosie, who had just finished insisting to Anne that she would never give permission for her to marry Charlie's son, now screamed at Charlie that she certainly hadn't sent Anne out for his son, but she'd be damned if she'd let him get away with saying that Anne wasn't good enough for him.

"In fact, Burrows," she went on, "I was about to tell Anne why I wouldn't let her marry into a crummy family such as yours! You're not good enough for her, and your son probably ain't neither!"

Anne would have laughed at the two of them acting like children, hurling insults at each other, if she didn't feel that her entire life's happiness hung in the balance. Also, she was worried over the fact that Edmund was nowhere in sight. Where could he be?

"Listen, Rosie my girl," Charlie Burrows growled as

he grasped her arm in a fierce grip. Then lowering his voice to an ominous whisper, he said, "You ain't nothin' but a whore, even if you are a good one. And your daughter ain't nothing but a whore's daughter—or maybe she's following her mother's footsteps! But my son ain't marrying a whore or the daughter of a whore either. If you're after my money, forget it. I'll write Edmund out of my will if he disobeys me." Then he flew out of the bar before the barman, who was advancing on him with a cudgel, could get in a blow. It was as if a tornado had ripped through the place, leaving consternation and shock in its wake. The air seemed electrically charged. Anne stood helplessly beside her mother, who was trembling with rage.

"Let's go upstairs," she urged. "We can talk there." She tugged gently on her mother's hand.

"I'll help you, Annie darling," Rosie said, her voice still strained and tense from her encounter with Charlie. "You just tell me what I can do."

"Come, Mother," Anne said. "I'll need your help! My God, Edmund's father is a madman!" She leaned over and kissed her mother's cheek. Together they made their way upstairs, feeling rather like the victims of some violent crime.

"But, Mother," Anne protested, sitting down on the edge of the bed, "where is Edmund? Why didn't he come?"

"Don't worry, darling. If I know Charlie, he locked Edmund up or put somebody in charge of making sure he didn't come. But if he's half the man you say he is, he'll find a way to come to you." Then she paused and her voice grew somber. "Unless you think the loss of his father's fortune will make him change his mind." There was a question in her voice, but Anne shook her head vehemently.

"I would stake my life on the fact that Edmund cares more for me than for any fortune." She spoke without reservation.

"Then we better get on with our planning," Rosie said. "You can marry and hold a reception right here in the Red Raven. If we plan it right, our friend Captain Thornburg may be able to give the bride away."

Anne noticed a softness in her mother's voice when she spoke of Dan Thornburg, the sea captain who had brought Anne to Australia.

"You're 'specially fond of him, aren't you, Ma?" she asked.

"Well, yes, I guess I am growing extra fond of him. . . ." She smiled into her daughter's eyes. "Let's not become foolish now. It must be this wedding talk that's doing it. He has his life—the life of the sea. And I've got mine right here. There's not much compromise possible to that."

"There's the future. Didn't you tell me he talks about possibly settling down here in Sydney in a few years?"

Rosie shook a finger of warning at Anne.

"Don't go matchmaking for your old lady, my girl. There's the future, you're right. But we'll let the future take care of itself. Right now we have enough to do to take care of right now! So let's leave it at that." She held out her arms for a hug, and Anne gladly moved into them. The two women had the same thought—that their days of closeness were coming to an end now that Anne would be moving on to a new life, the life of a married lady.

"Where will you two live? Have you talked of that, or have you been too excited to be so practical?"

"No, indeed. That has been a topic uppermost on our minds—particularly if Edmund's father were to disapprove. But, Mother, you must come sit down beside me, and promise me that you will hear me out before you give your opinion. . . . Promise?"

"What is it?" her mother inquired, sensing more trouble on the horizon. "You plan to move away from Sydney, is that it? Leave me here alone, eh?" She tried to make light of it, but her voice cracked, and she stopped talking before she gave herself away entirely by bursting into tears. That would never do. She must be strong for her daughter. There would be time enough for tears later, when she was alone.

Rosie sat down beside Anne, and Anne began to tell her about the Toowoomba opportunity. It would be a chance to do something meaningful, she insisted. Besides, it would be a way for her husband and her to work together, to make a good life.

"Now that the train line has been improved," she concluded, "visits back and forth will be no hardship at all."

Rosie's heart sank, but she knew there was no point in objecting. There was no defying youth. It was the force of the future driving through their veins, urging them on. She leaned toward her daughter and rested her head against Anne's. They sat on that way a while, until Anne couldn't resist asking, "Mother, you do think that Edmund will find a way to come to me, don't you?"

"Of course, he will," Rosie reassured her, hiding her own doubts as to whether the boy—a son of Charlie Burrows—could be man enough to withstand the pressure that his father could bring to bear against him. "I pray your young heart won't be broken, my darling Annie, her mother thought as she patted the girl's hand and smiled. "Of course, he'll come. He'll come tomorrow and everything will be just fine."

Both women would have been considerably more upset than they were if they had been able to see the subject of their conversation. At the very moment they spoke of him, Edmund was lying senseless in a locked room in the barn. His father, in a fit of rage, had struck him to the ground before rushing off to town to face Rosie Sullivan. He'd ordered the servants to throw him in the unused room and lock the door. They must not aid him in any way, he'd insisted. At that point, no one

knew whether the youth was alive or dead. No one
knew—not even Charlie Burrows, his father, who was
so beside himself with disappointment and frustration he
didn't even care.

22

DESPITE the fact that he spent every waking moment scheming and plotting, Lachlan McKenzie had yet to discover a means of escape from his foul prison. He worried the idea the way a dog will worry a bone until there is not a shred of meat or gristle left. That he hadn't found a way out of his cell was certainly not due to a lack of trying.

When he finally did regain his freedom, he did so through the efforts of another man. A man of whom Lachlan had never before heard and who had never laid eyes on Lachlan, a man known by various names around Australia's gamier areas, but most famously nicknamed "The Count." The Count had achieved his royal moniker not from any blue blood flowing in his veins, but rather from his rather foppish manner of dressing. He always wore a black morning coat, and he was never without his monocle attached by a velvet ribbon. This man had gotten himself quite a reputation in the field of horse racing, which was just becoming a major event in Australia in the 1860s.

In fact, in this year of 1866, he was furiously involved in setting up the first Grand National Hurdle. Now that the race seemed a certainty, he had to find the best damned rider in Australia to wear his colors. He intended to make his fortune on this one.

That's when he heard of the incredible riding feats of the wild bushranger, Bad Lachlan. He decided at once that

Lachlan was the rider he must have. The fact that he was currently rotting away in a dungeon didn't change his plans one whit. He felt sure he could arrange a release if he plied the right people with the right offers. He was also sure that he wouldn't have to split his profits with this jockey who would be grateful enough simply to be given his freedom. All in all, it sounded like he'd found the very man he needed.

The first that Lachlan heard about it was when his jailer came by and opened his cell, making a great show of rattling his set of keys.

"You're sprung, laddie," he said in a rough, but good-natured way. "The man what bought you is waiting for you. He looks like quite a swell."

Lachlan, though confused by every word the jailer uttered, was not one to look a gift horse in the mouth, and he followed along behind him down the narrow dank halls of this pit of humanity where he had already spent what seemed like several lifetimes.

The man who stood poised at the door to the daylight which shone in around him appeared the epitome of the dapper gentleman. Lachlan became aware of his own appearance by contrast. He had kept his body in shape; he was glad of that. But the prison had done nothing good for the few items of clothing he'd been forced to wear almost continuously and what with one thing and another, he looked like hell.

He rubbed his hand over his face before extending his hand in greeting toward his rescuer. He'd shaved just that morning, so his skin was smooth. Perhaps he told himself, he didn't look as bad as he thought. One thing he was sure of, within a few days away from this hell-hole he'd look a whole heap better!

The two men shook hands. The Count answered the questions in Lachlan's eyes by saying, "I'd like to stand you to a drink, sir. Shall we retire to the saloon around the corner?"

He knew the hirelings lounging around the stone entry hall were paid to pick up any tidbits of gossip such as might fall innocently enough from anyone's lips. He didn't intend to make any of his plans public property.

"Y' got to sign out, mate," the jailer said, holding a pen out toward the man he'd come to regard with some respect over the time they'd been forced to spend together on different sides of the bars. Sometimes he wondered, in fact, if he wasn't just as much a prisoner as the convicts.

Lachlan signed, clapped the man's shoulder in a farewell gesture, then walked back over to where the Count waited. He still had no idea who this man was, but if he was going to get him out of prison, Lachlan would go with him gladly. He whispered something to the Count now, and the Count dug in his pocket and came out with a coin which Lachlan flipped over to the jailer.

"Thanks," Lachlan said at the same time, "you did what you could."

The jailer, an old man whose skin was almost as grey as the rock walls around him, nodded at the bushranger with a smile that revealed the missing teeth and stained gums common to the lower classes who had too little good food and who too frequently tried to make up for that with alcohol and chewing tobacco.

It was with no regret that Lachlan turned from him and the jail behind him to the light of the street and the stranger who ushered him out the door.

When they were seated over a brew, Lachlan's rescuer explained the conditions of his release to him. He was an assigned man. He must serve the Count or return to prison. Lachlan began to fidget upon hearing these terms, but when the Count went on to tell him that the service he required was that of a jockey, Lachlan relaxed again, lifted his glass high and offered a toast: "To the best rider in the territory—myself—and the wisest man—the Count."

The Count raised his glass as well. A thin smile flickered about his lips.

"To Victory," he said.

Both men drank heartily.

"I have taken the liberty of retaining a room for you in the hotel. You must need a bit of time to realize fully that you are no longer forced to pace your six-by-four."

Lachlan realized from these words that his companion was no stranger to the world of prisons himself.

"Tomorrow we'll buy you some regular street clothes and riding silks as well. I want you to be the most gorgeous creature on the track. You'll have the most gorgeous creature under you, I can guarantee."

"When's the big race?" Lachlan asked.

"In two weeks time," came the answer. "Can you be ready?"

"It would take more than time in prison to make me forget how to handle a horse," Lachlan answered. "I'll be ready."

"Good. Then I'll show you to your room now. Oh, here's some cash for you," he added, passing over a wad of bills to Lachlan. "I assume we are both gentlemen of honor, and I will continue under that assumption until I am proved in error. Your reputation speaks well for you in my book."

"I won't betray your trust," Lachlan affirmed, putting the money casually into his pocket, as though a stranger came up to him and offered him large sums of money every day. In truth, Lachlan was not so much affected by money as most men—neither the having of it nor the lack of it. He was, to a great extent, the self-contained man. Prison had not robbed him of himself. Neither could sudden freedom.

When, a short time later, he found himself alone in a private room with no bars on the window and the lock on his side of the door, Lachlan smiled a smile that expressed the joyful peace he felt. He stretched out on the bed and pondered the strange turns of fate.

But the whirlwind events of the past few hours had left

him too keyed-up to remain in the confines of the hotel. So
soon he was up and about wandering around the town,
savoring the joys of ordinary liberty. The thought of Flanders flitted through his mind when he passed by some ladies
who were not above giving him the eye. He returned their
smiles, but he didn't pursue the situation any further. But
Flanders . . . Now that was a different issue. He wished he
could see her right now, wished it so strongly that he felt
the desire like a blow.

There was no way, though, to take that much time out if
he were going to be the winner of the first Grand National
Hurdle in two weeks. No, he would just have to wait until
the race was over to reclaim his woman. He wondered if
she still thought about him. Perhaps she would spurn him.
Then he remembered the passionate way she'd kissed him
when she found him sitting on her porch. How could he
doubt that she still thought of him just as he thought of
her?

Well, he'd had to wait this long, so he could certainly wait
another few weeks, he reasoned. After the race, though,
that would be a different kettle of fish. He laughed out
loud at the thought of holding Flanders in his arms again,
so happy did the image make him. It wouldn't be long
now. And wouldn't she be astounded to see him! These
ideas gave a jauntiness to his steps as he returned to the
hotel to turn in for the night.

The next day and the days that followed were full of
excitement for Lachlan. After the semi-retirement of prison,
he couldn't seem to do enough. He never tired. The Count
marveled at his endurance as he trained and trained and
trained. To his surprise, the Count found himself becoming
fond of this fellow—this bushranger. He had to urge him
to stop at the day's end, and that was a rarity between
master and man. Yes, choosing this fellow for his jockey
was the best decision he'd ever made.

The silks they'd chosen together were a flashy blend of
magenta and forest green. When Lachlan dressed in them,

he could be seen the length of Brisbane's main street. The Count knew that most of the riders would be wearing street clothes. Most Australians considered riding in colors a foolish affectation. Good, he thought, let them think my boy's a fop. They can enjoy betting against him, and I'll enjoy taking their money. Lachlan, looking at himself in the mirror, thought he looked quite splendid—splendid, and a bit foolish, but he didn't mind that. He'd never cared much for most people's opinions anyway.

The Count had another secret up his sleeve. A bit of magic that, combined Lachlan's skill with horses, guaranteed them the race, he believed. It was an American way of riding that placed the jockey's weight high up on the horse's withers and added considerably to its speed. Australians, even the few who'd seen a rider in that crouched position, thought it an ungentlemanly way to ride a horse. Good! They could remain gentlemen if they chose; he preferred to win races. He'd taught Lachlan the position, and Lachlan had seen its advantages at once. The Count appreciated the fact that Lachlan, like himself, didn't give a hoot for labels. People could call him outlaw or fool or any damn thing they wanted. Lachlan and the Count both cared only for reality—not words. The Count knew—just knew—they were going to make a winning team. He'd already decided that after this race he would cut Lachlan in on the profits and set up a regular circuit of races.

Lachlan, however, had no thought of remaining a hireling, for that's how he thought of himself at the moment. He liked the Count well enough, but he liked being a loner even better—even if it meant exchanging his current semi-legal status for the criminal route again. They didn't discuss this issue as they prepared for the big race. They had quite different opinions on the matter, but kept those opinions to themselves.

Then it was the night before the race. Lachlan and the Count had taken the day off to rest themselves and the horse. Lachlan thought his mount, Victory, was almost as beautiful a creature as Bandit. He wondered what had happened to his beloved Bandit, but he resolutely put that thought aside. He felt a closeness with Victory that he knew meant the horse would give his all when he urged him to.

The Count sat across the table from Lachlan and discussed the strategy he wanted him to follow in the race the next day. Lachlan listened calmly, nodding every now and then. He hadn't tried to explain to the older man that he could feel the power in the horse and that he would know how to unleash that power at the proper moment. There was no need to explain, he figured. What the Count really wanted was to win, and that was exactly what Lachlan intended to do.

When they parted for the night, the older man told him to sleep well.

"You'll need every bit of strength and energy you can muster tomorrow," he said.

"I won't disappoint you," Lachlan answered, and both men smiled.

But when Lachlan was alone, lying across the soft hotel bed, doubts began to assail him. He really knew next to nothing about organized racing. In addition, he knew absolutely nothing about his competition. The Count had assured him there wasn't a racer around who could beat him, nor a horse in the area who could outrun Victory. Lachlan believed those things, yet he found that sleep eluded him nonetheless. When daylight's pink fingers stretched through his window, he was grateful to be able to get up and bathe. He felt that he hadn't slept a wink all night. He just had to win, he told himself, and wondered how he'd managed to get so involved in the foolishness of horse racing. Still, to win a national race, that would somehow seem to vindicate his desperado's life in Australia. With trembling fingers he dressed in his silks. He couldn't wait to get down to Victory and walk him around a bit before race time.

23

As race time neared, the crowd that gathered was as colorful a spectacle as one was likely to find anywhere. The local ladies had quite outdone themselves. Some, in fact, did away with decorum altogether and dressed in quite a scandalous fashion. One of the squatter's wives, for example, had goldpieces sewn across her bodice, and another wore a gown so daringly low that she could not bend forward for fear of revealing her private treasures to every wandering eye. The assortment of bonnets, many of them more than a foot-and-a—half in diameter, was like a vast bouquet of brilliantly colored flowers.

Another vivid aspect of the day's crowd were the bookmakers who appeared every few feet dressed in their large plaid suits and sporting bowler hats. It was the costume that identified them in case anyone wanted to place a bet. Not that there was any doubt as to who they were since they insisted on shouting out the current odds at the top of their lungs. The Count, of course, was unique in this group. He continued to dress in his black morning coat, his monocle dangling from its string, his hat a conservative one, and his manner decidedly disinterested, as far as the casual observor could determine.

The serious money, though, found its way to him. The men whose lives were spent going from gambling spot to gambling spot all knew the Count. They knew he never turned down a bet, no matter how big the stakes were.

They knew, too, he paid up honorably if he lost. This in itself made him a rarity among bookmakers, many of whom ran a race that was almost as fast as that of the horses in order to escape paying off their debts. Many a horse race had ended with people chasing after the checkered-suited men. Many a checkered-suited man ended the race day with a soaking in the river, or worse. Some ended it with cracked heads.

With all this money readily at hand, the day also belonged to the pickpocket, of course. Young scamps could be seen wherever one looked. In the excitement of the actual race, they could always count on someone being too distracted to notice a jostle or poke that quickly transferred a watch or a pocketbook from its rightful owner to them. It was easy to strike and then disappear; that was the reason for the pockpockets' love of crowds.

The noise and the smells and the crowds created an excitement on the flats outside of town that easily equalled anything merry old England had to offer. The horses moved nervously under the weight of their riders. Sensing the special electric tension of the day, the animals were harder to control than usual. Lachlan, not one of the regulars, was regarded by the other riders with suspicion. Many of them knew him from his reputation as a bandit, but what was he doing on their territory, they wondered. Mostly they gave him wide berth, neither speaking to him nor making their deservation of him too obvious. All of which was fine with Lachlan. He just wanted to be left alone. He wanted to run his race; he wanted to win his race. Then he wanted to get away from this claustrophobic town life as quickly as possible. Those were the only thoughts on his mind as he gentled his horse to keep him calm until the start of the race.

Then it was time. The horses were lined up for the start of the race. This was it!

The crowd of horses jostled for position as the cry of "They're off!" rang through the air. Lachlan fought to keep control of Victory who was trying to get the bit between his teeth so he could take off at top speed. Lachlan knew that if Victory took the lead this early, the horse would tire before the finish. He'd spend too much energy getting through the mass of horses. Soon, Lachlan knew, many of them would drop back. Lachlan held the reins tight. He'd never had any trouble making horses know that he was the one in charge. The pounding in his chest mingled with the pounding of flashing hooves and the surging roar of the crowds to produce an excitement almost too powerful to bear.

The distance passed in a blur. The fastest horse in the race, aside from Victory, was a powerful black stallion called Pitchman. Before long they moved to the front of the pack. There the two of them thundered along neck and neck long after the other horses had been left behind. Now, as Lachlan looked over at the horse beside him and tried to gauge his remaining strength, he saw the jockey—a mean-looking little man with squinty eyes—draw his arm high over his head. Before Lachlan fully realized what was happening, the other jockey brought his whip down on Victory's flanks. The horse reared up in pain, allowing Pitchman to pull momentarily ahead. Lachlan uttered a howl of fury. So that's the way it's going to be, he thought. He spurred Victory sharply, and then he gave him his head. The mighty horse needed no further urging. He caught up with Pitchman in a short series of enormous strides. When the other rider saw Victory's approach out of the corner of his eye, he again lifted his hand. Only this time Lachlan was ready for him. When the arm was at its uppermost point, Lachlan reached over and caught hold of the whip's edge and gave it an enormous jerk. It flew from the rider's hand after lifting him halfway out of the saddle. Pitchman, thrown off his stride by the jockey's shift in balance, dropped behind as Victory galloped easily past. The finish line was in sight at last.

Lachlan knew the horse, despite his gallant heart, was nearing the end of his endurance. Flecks of foam flew from his mouth. His sides heaved, glistening with sweat. Lachlan himself found his breath coming heavily. He, too, was exhausted as the race's end neared.

Pitchman was closing the gap again. Lachlan knew Victory had to make one final effort or he'd lose. This was the moment when Victory had to give it his all. Lachlan leaned as far forward as he dared.

"Go, boy," he shouted into the horse's ear. "Run like you've never run before." Then he squeezed his legs against the horse's sides just enough to reinforce his words. That was all the urging this great horse needed. Lachlan felt a keen sense of admiration for the animal. There was no weakness of spirit within him. Despite his exhaustion, the horse extended his stride yet further. The powerful legs took in more land with each bound. Still, PItchman's nose was right on Victory's tail. Then he drew closer, so that his nose was even with Lachlan's knee. Oh no, Lachlan despaired, we can't lose it now. Not now.

"C'mon, Victory," he shouted, but his shouts were drowned by the shouts of the crowd cheering the horses on to the finish line. Luckily, though, his shouts weren't needed. Victory himself seemed to be aware of the crucial nature of these last few yards. Pitchman, too, was straining to the utmost. Then, in a flash that left each Lachlan uncertain as to who had won, they were across the finish line. He thought he'd done it, but he couldn't be sure until he reined Victory in and saw the Count beaming at him from the sidelines. It was the first time he'd ever seen the fellow really smile. So, he—Lachlan McKenzie—was the champion. He'd ridden Victory to victory!

Then they were surrounded by well-wishers and the variety of hangers-on who seem always to surround a winner. Ladies rushed to kiss Lachlan's cheek as soon as he'd dismounted. He smiled at how respectable he'd suddenly become, but he also turned mute, pleading eyes up to the Count to be saved from such a surplus of attention.

The Count took him by the arm and led him through the throng.

"Enough adulation, eh, old man?" he asked. His tone suggested that, although he'd had his share of ladies' attentions, he could perfectly understand the need a man might feel to be free of this burden.

"What I need most is a hot bath. Is someone seeing to Victory?" he asked, suddenly remembering the horse's exhaustion, which he knew was at least equal to his own.

"Yes, yes, I've a good lad taking care of him," the Count assured him. "Why don't you have a bath while I run around collecting my winnings? Then we'll have some scotch and discuss our future!"

"Yes," Lachlan muttered, his body aching as he walked. "The future. We must talk of that. I should be relatively recovered within the hour. I'll meet you then in the bar."

On that note they parted, each with an entirely different sense of the direction their conversation should take.

24

EDMUND had lain insensible for an indeterminate period after his father had struck him and stormed off. At last, though, he became conscious enough to distinguish light from dark, to see that he was in some dark room where just a crack of light slid under the place where a door must stand, and to acknowledge that he was in serious trouble— the most serious trouble of his young life. He had not yet rallied enough to move. He didn't yet realize, therefore, that he was locked in. Had he come to this realization, his mood would have sunk lower still. His own father had struck him and left him, not knowing or caring whether he was alive or dead. How could it be?

For the first time since that doleful day so many years ago when he was told that his beloved mother had died, Edmund felt tears rise in his eyes. What of Anne, he fretted, what would his father do to Anne? Then he remembered that Anne's mother was a friend of his father's. Also, she was a good strong woman. Surely she wouldn't allow anything evil to befall her daughter. He swallowed the lump in his throat, and at the very same instant he heard the scrape of a key in the lock in the door. He scrambled up on his knees.

Then the door opened.

"Edmund," a frail trembling voice called. "Edmund, where are you?"

It was Clara, his father's wife! As far as Edmund could

remember, she hardly ever set foot out of her bedroom. Could she really be coming to his rescue?

She raised a lamp overhead, so that its light would fall on her stepson—a young man her own age. Then she gasped at the sight of him on his knees, his head covered with blood.

"My God, what has he done? I heard the two of you arguing. Then he rushed from the house. But I didn't hear any more from you. Then I heard the servants muttering about locking you up at his command! I had to come and find you."

While she talked, she had placed the lantern on the earth, had taken her handkerchief from her bosom, and was attempting to blot the blood away from Edmund's eyes.

"Never mind that," Edmund said, removing her hand. "Just help me up if you will. I can rid myself of this mess, I'm sure. No need for you to dirty your lovely clothes."

She placed her arm under his and helped him to his feet. She picked up the lantern with her free hand.

"Lean on me. Don't worry about my clothes. I'll get you up to your room, and then we'll see about the extent of your injuries."

"Clara," he began, but couldn't think how to say what he wanted to say, and so he fell silent.

They stumbled along from the barn to the main house. By the time she had gotten him to his room, Clara's arms ached.

What was worse, though, was that Edmund, who had sat down heavily on the edge of his bed, now raised his arm beseechingly.

"Help me," he cried. Then he clapped his hand to his head, as though in terrible pain, and collapsed back onto the bed. Clara watched helplessly as his eyes rolled back in his head.

"Edmund," she screamed. "Edmund, speak to me."

But Edmund was in a dark land where speech is neither necessary nor possible.

"Help!" she cried, "Help!" unconsciously mimicking Edmund's last words to her. At her shouts, two servants rushed into the room. "We must get him a doctor," she urged.

The servants looked at each other in amazement, not knowing which was the more shocking sight—their mistress dressed and on her feet or their young master unconscious and bloody on his bed. In any case, they had no time to stop and ponder the oddities of the situation. It was obviously necessary to take action. They nodded and rushed from the room. Clara, now robbed of any useful function, continued to stand beside the inert body of her stepson with tears streaming down her face.

He's dead, she thought, and I'm as good as dead. Buried alive with a man old enough to be my father.

By the time the doctor arrived hours later, the only difference in the scene was that Clara was by now seated beside Edmund's still-unconscious body. The doctor realized at once that he had two patients to look after, the young woman and the young man both. The young woman seemed to be in shock. Well, he could have the servants put her to bed for the moment. The young man's needs seemed to be more urgent. It was obvious that his head wound was very serious.

Upon checking the eyes and reflexes, the doctor felt convinced that Edmund had suffered a severe concussion with, perhaps, a concomitant skull fracture. Unfortunately, there wasn't much to be done. The boy's youth and strength were on his side, but as to medication—well, nature provided the best: rest and sleep, even that sleep that was so deep it was labeled coma. Even coma could be healing. The problem was that it could also be the prelude to death!

The doctor spent some time talking to the servants trying to figure out exactly how Edmund Burrows had sustained such a terrible injury. He could tell from the hesitant way his questions were being answered that he was getting less than the truth. But what the truth was he

couldn't tell. He supposed he'd just have to wait for
Charlie Burrows' return from wherever he was and find
out from him. Meanwhile, he'd done all that he could;
he'd stitched the boys wound and cleansed his head with
disinfectant. Now he might as well use his extra time to
check on the wife's condition.

The woman, he found, had recovered sufficiently to be
weeping copiously.

"He's a brute!" she exclaimed. "He's killed his son
Edmund and now he'll probably kill me."

The doctor found it no small task to calm the woman
down. But, at last, he was able to leave her side, knowing
she would sleep easily through the night with the aid of a
sedative. My God, the doctor thought as he pulled the door
to the wife's room shut, what has been going on in this
household? He ordered one of the servants to bring him a
pot of tea, and then he settled in to wait for Charlie
Burrows' return.

When Charlie did finally return, almost as furious as
when he'd left, he was confronted with the doctor, tales of
a possibly dying son, and the news that his wife had
succumbed to hysteria. He poured himself a double shot of
whiskey and downed it in a couple of swallows.

"If it don't beat all, Doc," he said then. "You try to do
the best you can for folks and they won't have it. No sir,
they insist on turning everything around so that it looks
like you're nothing but a bum. You know what I mean?"

The doctor hadn't any idea what he meant, particularly
since Charlie Burrows was hardly noted for his kindliness,
and so merely nodded his head and remained silent.

"That damn boy wants to marry a floozy!" He pounded
his fist on the table. "And that no-good woman I married
wants to pretend that nobody but a floozy spreads her legs.
Well, don't it beat all."

"Well, I have one good child—my son Hugh—you
know him, Doc? A good boy away at school. He'll be a
proper gentleman!"

He poured another drink, offering the bottle to the doctor who refused it.

"Well, as far as I'm concerned, he's my only son now. You can take care of that other no-good, and I'll pay your bill. But that's the last thing that ungrateful brat will get from me. You tell him that, soon as he can move, to get his butt out of here! He's no longer a son of Charlie Burrows, no sir."

"I think you're just upset," the doctor offered. "Shall I call the servants to help you to bed? You'll feel different in the morning."

Charlie got unsteadily to his feet.

"I can put myself to bed," he insisted. "But I won't feel no different. I give those kids what I never had. Money. And the power that goes along with it. That one doesn't want it. So, good for him. Let him make his own way. Like I did in the first place."

On those words he staggered from the room. The doctor followed him into the hall and, seeing that he could navigate the stairs alone, left Burrows to make his solitary way. The doctor shook his head. There was a lonely man, he thought. Underneath the angry words he had sensed that the man's heart had really been attached to the son he was now disowning. Heartbreak for all, he thought. Foolish pride and heartbreak. He checked on the boy once more and left the house.

During the days that followed, Edmund slowly recovered, and he and Clara, who had taken to ministering to his needs, became friends. When he was conscious enough to realize what had happened, he begged Clara to contact Anne. He told his stepmother—odd to think of her that way when she wasn't much older than Anne, he realized— the entire story of his altercation with his father.

"Clara," he asked during one of their talks, "how did it ever happen that you ended up married to my father? I have never understood it."

"In a way," she answered, looking up from the needlework that she had taken to doing during their times together, "my story isn't so unlike your own. I loved a young man." She stopped a moment to calm herself. Strange that after such a long time it could still upset her so, she thought. "My parents had titles, but you know how it is with titles . . . After a while they are simply empty labels. They no longer had the wealth to back them up. Soon they would have to sell our family estate in order to live. Well, neither of them had ever had to work for money. The idea absolutely terrified them!"

"But what has all this to do with your love?" Edmund interrupted.

"He was a commoner. A poor commoner, at that."

"Then they refused to give permission, is that it?"

"Oh, worse than that. They found out about your father's offer to buy a titled bride! He offered enough money so that they would be able to save their estate . . . you understand?"

"Oh God, Clara. No! They didn't *sell* you to my father. . . ."

"I'm afraid they did. I should have run away, I suppose, but I'd always been a good obedient daughter and I didn't know how to save myself." She burst into tears.

Edmund patted her hand. He'd never felt so absolutely helpless. "And your love?" he asked when she'd swallowed her tears.

"I never saw him again. My life here has not been happy, you know that."

Edmund nodded. Both Clara and his father had always seemed more like father and daughter than husband and wife. An angry, unhappy father and daughter, at that.

"I've never been a proper wife to him. I just could never learn to love him. Nor forget my true love."

"Poor Clara." The pity in Edmund's voice brought a new round of tears to Clara's eyes.

"That's in the past now," she sighed. "I can't bear to think that the same unhappiness could come to you. How can I help you? It will be good to have something to focus on, rather than simply lying around feeling sorry for myself. I've done enough of that for a lifetime, I think.''

At that, both young people laughed and something of their natural good spirits reasserted itself. Silently Edmund vowed that, once he got free of this place, he would try somehow to help Clara in return. For now, he had to get well.

Clara made sure that a message reached Anne, who had been frantic with worry, but who had been unable to get a message past the barrier of guards surrounding the Burrows' homestead. She had heard almost at once that Edmund was injured. Rosie's network of friends had discovered that for her through contact with the doctor. But as to his condition, no one could say. When at last Clara's letter arrived in the hands of ''little Sam, the shoe-shine boy'' who had become a man long since and now worked most of his days on the dock, Anne was almost afraid to read it. But, on the other hand, she could hardly bear to have someone else read it first. So she tore open the seal with trembling fingers.

At once relief flooded her. Edmund was alive! He was recovering, albeit slowly. Soon, he assured her they could be together—and they would never be separated again. He had been disowned, he told her. There would be no money. Poor Edmund. He'd always believed that his father would understand their love. She would happily reassure him, when she got the chance, that she didn't care a bit about his family's money. She loved him for himself alone. All she wanted was for him to recover fully and for them to marry. They would have a happy life together, whatever they did.

In order to distract herself from her worry over Edmund and to forward their plans, she sent word to Flanders.

When Edmund is well, we will marry at once. Then we have agreed to come and devote ourselves to your vision. It excites us both. I only hope we will not disappoint you.

In the meantime, I am continuing my drawing as you suggested. What is more, I have begun to apprentice myself to a local photographer. He has not much talent that I can see, but he can teach me the skills needed. He limits himself, I am afraid, to the most shocking topics privately—pictures of loose women in their bedrooms—while publically he supports himself by taking the most mundane portraits of local worthies. I know it will not surprise you that my mother introduced him to me when he came into the Red Raven wanting to take her photograph. In fact, I have urged her to agree—on her own terms, of course. I would so love to have a portrait of my mother to take with me to Toowoomba. But while most of his models are somehow induced to pose nude, my mother will remain clothed. He would actually like to have us both—mother and daughter—and I have no objection.

He is teaching me both the taking of pictures and the process by means of which the film is transformed into a correct copy. If you wish, I can try to bring equipment with me. I shall enclose a list with prices. If you do not think it is too dear, and you are still interested, let me know.

Meanwhile, my love to you and your darling baby Tarleton. Oh, how he must have grown since I saw him last. Not a baby anymore, I suppose. But since I hope that Edmund and I will start a family as soon as possible after our marriage, another baby may soon be playing about the grounds! I know I should blush for my boldness, but I also know that I can be completely open with you. It is one of the joys of knowing you, Flanders.

I can never thank you adequately for having provided Edmund and me with a future! For that is what, quite simply, you have done.

I must close for now. I hope that, the next time you hear from me, I'll be a married lady.

She signed and sealed her letter and sent it off. So accurate was her prediction of her imminent marriage, though, that on the same day Flanders received the mail, Edmund arrived at the Red Raven ready to claim his long-waiting bride.

"Edmund," she cried upon seeing him enter the doors one morning. "Why didn't you let me know you were coming so that I could have dressed properly to greet you?"

"You could never be dressed any other way," he replied, smiling into her eyes. The only difference that she noted in him was a certain sadness somewhere behind his eyes. Then he moved toward her, and she was in his arms.

When they stopped kissing, she asked, "How did you get away from your father? Come sit by me and let me get us some tea while you tell me everything."

"I'll gladly sit. I must admit that the trip into town was more of a strain than I had imagined it would be. I suppose I'm not perfectly recovered yet, but I will be soon, my darling. I assure you of that. Just seeing you is the best medicine in the world."

They sat together for a long time then, talking and touching and planning.

"Let us marry at once, darling," Edmund said at last. "If you still want me."

Anne's bright smile and the pressure with which she squeezed his hand convinced him that she did.

"When?" she asked. "Just tell me the day, the hour, and I'll be ready. You must take me plain, of course. I have no fancy gown, you know."

"And you must take me plain," he answered, "for I have no fancy wealth nor power to offer you anymore."

"Edmund, surely you haven't forgotten that I never

thought you had any power or wealth until after I'd accepted your proposal.''

They exchanged happy smiles.

''There's something else . . . related to that business with my father . . . that I want to discuss with you. Since my father has absolutely and completely refused to have anything to do with me since that night when he struck me down, I have no desire to have anything further to do with him!''

''Oh Edmund,'' Anne interrupted. ''Surely you only say that now. Surely someday he will come to accept us.''

''Frankly, I doubt it. But if it is to be, it will be. Not now, though. And not through my doing. For now, I'd like you to consider the possibility of using my middle name, Knight. I want to renounce Burrows.''

Anne remained silent a moment, a frown furrowing her forehead. Then she said, ''Edmund Knight. Yes, that's a pretty name. Edmund and Anne Knight . . . Mr. and Mrs. Knight . . . I like it! Moreover, it was only recently that I learned you were a Burrows. It won't be hard to think of you as a Knight!'' She smiled, aware of the play on words. After all, he was her knight, wasn't he?

''What?'' Rosie said, coming up to them just then. ''Making plans without me?''

''Do you want some tea, Momma?'' Anne asked. ''I'll gladly get you some.''

''Yes, thank you. I'll sit here with my new son-to-be and quiz him.''

''Oh Momma, be kind,'' Anne pleaded.

Edmund had risen and extended his hand. This was his first meeting with Anne's mother, and he realized he should have sought her out at once, not lingered here beside his love.

''Forgive my rudeness,'' he said. ''I should have come at once to plead my cause before you.''

''Sit, sit. I understand you are recently recovered from a grave injury.'' She shook the boy's hand, then held it a moment in hers. "The only question I have for you is whether you love my daughter, and I think I can read the answer in your eyes."

Anne returned with the tea just in time to hear Edmund answer, "I love Anne better than any one or any thing. Although my father has sworn to disown me, so I cannot promise her riches, I promise your daughter all my love forever. . . ."

"Riches enough," Anne interrupted, and Rosie shook her head in agreement.

"Good. Then I give my blessings. We can have the marriage—very simple, I assure you—right here in the saloon, if that is not beneath you . . ."

"It is your home and has been Anne's home," Edmund answered, "how could it be beneath me? Only there is one thing that I must discuss with you both, and that's my stepmother Clara. She is desperately unhappy with my father. It is not a marriage made in heaven. . . ."

At that Rosie threw back her head and laughed.

"You say right there, boy."

"She has been kind to me during this time. I would like to help her escape."

"Escape!" both women cried in unison.

"Yes, she wants to return to England, but she is afraid that my father will kill her rather than let her leave. Considering the damage he did to my skull for less cause, she may not be far wrong."

"Oh, I forgot to tell you, Annie," Rosie said. "Dan, my captain friend," she explained to Edmund, "is in port. He should be here shortly. I thought he'd made a splendid best man—unless you have other plans . . ."

"No, no," the young people reassured her. Her choice would be fine with them. "But what has that to do with my stepmother?" Edmund asked.

"He's the very person you could trust to help you get her secretly out of Australia," she answered. "We can ask him about it today. Oh, suddenly I have the feeling that everything is moving too fast for me. Losing my little Annie,'' Rosie's voice broke. Tears streaked her cheeks. She'd always found herself easily moved to tears, but she'd promised that she wouldn't cry at her daughter's wedding. Well, it was clear that that was simply going to be one more promise which she couldn't keep. She accepted the linen handkerchief that Edmund passed to her. She wiped her eyes, and the three of them laughed a bit together. But they were each moved by the emotional intensity of the situation.

Fortunately, at that moment Captain Dan Thornburg came bounding into the saloon, and all attention turned to him.

''Speaking of the devil,'' Rosie cried, grinning broadly.

He came over to her and planted a kiss on the top of her head. It was clear to the two young lovers that a romance was brewing here they hadn't known about before.

''I believe the expression is, 'speak of the devil and he appears,' '' Dan said. He offered smiles all around, but he took Rosie's hand and gave it a special, private squeeze.

''We need your help to rescue a maiden in distress, Dan,'' Rosie said with no further preliminaries.

''Annie, you don't look the least bit distressed to me,'' he teased, moving around the table to take the young woman in his arms. ''And this must be the fortunate lad,'' he added, extending his hand in greeting. ''But surely our little Annie isn't the damsel in distress. So,'' he said, lowering himself into a seat, ''tell me about the problem.''

Edmund briefly outlined the situation between his father and his father's young wife. He explained his feeling of responsiblity for having placed her, unwittingly, in a worse position than she'd ever been in before, simply because she had offered him help against her husband's wishes.

''I cannot,'' he concluded, ''marry Annie and go off to Toowoomba leaving Clara behind to who knows what fate.''

"What's this about Toowoomba?" Dan asked, and Anne did the explaining while holding her dear old friend's hand. "You were really responsible for finding my mother and my teacher," she added. "You've been so important to my life. Now that I'm on the brink of a new phase of that life, I'd like to know you were part of that transition. What I'm leading up to is that Edmund and I—and mother, too—would like to have you be the best man at the wedding we're going to celebrate as soon as Clara is safe!"

"Bravo!" Dan cried. "Let's get rid of the tea and break out the champagne! It may be a bit early for drinking on a normal day, but on such a day as this there is no wrong time."

Their celebration extended throughout the day, heightened in intensity by the joy the two lovers felt at being reunited. Even the fear that Charlie Burrows would once again attempt to destroy their happiness receded until it was no more than a wisp of fog across a lovely morning's sunlit field.

But, of course, daylight inevitably wanes toward dusk, and so did their thoughts inevitably return to the need for planning and secrecy if they were to effect their own escape and that of Clara. As it turned out, they had less need of cleverness than they thought. Charlie, realizing that he had lost a son, had gone on a spree that left him stuporous with drink. Whenever consciousness threatened to awaken within him the notion that he was ruining his life or perhaps had already done so, he searched out another bottle and drank it down. He was, therefore, totally unaware of the fact that his wife, no longer the passive creature he had tolerated for so long now, was busily rushing around packing up her goods and making arrangements for them to be carried to the port. He remained unaware, too, of his son's absence when Edmund went to town to claim Anne, just as he remained oblivious to Edmund's return for his few clothes and to gather up Clara.

When, at last, as Edmund and Clara in the family coach

were just disappearing down the road, one of Charlie
Burrows's servants shook him awake to tell him of their
departure, Charlie just shook his head disgruntledly and
mumbled, ''Aw, the hell with them both,'' and sank back
onto his bed.

So the moment when Anne and Edmund were to be
joined in wedlock had finally arrived. Rosie, who had
brought with her to Australia her mother's wedding gown
in hopes that she would one day wear it, had spent her
time adjusting it to Anne's slim figure. Now she looked at
her daughter and beamed with satisfaction. She looked as
lovely as any bride could ever have looked. The gown was
a soft off-white silk with seed pearls rimming the neckline.
The bodice was snug after Rosie's adjustments and showed
off Anne's slim waist to advantage. From the waist, though,
the gown flowed freely, cascading to the floor in full,
heavy folds. Rosie had made a new headpiece and veil
after she discovered that the one she had saved for so long
was in decay. The new one was so sheer that the radiant
glow from Anne's cheeks shone through it clearly. Dan
provided the bouquet, a small grouping of some lovely
Australian wildflowers laced together by a blue silk ribbon.

''In case,'' he said, ''you're going by the old rules of
something borrowed, something blue, here's the blue.''
Anne sniffed the flowers, rich with the smells of fields and
sunlight. Oh, she thought, how I long to be off on the
adventure of my new life.

''Well, the gown is borrowed,'' answered Anne. ''How
does the rest of it go? 'Something old, something new.'
Oh dear, what can that be?''

Rose laughed. ''Why your love is new! And getting
married—well, I suppose that's about the oldest thing on
this earth. Do you suppose those will do?''

Dan gave Rosie a hug.

''I don't know about these youngsters, but that sounds
like good thinking to me,'' he said.

Edmund had been kept out of these preparations lest he

spy the bride before the ceremony and bring bad luck down on all their heads. But he was listening from beyond the door to Rosie's room where the others were gathered. And now he shouted in to them, "The idea sounds fine, and the idea of being married sounds fine, and the idea of being married while I'm still young enough to enjoy it sounds fine. So how about hurrying the good times up and coming on out here, folks. Standing in the hall is beginning to make me feel I'm a little boy being punished for something.''

Almost as soon as he spoke, the door opened and with a flourish Dan waved Anne ahead of him. When Edmund caught his first sight of his bride-to-be, he had no words for what he was feeling.

The older couple, who were watching from the doorway, just smiled. So young, so healthy, so full of life and love for each other—Edmund and Anne looked already united in a union that would prove ever indissoluble.

The minister was awaiting them downstairs. It was time to make the union legal under Australian law. And under God's. Dan took Anne's hand and led her down the stairs.

I'm leaving my home behind, the girl thought, once again. This thought introduced a faint note of melancholy into what was still the happiest day of her life.

Anne had noticed earlier in the day that Rosie had turned away from her several times to wipe a tear from her eyes. She knew her mother had much greater reason for sadness than she. How she hoped that Dan would prove to be more than just a friend. She had asked him yesterday whether he would be staying in Sydney for a long time now, but he had told her he must be off almost at once. The company had given him another ship to take back— one that was already set to leave. That would be good for Clara anyway, Anne thought. But her poor mother. She'd be all alone except for Bart. Anne knew that Bart loved Rosie and wanted to marry her, but such were the vagaries of love that Rosie didn't seem to return his affectons.

Anne sighed. She put all such thoughts from her mind. They stood before the minister. This was the day she would bind herself forever to her Edmund. Her first thoughts must ever be for his happiness. She looked over at the handsome, earnest man beside her. His face assured her that she could safely entrust her life into his hands.

How had he resisted the influence of his brutal father, she wondered. Surely no one could have predicted that he could grow up as noble as he had. Of course, she realized, very few people would have laid odds on her turning out anything but a bar girl, what with her upbringing in the Red Raven Saloon.

Then the precious eternal words were spoken and she was asked to commit her life to Edmund.

"I do," she said softly, and to herself she added, I promise more than simply to love and honor you, Edmund, I promise to make you the best-loved man in all of Australia.

Then she heard the minister saying "I now pronounce you man and wife." It was strange that she could hardly force herself to listen or to concentrate during this most important moment in her life. It all was passing by as though it were part of a dream. Then Edmund was kissing her, and she knew it was real.

Everyone burst into applause as they turned from the minister to face the assembled guests. There would be a party now, food and drink and dancing, but the important celebration would take place later—later, when they were alone, when they could at last share the passion they felt for each other. Now they were Mr. and Mrs. Edmund Knight, and they could spend tonight together. Tonight and every night.

"Oh, Edmund, I love you so much," Anne whispered.

25

WHILE Anne and Edmund were saying their farewells in Sydney and making preparations to be on their way to Toowoomba, Lachlan was attempting to make the Count understand the necessity for his visit to the same place. The Count kept insisting that Lachlan be his rider, and Lachlan kept reiterating his belief that he must be a free man. Finally, the Count ended the dispute not—as might have been expected—by reminding Lachlan that he was an assigned man, still in essence a convict, but by talking terms with Lachlan for their partnership.

"Two free men," he said, "working together for the benefit of both. How's that?"

Lachlan felt suspicious of this sudden relinquishing of power on the Count's part. When he voiced his disbelief, however, the Count reassured him by saying, "My dear boy, you have already earned me, by winning that one big race, more than I could have reasonably supposed I would ever gain from our alliance. You, on the other hand, didn't even ask for one penny from those profits. I am not insensitive to a noble nature, and I sense one in you. I would be proud to have you as my partner."

Lachlan now found himself intrigued by the notion of a legitimate profession. He had to admit he liked the Count. Still, his natural leeriness of human beings made him ask, "What's in it for you? You can find riders for hire, I'm sure. You don't need to offer partnership for that."

"Indeed not," the Count agreed, "but riders such as you—well, that's a different matter. You sense *with* the horse. Most riders work against their mounts. No, I think the bargain between us would be fairly struck. I'd provide the mounts and make the book; you'd ride us into the winner's circle!"

The Count, with the casual ease with which he did everything, held his hand out toward Lachlan. But Lachlan refused to accept it.

"Stay," he said. The Count put his hand back down on the table. "Before I can shake on it, I must discuss one other problem with you, Count."

"Very well." The Count eased back in his chair. His sharp eyes didn't fail to take in Lachlan's sudden discomfort. Well, he thought to himself, I wonder what new topic this gentleman-robber is about to introduce. Obviously one that he's more uncomfortable with than he is with horses!

"I must borrow your time and your horse before we set out," Lachlan began. "Before we form an alliance, I have urgent business in Toowoomba."

"Might I, as a gentleman who would honor a confidence and as your friend, inquire as to the purpose of that visit, Lachlan?"

"Please don't laugh. I assure you that my reputation as a lady's man is ludicrously exaggerated, but it is a lady I must see before I can leave the area."

The Count, well aware of Lachlan's ways with the women—it was a vital part of the man's legend—attempted to suppress the smile that rose unbidden to his lips.

"How long a time do you require?" he asked.

"A fortnight," Lachlan answered promptly, having thought through that question for some time now.

The Count nodded. "Two weeks, eh? She must be quite the lady! You need a horse and—I'm sure—some small amount of money in order to be your own man. Right you are. Those terms are agreeable with me. Now will you shake on it?"

The smile that broke across Lachlan's face at those words of the Count's was as brilliant as the sun shimmering across the ocean's waves. The Count could see why this man had found admirers. He also believed they would make a formidable team—formidable. He would spend the next two weeks arranging races and setting up a stable of fast horses. Then they'd be on their way.

Lachlan, on the other hand, had no thoughts just now for the future beyond the next two weeks. All he could think about was the fact that the next day he'd be on his way to see Flanders. He could hardly concentrate on the rest of the evening's conversation with that thought in mind. Before they parted, the Count had given Lachlan money and had arranged with him as to which horse he could saddle up the next day.

Lachlan spent the next hours in a nervous state the like of which he'd never felt, not even on the night before the big race. He didn't want to set out before it was fully light. After all, it would never do to have his horse stumble in a hole and pull up lame. No, he'd best rein in his own anticipation the way he had reined in Victory's during the race. He really needed a good night's sleep anyway, he told himself. Finally, he did fall into a deep sleep, and by the time he awoke, it was fully morning, so he could get up and be on his way with no qualms about the safety of the ride.

Lachlan had considered other dangers enough to have armed himself while he was still in town, but now that he was safely underway, the idea of danger had receded from his mind. His mind was, in fact, filled with quite other thoughts as he crossed the miles of rugged terrain that brought him ever closer to Flanders' home.

He let his mind drift as he rode. The route was direct enough. No worry about directing the horse. Instead, Lachlan's mind was a jumble of memories. The first night in his hideout with Flanders. Certainly at that point he never expected to have anything more to do with the strange British scientist-lady. Now, as he sped toward a new encounter with her, he thought that her Toowoomba homestead was as close to a home as he'd had since he came to Australia. Maybe as close to a home as he would ever have.

"Not much longer, boy," he whispered to his horse, "and you shall have a rest."

And so will I, he added to himself.

Nothing was further from his mind at that moment than the driver who had vowed vengeance against him that first day he'd met Flanders. But having heard that Lachlan McKenzie had just won the biggest horse race in Australia's history, Blade Parker had Lachlan very much on his mind.

Big Harris Wakefield had ordered him that morning to ready the coach for a ride into Brisbane, and he hoped that he would be able to hunt Lachlan down when they arrived. With this thought in mind, he goaded the horses on faster and faster toward town.

Just then he spotted a dark dot in the distance. He realized it was a single rider. It better not be some bushranger, he thought, or he'd be a dead bushranger. He reached behind his neck to check the position of his Green River knife.

At the same time, Lachlan spotted a coach coming toward him on the narrow road. It occurred to him that in days past this would have been the moment when he went charging in to attack the coach's driver. Today, though, he was just another traveler on the road. He was alert now, but still unconcerned.

There are people who spend their lives preparing for the moment of death; then there are others who believe that the death that comes for them will find them no matter what they do and, therefore, don't give any thought to it at all. What will be, will be, seems to be their motto. Lachlan was among the latter. He thought of safety, but only peripherally. Mostly he thought about life. So when he heard his name called as he galloped past the coach as they crossed paths, he had no thought of danger. He half-reined in his horse and looked back over his shoulder, trying to identify the person who called to him.

At the same moment that Blade drew his knife, Lachlan veered off the road and spurred his horse on to a full-speed gallop. The Green River knife whizzed through the air as its hurler cried out, "It's me, McKenzie. John Blade Parker! You remember?" Then, as he saw his missile hit its mark, saw Lachlan jerk back in the saddle as the knife entered his back, saw him waver in the saddle trying desperately to hang on, Blade's laughter howled through the air in a maniacal shriek of triumph. This moment, Blade felt, vindicated his years of waiting. This moment made up for his humiliation at Lachlan's hands. He wanted to pursue the man to make sure he was dead. He'd disappeared from view still clinging to his horse's neck. But Wakefield was already calling up from inside the coach, "What's going on, man? Are you in another fight, you feisty son-of-a-bitch? If you are, I swear I'll fire you!"

Besides, he knew that, driving a coach, he'd never be able to catch up with a man on horseback, not even a wounded man. And if Lachlan had already fallen from the horse, he was as good as dead anyway. He'd count it a kill, Blade decided, and continue into town.

As a matter of fact, he wasn't far wrong. Lachlan, who had managed to cling to his horse's neck and urge him on in the direction of Toowoomba, had taken the knife in the left side of his back not far from his heart. He struggled to remain conscious as the horse galloped on. He knew that if he fell, he would die. No one would find him lying along this mostly deserted road in time to tend to him even if the person were kind enough to want to do so. Still, the horse's every step seemed to tear open his wound further. He thought he could feel his heart's blood pumping out of his body with every stride. The landscape blurred before his eyes. Well, he thought as he felt himself drifting away from the reality of the Australian plains, I would have liked to hold Flanders in my arms one more time, but I guess that wasn't meant to be. Then, in a last effort to maintain life, he locked his fingers tightly into the horse's main, leaned along his neck, and resigned himself to his fate. The horse was on a straight course, he knew. If the horse kept going, and if anyone from Flanders' place saw him and if he were still alive by that time. . . . the thoughts went round and round in his head. Then all was blackness.

26

MORE than an hour later, Flanders stood in her front yard reading over the letter that had just arrived telling her of Anne's plans to join her soon with her new husband. She felt delighted by the news. It helped make up for the fact that her attempt at a herb garden was a disastrous failure. She regarded the ground in front of her. The plants had shriveled and died. They remained rooted in little patches, as though to remind her that she had not cared for them adequately. This land is unsuited for you, she addressed them silently. I did my best, after all. She would just have to do without crushed, fresh mint leaves in her tea. Hardly a disaster, she thought, laughing at herself. But it would have been so nice to have a touch of home about her still. She sighed. Lately she seemed to be doing too much sighing.

She would go and find Tarleton, she decided. They could have a reading lesson. Her four year old son was always able to bring a smile to her face. What a joy he was. Then, as she started to turn back to the house, she heard a horse approaching at the gallop. It wasn't completely unprecedented, but it was certainly unusual—unusual enough to warrant some interest, if not alarm. She called to Elizabeth, but there was no answer. Flanders stood looking toward the sound.

In the distance, some way down the road, she spotted the horse coming toward her. At first, he seemed to be riderless, but then she saw that he carried a rider draped across him . . . a rider who seemed lifeless. Now alarm filled her, but not alarm for her own safety. It seemed to her that she had seen so much violence since she had arrived in Australia. When was it ever going to end, she wondered. The country had an energy that was exciting, but it was matched by a brutality that was terrifying. Now what was this coming toward her? More evidence of man's cruelty to man, no doubt. Doogalook had heard her call and came to join her. She was glad of that. He had a calm way that she admired. No doubt he could stop the horse better than she. Also, he could help her get the man down from the saddle so that they could see if he was living or dead. He certainly looked dead. By now the horse had drawn quite close, and Flanders had her first look at the rider's face. My God, she gasped, it looks like . . . But no, it surely cannot be . . . But it is! "Lachlan," she cried. "Lachlan." But the corpse-like rider gave no sign of hearing her cry.

Doogalook made a number of gestures to the advancing horse, and the horse slowed, then stopped as Doogalook reached up and secured his reins. Flanders had no time to ponder his magical powers. She had seen them in action many times since he came to live with her in Toowoomba. Now her only concern was for the rider.

"My love," she cried as Doogalook eased the man to the ground and she saw that it was, in fact, her own beloved Lachlan. "My love, my only love, I can't have found you again only to lose you again! Please be alive, please." She was beside herself with fear and hardly knew what she was saying. She sank to the ground next to the limp body of Lachlan. Her hands lifted his head onto her lap. Her long tapered fingers stroked his brow, tenderly moving the strands of hair away from his closed eyes.

Doogalook, squatting beside her, supported his left side so that the knife, which was still firmly implanted in Lachlan's back, would not be pushed further into his body.

He probed the man's neck for a pulse and felt a weak, rapid one under his fingers.

"He lives!"

"Thank God," Flanders exclaimed. Suddenly the afternoon, which had grown unnaturally still, resumed its normal sounds to her ears. She heard the raucous noises of the thousand insects hidden in the low, dense shrubbery. Flanders could hear voices from the house. She heard Elizabeth call to her husband to go see what was going on in the yard. She heard Tar whine that he didn't have anybody to play with.

"Allen," she called, knowing that the man would be hurrying toward them. "Help Doogalook carry this man inside." She stood as soon as Allen's strong hands replaced her own in supporting Lachlan's head. "I'll alert Elizabeth," she said to the two men, and she turned at once toward the house. Her feet seemed to be creatures with a will of their own and started to run toward the house. Her full skirts swirled around her ankles.

"Elizabeth," she cried when she was still a hundred feet away from the kitchen. "Quick! We need your medicines. As fast as you can. It's Mr. McKenzie, and he's badly wounded."

The serving woman dried her hands on her apron, as soon as she heard Flanders' voice calling. She went out to meet her mistress, and the two women met in the hallway outside the kitchen at the back of the house.

"What kind of wound?" Elizabeth asked. She wasn't a woman to waste time with foolish words or useless emoting.

"A knife. He's hardly alive."

"I'll get clean sheets for bandages. You know the herbs I gathered that are drying out on the back porch?"

Flanders nodded. Her heart felt frozen in such terror that it paralyzed her rational abilities. She was grateful to have her servant take over the responsibility of thinking what to do.

"Quickly, go and fetch them. Bring them to the extra

room. I'll tell the men to put him there. And boil water. I have to make up compresses.'' She didn't wait to see if Flanders would obey. She knew that she would. The man they were discussing was after all her lover. Elizabeth had prior dealings with knifings; they were bad. She gave orders to the men as they came through the door with their burden.

"Place him on his stomach, men,'' She followed along behind them as they all three made a cluster of movement down the narrow hallway. "Tear his shirt away from the knife,'' she ordered. "Careful! Don't jostle him anymore than need be.''

"A little late to worry about that,'' her husband said. "He looks like he's been riding with that knife sticking through his ribs for a good long ways now. The blood's congealed and turned brown around the tear in his shirt.''

"He's lost plenty of blood, that's clear,'' she agreed. "But he'll lose a bit more, I'm afraid, before I can get him and that knife to part company.''

She knelt beside the bed and peered closely at the half-dead man's back. The knife had penetrated well into his chest cavity from the rear. If it had knicked the heart, Elizabeth reasoned, all their work would be to no avail. If the bleeding had stopped on the outside but was continuing at a good pace internally, then he would die as sure as morning brought daylight. She'd have to hope that wasn't the case. If the heart wasn't affected, he might make it.

When she withdrew the knife from his back, thick maroon blood oozed up from the deep wound. There were no bubbles, and she breathed a sigh of relief. The knife hadn't punctured either the heart or the lungs. The color of the blood told her that Lachlan wasn't bleeding from a major artery.

"There's lots to be thankful for,'' she said to Flanders, who had arrived breathlessly with the basket of herbs and a kettle of water. "Allen, fetch some of them clean sheets and tear them in good strips for me to bind up this man's chest.''

"Oh Elizabeth, tell me he'll live," Flanders pleaded.

"I can't do that yet. But at least I don't have to pronounce his death sentence yet either. From the angle of the wound as I withdrew the knife, it looks like the knife embedded itself between the chest wall and the collarbone. He might not shoot so good with his left arm after this. It looks like there's lots of muscles damage.''

"He's right-handed," Flanders interrupted irrelevantly. "Oh God, Elizabeth, he just has to live. I haven't even told him that I love him!''

Elizabeth eyed Flanders with a sardonic smile. "Not to mention the fact that you haven't yet told him about little Tarleton.''

Flanders bit her lip. She nodded. The older woman, sharing her mistress's pain at the sight of the beautiful man so close to death, turned back to her patient, saying over her shoulder as she did so, "I'll do my best. There'll be no change tonight. Why don't you go take care of the boy while I see what I can do about tending this wound. If there's any change, I'll call you.''

Flanders leaned over Lachlan's inert body and planted a tender kiss on his hand which lay limply beside his head, the fingers curled unconsciously in a graceful pose.

"I'll get Tar ready for bed, read him a story. Then I'll be back. Meanwhile, I'll pray . . .''

Elizabeth, busy with applying the herbal ointments she had made and accepting the wads of bandage that John was handing her, didn't answer. There was nothing to say. Words have no power at the most crucial moments of our lives, Flanders thought as she went in search of her son.

"Tar," she called, "Tarleton, come to Mommy, and I'll read you a story." She knew that wherever the little boy was, the lure of a story would bring him to her, whereas the threat of a bath and bed would only send him scurrying into hiding.

"Here," a small voice cried. "I'm here, Mommy."

She saw her son's beautiful strong body curled around the newest kitten that had made its way into their household. The two baby creatures—kid and kit—showed all the beauty possible in the world. She looked at Tarleton as though she hadn't seen him for a week instead of an hour. He had hair that was fairer than hers. She thought how odd that was, considering the fact that Lachlan was so dark.

"Come here, baby," she said.

He stood at once, lifting the kitten by its two front paws, and came toward her with a smile on his face.

"Darling, put the kitten down and give me a hug. I need a nice strong hug from my boy right now."

He dropped the kitten, who meowed and dashed to safety. Then he stretched out his arms to his mother and was lifted up into her arms.

"My, you are certainly my big boy now," she said. "You must weigh forty pounds! Today I'm going to tell you a story about your father."

"Lachlan McKenzie?" the boy asked in his boyish lisping voice.

"Yes, Lachlan McKenzie," Flanders repeated the name, as though offering up a prayer for his safety. He's not dead, she thought! He's still alive. My dear love. She hugged Tarleton tightly to her. She had always told him stories in which his father took the part of the hero. Tonight she would tell the true story of how famous he was. Naturally, she altered the facts to make his livelihood one that a young boy could proudly emulate. But the main thing was that he must know how wonderful a man his father was. *Is*, she corrected herself! Perhaps in the morning she would be able to introduce them to each other.

27

BY morning, it was clear that Flanders' early optimism was unfounded. Lachlan was out of the coma he had been in, but he was aflame with fever. He couldn't recognize anyone and thought he was back in prison. It was a terrible anguish to hear him shout out blasphemies or beg piteously for mercy.

"What is going on?" Flanders asked Elizabeth.

The two women had spent the night sitting beside the sick man's bed and watching him grow more and more restless. Then, at daybreak, he began to vomit, shake uncontrollably, and rant about prison conditions.

"He must be poisoned," the woman answered. "Either the tip of the knife was dipped in something deadly, or the wound is getting infected. Both possibilities are rotten."

"Can't we do something?"

"Send for the doctor. Lachlan should hold until then. Maybe he can cut him open and bleed him. I wouldn't want to try it on my own. Better a doctor should be here. Just in case . . ."

The words she didn't speak, the conclusion of her thought, was that it would be better if there were a doctor around in case Lachlan died. Elizabeth didn't want to be responsible for any move that would lead directly to that. And she wasn't pleased with the way the man's lips had taken on a blue color that deepened with each passing hour. "Send for the doctor," she said again.

"Go on, Elizabeth. Send John. But tell him, for the love of God, to hurry!"

Flanders was glad that Elizabeth had left the room. It allowed her to weep without worrying about looking weak. "Lachlan," she whispered, resting her head on the pillow beside his heaving chest. "Please come back to me." Tears dripped from her cheeks onto his. At their touch, he shivered and for a moment seemed to come to himself. He sat up, gazing about him wildly. His eyes focused on Flanders' face. She was sitting up now also, with a look nearly as wild as his.

"You!" he cried out. "Are you real or are you a dream?" His eyes snapped shut again, and he collapsed back onto the pillow where he lay unmoving as though death had, in reality, taken him away.

"Wait!" Flanders shrieked. She could no more say what she was doing than she could reason out her deep love for this man, but she knew that if he died, right here before her, she would never be whole again.

"I love you," she said in a calmer voice. She leaned over to see if she could feel his soft breath on her cheek. Yes, he was still alive! "Lachlan, it is I—Flanders Wilde. It's no dream." But she saw as she spoke that he was once again unconscious of his surroundings. He drifted in that peculiar dream world of pain and fever from which he was unable to wake. Soon, without being aware of it, the exhausted woman beside him drifted into a sleep that resembled the tortured slumber of her lover.

At least she though, was roused from her sleep later in the day by the arrival of the doctor. Lachlan, on the other hand, remained fitfully tossing in his nightmares.

"Please, Doctor," Flanders begged, "save him."

"Get her out of here," he ordered Elizabeth. "She'll wear herself out and do him no good neither." To Flanders he said, "I'll do what I can. I'll have a good look and do what I can. Then I'll come talk to you and tell you what I think."

Flanders blanched but did not respond. Nor did she resist as Elizabeth led her from the room.

"Rest a while," Elizabeth suggested. "I'll be sure to come get you when the doctor is finished."

"Bring me the boy," Flanders ordered.

"Not now, child. Just rest."

"Bring him!" Flanders' tone made it impossible for Elizabeth to deny her. She went in search of Tarleton. Flanders sank into the stuffed rocker that she'd had built when she was carrying her baby. She had to hold him. She knew that if she could hold onto him, she wouldn't lose her senses. She must be strong, she cautioned herself. She'd be no good to anyone if she didn't manage that. But what if he died? Tears rose again to her eyes. She commanded herself to stop the self-pity!

Elizabeth returned, dragging Tar by the hand.

"Stay with your mother," she said to him. "Your mother don't feel too good and she needs you."

"Aw, I was having fun," he said.

"That's enough," Elizabeth warned, raising a finger and shaking it at him. Then she lifted the thin boy onto his mother's lap. Flanders' arms clasped him like two steel bands until he squirmed and said, "That hurts, Mommy." She loosened her hold then. He began to prattle on about a game he had made up, and his mother, staring off into an empty void that seemed to stretch before her like eternity, let him ramble on without a single interruption.

After an indeterminate period of time, during which the light in the room that filtered in through the curtains turned from murky gold to sodden gray, the doctor entered the room and stood before the mother and child.

Flanders gently pushed the boy from her lap. "Tell

Elizabeth to give you one of her special tarts,'' she said. ''Mommy has to talk to the doctor now.''

''Are you sick, Mommy?'' the boy asked.

''No, Mommy's fine,'' she answered. ''Someone else is sick. Run along now, and I'll tell you all about it later.''

''Bye,'' he called over his shoulder as he scooted from the room. ''Elizabeth,'' they could hear him shouting as soon as he got into the hall.

The mother and the doctor exchanged brief smiles over the antics of youth, but their mood was too somber for them to sustain more than a fleeting moment of mirth.

''Tell me,'' the woman said curtly.

She knew this ''doctor'' from stories the assigned convicts who were her extra servants told. He had cared for them in prison or on the road gangs. The way they told it, he was a convict himself, who had more or less won his freedom because of his medical skill and knowledge gathered from God-knows-where. They had no complaints about his ability, however. Flanders doubted that he was a real medical doctor, but in this land, where every second person had been a convict or was the child of one, she wasn't about to hold that against him.

''How about a cup of tea or a glass of something stronger while we talk?'' he asked.

His words shot a rocket of alarm up along Flanders' spine that registered in her face as a tightening of her lips and a flaring of her eyes. He would die. She wasn't meant to find happiness in this life, she decided. She would have to adjust to his death yet a second time. She didn't know if she could bear it. Losing one's love once—that was surely enough pain for anyone's lifetime. But twice!

She rose without a word and went to the sideboard cabinet. She took the key from her pocket—she had long ago learned that if she left the liquor unlocked, it disappeared. She turned the key, swung open the wood door, and reached inside for the decanter of rum. Despite her distress, Flanders couldn't help but admire the beautiful artistry of the cabinet. She'd had it built of mountain ash, a native hardwood that could polish up to a shine like no other wood she'd ever seen. The grain had a beauty to match anything England could offer, even mahogany. The craftsman had carved its mantel in a pattern that resembled gum tree leaves and acacia flowers. It was a magnificent piece, a true work of contemporary Australian art, Flanders thought. Then she closed the cabinet and turned back to the doctor who had seated himself in a chair close by the one in which Flanders had been sitting.

She handed him the heavy glass half filled with rum as she said, ''Well?''

He drank off a good half of the drink before answering.

''Sit,'' he said. ''The man has a bad infection. I've cut it open and drained it off as best I could. Your woman mentioned to me that it might have been a poisoned knife. If so, his chances are worse, because the poison would have entered his bloodstream.''

''What else can be done?''

''Frankly, nothing. He's young and strong. That's the best thing going for him.''

''What are the odds?'' Flanders wondered at the icy, calm tone of her own voice. It sounded to her ears like a stranger speaking. She didn't want to be pacified. She wanted the truth.

''Fifty-fifty. But I know you're a scientific lady; you know those numbers mean nothing. What good are statistics when you want to know about a particular case?''

She knew he was right. At least he wasn't trying to sugar-coat his words. He immediately rose in her estimation, and she relaxed her guard against him a bit.

''When will you come back?'' she asked.

''I'll be back tomorrow to see if the wound needs draining again. I don't believe in bleeding. Doesn't make sense to me that somebody who's already lost a bunch of the precious stuff would be helped by losing more. Meanwhile, there's not much you can do but change the dressing.'' He stood up, planting his glass on the table between them. ''And pray,'' he added.

Flanders accompanied him to the front door. There he paused and faced her.

''I know who that man is. I don't suppose you want it mentioned that he's here.''

Flanders winced. She hadn't really given a thought to the need for secrecy. She remembered Lachlan's last visit, and the posse that hounded him from her door.

''I'll pay for your silence,'' she said grimly.

''Don't be a damn fool,'' the doctor roared. ''I'm not trying to blackmail you. I just wanted to tell you. You'll pay for my professional services, and that's all.''

Flanders, contrite, said, ''I'm sorry, I didn't mean to offend you. I just thought . . .''

''I know what you thought. And there's no offense taken. Australia is a place where a lot of men take a buck any place they can find one. Go tend your patient. I'll be back tomorrow.''

Flanders held out her hand. The doctor looked at it a moment. Unusual for a woman to offer to shake, he thought. Then he grasped it in his own and was impressed with the firm grip on the woman's part. There was something solid to this woman. The tantalizing stories he'd heard about a crazy lady scientist had more to them than he'd suspected.

''Good-bye,'' she said in a friendlier tone than he'd heard from her before. ''Thanks for what you've done.''

''I only hope it's enough.'' He waved his hand in a farewell gesture and stamped down the porch stairs.

Flanders closed the door and returned to Lachlan's side. She felt almost afraid to look at him too closely—afraid that he might not be breathing. She took a deep breath and forced herself to examine his form. His chest still rose and fell. Thank God, she sighed.

In fact, she thought he looked a little better. The color in his cheeks seemed more natural, not the high flush of fever. She placed her hand on his forehead. He was still so terribly hot. She saw that Elizabeth had placed a basin of cool water and a cloth nearby. Flanders dipped the cloth in the water, squeezed it out, and softly bathed Lachlan's face. She let a few drops of water drip onto his cracked lips and was encouraged to see him move them slightly and then swallow. She offered him a few more drops of water. He looked so parched. Again she was rewarded by movement. A bird began to flutter in her chest, or so it felt. Happiness, hope, something wonderful—feelings that she had not allowed herself to feel for so very long.

She looked at Lachlan's face. He was a handsome man, she thought, not for the first time. Her fingers traced the shape of his eyebrows, his aquiline nose, the fringe of his eyelashes.

To her amazement, Flanders saw Lachlan's face quiver and then—and then Lachlan opened his eyes. He opened his eyes and within those pitch-black coals Flanders thought she could see her own Lachlan.

"Lachlan," she whispered.

He struggled to move his mouth, to force his lips to shape a word. She leaned closer, placing her ear near his face.

"Flanders." She heard it. He had spoken her name. She sat back up, but his eyes had closed once more. He had spoken her name! Perhaps he would live. He just had to.

"You're safe now," she said. She didn't know if he could hear her, but in case he could, she wanted to offer her encouragement. "You're safe, and I'm right here beside you. Don't worry about a thing. You just rest and get well. Oh, and then I have so much to tell you. So much."

She fell silent. Lachlan looked as though he were sleeping.

He wasn't tossing or turning. Perhaps he was on the way to recovery. If so, she would have to find a way to tell him about Tarleton. Tarleton Wilde—not Tarleton McKenzie! In fact, though, he was a McKenzie!

As if summoned by the magic of her thoughts, Tarleton appeared at the door.

"Who's that sick man?" he asked coming over to her and climbing up on her lap.

"Tar, it's polite to knock. I swear you're growing up a regular wild Australian, aren't you?" She kissed the boy's ear where the blonde hair was curling over the rim. "This is the sick man." She paused a moment wondering if she dared tell him, then she added, "This is your father, Tarleton."

Flanders didn't know what reaction she had expected, but she certainly didn't expect the reaction that she got. The boy, without a word, slid from her lap, went over to the bed, wrapped his arms around the sleeping man's neck, and kissed his cheek.

"He can't hear you," she said, gently drawing him back. "He's too badly hurt. But when he's better," she realized she was taking a chance by assuming that he was going to get better, but she went doggedly on, "then he'll give you great big kisses back. But come on now, let's go hear what you've managed to do with your reading. Have you figured out anything of what Mister Darwin is saying?"

Flanders had been reading Charles Darwin's *On the Origin of Species* which had been published in England in 1859 and had caused such a stir that word of it had even reached her in Australia. She had ordered the book at once, of course. Darwin's theory of the development of man was quite the most exciting thing she had ever read. Now, realizing that Tar was quite a bright boy, she had attempted to give him short passages from it to practice his reading on. No use filling his head with foolishness when he could begin to think scientifically, she reasoned.

"It's hard words, Mum," he said as they walked from the sick man's room.

"Yes, that's true, but you must begin to understand hard words as well as easy ones. We'll read it together, and I'll explain to you what you don't understand."

She led the reluctant boy from the room where his father lay. She would try to use this time to keep both their minds off him as he struggled to stay alive.

28

IT wasn't many days later that Flanders entered Lachlan's room as silently as she had always done before only to discover that he was alertly watching her approach. A smile crossed her face, and she accelerated her pace, throwing herself into his arms. He welcomed her there with delight. The kisses they exchanged spoke more than words could ever have done of the longing and anguish each had felt at their lengthy separation.

"You're alive," Flanders said when at last they pulled apart.

"Thanks to you," Lachlan answered. Then he laughed.

It was the most beautiful sound Flanders had ever heard. It was silver bells on Christmas morning. It was the musical song of the menura, or lyre-bird, whose song often thrilled Flanders when she first opened her eyes in the mornings. It was the magic of Tarleton's baby laughter magnified into the rich lushness of the adult male. It was life, Flanders thought.

"Lachlan McKenzie, now that you seem to be on the mend, I should kill you for abandoning me for this long! I thought you were dead. No, I *knew* you were dead. And then you finally come back to me and I thought you were going to die on me all over again! Damn it all, man." Here Flanders' voice broke and she began to sob. She raised her hands to cover her face, but Lachlan reached up and pulled them back down. She tried to pull free of him, but he wouldn't let her go. She swallowed hard and stopped crying. "Damn you, Lachlan, I love you," she said.

He pulled her to his chest, wincing slightly as he felt a burning pain flame through his back.

"I love you, too, woman; now don't be a damn fool!"

How sweet those words sounded to Flanders' ears! How often she'd dreamed of hearing them, only to awaken to the reality of empty arms, and an empty bed. "Where were you? I went back to the cave, but you were gone."

"I was in a different darker cave than that one, I can assure you. A dark pit, that would be more like it."

His voice had grown tense as he spoke these words, and Flanders could only wonder at what terrible things had befallen this man since last they'd met. "If I should meet thee," she said, quoting the line Lachlan had spoken to her so many years ago that first night in his hideaway, "If I should meet thee, after long years . . ."

"How should I greet thee," he completed the line for her, "with silence and tears."

"Oh Lachlan," Flanders cried, burying her head in the curve of his neck. "I've missed you so."

"I was sure you'd be married and have a kid at your knees by now," he answered.

This was her chance. The topic of kids had been introduced. She told herself to go ahead and tell him, but still she held back. Then he went on talking, telling her that he'd been in prison, that only the thought of her had kept him sane, that he'd realized then how much he cared for her. And the moment when she could have spoken was passed.

But his words, the things he was murmuring against her head, were so sweet. It was a sweeter moment, she thought, than any she had ever dreamed. She could never have dreamed that "Bad" Lachlan McKenzie would be telling her that she was a strength to him in his worst hours.

"Lock the door," he said, his voice rough with the passion he'd waited so long to express.

"Oh, Lachlan. Your back!"

"Lock the door, woman. I'll watch out for my back."

At his first touch, Flanders had felt the old flame of desire warming her body, so she was hardly in a position to resist the suggestion he was making. She hurried to comply with his wishes and, after locking the door, fumbled with her clothing in her eagerness to be rid of it. On his part, Lachlan just lay there and watched her. Since his arrival he'd been dressed in only a loose nightshirt. It would present no problem to their closeness. Then she stood before him naked, shining in her nakedness, and so incredibly beautiful to his eyes.

"Come to me," he ordered, lifting the sheet with his uninjured arm to welcome her into the bed.

She stretched herself out along his length, trying to take care to avoid any contact with his left arm. The touch of his skin was like the embrace of velvet or the comfort of rain on a hot day. She couldn't think of an image powerful enough to express her feelings as his hand moved down her body and caressed her thighs, spreading them gently apart. Thought left her as she focused totally on sensation. She stroked the hair on his chest under his shirt.

She could feel the hardness of his body against her. Then, with a single swift shift in position, he had placed her beneath him and he was lying over her. She looked up into his face, fierce with the play of passion upon it.

"I want you," he said hoarsely, as he found his way into her.

At the moment that she felt him enter her, Flanders' eyes closed involuntarily. She thought, I am one with my love once again.

Lachlan began the rhythmical movements that spoke the eternal language of love. Closer, closer, he thought, with each stroke. With his good arm, he gathered Flanders tight against him.

Flanders could imagine a sailor on the high seas as he considered his insignificance against the might of the ocean's swells. That was her feeling as a mortal in the throes of immortal ecstasy. Then, as Lachlan's movements sped toward their inevitable climax, as her breathing turned to jagged gasps, as wave after wave of excitement filled her, she was lifted outside herself, to a place of rapture she had never been before. She called out at the last moment, "Lachlan!" And in her own ears the cry echoed through all the eons of time . . . through all the celestial miles of space.

When she came back into herself, into an awareness of where she was and who she was and with whom she was, she smiled contentedly. Life could hold fulfillment. She'd forgotten that. Lachlan lay beside her, looking as though he were asleep. He looked paler, too, than he'd been earlier. She became alarmed, watching him, and whispered, "Lachlan, speak to me. Are you all right?"

He opened his eyes slowly and took her concerned face in.

He nodded.

"Are you in pain?"

He nodded again, but then he added, "It was worth it, though." And they were both able to laugh at that.

"Lachlan, before my courage fails me as it has before, I must tell you something important. Very important. Please try to listen calmly. Say nothing until you've heard me out. Even then, perhaps, say nothing. I'll just tell you. You think it over. Tomorrow . . . or later today, maybe, we can talk about it. . . ."

"My God, you're certainly making me curious. Have you become a murderess? What is it? Tell me quick. You have me imagining the worst."

"I have a child!"

The silence which followed her words was so intense that it made Flanders imagine that she had gone stone-deaf. The silence seemed a palpable shape filling the room, forcing a distance between the two people lying so close together on the bed.

"A child," Lachlan repeated as though trying out the sound of those words.

Flanders nodded her head.

"Yes, a son."

"So," he said bitterly, "you are married after all! Why didn't you say so? Why did you let me make a fool of myself?" He turned away from her so that he was staring at the wall.

"Hell, no, I'm not married!" Flanders exploded. "Who do you think I could be married to?"

Lachlan turned back toward her. He'd never heard her sound so enraged, but he was enraged himself.

"The brat's father, that's who," he answered.

"Oh my God." Flanders blushed. It hadn't ever entered her mind that he might not realize he was the boy's father. Now she said, "You are a fool," but the tenderness in her tone belied her words. "The child is *our* child. Yours and mine! You're the brat's father, as you so delicately put it."

The expression that crossed Lachlan's face was so comical that Flanders laughed out loud. His mouth fell open. His eyes widened.

"Close your mouth or you'll catch flies," she teased.

"I don't know what to say."

"Don't say anything. I think you need to rest now anyway. Why don't I leave you alone, and I'll come back later? We can talk then . . . when you've had a little time to get used to the idea."

She was hurriedly dressing as she spoke. Now she planted a kiss on his cheek and turned toward the door. Before she reached it, though, his voice stopped her.

"What's his name?" he asked.

Flanders took a deep breath. She hoped he would approve her choice. She hoped his question meant he was going to be able to accept the idea of being a father.

"Tarleton," she answered. "I call him Tar sometimes."

He nodded, but he said nothing, and Flanders took this

as a sign of dismissal and left. In the hall she stopped and leaned against the wall. Well, she'd done it! She'd told him. After all this time, Lachlan McKenzie knew that he had a son. How she wished she could hear his thoughts now, she told herself. She went off to her room to do some cataloguing. Her work had been completely abandoned since Lachlan arrived half-dead. Today she needed something to get her mind off of him.

Flanders quickly became so completely absorbed in her work that it was with a sense of surprise that she looked up some time later to discover that the light was already fading from the sky. What a blessing work could be, she realized not for the first time. A distraction and a blessing both.

She yawned and stretched her arms up over her head to relieve their stiffness. She massaged her neck. She always carried tension in her neck. She went over to the mirror to see if she looked presentable enough to go down into the household. She took the pins from her hair and let it tumble onto her shoulders. Then she twisted it into a heavy coil and pinned it back up more neatly. She noticed a bruise on the side of her neck. Lachlan must have given it to her, although she hadn't felt it. Well, she would cover it as best she could with cornsilk powder. Suddenly she was flooded with the memory of Lachlan poised over her. Just remembering quickened her breathing and filled her with tingling warmth.

Then, for the first time, the thought entered her mind that she might have gotten pregnant again. Oh no, she prayed, let it not be so. One child and all her work were enough for one lifetime. She remembered that Elizabeth had talked to her once when she was pregnant with Tar about how there were herbs that could keep you from getting that way. A special potion you could brew up and drink. She would go and ask Elizabeth about it. The question wouldn't shock that sturdy soul, she knew.

Then she would check on Lachlan. If he agreed, she

might introduce him to his son this very day. Her heart began to pound in her chest. The moment she had dreaded and longed for during all this time might very well be at hand. Today. She went back to her desk, closed her notebook, put away the pen and ink. Today, she repeated to herself as she left her room.

By the time she re-entered Lachlan's room, the servants had already lit the kerosene lamp beside his bed. It was an early dusk, and the light that came through the curtained window was almost lavender. Lachlan was propped up on the pillows looking even more recovered than he had earlier that morning.

"Don't you look remarkably well!" Flanders exclaimed.

"And you look like the woman I dreamed about all those nights when I was locked away in that horrible hell-hole. Come closer and let me get a good look at you. This morning I wasn't seeing all that clearly."

Flanders didn't know if he meant because he was still feverish or because he was looking at her with lustful eyes, but she didn't ask him to clarify his statement. She approached the bed, made a curtsy, and then stood up and made a slow circle in place so he could survey her from every angle.

"The years haven't treated you too badly," he commented, and grinned. "You don't look like an old lady yet. Now let's see, how old are you now? I know you've past that crucial mark—thirty. And you're still a bit under forty . . ."

"Forty!" Flanders shouted. "Why you no-good . . ."

"Now, now, temper, temper," he admonished her, looking perfectly pleased with himself for having stirred up a fire in Flanders' spirit.

"I'm thirty-one, if you don't mind. And 'almost forty' is quite an exaggeration, wouldn't you agree?"

"Oh, I don't know about that. The years after thirty fly by so much faster than the ones before."

She knew he was teasing, but she couldn't ignore the

game. "You are showing that the recovering patient is a perfectly feisty creature," she said. "And I do not have any need to stand here and be insulted by such a creature! So, Mr. McKenzie, I'm mighty pleased that you're feeling better, and I'll look in on you again in the morning."

With that she turned away from him with a flounce of her skirts, but she would have been devastated and amazed if he hadn't called her back. The fact that he did call her back, therefore, came as no surprise to her. What astounded her was what he said next.

"Bring the boy in, Flanders," he said, and his voice had lost its teasing tone.

"Really?" she asked.

"Go get him."

The rush of feelings that Flanders experienced as she left the room to get Tarleton was a mixture of delight and terror. Fortunately, she didn't stop to analyze these feelings—she simply went to get the boy. She found him with Allen taking care of the horses.

"I love Bandit, Mommy," the boy said as he saw her coming. "And he loves me. Look." The boy approached the wild horse.

"*No,* Tar!" his mother cried, hurrying toward him.

But the boy was already beside the horse, stroking his side. The giant stallion was stretching his neck down to be patted by the boy. She stopped where she was.

"Allen," she said in an icy tone, "I warned you not to let anybody near that horse. Anybody! Especially not my son!"

"I'm sorry, ma'am. But the horse just seemed to gentle down whenever Tar was around. I plum forgot your instructions. Just look how they get on."

Flanders was looking, and she could hardly believe her eyes. The only person who had been able to treat Bandit with that easy familiarity had been Lachlan. My God, she realized, she hadn't even told Lachlan about Bandit!

Still, she wasn't quite ready to show Allen that she

forgave him. After all, the boy could have been trampled to death. She kept her face stern as she called Tar to her side.

"Finish up, Allen. We'll talk more about this later. Then bring Bandit around to Mr. McKenzie's window. Meanwhile, Tarleton, you must come with me. We've got to get you out of those ragged play clothes and into something fancier. Come on now."

"Why, Mom, why?"

But his mother took hold of his hand and began walking rapidly toward the house without answering.

When they were out of earshot of the stable, Flanders whispered to the boy, "Let's go get you dressed up. You're going to meet your daddy!"

But when, a short time later, he stood before her in a white shirt and tight flannel trousers, his hair meticulously combed, a velvet bow under his collar in the fashion of little boy's dress-up clothes, he didn't look a bit like her Tar. Not a bit like his father either. She shook her head.

"No, Tar," she said. "Let's get you into some play clothes. This is too much like a party outfit."

She changed the shirt for a red and black checked wool flannel, discarded the velvet bow entirely, and rumpled his hair.

"There," she said then. "Now you look like my boy again. Come on, son."

Tarleton, aware, despite his youth, that this was a momentous occasion, wore a somber expression as he followed his mother through the house to the room with the stranger in it. The stranger who was Lachlan McKenzie. The stranger who was his daddy!

Then they were there.

The room was bright with light. Tarleton blinked.

"Lachlan, this is Tar. Tarleton. Your son."

Flanders clung to the boy's hand nervously. Then Lachlan beckoned to him.

"Come here, boy," he said.

Flanders gave the boy a soft push forward, but there was no need. The boy, having been raised without the constraints of "civilization," felt no constraint about showing his feelings. He went directly up to the hero he'd heard about all his life, his father Lachlan McKenzie. He held out his hand manfully as his mother had taught him to do.

Lachlan threw back his head and laughed, revealing the beautiful white teeth that had always attracted Flanders so strongly. Instead of shaking the boy's hand, he swept him into his arms and gave him a hug. The boy, giggling in response to the sudden excitement, wrapped his arms around his father's neck.

"Hello, Daddy," he said. "I'm glad you came back to meet me!"

"What a charmer," Lachlan said to Flanders over the boy's head. Then he set the boy on his knees and said, "Tell me about your life, boy. We've got a lot of catching up to do."

"My name is Tarleton. Tarleton Wilde."

Lachlan raised his eyebrows and looked over at Flanders, but he said nothing. Flanders' heart was beating strongly. The vision of her boy on Lachlan's lap was the most beautiful sight she'd ever seen. It was going to be all right. Everything was going to be all right.

Then her attention shifted as she heard a soft whinny from the yard outside the window.

"Oh, Tar," she said. "Raise the curtain so your father can see what's out in the yard for him."

"You mean . . ." the little boy began, but his mother hissed him silent.

Dutifully, he went over to the window and raised the shade. Bandit's beautiful shape was framed in the glass almost as though it were a large painting of a horse.

Lachlan stared unbelieving.

"Bandit?" he asked.

"Oh, yes, Daddy, I love Bandit. He's nice to me, too, isn't he, Mommy?"

The two adults exchanged glances. Flanders nodded.

"I found him and bought him back for you," she said. "The boy's right. He's the only one who can gentle that horse."

"A sure test for any son of mine!" Lachlan said. "I can't wait to get back on Bandit. And just you wait, Tarleton. I'll teach you how to ride him!"

Flanders felt her face must split apart from smiling. Unbelievably, they were a family. She and Tar and Lachlan.

29

By this time Gil Tylers community was well on its way to becoming a true democracy. Though others who heard of the exploit merely scoffed at it, he believed it was an idea whose time was rapidly coming. Cooperation and community were the only way to survive, he told his fellow selectors. They had held elections and voted him their leader. They'd also decided to name their land with its settlement of clustered housing Tylertown in his honor. Others who saw the random collection of tents and shacks of one sort or another usually called it Shantytown. And despite the bright promise of his dream, Gil Tyler had to admit that they were living in poverty by anyone's definition.

So far, he reminded himself. So far. But better times must surely lie ahead. At least they had thwarted the attempt to drive them into bankruptcy. That had been the hard fate of so many other selectors. Still, when he looked around Tylertown, he had to admit that he and his comrades were living in appalling squalor. Their floors were the earth beneath their feet, the decorations on their walls were cut from newspapers and journals such as the *London Illustrated News* and the *Brisbane Age*. But "poor and honest" had been the fate of many good men, he told himself.

What really troubled him more deeply this February morning in 1867 was the fact that not all the people who shared the land shared the dream as well. He'd closed his eyes to the evidence of "duffing" or stealing sheep and cattle, but he knew it was going on. There were also those men who didn't do their fair share of the agricultural work, but who still claimed full share of the food. Hell, Gil thought, I never wanted to be a governor; I just wanted to be a farmer . . . and maybe a little bit of a philosopher, if I ever got the time.

His reverie was interrupted by the tugging on his leg of one of the children—the community had thirteen adults and thirteen children as well. He pointed out to everyone that thirteen wasn't really an unlucky number; it was a magic number, and that was why it scared superstitious people. Anyway, two of the women were pregnant, so that number would soon change.

"What is it?" he asked the dirty child whose name he couldn't for the moment remember. "Aren't you supposed to be working on the flower bed for my front yard?" He'd tried to assign the smaller children jobs in which they might take some light-hearted pleasure. After all, he told himself, we don't want to become a society of barbarians just because we're poor and have to work hard.

"Well, yes, but there's a lady came to see you. She's waiting for you."

Louisa, Gil thought hopefully. He hadn't seen her for months. He wondered that she would have taken the risk of coming here. But who else could it be? He hurried after the child toward his house, a log cabin that was the most solidly built domicile in Tylertown. As he approached, he saw a woman's form kneeling in front of his porch. She had a trowel in her hand and was hard at work on the flower bed. As she heard him approaching, she looked up with a smile.

"Louisa!" he called out to her.

She stood up then, ignoring the dirt that still clung to her ankle length skirt and ignoring the trowel in her hand.

"I'm tired of being a lady, Gil," she said. Her face still bore a smile, but there was a slight trembling to her lips that gave evidence of how much effort the control over her emotions was costing her.

"Come inside," he said. He took the trowel from her hand and let it fall to the ground. He took her arm and led her into the house. Then, as soon as the door was closed behind them, he took her in his arms and kissed her long and deep.

"I've missed you," he said with intensity. Louisa didn't doubt it—either Gil's love or his loyalty from that first meeting on, even though they had never spoken a word of love nor made any promises.

"I've missed you too. More than I can say. And almost more than I can bear. I don't want to be proper and wait for you to come for me, Gil. When we met, I was a girl on the brink of womanhood, but now I am truly a woman. I hope I am the woman for you because I have come to stay!"

"What are you saying? You can't stay here. Look around you." He pointed to the curtainless windows, the roughhewn furniture, the cupboard with its few cracked dishes. "There's nothing here that's good enough for you."

"There's one thing here that is absolutely good enough for me—the owner! I care nothing at all for possessions. I have lived all my life with possessions and they're nothing to me. Whereas you are everything. Will you have me?" Two circles of color appeared on her cheeks as she gazed shyly up into his face.

Gil took her face in his hands tenderly. This rare flower, this lovely child, this woman, had come to him to be his own. She had chosen him. He felt humble, and for a moment he who always had words ready for any occasion found himself unable to think of a thing to say. He bent to kiss her. Softly he pressed his mouth to hers.

Then he said, "I'll have you and gladly. I only hope you'll never live to regret it. I'll try, Louisa, I swear, I'll try to make you happy."

She kissed his cheek.

"Gil," she said, "you already have!"

He felt such a longing for the sweetness of her that it took all of his will power not to grab her and carry her to the bed. But he knew she was pure, so pure. Just a while ago she was a girl. Now, though she insisted she was a full woman, he knew she was still innocent. He had to control himself.

"Louisa, you know that your father will never accept this. He'll come for you. What then?"

Louisa sat down on one of the two chairs by the small table Gil ate his meals on. She took her time replying, first straightening her skirt and brushing the dirt from it. Finally, she looked up at him.

"I left him a note," she said. "I don't think he'll come looking for me right away. At least not here. I said I wanted to see the life in the city, and I was going to try to make my way in Sydney. I hope I was convincing enough!"

"God, woman, I would never have suspected you of such deviousness. But now what are we to do? Here you are. It's getting on in the day. I can't make arrangements for a wedding at this time of day. What shall we do for the night?"

Louisa's face took on a very womanly air. Almost worldly wise, Gil thought.

"Wedding!" she exclaimed. "Who said anything about a wedding? I've just come to be your mate! You don't have to marry me."

Although Louisa had imagined being married to Gilbert Tyler a thousand times, she had no intention of forcing him into such a condition against his will. She brushed from her mind any misgivings about the kind of spot her just turning up like this might be putting him on. She intended to make it clear that she was a modern woman— that was the phrase she had been reading lately in the magazines from England. She'd read an article in *Blackwood's* just recently on that very topic.

"*I* said something about a wedding, you little fool!" Gil

said. "Of course, I don't *have* to marry you. I don't *have* to let you stay here either. But if I want to spend my life with you—and I do—then it follows that I would want to marry you! *And I do!*"

"Oh Gil." Louisa stood up and threw herself into his arms, almost knocking him off balance. He hugged her to him with so much strength that she cried out, "You're squeezing me to death, love. You don't want to murder the bride-to-be, do you?"

Gil's face paled. "Don't talk of murder," he said. "We're going to have a long, happy life, God willing. That's what we have to concentrate on. But we still haven't resolved the issue of where you are going to spend the night. I suppose I could ask one of the other women to take you in. You wouldn't mind staying with a poor Tylertown family, would you?"

"I would mind anything that kept me away from you."

"But Louisa, be reasonable . . ."

"If I were reasonable, I wouldn't be here in the first place, now would I?"

"But . . ."

"No buts, darling. You can sleep on the bed while I sleep in your reading chair. It looks comfortable enough. Or we can share the bed." At his shocked look, she added, "Like brother and sister, I mean. I've spent my entire life so far sharing my bed with my brother. Then, tomorrow . . ."

"Tomorrow we'll marry. I'll send one of the men off tonight for the preacher. He can be here by tomorrow afternoon."

"Good," Louisa agreed. "You go do that, and I'll see about getting some supper on the table"

Louisa's practicality came as a surprise to Gil, who left his cabin shaking his head in bewilderment. I swear, he said to himself, women are a different kind of creature. I'll probably never understand them.

Then he started to whistle from the sheer exuberance

and delight he felt because this woman had come to share his life. In a matter of moments, his whole world had been transformed, because she was in it now.

The sense of how quickly life can change struck him over and over again during the next few days. Events spun his life into such a whirlwind that for a while he doubted anyone or anything would be able to survive the force of it. It began that very night when he and Louisa made themselves ready for bed. Louisa had come to him with only a little bag full of clothes, including a maroon flannel nightdress that she had always loved. She went into the bathroom to change into it—Gil's house was the only one in the community that boasted such a luxury.

Now she stood before the mirror and surveyed herself as she prepared to return to the main room which contained all the rest of the living facilities. The one room served as kitchen, dining room, living room and bedroom combined. She still wished she were more beautiful, especially tonight. She fretted as she gazed at herself. But the excitement of having run away from home and of being about to spend the night with the man she loved had put a high color in her face that she knew did wonders for her. He certainly seemed to like her as she was, she reflected happily.

She came back out and was glad that Gil had dimmed the lamp down to a soft flicker. He was already in the bed. His chest was bare, which Louisa found exciting in a way she'd never before been excited. Could he be naked under the covers, she wondered. But she knew that couldn't be so. It was he who had insisted they be married at once. Still, she hardly felt she was joining her brother as she crept into the bed beside Gil.

He reached over and stroked her hair.

"Oh, darling," she sighed.

Then he pulled her to him and began to kiss her neck.

"Stop me, Louisa," he whispered. "Pretty soon I won't be able to stop myself."

"I don't want to stop you, love," she said. "What

difference does a ritual make to true love? In God's eyes the words we spoke this afternoon already make us husband and wife, I'm sure.''

Then she kissed him with a kiss at once so deep and passionate and loving, that he could not resist the longing within him. With a sob, he gathered her to him, his free hand working to lift the hem of her nightdress.

His fingers caressed the smooth skin of her legs, her thighs, her soft belly.

''I don't want to hurt you,'' he said. ''Don't let me hurt you.''

Then he stretched himself out on top of her and entered her. She cried out once briefly, but by then he was utterly in the grip of his own fierce desire for her. He thrust himself into her again and again, hoarsely whispering words of passion.

Afterward, they lay in each other's arms in a warm joy of fulfillment. Louisa knew now that they would be together forever, and she felt a serenity she had never known before. Gil felt that there was no problem life could throw at him that he couldn't handle now that he had Louisa by his side. They hardly slept at all that night.

They spent their time between kisses talking about their plans for a life together. Then without their noticing it, the night had passed and light was beginning to fill the sky.

Gilbert leaned over and kissed Louisa's eyelids solemnly.

''Good morning,'' he said. ''This is our wedding day!''

30

THAT same day, Louisa's father demanded to know why he hadn't seen his daughter around for the last twenty-four hours. She'd been a moody soul, he thought, ever since he'd rescued her from that Tyler's shack. Now she'd probably taken to her bed again, pretending to be sick to get out of doing the extra work he'd assigned to her.

His wife Bertha reached in her kitchen drawer and retrieved the letter she'd read and then hidden from her husband's eyes. Now she handed it over to him without a word. She knew from the years of living with this hot-tempered man that there was terrible trouble ahead. As soon as he learned that his daughter had run off, she figured there would be fireworks. And she was right, she realized now, as he pounded his one fist on the table and crumpled the letter in his other huge hand.

"Sydney, my ass!" he shouted. "She's gone off to that no-good bum. He's gone too far this time." He scowled.

"What are you going to do, Harris?" his wife asked nervously.

"I'm going to get our daughter back, that you can be sure of. I'm going to get even with that blackguard, too." He stormed from the room and Bertha could hear him calling some of the men together. Then she heard them clomp into the men's study, off the parlor, and slam the door shut.

"Stephen Gray," she called to her youngest child and only son, who was never far out of earshot.

Almost at once he appeared at the kitchen door.

"Lou's gone away, hasn't she?" he asked. "She's in love."

"Why, Stephen, how do you know that?" his mother asked. She always found herself amazed at how much this child knew. He was the youngest but the brightest, of the three. He was also the one person who was closest to Louisa in every way.

"Did she tell you that?" Bertha persisted.

"No, but I know it's true. She's in love with that selector Dad hates, isn't she?"

Bertha shook her head yes. "Daddy's very upset. I'm worried about what he might do. He's in there," she pointed, "with some of the men—the toughest ones—and they're making plans. But I don't know what plans."

"You want me to find out?" the boy asked, catching on to his mother's idea at once.

Again she nodded, and he scooted from the room as quickly and silently as a ghost. Bertha stood where she was, unable to act further, wondering if she had done the right thing to make the young boy her accomplice. She wanted desperately to help Louisa, but desired just as much not to be disloyal to her husband.

She looked around her at the beautiful kitchen Harris had installed for her when she'd refused to let him bring servants in to do the cooking. He was a good man really, just a bit pig-headed. Well, a lot pig-headed, she admitted to herself. But they'd had a good life. Virginia, their oldest child, was twenty-one now and should really be married. But she didn't seem to attract the men, despite her father's fortune. He'd been talking about setting up a marriage to the son of one of his cronies. Well, that might work out.

Louisa had obviously found her own way. If only Harris could make peace with it. The selectors weren't a different breed of men, just a poorer bunch. But this Gilbert Tyler certainly rubbed Harris Wakefield the wrong way. He wasn't about to share his land with the man, let alone share his daughter with him. So one daughter had no man, and the other one had the wrong man. What a headache it was raising daughters!

But then she thought about young Stephen Gray. What a joy he was! He hadn't given her a minute's worth of real trouble in his whole life. Even when he got older, she couldn't envision him as any kind of troublemaker or hell-raiser. He'd grow up and find a woman and make a good life. She was sure of that.

Then he came rushing into the room, scattering her thoughts.

"Mom, it's bad, what they're planning to do! Real bad!" The boy looked so scared that Bertha's heart began to pound in alarm.

"Tell me quick," she demanded.

"They're going to wait for dark, and then ride over to Tylertown, kidnap Louisa, and burn the place to the ground. What are we going to do to stop them? We have to stop them!"

"I don't know. Let me think a while. Sit down and be still."

The two of them sat at the kitchen table and sank into gloomy silence.

"I could ride over and warn them," Stephen Gray offered.

"No, you might get hurt. Besides, your father would never forgive you. I have to bring him to his senses somehow, stop all of them before they ever leave here. Otherwise we'll have a real tragedy on our hands for sure."

She forced herself to smile at the boy reassuringly, though she was inwardly sick with worry. No need to upset him further. "Don't you worry any more about it," she told him. "I'll talk to your father. He'll *have* to listen to reason."

"Make sure, Mom. They might hurt Louisa by mistake.
I'd kill them if they did that."

Bertha was amazed at the passion in the boy's voice. He
was a true son of "Big" Harris Wakefield after all. Underneath all his tenderness was the same ferocity she'd seen
over and over again in her husband.

"Don't worry," she repeated. "I'll make sure your
father doesn't do anything rash." She spoke with far more
assurance than she actually felt.

But she convinced her son, who stood up at that, gave
her a kiss on the cheek, and said, "Good, I'm going out
for a short ride. Then I'll come back for my lessons."

Smiling after him, Bertha was glad to see him go. He
was best left out of this from now on. Now her hard work
would start. She went over to the stove and put up a pot of
coffee. Then she heard the men filing out of the room
where they'd held their meeting.

"Harris," she called, "come have a cup of coffee with
me, dear."

She heard him whispering final warnings to the men,
and then he came in to join her. His face had the ruddy
glow it often got when he was in the midst of some daring
exploit or other. She pretended not to notice. When they
sat down together, she took a deep breath—and prayed
she'd find the right words.

Meanwhile, the men had been given their instructions
and were preparing the horses for the afternoon's ride.
They were a rough gang who sat about shining pistols and
making sure they had plenty of artillery.

"Sweetheart," she began, as she poured him a steamy
cup of coffee strong enough to make a mouth pucker,
which was just the way he liked it, "I know you have a lot
of pride and that you think of your children as part of
you."

At that, Harris wiggled in his chair uncomfortably and
said, "It's no good, Bertha. You're not going to talk me
out of going after her."

"You have to listen to me this time," Bertha said, her voice dull as she sank into the seat beside him. "No good will come of your riding out with guns a-blazing. Louisa is a woman now. You must treat her that way."

"And how is she to treat me? I'm her father! Did she come to me and talk over her plans like an adult? No. She ran off like a young flibbertegibbet! Why should I treat her like one?"

Bertha realized she was getting nowhere. She decided that she had to try to buy a little time at least—time in which to think over what to do, or time to contact Louisa.

"Maybe you're right," she sighed. "But tonight isn't the time to make a decision. Please let's sleep on it. Then, tomorrow we'll figure out what would be the best thing to do. Together. All right, dear?" She used her best wheedling tone on him.

Harris looked over at her. She was a fine, robust woman. She'd been a boon to his life.

"That's a deal," he agreed.

Bertha took a deep breath. She hadn't realized she'd been holding her breath. "Thanks, darling," she said. "You're a good man when you put your mind to it."

He stood up and walked over to the door. There, he shouted out to the men in the yard, "Hey, you. Hey, Blade. Hold up on those plans we made. We'll talk again tomorrow. Just go on about your work for now."

There was a chorus of "Okay, Boss," and "Right-o."

Bertha happily kissed her husband's cheeks. In return, he gave her a strong hug. She didn't know that he'd told the men to pay him no mind if he seemed to be calling off the plans, he'd only be doing it to gull and pacify his missus. They were to go on without him. He felt certain that in the long run—with Louisa back at home where she belonged—Bertha would be grateful to him for going after her. After all, he'd spent his lifetime making decisions that were in her best interest.

He heard the men talking outside and then split up as

though to go on with their routine business. He knew
Blade would keep things well in hand. Tonight, under
cover of darkness, they'd ride in on Tylertown. And bring
Louisa home.

The night that fell seemed to be part of Harris's plan.
Usually the skies were ablaze with a million points of
light. But this night was totally black, unlit by moon or
stars. This night held only darkness.

31

THE pack of men riding up on Tylertown heard what might have been a shout blown to them by the wind. At first they rode on, thinking it must have been their imaginations. The night stood still, except for the rush of their movements upon it. Then the shout came again—a shout of warning.

Although they didn't recognize the wind-whipped voice hidden by darkness and by the thunder of hooves and by their own pounding hearts, they did realize that their boss's plan was about to be ruined. Blade, out in front of the pack, could just barely make out the shape of the horse ahead. He couldn't see the rider. But he could estimate where the rider was. He raised his rifle.

Stephen Gray, riding to warn his sister, heard the galloping hooves of the men behind him growing ever nearer. He urged his horse to go faster and faster. They were catching up with him. He'd never make it, never. They would force him to go back. They would laugh at him for being just a kid. He kicked at his horse's sides to force that extra speed he needed from him.

"Louisa," he shouted again at the top of his lungs, but the sound barely reached the outskirts of the collection of houses he spied ahead of him. He saw points of light shining at their windows. His sister was there somewhere. He had to warn her, protect her. "Louisa," he shouted again. The wind carried his young voice away.

Then a shot split open the night. A terrifying howl, like
the cry of a wounded animal, pierced the air. It went on
and on. It was like the soul-rending wail of a banshee or
the hysterical cry of the loon.

Louisa, lying in her new husband's arms, thought she
heard her brother's voice calling her name. No, she told
herself, it couldn't be. I'm letting my imagination run
away with me again. Then came the shot and the scream.
She jumped up.

Gil was up too, already fastening his pants and heading
for the door. He grabbed his rifle on the way. Louisa
hurried after him.

Other people were pouring from their huts, shouting and
running. Lights sprang up all over Tylertown. A line of
Tylertown folks began firing at the men riding up on them.

"Wait!" Blade shouted to his men who drew in their
horses and formed a cluster. They were still some distance
from the Tylertown houses. But with all the lights on, they
could see the people armed against them. They could see
Louisa bent over the body of a boy.

"The boss wouldn't like this," one of the men next to
Blade muttered. "Who was that you shot?"

No one answered.

Indecision broke their ranks. Should they go on, grab
Louisa, and destroy any witnesses? Should they go back
and get further instructions?

Now the Tylertown people had formed a line that began
advancing toward them, firing weapons with every step.

"Better go back," the men muttered. All except Blade
who, having committed the unforgivable sin, felt he had
nothing more to lose and might as well finish what he'd
started. But when all the others turned away, his nerve
faltered, and he lingered only a moment longer, glaring
hostilely at the ratty community of selectors. Then he
wheeled around and galloped after his crew.

Louisa bent low over the wounded body of her brother.

"Stephen Gray, my darling," she cried. "Oh, what are

you doing here? What's happening? Gil!'' she shouted, turning toward her husband, who was busy congratulating his comrades. They'd rehearsed for this moment, or a moment just like this one, many times, and he was pleased with how well they had all kept their heads and responded just as they'd planned. Now he hurried to Louisa's side.

"It's my brother," she said. "He came to warn us."

"Help me get him inside," Gil said. "I think he's hurt pretty badly."

There was blood spreading like a grotesque crimson flower across the boy's chest. Louisa's gown and hands were covered in gore where she had held her brother to her. The boy struggled to talk, but there was an ominous gurgling sound to his voice, and he seemed terrifyingly weak.

"Daddy wants you back, Lou," he managed. "He wants to destroy Tylertown."

"Hush, dearest," she urged. "I know, I know. You were very heroic to come and warn me. You've saved my life, I'm sure, and many others as well. But hush, now, brother, while we tend to your wounds."

Gil lifted the slight body in his arms, but the look he shared with the other men who'd gathered round gave away how serious he thought the boy's injuries were. One of the men, the one who knew the most about doctoring, stepped forward and followed Gil into his house. Louisa could hardly bear to take her eyes from her brother's face as she led the way. The others milled around in front of the house, unwilling to disperse until they learned the fate of the boy who had risked everything to come and warn them.

Inside Gil's cabin, the three people bent over the boy, but there was no need for any of them to speak. There was no need for anyone with special medical knowledge to be there, because it was obvious to even the most untrained eye that the boy was losing color and life as fast as he was losing blood.

"Lou," he whimpered, "it hurts me, Lou. I can't breathe, and . . . and . . . I'm scared."

Louisa signaled the men to move away. She could see there was nothing to be done for the boy, and she wanted to have these last few precious moments alone with him.

"Don't be scared, Stevie," she said, using the name she hadn't called him since he was little more than a baby. "It'll be better soon. And I'm right here. I'll sing to you. Would you like that? You used to love to hear me sing."

Stephen Gray nodded, though his eyes seemed to look right through his sister. She bent down, as much to hide her own tears as to kiss his cheeks. Then she straightened back up, swallowed hard, and tried to make her voice as natural as possible as she started his favorite song, "Summer Is a'Coming In." As she finished the first stanza and started the chorus, Stephen's eyes closed.

"Oh, Stephen," she cried. "What have I done to you?"

Gil had come to stand over her, and he now knelt beside her and took her in his arms.

The sobs that came from her spoke of a heartbreak that could never heal. Surely this was the cruellest blow that fate could possibly have dealt her and hers, to rob them of this lovely child!

Finally, though, she stopped weeping. In a much calmer manner, she said, "My father won't stop simply because he didn't succeed this time. When he learns of this, it'll only redouble his fury. Perhaps we should give up. Give up and run away."

"Lou! How can you say such a thing? Run away? How could we live with ourselves? Besides, if your father really wants to find us, there will never be any hiding from him. No, there has to be a better way." He paused, and then asked her as gently as he could, "Did your father love Stephen Gray?"

"Did he love Stephen Gray, you ask? It's the one thing about him I know for a certainty. Yes, he loved him. He adored him."

"Then that's our answer."

"What's our answer? He's managed to kill the thing he loved best." Her voice had taken on a hysterical edge."

"You and I must take the boy's body back. We must show your father the result of his desire for vengeance. 'Big' Harris Wakefield won't feel so 'Big' then. We'll try to make peace with him, but if we can't, then it must be war. But we'll try."

Louisa stood up beside Gil. She took his hand in hers.

"My mother will be our ally, I know, although I can hardly bear to think of what will become of her when she sees the body of her boy."

"Let's go at once," Gil said. "We don't buy anything by delay."

He went to see to the carriage, and Louisa had a last few moments to say her private farewells to the boy who had only so recently been so full of life and promise.

Then, not long after, she was in the carriage with Gil, and her brother's body carefully cleaned and wrapped in cloths in the wagon behind them. They rode across the pitch-black terrain in silence. In each of their hearts was sorrow. And dread of the encounter that lay ahead.

This was to be my first night of wedded bliss, Louisa thought. She wasn't normally superstitious, but she had to struggle not to take this as an evil omen.

Then she spotted the lights that marked her parents' home. It looked as though every light in every building was buring tonight. She knew they must already know that their son was hurt, at least that much. What else they might know or surmise, she wasn't sure.

"Maybe I should go in alone," she said.

"And I should hide behind your skirts?"

She looked over at this almost-stranger who was now her husband. She sensed the power within him. They would face her implacable father together.

They pulled into the courtyard, and she could see her

father standing on the porch. He had a rifle in his hands, which he aimed directly at them.

"Wait, Father," she cried, "It is your daughter, Louisa." Her father lowered his arms.

"Where is Stephen Gray?" he roared.

"With me," she called back.

"And who is that man beside you?"

"Gilbert Tyler, Mr. Wakefield," Gil answered for her.

"You destroyer! You corrupter!" Harris raised the gun again. "You've abused my daughter and you dare to come and face me?"

"Abused? Father," Louisa cried, "we are married! He is my husband."

The carriage had come to a stop less than a hundred feet from the porch where the man stood. Harris began slowly to descend the steps toward them. Bertha came out of the house behind him.

"Louisa," she called, "Louisa, is that you?"

"Yes, Momma," Louisa answered, climbing down from the carriage without waiting for Gil's assistance. She ran to her mother's arms.

"What did I hear?" her mother asked, hugging Louisa to her. "Married?"

"Yes, I am. But there's terrible news to talk of first. Your men, Daddy, shot Stephen Gray!" Louisa tugged on her mother's arm, pulling her toward the wagon where Gil Tyler still sat. At her first sight of her boy in the wagon, Bertha gave a terrible cry. Harris rushed over to her.

"My son!" he shouted, as though he could awaken the dead boy. Then he looked up at Tyler and screamed, "What have you done to my son?"

"I? What have *I* done?" Tyler answered, his rage just barely under control. "It's you! *You* have murdered your own child! *Fool!*"

"Stop it, both of you," Louisa interrupted the two men. "How can you keep up this mindless quarrelling with

Stephen Gray lying there? Can't you, for God's sake, at least control yourselves under the circumstances?''

Louisa's words echoed in the still air. The scene was as age-old as death itself. The death of a child and the grief it brings are so much greater than any words can ever express.

Without comment, Harris held out his hand to Gil, who now stood beside Louisa, his bride. Gil accepted the man's handshake solemnly.

"I love your daughter," he said simply. "I intend to take as good care of her as it's in my power to do."

Harris looked at the man before him. He saw a man of youthful vigor, a man much like the man he had been once. How had life become so warped in this primitive landscape that he had allowed hatred to cloud so completely his eyesight? He looked over at his daughter. She gazed at him with pleading eyes. She was a lovely young thing, but he couldn't overlook the fact that she was definitely a woman now. She had made her choice. He would try not to ruin it for her.

"Live well and happily, daughter," Harris Wakefield said finally. "But I won't let the death of my boy go unavenged. Who is the man who fired the shot that killed my boy?"

"One of yours," Gil answered.

"Who did it?" Harris yelled to the group of men who hovered in the background.

"Blade Parker," a disembodied voice answered, "but he's long gone now."

"What do you mean long gone," Harris thundered.

"He packed his gear and headed out the minute we got back here," another man answered. "I guess he figured his life wouldn't be worth a plugged nickle once you'd found out about young Stephen Gray."

"He can't run far enough!" Harris vowed to everyone within earshot. "I'll track him to the ends of the earth!"

"Father, it won't bring Stephen Gray back," Louisa said pleadingly, laying her hand on her father's arm.

He nodded, but refused to take back his words. He did, though, clutch his daughter to his breast and hold her tight against him as he hadn't done since she was a small child.

Bertha wept openly, her apron raised to cover her eyes. "My baby boy," she moaned. "My precious lambie."

Gil looked down at the earth, kicking at the dust in helpless sorrow and dismay.

Louisa and her father clung to each other in the silence of night, feeling all around them the presence of darkness and death.

32

MR. and Mrs. Edmund Knight had settled in at the Toowoomba estate and taken up their new tasks and their new life as married people with energy and enthusiasm. It wasn't long, in fact, before it seemed to everyone that both the Knights and Lachlan McKenzie had always been a part of the Toowoomba household.

Flanders never dared raise the subject of Lachlan's return to good health, for fear that he would take it as a sign that it was time to leave. Meanwhile, she lived in the glory of these days as though life had at last fulfilled its promises.

Then Anne came to her with other exciting news: she was going to have a baby. Everyone joined in a party to celebrate the coming increase in their number. Flanders found herself praying that Lachlan would still be with her when the baby was born. In some strange way she felt it would be a chance for them to experience Tarleton's birth together. But that was months away. And Lachlan had already started talking about having to get in touch with his backer, the Count.

"Deep thoughts for such a festive night," Lachlan said, coming up to her with a glass of punch.

"How do you know?" Flanders asked, guiltily feeling that he must have read her mind.

"Know? What should I know? I only know that your beautiful eyes were full of sadness just then, and I don't ever want to see them that way."

"Then don't ever leave me," Flanders blurted out impulsively. Immediately, she regretted her words. Nothing would be more likely to scare him off than her urging him to stay. She saw him look away; she dreaded his next words.

"You know I can't stay here forever."

"Why not?" The words burst from her unbidden. They sounded like the broken cry of the kookaburra in her ears. Though other people described that bird's song as a sort of maniacal laugh, she had always heard a demonic wail buried in its heart. That same wail she now heard in her own words and felt in her own heart.

"A man doesn't live off his woman," Lachlan answered with characteristic adamancy.

"Nonsense!" Since she'd already begun this, she might just as well continue it. "A gentleman doesn't go around robbing people either."

He flushed, but then he chose to treat her comment as a joke rather than an insult.

"I may just have given that up," he teased. "I heard from the Count today." He knew that announcement was going to have repercussions, and he had purposely waited to bring it up until they were in the midst of the party, hoping the general air of joviality would defuse her reaction.

"Oh?" Flanders didn't trust her voice to stay calm, so she said no more. Her heart had begun a furious tattoo the moment Lachlan had mentioned the Count. So she was going to lose him again, she thought in anguish. How could she bear it?

"My letter had to chase him quite a ways across Australia. He's finishing up one more race. Then he plans to meet me back in Brisbane. He thought I was dead. Everyone seems to think that, as soon as I'm out of sight, I've gone to my reward. I guess one of the days," he paused and looked across the long terrain outside the window, "they'll be right."

Flanders shuddered.

"Why don't you marry me and make an honest woman of me? Maybe then you could see your way clear to staying here and helping out with the Australian Institute's work."

"No, honey, I have to be my own man. You *know* that, Flanders. But I'd marry you if you want my name for Tar. He's a fine lad."

Marriage wasn't really what Flanders wanted. She'd never been able to see how the arrangement was all that beneficial to women. All she wanted was a means to keep her man close by. But she could see that this wasn't meant to be. No argument could counter his need for freedom. All she could do was wave good-bye to him when he left with as much good-humor as she could muster, and then welcome him back to her arms when he returned. The eternal lot of women, she thought sardonically.

She'd thought she'd eluded that fate by crossing the world on her own, by having a child on her own, by having established a professional life that was the equal to any man's. But no. Not inside, not where it really counted. There she had the same yearning for love and security that ruled all the others of her sex as well. But she'd be damned if she'd give up. Her work would continue to sustain her, no matter what. It *had* to!

"Shall we say good night to the gathered revelers?" she asked. "If our days together are to be so limited, we'd better take full advantage of our nights. She smiled as she said those words, and Lachlan smiled back at her. Their exchanged look spoke more powerfully than their words.

As they walked toward the bedroom, the slightest touch of Lachlan's hand set Flanders afire. The renewed knowledge of the transiency of their time together made her especially hungry for closeness. And as she strained to be patient while Lachlan began the slow and tantalizing unbuttoning of her bodice, a performance that had become a ritual between them, she knew that this night would be like no other they had ever shared. She felt, as she never had before, the full power of her womanhood. She would show it all to her love, Lachlan, that he might admire and enjoy the woman within her that he had created by loving her.

And indeed she was right. There had never been a night of love like this one! It began with a bouquet of tender touches flowering across the landscape of their bodies. Neither of them was in any hurry. They touched, they kissed, and they whispered the tenderest words of adoration they had ever exchanged.

When they seemed to have exhausted the possibilities of this delicious fore play, they discovered new territories yet to be fondled and caressed. Their intimacy was total, their passion unending.

But as all nights must, this one inevitably came to a close. The ensuing days sped by with a terrifying swiftness, and at last Lachlan was gone. He rode off with a wave and a kiss and a promise to come back as soon as possible. Flanders was left once again to consider her life as a woman alone on the Darling Downs in Queensland, Australia.

She was pacing the length of the veranda feeling very dejected about her abandonment when the realization came to her that, in fact, she was far from alone. True, she didn't have her man with her full-time to share her life. But she had established a veritable community.

She counted off the people in her little enclave. There were Elizabeth and Allen first of all. Whatever could she have done without them? The other servants had come and gone, never making much of a mark on her consciousness. But these two were a real part of the Toowoomba homestead. It was too bad they had never had any children. Flanders supposed that Elizabeth was too old now. Well, they were like grandparents to Tarleton, and wasn't he lucky to have them!

Next in the ranks of "family" Flanders thought of Doogalook, who had recently surprised everyone by reappearing from one of his forays into the desert area with a pregnant young girl, Yala, whom he introduced as his "wife." She would have her baby any day now, and that would add a new "citizen" of Tarleton's generation to their ranks.

And Anne Finch, who had been not more than a girl when Flanders first met her, was now Mrs. Edmund Knight and about to have a baby of her own. Anne and Edmund were vital members of the group. Ever since the day of their arrival, they had made themselves useful by innumerable acts around the grounds, but more importantly by their eagerness to pursue the art and excavation work so necessary for the furtherance of the museum Flanders envisioned as her ultimate gift to Australia.

The evening was covering the land with its purple shadows even as she continued her pacing. The change in light called her to herself, and Flanders leaned against the railing to gaze out at the land she had learned to love so well.

She saw the lumpy boulders and low hills that preceded the mountain chain and recalled the unweathered basalt. The bland neutral colors of the basalt ridges, scarps sometimes twenty meters high, rising from the chocolate earth pleased her eye. The soft color of the soil was indicative of the limited rainfall. Further north there was soil so rich and dark it looked absolutely black.

She rested her eyes on a distant stand of trees and pretended she saw Lachlan riding toward her. Thinking about Lachlan again, she smiled to remember the way he had taught her some manly skills during his recuperation. "For your protection when you ride out alone," he'd said. He'd taught her to ride like a man instead of sidesaddle. She loved it and could hardly wait to gallop across the terrain she now surveyed. He'd also taught her to shoot. She was glad to have both those skills. Yes, she decided, the answer to loneliness was work. That was what had always saved her. And she had been neglecting it during these happy days with Lachlan. Now she felt a renewed sense of dedication. Tomorrow she would have to arrange the sojourn into the northern aborigine region that she had wanted to explore.

33

THE seasons passed with their profoundly moving regularity, and Flanders' household increased by two. Doogalook named his boy baby Makatakaba in honor of his tribe's mythic god of fire. It was a very powerful gesture, because life without fire was unthinkable to the aborigines. To name his son thus would make him a powerful man, Doogalook explained. Yala, his wife, agreed, nodding her head and smiling. She hadn't yet learned much English, so Doogalook said everything over twice—once in English and once in his tribal tongue.

Little baby Makatakaba happily nursed at his mother's breast as his father told something of the story of Makatakaba. Tarleton, sitting on his mother's lap, thought how wonderful it was to be named after a god. "Momma," he whispered, "isn't my daddy kind of a god, too?"

Flanders smiled and kissed the top of his head.

A while later, they were welcoming in another new baby, Anne's daughter Krystal. She was so fair that her parents named her after a glass you can see right through. Tarleton found the babies boring at first, but it wasn't long before they were old enough to be his playmates. It wasn't many more turns of the calendar before the three of them— Tarleton, Krystal, and Makatakaba—were as inseparable as the three storybook adventurers who vowed never to part. Tar read parts of it to the others from the magazine where it was printed one section per issue, the tale of *The Three Musketeers*.

"That's us," he urged, "the three musketeers! One for all, and all for one."

It was a childhood vow that was to become a lifelong commitment. Doogalook's son was soon teaching the other two aborigine ways and the tribal tongue of his parents. Krystal passed on the artistry that her mother spent hours teaching her. And Tarleton, the oldest, bravest, strongest, and smartest of the three, taught the others to read and write and make up wonderful adventures which they acted out in their unfettered childhood roamings through the wild landscapes of the Australia that was not only their home, but also the land of their births. The trio of true Australians bloomed with a pride and ease of place that bespoke the enduring strength of this ages-old continent.

Looking at them as they grew toward adulthood, it was hard to realize that the first white settlers had arrived less than a hundred years before, a handful of convicts whose only interest was in getting back to England as fast as ever they could, or at the least, surviving the monstrously brutalizing conditions of their captivity.

Flanders, busy with her endless work, was happy for her occasional visits from Lachlan, who seemed to have thoroughly transformed himself from a bushranger to a racer. She felt the amazement of someone much older than her thirty-five years when she realized that she had been in Australia more than a decade. In fact, almost fifteen years! Only her sense of self-mockery kept her from shaking her head and remarking to Elizabeth that time certainly did fly. Well, Flanders my girl, she warned herself, you're becoming a member of the older generation after all. No way to escape that, no matter how many miles you ride across.

Everyone on the Toowoomba land was busy with the work around which their lives centered, the work of the Australian Institute. Despite the size of the house, the rooms were beginning to bulge with specimens and sketches and reports until it became a household joke that, if you wanted a cup of coffee, you'd better check first to make sure the coffeepot wasn't housing some precious artifact.

Flanders was forced to the realization that she just wasn't going to have enough room to house her collection much longer. More over, she saw that the Australian population was growing and that more and more of the people lived in the cities. She should really think in terms of making her collections available to them, to the city people who were losing touch with the land. Australia had about two million people now, she had heard. The number amazed her—especially when the majority of the continent remained undeveloped, unsettled and uninhabited. But that wasn't the point, she told herself, making herself stay with the idea of moving her collection to a city, although it was a somewhat distasteful idea to her. She loved the rural land best.

She wished Lachlan were nearby; she wanted to talk this whole new idea over with him. Maybe if she were willing to move to Brisbane or Sydney, he'd be willing to settle down with her. She wondered where he was right now. Well, she could wait. Someday soon she would have to make the move, she knew, but not right now. Not this year.

34

As fate would have it, at that moment in the late months of 1872, Lachlan had no time for idle thoughts of love. He'd spent the last ten days racing horses for the Count at a rate that would have tired the most professional rider. He was glad that they would be taking a few days off now, as they moved across the land to the races at Newcastle. He'd had quite enough of Grafton for the moment, but more than that he'd had quite enough of his backside in the saddle of a horse galloping around an oval. He looked forward to the ride south along the New South Wales coast in a carriage like a civilized man.

There would be a group of races in the early months of 1873 that would be worth many pennies. He would win his share, he was sure.

Lachlan and the Count had been making good use of their time together. Lachlan had even opened up an account in a Sydney bank in his son's name, so well had he been doing at earning money.

"Better than the life of the bushranger," he often toasted the Count over their wine at dinner.

The Count would smile and nod. He'd made the best purchase of his life, he knew, when he'd bought this man's freedom. So they shared their fortunes across the continent and across the racecourses of Australia during the early years of the 1870s.

Ever since its earliest days, the racecourse scene had

been a colorful blend of decent folk and outrageous scoundrels. Many a bookie had fled across the commons in order to escape paying off a debt. Many a thief had been caught and punished for the same reason. But neither Lachlan nor the Count took much notice of this skull-duggery. The Count was scrupulously honest in his dealings with gamblers. Lachlan rode so well he had no conceivable need for cheating.

It was doubly strange, then, that they should be brought to ruin by a struggle over a gambling debt. The issue was a two-fold one. First, a snaky little man nicknamed Oiler called Lachlan's win in a race into question. Second, Oiler found a ready ally in a man called B.W., who was the Count's major competitor in the racing game. The year was 1875 and drawing to a close. These races had been scheduled to welcome in 1876.

The Count attempted to laugh off Oiler's charges, and he advised Lachlan to do the same.

"He's well-known as a trouble-maker," he said. "Pay him no mind, and he'll disappear into the woodwork like the nasty insect he is."

Though it went against Lachlan's grain, he allowed the Count to convince him.

Oiler would have come into a good bit of money if he had been able to prove his win against Lachlan, but everyone in racing circles knew that he was a bad jockey and a liar. He was always making claims against some other rider. No one paid him much mind. The prize money had already been awarded and that was that.

Then, though, Oiler convinced a big-time gambler known only as B.W. to join him in taking action against Lachlan and the Count. B.W. had been a rival of the Count's for as long as either had been working the gambling racket. Both were successful at it, but each was leary of the other.

B.W. felt particularly peeved by the Count's latest round of wins. His general dislike had grown into an acute animosity. He'd be glad to see the man brought down. Or vanquished completely, for that matter. So, when Oiler suggested they bring a claim in the magistrate's office—a claim that might force the Count to take off for other parts—he accepted.

"I'll back you, Oiler," he said. "Now shout me to a beer, why don't you?"

The news of the investigation deeply troubled Lachlan. He almost panicked at the thought that it might land him back in prison.

"I'd sooner die than go back to that hell-hole," he insisted to the Count on the eve of their scheduled appearance before the court.

The Count shook his head sympathetically. He'd begun to realize that he was growing too old for this sporting life. This trouble would have once seemed great fun to him, a trouble worth outwitting, but now it seemed merely a bother—an enormous bother. But he'd try to make things right for Lachlan's sake.

Without discussing it with Lachlan, the Count sent a message to B.W., who was nothing if not a gambler, that he would establish a contest of any sort B.W. wished and for any stakes he wished, if only he and Oiler withdrew their suit. It griped him to send this message, as it implied a confession of guilt, and the Count felt no guilt in the matter at all. He knew full-well that he was being swindled front-side and back. Nonetheless, he was enough of a practical man to realize that an appearance in court could do nothing but bad things to both his reputation and Lachlan's spirit. He was willing to settle.

He blanched, however, when he received B.W.'s answer. "I will gladly release my suit against you," B.W. wrote, "if you agree to a duel. Surely a man of honor, such as yourself, would not hesitate to settle accounts in the traditional manner. If you agree, we can make arrangements as to time and place, seconds to stand behind us, and so on. I await your answer. If I do not hear from you in the affirmative by midnight tonight, I shall expect to see you in court at midday tomorrow.''

B.W. was known not only as a man who spent with one hand what he gathered in with the other, but also as the best swordsman in all of Australia. If he agreed to the duel, the Count knew he was signing his death warrant. If he sent Lachlan in his place, then the younger man would surely die. If he refused the offer of appeasement altogether, then he and Lachlan must stand up in court and deny a charge which, though patently untrue, might destroy them both.

He had not shut his eye for a moment by the middle of the night when his answer was expected. The dilemma that faced him filled his mind, driving sleep into some other region where life was fair and innocent people could sleep and have happy dreams.

It was the hour of his deadline when he finally seated himself at his writing desk to formulate his answer. He found that, once he'd dipped his pen in ink, the answer came without any effort at all. The answer took only seconds to write out, in fact. He looked at the message before him as he waited for the ink to dry . . . ink that had the sheen of blood on the white page.

He'd only written two words: ''I agree.'' Nothing more.

Then he went to sleep, having dispatched his note by messenger boy. He went to sleep telling himself that in the morning, along with plans for the duel at some undetermined time in the future, he must see a lawyer about setting out his will. Since it looked like it was almost over, he had to get his life in order. His last thought before sleep was almost a prayer. It was a feeling rather than words, but if he had put it into words it would probably have been: Thy will be done.

The duel was set for New Year's Day, which was only a few days away. As far as the Count was concerned, the sooner, the better. He finally told Lachlan what was going on when Lachlan refused to believe his fabrications about how they had been saved from a court appearance. However, he absolutely forbade the younger man to intervene. He pretended that this was because he was the better swordsman, but they both knew it was because he was the older person and therefore closer to the grim reaper naturally.

On the day of the duel, the Count spent an inordinate amount of time on his toilet. He wanted to look his best. If he could win, he would. If not, he would die in elegant attire. He chose a pleated shirt with a grey sheen to it and paired it with a silver cravat. His black morning coat and his best trousers, the ones with the faint silver line in them, were freshly pressed. Lachlan had taken charge of providing him with the best weapon money could buy.

"However," he said as he handed it over, "I find it preferable to run away and live than look beautiful and be felled by a pompous fool!"

"Nonsense, son," the Count admonished him, "you say that only because you are trying to spare me. In fact, you yourself seem to have always put honor before personal safety."

Lachlan wasn't at all sure that was a valid interpretation of his life, but he was so flattered by it that he held his peace. It might very well have been the highest compliment that the Count had ever paid him. He prepared to be the second, although the Count told him to forget about revenge and get himself safely away from the whole scene before the duel was set to start.

Lachlan was no master at the sword; he relied more on his wits and, at last resort, on a pistol. A sword, he insisted, was a gentleman's weapon. Gentleman was a word Lachlan treated with scorn. To him, it meant a fop, a fool, a poseur. He begged the Count to insist upon a change of weapon up until the last hour. Unfortunately, the Count had been raised to be a gentleman, and so he found himself forced to accept a position that he realized was disadvantageous to him in every way.

"I have written a note which you shall find upon my

person in the worst event," the Count said shortly before the start of the duel, "which grants you your freedom from service to me. It is pure legality, of course, since you have been free during our entire association. Good-bye, dear friend." The Count's voice was shaken by emotion, and Lachlan had to look away to get his own surging feelings under control. Then the arbiter called the combatants into position.

The Count stood regally before the small number of gathered spectators. God, he felt old! Like an ancient. Well, he told himself, it's as it should be to feel old at the hour of one's death. Besides, he might feel old, but he would not let anyone else see that. He held his blade before his face, his other hand fisted behind his back, and saluted his enemy. Then there was the call to begin. B.W. charged in on him. There was no time for anything but a feeble riposte, and then he felt B.W.'s blade enter him with a pain unlike any he had ever experienced. His blade clattered to the ground as the arbiter called a halt. The duel was to be for first blood only. Nonetheless, the Count knew as Lachlan caught him and lowered him to a sitting position on the ground that the blood that gushed from his chest was pulsing with lethal energy. The precious fluid that should be coursing through the avenues of his body was coloring the streets of the town.

"I'll get help," Lachlan said, knowing as he said it that it was of no use.

The Count clutched his hand.

"Stay," he implored. His voice was as pale as his countenance, and Lachlan had to bend forward to hear him. "A friend at a moment like this is far more valuable than a doctor."

Then his eyes closed, his head slumped against Lachlan's shoulder, and the energy that had been the man vanished. Lachlan was left holding the empty shell of the once vital man who had been the only real friend he'd ever had.

Oiler, who had slunk along the sidelines of the crowd to get nearer to Lachlan, laughed.

"Fool," he sneered. "The court case is still on! It was only postponed! Now it'll be your turn, Lachlan McKenzie. The Count was a fool."

Fury coursed through Lachlan's body like a flash flood. As soon as he heard the words, Lachlan felt the truth in them. B.W. and Oiler had set this whole thing up. They had never intended to release the others from the court suit, but the Count was too honorable to have suspected such foul play. Now the Oiler laughed, a high squeal that reminded Lachlan of a rutting hog. Without thought, without a word, without releasing his hold on the Count, without rising from his crouch on the ground, Lachlan reached inside his waistband, withdrew his pistol, and shot the giggling man through the heart. Oiler fell like a stone and was dead before he hit the ground.

Then, in the consternation that followed—amid yells of "Stop that man!" and "Catch him!"—Lachlan leapt to his feet and tore through the street in search of Bandit. He'd tied him to a post not far away. He bounded into the saddle, pausing only long enough for a last look back at his fallen friend, the Count, lying in the dust. Then "On, Bandit," he cried, and they galloped out of the town. He'd be a hunted man again, he knew, but the sweet pleasure of revenge made it seem worth it.

As Lachlan rode, he avoided the most heavily frequented roads. which were the coastal ones. Population in Australia continued to cling to the coast so as to be within reach of life-giving water. Further inland, the availability of water or lack of it could and often did make the difference between life and death. In fact, Lachlan realized, he'd have to watch out for that himself. He'd been a "civilized" man so long that he'd gotten soft. He had to remember the tricks that had kept him alive when he was on the run. He had to remember, and remember fast, or he wouldn't make it.

He headed naturally toward Flanders' place, but that was a long ride away. He headed straight west for a start, along the Gwydir Road. If anyone was setting out in pursuit of him, they'd expect him to head north instead. When he got to Glen Innes, he'd turn north. He might stock up on water there at the same time. It would be a hard ride up into Queensland from the small town in northern New South Wales.

He was already beginning to enjoy the adventurous aspect of it, though. And wouldn't Flanders be surprised! He also looked forward to seeing his boy, Tarleton, again.

If he could just evade any gun-happy fools between here and there. Well, he had his wits about him, and most of his pursuers were witless. He'd manage, he told himself.

Blade Parker was the only enemy who seemed to care much about his whereabouts these days, and even he hadn't been heard of for so long that Lachlan thought he had probably gotten himself killed off somewhere along the line. At least he hoped so.

In fact, Blade Parker had been mostly a drifter since the accidental murder of Wakefield's son, Stephen, which forced him to flee from the Wakefield homestead. He tried to stay undercover as best he could, because he'd heard rumors that Wakefield wanted him dead.

It gave him a lot of time to think.

Yes, he'd had a lot of time to think, but in his case thinking was on a very rudimentary level. He had a head of large proportions but not a lot of mind. In his brutish way, though, he had traced all his troubles back to the first time he encountered that damned bushranger, "Bad" Lachlan McKenzie. Therefore, having nothing more profitable to do with his time, Blade began to track McKenzie. He arrived in Grafton at a time when Oiler's murder was still being discussed. The mood of the times was such, in fact, that although the entire community knew that Oiler was a worthless human being, they felt steps had to be taken to make sure this kind of killing didn't go unpunished. It was time they took a stand for law and order.

As a result, a handbill dotted the area offering a reward for McKenzie "dead or alive." Blade held the paper in his hands, read the descriptions, and smiled. He didn't stop to wonder whether a similar paper was being circulated elsewhere to offer a reward for his own capture. He simply decided that this gave him even stronger reasons for hunting down the bushranger. Now he could gain his personal satisfaction by murdering the cause of all his bad luck— and get paid for doing it in the bargain. Not a bad deal, he figured. He shifted his stogie to the other side of his mouth, spat out the extra tobacco juice, and wiped his thick lips on the sleeve of his checked flannel shirt.

He hung around town long enough to learn that Lachlan had headed north. Then he packed up a long-lasting pile of provisions and started off in that direction. He knew it was a long shot. But hell, he figured, he didn't have anything better to do with his time. He lost the trail as soon as he started into the outback, however, and traveled around more or less aimlessly in the southern regions of Queensland.

Then it entered his dim mind that if he returned to the scene of the first encounter, he might be able to locate some hint of the bushranger's hiding place. It was probably the most intelligent idea that Blade had ever had. And, unfortunately for Lachlan and Flanders, it came to him at the very most deadly time.

Once Blade was back on the road where he'd been bushwhacked, he found it fairly easy to figure out that the mountains must hold numerous caves, and caves would provide excellent hiding places. It might have gone no farther, though, if Blade had not been the particularly vicious person he was. After all, the mountain ranges dividing the coast from the inland was extensive. But he knew he had to stick to the Cunningham Slopes; he figured that, after going through the gap, the outlaw—that's how he thought of Lachlan, but not of himself; such is the blindness of the personal ego—must have stopped some-where pretty close by. So it was in that area that he set up camp. He was patient. He'd learned means of survival. Then an aborigine from Doogalook's tribe happened to pass nearby on a hunting foray.

Blade caught him and bound him. Then he tortured him, as much for the sheer pleasure of it as anything else. Finally, though, he did extract the information he sought— the location of a particular cave where a white man used to make his home. In this way Blade Parker found the cave that had sheltered Lachlan during so much of his life in Australia. The cave had obviously not been used in a long time. Damn, Blade thought, he's probably found a new place. But, since he was already there, it seemed the best course of action to set up the cave as his own hideout. Then he could make his way over to Brisbane and re-provision himself before starting out in some other direction.

35

THE first day of 1877 was ushered in by the most glorious summer weather any Australian could remember. The skies were azure with only a trace of cloud, which only served to enhance the wonder of the sky's clarity. There had been an unusual amount of rain; Flanders counted four days of rain in the last two weeks. She stood on her veranda, breathed in the warm air, looked at the lush greenness of her yard where just a hint of rain caused plants to riot in response, and thought that her happiness was total.

She remembered Lachlan's arrival after his escape from the scene of the Count's death. He'd told her, after the first kisses, that he was a wanted man again. It hardly touched the surface of her joy at having him back. After all, he'd always been a wanted man. She'd made peace with that. And here, in the Downs, she felt sure that no one would touch them. No one would mar their pleasure.

Lachlan had been with her a long enough time now so that she almost dared relax into the comfortable belief that this time he would stay forever. Tarleton would soon be fourteen, and he had blossomed just like one of the plants in the yard in response to his father's attention.

Another blessing she counted, on this glorious morning that was like a demonstration of God's goodness was the work she had just completed with Anne. Together they had designed a portfolio of photographs to display to the scientific community the wonders of the Australian terrain. It had been years in the making, and at times Flanders had despaired of its completion. But at last it was ready to send off along with her accumulated records of cataloged flora and fauna. Her data had been as much a stumbling block as the photographic record. First she had had to complete the work—well, actually it could never be completed; she had simply decided on a point to stop for the moment— then it all had to be laboriously duplicated. She had no desire to lose even one line of it. Sometimes, when she looked at the collection of papers which covered every shelf and filled every drawer in her house, she thought it was the only true account of her life. Everything personal seemed to fall into cracks and disappear by comparison. A sample of Doogalook's work duplicating the aboriginal cave art would accompany the material. Oh, it was all so wonderful! At last the world would have to acknowledge the importance of the work she had been doing and of the place itself—her Australia. She stretched her hands high overhead, letting her head fall back so that her face could feel the full force of the sun's heat.

Lachlan, coming out of the door behind her, admired once again the womanliness of this body he now knew so well. Flanders was wearing a red shirt with yellow stripes, much gayer clothing than she used to wear when he first met her. The shirt was tucked into a pair of wool trousers. She had adopted the male style of dress after he'd taught her to ride like a man. He knew other people might find it strange and unappealing, but he personally found it sexy to see the cloth cup the roundness of her buttocks and to see the slimness of her waist emphasized by the waistband of the trousers. Now, as he watched her stretch like a cat, he felt a yearning to make her his once again. It was wonderful how his desire for her never diminished. Lately he had begun to think that his life with this woman, Flanders Wilde, was the best thing he could ever have been lucky enough to experience. He had just about decided to stay here, help with her work and the work around the land—

maybe capture and train some of those wild horses that still ran free across the inland plains—and marry his woman! Yes, he felt quite sure that was what he wanted to do. He wanted to make Flanders and Tarleton truly and legally his own.

"Good morning, woman," he said gruffly, coming up behind Flanders and putting his arms around her waist. She slid around in his arms to face him. Her arms curled around his neck. The smile she greeted him with warmed him more than the sun shining down from the heavens.

"The package leaves today!" Flanders' voice held the excitement she had just been feeling about the work she was about to send off to England, but it was intensified by the excitement she always felt when she was close to Lachlan. While he, with his greater experience, found their continued delight in each other a source of wonder, she accepted it as the natural course of events. Lachlan was the only man she had ever loved and given herself to. He kissed the soft spot directly behind her ear.

"You're so tender," he whispered, his voice revealing to her the passion that was growing in him.

"Lachlan," she teased, "we've just barely gotten dressed. Do you really want us to get all undressed?"

He didn't answer, but simply nodded. And smiled. The smile had just a glint of wickedness in it, Flanders thought. Just a hint of the special knowledge they shared of each other's delights.

She took his hand and began to lead him back into the house. He followed willingly, unbuttoning his leather vest as he walked. When they were alone in the room that used to be Flanders' but which they both now thought of as theirs, he grabbed her to him and pressed his mouth to hers. The urgency in the kiss startled Flanders, who immediately began to suspect that he was planning to tell her he was taking off again. But this time, she was to learn, he had quite other issues in mind. Meanwhile, she gave herself wholly to the moment's kiss. His tongue probed the inside of her mouth. His hand crushed her bosom within the confines of her red shirtwaist. It was as though they'd just come back together; it was like the night he returned to her after the Count's death. What it wasn't like was the ardor of a man who had risen from her side just hours ago.

"Lachlan," she urged, "is something wrong? Dear love, you can tell me anything, you know. You are my very soul. Nothing is forbidden!"

"Nothing?" Lachlan asked, mimicking her serious tone of voice.

She drew him with her to the bed where they sat side by side.

"Of course not." Flanders reached up and stroked the dark hair that curled low on Lachlan's neck. Her other hand rested on his thigh. She'd grown bold during this last visit of his. She was often the one who urged him to come closer to her in the night. But now his strange mood intimidated her. She wasn't sure what he wanted.

He reached over and pressed her to the bed, leaving no doubt about his intentions. But even as she felt his hand slide inside the waistband of her trousers, touch the flesh of her stomach and then move further down, even then she knew it wasn't just lovemaking that he wanted.

"Wait a minute," she urged, "and I'll get these clothes off." She slid out from under him and hurried to get her clothes undone. Unmoving, lying on his back on the bed, one arm propped under his head, he watched her. The strange smile had returned to his face.

"You're making me self-conscious," she whispered. "Why are you staring at me instead of getting undressed? Lachlan . . ." Laughing, Flanders advanced on the seemingly imperturbable man sprawled across her bed. His smile broadened, and he spread his arms wide to receive her as she flung herself naked on top of him.

"Now I've got you in my power," he teased. "You're undressed, and I'm not. Cool as a cucumber!"

She reached down her hand and grasped the bulge that was evident through his tight trousers.

"Cool as a cucumber?" she asked.

He joined in her laughter, then the laughter faded away from both their faces as he rolled over on top of her. She began kissing him ardently, and she felt she couldn't kiss him fully enough, deeply enough. She could never get enough of this man, she thought exultantly. Then she felt him loosening his clothes with his free hand, all the while continuing to kiss her lips and her neck and her breasts. The bed beneath her felt like a cloud, and she thought she had somehow been transported to heaven. Then their bodies were touching, flesh to flesh.

"I love you more than I can ever say, Lachlan."

Without answering her, he began the slow thrust that was a prelude to their most thrilling peaks of passion. Like a storm at sea, the waves grew higher and higher until they were lost within them.

In the silence and ease that followed their passion, a silence that felt like the desert at night, Lachlan spoke what was in his heart. He spoke the words he had practiced and rejected over the miles and over the years. He spoke the words that Flanders had never expected to hear from him.

"You are my woman," he said, "for good and always, but I would like you to be my wife as well."

"What?" Flanders asked, unable to believe the words she had just heard.

"Will you marry me, Flanders, and make us a family? Make Tarleton Wilde into Tarleton Wilde McKenzie? Make Flanders Wilde into Flanders Wilde McKenzie? Make Lachlan McKenzie into less of a fool than he has been during most of the fifteen years we have known each other?"

Suddenly, having finally uttered the thought, Lachlan felt terrified that he had revealed too much. He should have adopted a more teasing tone. What if she rejected him? But he didn't have to wonder long, because Flanders leaned over to place her lips next to his ear and whispered, "If that is not just temporary insanity speaking, I accept!"

"Oh God, Flanders," Lachlan exploded, grabbing her face in his hands and kissing her lips tenderly. "If it is anything, it's sanity at last! I don't know what has been the matter with me all along. This is what I want from life. Just you and my son and the pleasure of days like this one."

"Wonderful! When shall we do it?"

"Oh, I don't know. I never thought beyond asking you. The practical stuff never entered my mind. What do you think?"

She frowned, trying to think, which was hard to do, not only because of the immensity of the issue thrust upon her so suddenly, but also because Lachlan, enjoying her discomfiture, was lazily but provocatively stroking the silky softness of her inner thighs.

"You're distracting me," Flanders said, feeling new heat rising in her.

"I know," he answered, leaning over to nibble at her hardening nipples. "Come here and give me a kiss." Soon they were enveloped by passion once again, and it was hours before their talk could resume.

Once they'd come back down to earth, Flanders proposed that they marry on Tar's birthday, which was coming up soon.

Lachlan nodded seriously. "If he doesn't mind sharing his day with us, that sounds good to me. Also, I won't have another date to remember. Just one present for each of you on the same day."

"Hah!" Flanders sneered. "I won't hold my breath until I get a present from you!" And on that teasing note, she jumped up from the bed, trounced over to the heap of clothes lying on the floor where she had dropped them in her earlier haste, and began to dress.

Lachlan followed her example.

"You know what I'd like us to do to confirm our engagement? Here, grab hold of this bedspread and let's shake it smooth, so we don't absolutely scandalize the entire household."

"As if we haven't already," Lachlan answered. "No, I can't imagine what you want us to do. It would be unlike you to want an engagement ring, so surely it's not that."

"Dummy! Of course, it's not that. I thought we might go back to your old hideout and spend the night. Relive our first night together. What do you think?"

She went over to him and blew a kiss in his ear.

"I think, my dear lady, that you are a hopeless romantic. That's what I think. And despite your scientific mind and your masculine attire, I think you're a big fraud. Under that professorial surface, you are really a mushy schoolgirl."

He held up a finger forbidding interruption as Flanders, hands on hips, began a tirade in self-defense.

"I also think," he added, "that it's not a bad idea. Let's go there as soon as your big shipment is safely underway. That will be a good time for you to take a break anyway, right?"

"Right! I'll talk to Elizabeth about packing us a super-special basket of provisions so we can feast on other things in addition to love. We'll leave tomorrow. I can hardly wait!" Flanders blew him a kiss and left a totally happy man in the bedroom that had become their paradise.

The next day was as glorious as its predecessor had been. They decided not to take the coach, preferring to ride along together like the two comrades they were. The saddlebags were full of the goodies that their faithful Elizabeth had made when she heard where they were going and for what reason. She looked forward to another marriage taking place; she was always glad of an excuse to celebrate.

Lachlan, noticing that Flanders was wearing a gun in a back holster on her belt, asked her why she had taken a weapon along.

"You may be getting too rough and tough for me," he said. "I'd better not turn my back on you."

"I'm wearing it because you taught me always to be ready for anything. Didn't you? Besides, I noticed you readying your pistol, and I thought that meant I should bring mine along as well." She haughtily lifted her aquiline nose in the air and spurred her horse on so that for a while they rode with Bandit's nose close on Sunny Day's tail. Then Lachlan caught up with her and reached over to tug gently at the reins held tightly in Flanders' hands.

"Hey," he said, "this is a joyful trip. Let's not kill the horses or ourselves, what do you say?"

Flanders let Sunny Day slip back into a trot.

"Right you are," she agreed. "All joy this trip."

They rode on in silence, enjoying the day and the closeness they felt to each other. Gradually, though, the familiarity of the road brought back thoughts of their first encounter to Flanders' mind. The initial terror that she had felt when the unknown bushranger stopped her coach. She remembered how the night had transformed her feelings toward the dangerous man who had taken her as his prisoner and had brought her the first experience of love . . . the night that turned her from a maiden into a woman. She shuddered suddenly, as the face of "Blade" Parker flashed into her mind. She remembered disliking the surly brute at first sight. Then she'd found that feeling reinforced by the way he beat his horses. She remembered the last time she'd seen him—in that bar—vowing revenge against Lachlan. She shuddered again, and tried to put that idea from her mind. Why had his memory come back to haunt her, she wondered. Then she decided it must simply be because they were traveling the same roads. Returning to the same spot. Reliving that night. Reasons enough, she assured herself. No cause for any alarm.

As the two riders came in sight of the cave, they accelerated to a controlled gallop. The sound of the horses' hooves alerted Blade, who was still making the cave his

home. He hid behind a boulder in order to see who might
be approaching. He could hardly believe his eyes when he
saw that the riders were none other than Lachlan McKenzie himself and that same crazy woman who had been his
passenger in the coach so many years ago. Or at least it
looked like her. Although, from the way she was dressed
and from the way she was riding, it was impossible to tell
for sure. Blade would have laughed at her mannish appearance if he hadn't been busy instead taking aim at the rider
he knew for a fact was "Bad" Lachlan McKenzie, the
very man he sought.

If vanity didn't forbid, he could have shot them both
dead without their ever knowing who had undone them.
But Blade, while cunning enough to make sure he would
come out the winner, couldn't resist the desire to let
Lachlan know that the man who had brought him down
was none other than Blade Parker, avenging an ancient, but
still rankling humiliation. As the riders approached, Blade
stood up from his hiding place with his pistol aimed at the
spot exactly between Lachlan's eyes.

"McKenzie," Blade called. "Say your prayers. Blade
Parker has come for his revenge!"

As Lachlan reached for his gun, a single shot exploded
from the tip of Blade's pistol. His aim was deadly and
true. Without a word, Lachlan pitched forward in the
saddle.

Blade, savoring his triumph, strode toward his victim
and the woman who had always been so scornful of him.
Well, he'd shown them both. Blade Parker might be down,
but he wasn't out. He was having the last laugh and he
was going to enjoy it!

Flanders, confused by the suddenness of the attack and
suffused with concern for her Lachlan, had nonetheless
been well enough trained by Lachlan so that she'd
unholstered her own gun secretively. Then, as Blade called
to her, "Hey, lady, I guess I'm going to have my turn

under your skirts after all,'' she emptied it into the body of the gloating Parker.

As he fell, Parker had a dim awareness that it was the woman who had shot him, not the man. But how could that be, he wondered. It had never entered his mind that she would present any danger to him. He had only worried about the man. Then his eyes closed; it was his last error in judgment.

Meanwhile, Flanders had jumped from the saddle and eased Lachlan to the ground. The horses, skittish and upset, still stayed close by their owners. Lachlan's eyes were wide open, staring into the sky, staring into eternity, but seeing nothing. Flanders knew, even before she bent over him trying to find a pulse, that he was dead. The bullet hole, a clear red circle in the middle of his forehead, hardly bled. Flanders clutched her lover's body to her. A kind of keening sound came from her, but she shed no tears. This moment seemed foretold somehow. In its inevitability lay its true horror. She half-remembered a line of poetry that Lachlan had taught her . . . something about thoughts that lie too deep for tears. That was how she felt now as she held her first and only love dead in her arms.

36

THE morning of April 10, 1877 held a heaviness in the air that spoke of a coming storm. Tarleton opened his eyes and saw that, although the sky was grey, it was definitely morning. I'm fourteen now, he thought. Almost a man. He jumped out of bed and dressed as quickly as he could. He and Krystal had planned to get up before the rest of the household and sneak away for a private outing. It would probably be their last chance to have time alone together because most of the day would be devoted to party activities and the next day Tarleton would be leaving for Sydney with his mother for who knew how long.

Fourteen, Tarleton thought as he tucked his wool shirt into his pants and fastened his belt. He dressed now in conscious imitation of his father. He put on his father's leather vest. His mother had given it to him after they'd buried Lachlan McKenzie in their cemetery plot. One of the things he wanted to do today with Krystal was go and visit his father's grave. He wanted to tell his father good-bye, and he knew Krystal wouldn't laugh or make fun of him. Even though Krystal was young, still a little girl really, she seemed to understand Tar as nobody else did—not even his mother. That was the other item on his agenda for today: to tell Krystal how much she meant to him before he said good-bye to her.

As he hurried to their pre-arranged meeting place out behind the house, he heard the guttural growl of thunder, felt a chill wind prick his face. Winter was coming. There could be no doubt about that. The cold, stormy aspect of the day pleased him in a perverse way. It felt as much like a day of endings as a day of beginnings, and he had been sent serious weather for a serious day.

He saw Krystal huddled beside a tree, clutching her sweater around her.

"C'mon," he said, and they both began to run toward the beautiful oasis Flanders had created to be Lachlan's last home.

There, hidden from the house by the large tree that formed the center of the memorial space, Tarleton knelt beside the stone that marked his father's grave. He beckoned Krystal who fell on her knees next to him. The two children wore somber expressions. Thunder filled the air again, and Krystal grabbed Tar's hand. She'd always been afraid of thunderstorms.

"It's all right," he said, holding her little hand in both of his. Then he turned his attention back to his father's grave.

"Dad," he said aloud, "I wish you were here to see me on my fourteenth birthday. I hope that, wherever you are, you can hear me. I love you. I want you to know, before I leave for Sydney with Mom, that I'm going to take your name. From now on, I'll be Tarleton Wilde McKenzie. I already spoke to Mom about it, and she likes the idea. I'll try to make you proud of me."

As he spoke these last words, the sky burst with another enormous clap of thunder and seemed to split in pieces. Krystal screamed and leaped to her feet. Tarleton stood up too and looked at the sky which was almost pitch black now. Suddenly, huge rocks began to fall all around them. Marbles of ice. Hail!

"Let's run for home," Krystal said, but Tarleton caught her hand before she could turn and start to run.

"Wait," he shouted over the loud wind that had come up. "There's something else I have to do. I have to tell

you something.'' The two children stood frowning across
the mere inches that separated them, buffeted by the wind
and beaten upon by the hailstones.

"What is it?'' she asked.

"Krystal, you're my best friend in the whole world.''

"You're my best friend, too.''

"What I mean is,'' the boy stumbled on, not sure how
to express the new feelings he was having. "Even though
I'm going to be far away for a while, you'll still be my
special friend. And someday. . . .''

"Tarleton! Krystal!'' They could hear Elizabeth's voice
calling them through the wind's howl.

"What is it, Tarleton?'' Krystal asked.

"Nothing, I guess.''

"Go ahead,'' the girl urged. "Tell me.''

"Someday we'll be together again. And then I want us
to be together forever. I want to take care of you, Krystal.
I want . . .''

"Krystal! Tarleton!'' The voice came again, more insis-
tent this time.

Tarleton grabbed Krystal's hand and started back toward
the house. By the time they made it to the veranda, they
were both soaked.

"Shame on you children,'' Elizabeth scolded. "I swear,
Tar, if it wasn't your birthday, I'd whip you.''

Tarleton laughed at Elizabeth acting mad. He knew she
really loved him too much to whip him. Besides, he was
too big for whippings anymore. At his laugh, Elizabeth
boxed him playfully on the ear.

"Get in here, you two, and I'll make you some hot
chocolate.''

As soon as Elizabeth turned her back, Krystal tugged on
Tarleton's arm. He looked at her and she pulled him
closer.

"I promise,'' she whispered. Then she kissed him shyly
on the lips and ran into the house after Elizabeth.

The rest of the day followed the plans that Flanders had

made. There was a party where everyone gave Tarleton a present of some sort, and Flanders tried not to think about the fact that this was supposed to be her wedding day.

After the party, she reminded Tarleton he had to finish his packing, and she used the same reason to excuse herself. It was a relief to be able to escape the festivities and be alone. And, of course, she did have last-minute packing to do.

She had decided that it was time to open a museum in Sydney to house the Australian Institute. The very idea excited her, and she had to do things to keep herself interested in life, now that Lachlan was gone. There was nothing she could do to bring him back; he'd also never be any further from her than her thoughts and dreams. But she had to go on with the work she'd devoted her life to. Otherwise, nothing made any sense.

If she spent the next months getting everything in order, with Tar's help, of course—she was determined that he would learn the meaning of work in a good cause—she hoped she could open to the public by the beginning of 1878. Anyway, that would be her goal. Anne would be in charge of continuing the work on the Toowoomba end. Now that transportation between Toowoomba and Sydney had improved, they would be able to stay in fairly close touch with each other. Then she'd have the whole Toowoomba community invited to the Grand Opening. Ah, she smiled in satisfaction, imagining the glory of that moment.

But then she forced herself to put future thoughts aside and concentrate on what had to be done this moment in order to be ready to leave the following morning.

The trip itself was exhausting. First they had to take the coach over to Brisbane, and then they had the long journey by rail from Brisbane down to Sydney. Luckily, Tar was full of the excitement of the thousand sights he'd never before seen. Even when Flanders drifted off into a dream or busied herself with reading reports in scientific journals, the boy had no problem keeping himself amused. Just watching the myriad changes in the landscape outside the train window fascinated him. Not to mention the characters he got a chance to talk to. Why, he'd never known so many strange people existed. It seemed that everybody had a different way of looking at life in this remarkable world.

Watching him make conversation with strangers in an easy, natural way, Flanders was proud of him. She was also glad that she had made the decision to take him with her to Sydney. It was time for him to become a bit more cosmopolitan. He'd been raised in a completely protected environment, after all. Now he'd have a chance to see a different pattern of life. Australians recognized the schism between country and city in their expression, "Sydney or the bush!" Well, Tar had seen plenty of bush life; now it was time for him to have a go at Sydney. It was time for him to learn the way a gentleman behaves and dresses and so on, she thought, looking at the rough country way he was currently clothed. She herself had, of course, reverted to feminine styles and a city mode of dress. She wore a coral silk dress with an ankle-length skirt. It felt strangely sensuous to have petticoats flouncing around her legs, to hear the rustle of silk when she moved, and to be conscious of the fullness of her breasts as they strained against the fitted bodice with each breath she took. When Tar had first seen her dressed up this way, he'd been quite flabbergasted.

"Gawr," he'd mumbled. "Ain't you too beautiful to be my mum?" Then, embarrassed, he'd hung his head.

But Flanders had only laughed and kissed him.

"Just you wait and see all the changes in store for you during the next year," she'd said.

Remembering that now, as they rode through the night to the clickety sound of the wheels on the tracks, Flanders smiled and patted the cheek of the boy who'd fallen asleep against her shoulder. In the morning they should be arriving in Sydney. Her excitement at the prospect grew with each mile that passed.

They got there on a Saturday. That meant the narrow thoroughfares were crowded with strollers of every description. The boy and his mother wandered along Pitt Street and George Street and took it all in. Tarleton dragged his mother over to every shop window, so amazed was he by the vast array of goods offered for sale. Newsboys were noisily hawking the latest array of troubles spread across the latest edition of the paper. There were architectural wonders of iron and glass and granite fronts. When the two tourists at last made their way to the Adams Hotel, they were only too happy to spend a quiet time cloistered away from the hubbub.

Their respite was to be a brief one, because Flanders was eager to do as much work in as little time as possible toward the opening of the Australian Institute. She found the change of environment from the outback to the city amazingly envigorating. Although she had always been an energetic woman, she was absolutely indefatigable now. Tarleton found himself pressed to keep up with her, particularly since his days had never before been so strictly supervised. Gone were the lazy lounging afternoons. Gone were the easy mornings playing with his two friends or riding out into the dry desert lands. Now the schedule was set by Flanders, and her pace was full-speed ahead.

She arranged for them to be awakened by one of the hotel staff at five a.m. She was in the dining room having her tea by five-thirty, and she told Tar that she expected him to join her no later than six o'clock. At that time they made their agenda of the day's activities. Frequently their chores took them in opposite directions. Then they would not re-unite until supper which Flanders set late, in the European fashion, at eight at night. There was so much to do that she hated to call a halt to the day even then. But she knew that, for her own sanity as well as Tar's well-being, she had to leave them some time for relaxation and pleasure.

She was pleased to notice how quickly Tarleton assumed a more manly air, accepting the responsibility that was given to him. Within a matter of months she was able to talk to him like a colleague in an enormous venture, rather than as a mere child helping out his mother. Although he was only fourteen, he had a man's appearance, she saw now, as he began to dress the part. She also noticed how strikingly he resembled his father. At times she had to close her eyes to calm the pounding of her heart when she saw him across a room. Her son, she thought, her beautiful son. The ghost of Lachlan McKenzie alive and well.

Tarleton was six-feet tall and had a mass of dark curly hair that framed his face. His hair, once so fair, had darkened with the passing years, so it was now almost exactly the color of his father's. He had a broad forehead that bespoke a directness of manner, which was confirmed by his behavior. He hadn't yet fully grown into his features, but she could see that he was going to be as handsome as his father had been. A good sturdy man, he'd be, with a good mind.

These were happy days that they shared as 1877 sped toward its close. Busy and happy. Flanders felt it was probably her first chance to get to know her son as a person—maybe her last as well, since she thought he would probably marry young and leave her. His attachment to Krystal hadn't gone unnoticed by her. That was another reason she had been glad for this Sydney sojourn. They were both still children. They both needed time to grow up and to meet other people. Then, if their future was meant to be together, there would be time enough.

She was proud of Tarleton for the work he was doing, and she tried to make him aware of that. He grinned and ducked his head, surprised by his mother's compliment.

Flanders advertised in the *Sydney Morning Herald* for

workers to help her ready the building she had decided upon. Rather than start a new building project, she found a large hotel that had gone bankrupt and stood empty for more than a year. She was able to make a good deal, she thought, although it almost exhausted the last of her inheritance. Well, the homestead was just about self-supporting now. Besides, she couldn't think of a better way to spend the money than to bring Australia—the truth of the land's creatures—to the attention of other Australians.

Now the days were full of hammering and sawing and the rich smells of newly cut wood. Right before her eyes, the reality of her dream was taking shape. It had taken close to twenty years, but she could hardly believe in its actuality anyway. At times, standing in the doorway watching the workers busily arranging shelves and plastering walls, she felt truly blessed. Thank you, Lachlan, for love. Thank you, God, for my life. Those prayers came to her lips unbidden.

She could see that her original plan of an opening before the start of 1878 was unrealistic. Everything took so much more time than she ever anticipated. Even after all these years, she thought ruefully, she hadn't learned that she couldn't always bend reality to her will. Well, it was an inclination that had usually stood her in good stead nonetheless. Sheer faith and will power had brought her this far. She supposed it would carry her the rest of the way. The Australian Institute would open before 1879. Or early in 1879. That she was sure of.

She already had one section complete enough architecturally so that she and Tarleton could spend their days with him uncrating material from Toowoomba and her labeling and arranging the material. That first room began to look like a real museum. Not the British Museum perhaps, but nothing that anyone need feel ashamed of either!

Local citizens began to stick their heads in to find out what was going on. Flanders was always happy to take time out to talk to them about her ideas. After all, wasn't that the real purpose behind the museum? To get Australians deeply interested in their varied and unique land?

One of the people who began to stop in on a fairly regular basis was Rosie Sullivan, Anne Finch Knight's adopted mother. At first she came mostly to hear the latest news of her darling daughter Anne and her granddaughter Krystal. But then the two women began to become friends. Flanders, after all, knew no one in Sydney except for Tarleton. It was pleasant to be able to chat with a friendly woman. And they both loved Anne. So they had a common interest. As time passed, the friendship grew, much to both women's surprise and pleasure. Rosie was now the general manager of the Red Raven Saloon, which had, as a by-product of a new Sydney sense of propriety, become transformed into quite a posh establishment, happy to forget altogether its former existence as a brothel. Flanders and Rosie spent many delightful evenings trading stories of their earlier lives, as different as those lives had been. Rosie spoke of Bart, the bartender, who had tried for so long to make Rosie his wife and had finally abandoned the idea and taken one of the young girls from town as his bride. Now he lived in the suburb of North Sydney and seemed to have settled down happily enough to raising kids and crops. Rosie only saw him on an occasional Saturday night in town. When she did, she confided to Flanders, it was almost like seeing a ghost from another life.

Rosie also brought Flanders up to date about Charlie Burrows. "Well, he's got his come-uppance," she said with no real animus. With Edmund's help his wife went back to England. Since then, Charlie's been a loner. He even finally came to me and said he should have married me when he had the chance. Said, 'How about it, honey?' Can you believe it? Well, after the way he'd acted toward my little Anne and his own Edmund, I wouldn't have touched him with a ten-foot pole."

Flanders enjoyed hearing these tales of a life so full of

colorful adventures and men. My goodness, the men Rosie's known, she thought, more than a little incredulous. But the woman was so natural and so good-hearted, it was hard not to be charmed by her. And, in fact, Flanders was charmed.

These evenings helped her pass the time between one day's work at the museum and the next. For, in truth, now that it was getting ever closer to the opening date, Flanders was becoming almost hysterically obsessed with the Australian Institute.

She'd actually set the opening date at last. Founder's Day was always celebrated on January 26, and Flanders decided that would be the perfect occasion for her to open her doors to the citizenry. January 26, 1879. The Institute would be available to everyone free of charge. She hoped that many people would decide to satisfy their curiosity during their holiday by stopping in. She had sent word of the date to the Toowoomba household and expected everyone to arrive in good time. Now it was mostly a matter of waiting. That was almost harder than the twelve-hour work days she'd been putting in.

37

DURING these strange, dreamlike days of waiting, Flanders had an unexpected and thrilling bit of news. An official packet arrived for her which was covered with seals and ribbons. The return address indicated that it was from the British Society. Flanders held it in her hands tentatively, as though it were an explosive and the slightest disturbance might set it off. In fact, she realized the explosiveness—if she were to state it accurately—lay within herself. She remembered all too clearly the devastating effects of the last missive from the scientific group, the devastation she'd felt at the suicide of her professor, the rage against the fools who had hounded and under-valued him so. She had buried these feelings within her, but had never completely gotten over them. Now this new document had appeared. Her hands trembled, and she felt that, if she didn't sit down, she would faint.

She placed the package on the table and stared at it. Perhaps she should call Tar to come and be with her. But then what if it were more foolishness? Foolishness which cast doubts on her competence and integrity again. She wouldn't want her son to be exposed to that. She had too much vanity not to want him to see only her successes. Especially now, with the greatest one of all about to take place. No, she didn't want Tar nearby.

Oh, if only Elizabeth had arrived, but it would probably be another week before that happened. She couldn't sit and stare at the unopened material for a whole week! She'd be mad by then, if she even tried it, she was sure. Flanders my girl, she lectured herself, as she had so many times over the years when she began to lose courage, get a hold of yourself. How could they hurt her more than they already had? They really couldn't hurt her at all anymore. She was far from the naive girl she had been when she'd sent out her first materials so many years ago.

Flanders stood up and walked over to the lovely dressmaker's mirror that stood on the floor near her closet. There she was—herself—the familiar stranger! That's how she'd always felt about her image in the mirror, and the years hadn't changed that. That woman in the glass, that woman was in her forties now. Why did the inner person still hold the memory of an eighteen-year-old girl? Why did her heart still feel the pulsing of that first passionate night with the desperate, crazy bushranger, Lachlan McKenzie? Her hair had gray strands like streaks of cloud in it now, but otherwise it was the same thick hair he'd reached over and taken the combs out of that first night to watch it flow free down along her bare shoulders as he reached for her naked body. Flanders trembled now, remembering.

She was thicker in the waist now, but still had the definite hourglass shape that caused plenty of men to turn around in the streets and gaze at her appreciatively. Well, put those thoughts away! That part of her life was over now. Still, it was nice to know she was still woman enough to put a little fire in a man's loins. Flanders! Shame on you, she scolded herself, and turned away from the glass.

The packet on the table seemed to leap into her view. She couldn't put it off a second longer. Like a greedy child about to unwrap a box of chocolates, Flanders tore at the papers, not even pausing to preserve the official seals.

Honourable Flanders Wilde, it said.

That's how it was addressed!

Honourable Flanders Wilde.

Flanders drew in an enormous breath and sank down into one of the chairs. Her eyes quickly scanned the rest of the document. Remarkable, they said. Remarkable achievement. Further on there was some mention of an award. Someone was being sent to be at the Institute's opening and present her with an award for distinguished service to the scientific community. "Nothing like your work has ever been seen before in the annals of science. Not only the remarkable creatures you reveal to your colleagues through your work, but also the stunning beauty of your photographic plates."

There was more, but Flanders put the vellum papers back down on the table. There would be time to read it later. Time to read and re-read it, as she was sure she would do daily for the rest of her life. For now, it was enough to know that she had proven the worth of her work. She had justified her life's work in the eyes of the world.

The amazement of every day in this remarkable land of Australia was enough proof for her. Now everyone would know. People would come to see the Australian Institute and then go out into the outback and see the wonders for themselves. That's what she hoped would happen. She allowed herself a few more minutes in idle dreams before she forced herself out of her delightful reverie. It was time to make sure everything was in order for the grand opening.

She could hardly wait to show Anne the letter. Her name was mentioned, of course, as the photographer. She must make sure that somehow she found grant money so that Anne could go to England for a while. Anne could hardly recall that distant homeland. She and Edmund had never had a proper honeymoon. This would be the perfect trip for them. There was mention in the document of a sum of money that went along with the award. That would be the money to finance their trip. Yes, in her own mind that was settled. All she had to do was convince Anne and

Edmund. That shouldn't be too hard. Krystal would find it the best sort of education, too. Travel always was. She laughed at herself as she thought that. She hadn't left Australian soil for a single day since her arrival here twenty years ago. Well, she had no desire to travel. Australia was world enough for her.

Then, thinking of education, she began to think about Tar's future. He needed formal schooling. This time in Sydney made her acutely aware of that. He had an excellent mind. It was unfair not to provide him with the best education she could. He must become a university man. The University of Sydney was quite well-established. She thought that would be an excellent choice. After all, he was an Australian and he need not return to any foreign soil to further himself. No indeed. The University of Sydney it would be!

My, she thought, I seem to be settling everybody's futures at a great rate here. It must be the stimulation of recognition at last. In a way, she was glad it had been delayed for her. There was no danger that it would turn her head at this point. She'd just go on doing what she had been doing all along. She supposed that was maturity. Well, it wasn't so bad.

Flanders stood up and looked around the room as though she hadn't seen it before. She stared out the window at the clear spring sky. It was the middle of December. Bird songs came from invisible hiding places. The streets were jammed with horse carts and steam trams and pedestrians. Oh, it was a bloody jolly scene. She must run fetch Tarleton and drag him out with her for a walk. Oh, she could see the delight of the city. No wonder most Australians chose to live in the city. But still, it wasn't for her. Not for a permanent home. No, as soon as the Institute was set in motion, she'd be on her way back to Toowoomba. But for others, especially for the young, she could understand its charms.

She hurried from the room.

"Tar," she called, "Tar, let's go for a walk. I have wonderful news to tell you!"

As they walked along, jostled by the crowd, she reminded him of their first walk down these same streets.

"You're right," he agreed. "There's more comfort than fear in it now. But that first night! I thought I'd be trampled to death."

She linked her arm through his and leaned closer as she began to tell him of her news from London. Then she added her idea about his going to university. To her surprise, she discovered that he had already been thinking along those same lines. Well, that certainly simplified everything.

"It won't be long," she said, giving his arm a squeeze, "before we're going to the train station to greet all our friends from home."

They shared the smile of conspirators at that notion, each thinking of the pleasure that reunion would bring.

The last few days of waiting seemed to fly, and very soon mother and son found themselves walking arm and arm down toward the railroad station.

"Do you suppose they'll have an entire car to themselves?" Tarleton asked.

"If not," Flanders laughed in response, "they'll darn well take up every seat anyway. It's quite a good number coming . . . Elizabeth and Allen, Anne and Edmund, and Doogalook and Yala, and the two kids . . ."

"They're not kids anymore," Tar interrupted. Two red circles appeared on his cheeks to indicate how strongly he felt about the whole issue of whether they were kids or not.

"I understand that you have all grown up quite a bit during your few years in this world. Sometimes I think you young native-born Australians don't have any childhood at all. Of course . . ." She hesitated and smiled over at him to show that she was teasing, "other times I think you'll be kids and nothing but kids all your lives!"

"Let's hurry, Mum," he urged. "I think I hear the whistle."

"If so, you must have bloody good ears," she said, trying to keep up with him as he sailed along at double speed. "We must be at least an hour early."

They arrived at the station and checked the big clock. Still panting, Flanders said, "I don't suppose you want to hear me say 'I told you so.' "

"Right, you are. Come on, lady, I'll treat you to a brew."

"Well, all right!" Flanders agreed. "I guess you are growing up faster than I'd realized. We'll sit in the pub across the way and share a pint, mate." She pretended a mockery of the amazement she felt in earnest. Tar was quite the young man already. Children were only a temporary gift. She'd heard her own mother say that. Today she felt clearly how true the saying was.

They sat together and made stray comments about trivial things while their thoughts went their own ways. At last they really did hear the train's whistle, and they made their way back over to the station.

"There she is!" Tar cried, dashing away from his mother and rushing up to a young girl who had just stepped from the carriage to the train platform.

Sure enough, it was Krystal. He'd been able to spot her, whereas Flanders could not. She was all dressed up and was beginning to have the shape of a young lady, Flanders noticed. A trip to England with its resulting separation will be good for both of them, Flanders thought. Even if they don't agree just now. She hurried after him toward the cluster of people gathered now beside the train. Her people. Her family, if you will. How good it was to see them again. She'd be glad to get this week over with and head back to Toowoomba, she realized. Suddenly, seeing her old friends, she was overcome with homesickness.

They all greeted each other with the kind of high false

voices that people unused to public demonstrations of affection resort to when forced into them. And they all looked uncomfortably clean and starched in their dressy clothes.

"I know that journey isn't easy," Flanders exclaimed. "Why don't we go at once to the hotel where you can have a chance to bathe and rest? Then, at dinner, we'll gather together and have a proper party! Tar," she called to the lanky boy who was deep in talk with Krystal, "run fetch a coach for hire. Oh dear, I think we'll need two!"

She could hardly wait to tell them her news, but she remembered how exhausting that trip had been for Tar and for her. She would wait. Then she would tell them and they would celebrate.

On the morning of the opening, everyone dressed once again in their fancy clothes, but they seemed more comfortable in them now. In just a few days, the city and its magic had affected them as it had Tar and Flanders before them.

Doogalook and Yala had dressed in their tribal, manner, which meant that they were more naked than clothed. But Makakataba, their son, was caught in the dilemma faced by so many aboriginals once they had moved out of the tribe. He felt unnatural in tribal clothes because he had not been raised tribally, yet, being no white man, he felt a bit of the fool in western clothing. He decided finally on a simple white shirt and a pair of baggy trousers. Flanders assured him that he had such natural grace he would look at home in anything, but she knew she was really not answering the boy's unspoken questions. The question was too complex. It would take some other person to figure it out, she thought. She knew that probably there would not be a satisfactory answer for a number of generations, if ever. The situation with the aborigines was grim. They were essentially being wiped out. Their culture, too, not understood by the white settlers, was being destroyed or perverted. She shook these thoughts from her head. This wasn't the day for them. They shouldn't mar the festivities, nor diminish the moment's triumph. This was the day they had all worked hard for, and she the hardest and longest of all. It was her day!

38

FLANDERS had tried to surround the grand opening with a great deal of pomp and ceremony, because she thought it would serve the double purpose of offering the Sydneyites a bit of fun and giving the Institute a dramatic start. So the first ceremonies were to take place on the steps in front of the building. This way she hoped to attract the casual bystander who might not otherwise be tempted to walk inside.

To her amazement, though, as she stood now on those steps, Flanders saw that she had drawn an enormous throng of people who were bumping and pushing against one another to get close enough to see and hear. She may have made a mistake, she thought. In Australia, a group is always close to being a mob. She whispered to the legislator she'd invited to officiate that they'd best get on with it.

He began at once to make the speech he'd planned. The usual phrases flowed from him, with most of them drowned out by the buzz of the crowd. "Great occasion . . ." "Sign of world recognition of Australia's importance . . ."

Then he was ready to cut the ribbon Flanders had hung across the carved double doors. She stood beside him, and together they wielded the huge scissors with broad gestures so the crowd could make out what was going on. Then Doogalook on one side and Tarleton on the other swung open the doors. The Australian Institute was officially open!

Flanders stood next to the entrance and tried to greet every one of the people who passed her on their way into the hall. She smiled in as welcoming a way as she could to the known and the unknown alike. After a while she began to feel that her face was a plaster mask that would surely crack open if she couldn't stop smiling for just a moment. Fortunately, by then the initial bunches of people had passed through to the inside of the building so that she could pause a moment at the door and for a moment pretend to be an outsider looking in.

It was magnificent. Even to her own eyes, the achievement was great, worth a life's work. The British Society representative had arrived—on Captain Dan Thornburg's ship, at that—and would be presenting her award at a fancy dinner tonight, to which only the most influential people had been invited. No fear of mobs there. She was already planning her acceptance speech. She could tell them it was certainly about time that they recognized her work! Not an especially politic attitude, but an enormously satisfying one! She smiled, knowing she would, of course, do no such thing. She would make it short and to the point—the Australian way.

Deep in thought, as she walked through the people in the rooms, Flanders passed right by Rosie Sullivan.

"Why, ain't we gettin' snooty!" Rosie teased.

"Oh Rosie, after all these years, here it is!"

Rosie leaned over and gave her new friend a hug.

"Dan," Flanders cried. She had just focused on the man holding Rosie's arm—her old friend, the captain, the man who had brought Anne to Australia. "How are you? And don't you look just fine, all dressed up in your Sunday best!"

"We have big news for you. Can you take any more big news? We're getting married. I've retired from the sea, and Rosie and me have set the date."

"I don't know, today may just test my ability to handle happiness." Flanders beamed at the man and woman before her. They looked so blissfully happy. They both deserved it. They'd had plenty of the other kinds of experiences in their lives. "When?" she asked.

"Well, it wasn't going to be for a while. Maybe not for months. But when we realized that we had all our friends from Toowoomba here now . . ." Dan paused and squeezed Rosie's arm, letting her finish the announcement.

"The end of the week!" Rosie exclaimed. "Oh, I don't know how we'll get it all arranged, but we will somehow."

"So, a wedding. How wonderful. That will be a wonderful last memory for me to carry back to Toowoomba from Sydney. And you know I'll do whatever I can to help in the arrangements. After tonight, my work here will be about done."

"I'm counting on you," Rosie said. "You and Anne."

They parted then, to continue their meandering through the museum in different directions. Now it seemed that every few steps Flanders took brought her to another loving friend: Anne and Edmund who still remained an inseparable couple, Krystal and Tar who looked like the perfection of the new Australia, Doogalook and Yala who revealed the true dignity of the noble aborigines, and a score of new friends she'd made during this time in Sydney. Life was rich and good, and it offered more important rewards than medals and honors. Her smile felt like the sunlight, warming her whole body. Her breathing felt full and free. Flanders stood in the midst of this Grand Opening crowd and felt happiness define her being.

39

ROSIE'S wedding was the biggest bash of the summer.
Absolutely everyone who had ever touched Rosie's life
was invited, and that included a good portion of Sydney
and its suburbs! The Red Raven had been utterly transformed into a gala festival hall.

The entire length of the polished mahogany bar was a
mass of fancy platters heaped with delicacies. There was a
good selection of Australian seafood, including those miniature crustaceans known as Moreton Bay bugs and, of
course, the delicious Sydney rock oysters. There was plenty
of beef, too. Australians loved their meat. And Rosie was
never one to let men go hungry.

The tables in the saloon had been cleared away and the
wood floor newly finished to a high polish. On the floor
were strewn flower petals which gave the room a lovely
confetti look and the sweet aroma of a garden in bloom. It
was a far cry from its normal brewery ambience. Of
course, the beer flowed freely enough even today, so the
many gathered guests were a little louder and messier than
they might have been at a proper English wedding.

The back room had been turned into a private chapel.
There, with only Anne, Edmund, Krystal, Flanders and
Tar present, Rosie took the vows of holy matrimony. She
looked as lovely and vulnerable as any virgin, Flanders
thought. She also looked as dewy as any twenty-year-old,
and Flanders knew that Rosie must have been forty-five or

315

thereabouts. Well, here's to happiness at any and every age, she thought.

Dan, dressed in a double-breasted navy-blue suit, sounded a bit nervous as he said, "I do." But when the minister pronounced them man and wife, there was no hesitancy in the way he hugged his bride to him and kissed her.

The whole effect, Flanders thought, watching the couple embrace, was quite as lovely as anything she'd ever seen. Unbidden, tears rose to her eyes, blurring the scene before her. Mostly they were tears of happiness, admixed with some of grief for Lachlan that would never entirely leave her.

Then everybody was hugging and kissing and moving back out into the saloon's great, crowded main room. Soon, between the heat of the day, the additional heat brought on by so many bodies in such close contact, the unusual amount of drink, and the excitement of the occasion, she felt quite light-headed.

A couple of fiddlers had begun to play lively melodies, and some people were clearing a space in the center of the room for dancing. First, of course, Rosie and Dan had to have a waltz alone. Everyone insisted, and they were happy to oblige. They danced together with an elegant grace of movement. The crowd applauded as the music spun them faster and faster until, laughing and apologizing, they were forced to admit defeat. Then others took up the dance, and the floor became a mass of merrily whirling pairs.

The legislator who had officiated at Flanders' opening came up to her and asked for the pleasure of a dance. Flanders happily agreed. Soon they were one of the spinning couples. She hadn't danced in so long that she felt giddy. Also, she had to admit, it was lovely to be in a man's arms. Oh dear, she thought, Flanders, you'd better be saying your good-byes shortly. It's definitely time for you to be putting yourself to bed!

She soon found a way to get Rosie's attention. She gave

the bride a kiss and whispered that she really had to leave, but please not to make a fuss over it. They'd see each other tomorrow. Rosie and Dan were setting up housekeeping in Paramatta, just a short ways from Sydney. They planned no honeymoon. "Our whole lives will be our honeymoon," Dan had explained, so the family, which included Flanders, was invited for a supper the following night. "I'll see you then," Flanders whispered. Then she made her way out of doors.

Lying in bed, Flanders' head was swimming. She let her thoughts drift where they would. Soon she would be returning to Toowoomba, she told herself. Although she would actually be riding the railroad train back home, in her hazy, half-drunk state of mind she imagined herself once again aboard the Cobb & Co. coach that used to be the main means of locomotion. She felt the rocky terrain under the wheels, just as though she were back on board. The dust was pouring in through the open windows and she lifted her lace handkerchief to her lips to try to keep herself from coughing. Then, as she drifted closer and closer to sleep, she seemed to hear a voice call to the driver. She heard gunshots. The carriage shuddered to a stop. "Throw down your bloody guns!" insisted a voice that was so strange, yet so familiar and, with it all, so sweet. It was Lachlan. The bushranger, "Bad" Lachlan McKenzie. As she sank into her sweet dreams, Flanders smiled.

First in a Ten Book Series

RUM COLONY

by Terry Nelsen Bonner

New South Wales was the wild frontier, beautiful
and savage at once; the newly discovered continent
was a new land, and a new way of life. For the
young and spirited beauty Annie Hollister, the handsome and dangerous Captain Steven Rourke, and the
courageous and loyal Irish patriot Phillip Conroy, it
was the setting against which their ambitions, passions and conflicts were played out to a spellbinding
climax.

A DELL/EMERALD BOOK $3.50 (07469-X)

FIRST FAMILIES

by Terry Nelsen Bonner

An Irish convict and the daughter of an English peer vow to survive and triumph in a wild new land: New South Wales. Lady Evelyn Gilleland was bred for a life of elegance and privilege; Gavin Traver was condemned to a life of cruel labor for defending his human dignity. Together they overcome the barriers of society and the rugged challenges of the savage outback to found a brave new world of their own.

A DELL/EMERALD BOOK $3.50   (02745-4)

Second in a Ten Book Series

THE PIONEERS

by Terry Nelsen Bonner

The growing colony of New South Wales becomes a battleground between convict descendants and pioneering free settlers. Edward Carmichael, a young London aristocrat; Doreen Finnegan, a beautiful Irish convict; Elizabeth Hope, daughter of a huge landowner and ex-officer; and Tom Melville, son of convict parents: men and women kept apart by factions struggling for dominance in the new land. These natural enemies will be united through their valiant struggle and undeniable passions.

A DELL/EMERALD BOOK $3.50 (07166-6)